WIDOW TOWN

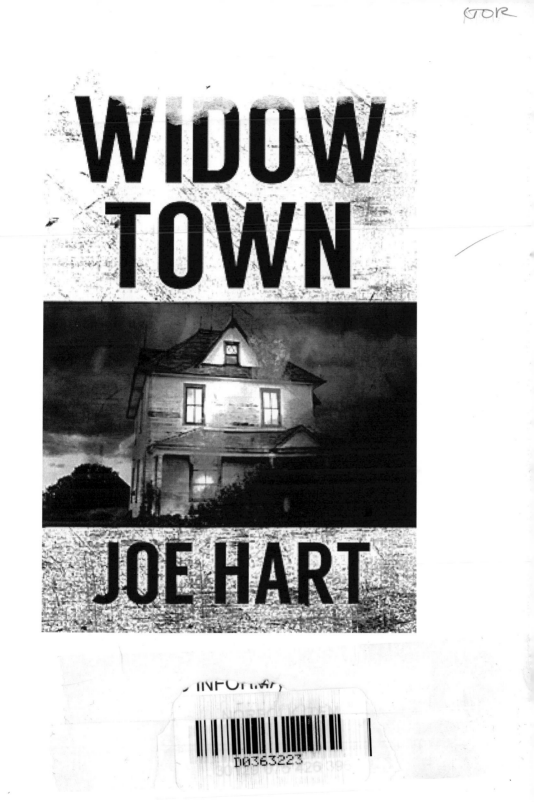

JOE HART

Widow Town

To Mr. Brown, wherever you are. Thanks for the guidance and inspiration and for believing in me when I was just a kid with ideas. Sorry I didn't stop to see you that last time. I didn't know it was the last time.

Special Thanks

Many people help construct a book that don't get their names on the cover, and this one's no different. Thanks to Neal Hock, my editor, for always helping make the words better. To Kealan Patrick Burke, my cover designer, who always makes sure my books get noticed. Thanks to Dylan Morgan, Craig McGray, and Griffin Hayes for your continued help and support, appreciate you guys. And thank you, readers, for your time and company on all the rides we take.

Contents

"It is of great use to the sailor to know the length of his line, though he cannot with it fathom all the depths of the ocean." —John Locke

Chapter 1

A scream woke him, cut off before it could reach its crescendo.

Ryan came to laying on a hardwood floor, tasting blood in his mouth, his blood. He tried to sit up and found he could. He was in a house, a hallway. Its walls were familiar but not home. He blinked and let the memories outside the door of his mind flood inward. A whoop came from nearby and Darrin walked through a doorway to the left carrying his big knife, the one that gleamed even in the dark. Darrin's dark eyes caught and pinned him to the floor.

"Whatcha doin' down there little brother?"

"Passed out, I think."

"You think? I'm pretty sure you did, so's that cooze you were supposed to be watching when she knocked you over. You cracked your head on the floor."

Ryan put a hand to the back of his skull, ran his fingers over a growing knob there, a golf ball half buried under his scalp.

"What'd you do to her?" Ryan asked.

Darrin knelt close to him, a reek of cigarettes, sweat, and something else coming off his skin. "What do you think I did, little brother?"

Adam clunked toward them through the hall, his big boots like hammers on the wood floor. A crooked grin hung off the side of his mouth, his right canine peeking out. He held the steel contraption in one hand. Darrin pivoted without standing.

"Done?"

"Done," Adam said, the smile getting wider.

"You didn't leave anything?"

"Nope."

"You're sure? Because one fucking drop of saliva and you're going to prison, my friend."

Adam seemed to consider it, the wheels turning, slow but sure. "Nope."

"Good." Darrin brought his attention back to Ryan. "Get up, your mouth's bleeding."

Ryan nodded, wiping at his teeth with his jacket sleeve. He pushed himself onto his feet and rubbed the back of his head again, the lump there feeling larger through the gloves he wore.

"We good?" Darrin asked, panning from Adam to Ryan and back again.

"Yep."

"Yeah," Ryan answered.

"Then let's go."

Outside the frogs harped from a slue somewhere in the dark. A swarm of gnats gathered around them as soon as their feet hit the ground and Ryan only had a moment to look up and see the half moon soaring overhead before he heard Darrin emptying out his little container on the front porch. There was a whoosh of the gas igniting and then orange light bloomed across the house, throwing their shadows into long shapes on the lawn. Ryan glanced at Darrin, his eyes alight with the dancing flames and with some internal burning. *He's on fire inside*, Ryan thought as Adam walked past him toward the van parked near the edge of the vegetable garden. Darrin followed him and made his eyebrows jump once as he passed Ryan, his eyes dark again.

"We go, little brother, we go."

They piled into the Ford. Darrin behind the wheel and Ryan in the middle. Adam rolled down his window, the sideways grin back on his face as Darrin rounded the van on the gravel drive, and pulled away from the burning farmhouse.

Chapter 2

"When did they start pissing in the coffee around here?"

MacArthur Gray lowered his own cup, tasting the bitter tang and gave his deputy a look.

"Joseph, how many times are you going to say that?"

"I suppose until they quit doing it over at the diner."

"I would say that's an awful rude assumption you're making."

"What? That they urinate in the coffee?"

"Yep, I find the flavor to be closer to cigarette butts and toilet bowl cleaner. Piss has a different taste entirely."

Deputy Ruthers gave the sheriff a glance and burst out laughing, slopping a little coffee onto his pants and the car seat.

"Now damn it, Joseph, look what you've done."

"Sorry, Sheriff, apologies."

Gray focused on the dirt road and the sun seeming to rise directly from its end. A field to the left rose and fell with head-high cornstalks for acres beyond measure, their green color standing out against everything else dead or dying. Dust plumed behind the cruiser in a cloud, the sky already a mocking blue. No rain in weeks.

"They sure it was a house fire? Could be Jacobs is just burning a brush pile or something?" Ruthers said.

"They didn't say, but any and all smoke has to be looked into right now, there's a burning ban and Jacobs knows better than most what a spark could do around here."

Gray saw Ruthers shoot him a look and then glance back at the road. "What do you really think, Sheriff?"

"I don't know."

"What's your gut tell you?"

"That I didn't eat enough this morning."

Gray piloted the cruiser around a sharp bend, a flock of blackbirds bursting from the roadside in a flay of wings and beaded eyes. A finger of smoke rose above the trees to the right and Gray turned the car into the long dirt drive, past a pitted relic of a mailbox, the letters worn away to almost nothing. When the house came into view Ruthers inhaled and set his coffee in the center console.

"Well shit," Gray said.

The front of the Jacobses' house was a blackened mess. The covered porch was gone and soot ran in vertical streams up the siding. The windows, trimmed with white decorative shutters before, were blackened, their glass shattered or cracked. The shingles were curled up in a greeting and a bit of rubble that might've been a glider swing still smoked.

Ruthers started speaking into the radio, calling back to Mary Jo, telling her they would need the fire truck from Wheaton. Gray parked a dozen yards from the

11

smoking structure and stepped out into the morning air that smelled of cooked paint and char.

"Get that hose going off the side of the house there will you, Joseph? And just wet the grass a little, don't spray the porch."

"Yes sir."

Gray picked his way toward the front porch, seeing the screen door gone, the brass knob blackened like a nub of coal. With long strides, he made his way around the side of the farmhouse, seeing that the rest of the structure looked untouched by the flames. The buzzing of flies sizzled to his left and he looked at the doghouse near the edge of the woods, the dead dog lying at its entrance. Its throat was slit, a red gap ringed by clotted fur gone from gold to burgundy like a sunset.

Gray drew his weapon.

The Colt 1911 Long Slide came out of the holster in a seamless glide of pitch-black steel. Gray made sure the safety was off before moving around to the back of the house. The backdoor was unlocked and opened without a sound into a small mudroom. Work boots stood in pairs beside brightly colored sandals. A wooden sitting-bench lined one wall and a low freezer stood against the opposite.

Gray waited, listening to the quiet. Except for the hush of Ruthers squirting water on the lawn, there was nothing. No sounds of life, no dishes banging or footsteps coming to investigate his presence. After another minute Ruthers approached from outside and stepped in behind him.

"Sheriff—"

"Get that fancy pistol out of your holster, Joseph, there's something wrong here."

Ruthers struggled with the nylon straps holding his Deacon .7 Striker and finally released it, touching the digital thumbprint reader on its handle twice in quick succession. The weapon issued a short click.

"What is it?"

Gray didn't answer for a long time, still listening, hoping. "The smell."

"I don't smell anything," Ruthers whispered, his eyes looking past the sheriff's wide back.

"You will."

They moved through the house, Ruthers pointing his gun into each doorway as they went, Gray holding his at the floor, his dark eyes watching. The kitchen stood empty, late August sunshine filling the space up with orange light so thick it looked solid. Pans sat on the counter, a layer of grease coating one, another half cleaned in the sink. The faucet dripped once, breaking the silence. Gray walked into the dining room, his boots clicking against the hardwood floor. A vase set with flowers lay on its side on the dinner table. Water pooled on the floor in Rorschach patterns, yellow petals became miniature boats on their surfaces.

The smell got stronger and Gray stopped, glancing to his right at a stairway that ran up into relative darkness. Ahead, the front entry and living room were empty, the TV blank except for an elongated reflection of his movement. A white door to the right stood closed, its paint clean and fresh as if applied the day before. A collage of pressed flowers against a blue paper background hung from its middle. Gray moved to the door, his breathing steady, still listening, waiting. He gripped the doorknob, pointing the long barreled Colt straight up. Ruthers moved in to his other side, the Deacon at shoulder level, its barrel flashing a small red light every three seconds. Gray nodded once and waited until Ruthers returned the signal. He flung the door open, readjusting his position, bending his knees, his finger tightening on the trigger.

The smell was awful and only the sight was worse.

"My God in heaven," Ruthers managed before he covered his mouth with one hand and stepped back. Gray stood in the doorway looking into the pink-walled bedroom and finally dropped his gaze to the splattered floor before closing his eyes to a sight he knew he'd never forget.

"So?" Enson said as he spread his arms apart.

"Joseph and I are going to go over to Wheaton Medical after this and wait for the autopsy results. After that we'll be in touch."

Enson's mouth twitched once and then he rubbed his foot in the dirt again. "Gray, I've no time for your bullshit today. You've got something on your brain that won't let things go."

"I suppose you're right, Mitchel."

"There's no reason for you to go over to the center because I know what you're going to do. You're going to stir up things that aren't there, make mountains from molehills, and I won't have it, not in my county. Your infatuations with history are irritating."

Gray slid from the hood in one motion and stood to his full height. He took two steps and loomed over Enson, looking down at him from beneath his hat.

"If you've forgotten how you drove here, Mitchel, this is not your county. Section 16 of the county arbiters states that if a county does not have the facilities to deal with a crime, the nearest county will assist and abide by all reliefs necessary in conceding the law's due order."

"I know what the damn law states, Gray, what I'm saying is—"

"Joseph and I will be over no later than noon. It's hotter than the devil's ass out here and we need some shade."

Gray walked to the driver's side door, nodding at Ruthers once before climbing inside. When their doors clicked shut, Gray watched Enson walk away, his heavy body laboring in the heat.

"I don't think he liked that, Sheriff," Ruthers said, still looking after Enson's awkward shape.

"Joseph, you could fit into a raindrop how much I care about what Sheriff Enson likes, but that would be a waste of good water." Gray looked at the younger man. "Can you hold down food?"

Ruthers considered it. "I think so."

Gray started the cruiser and flipped it into gear. "Then let's get something to eat before we go and hear all the details about what happened inside that house."

~

They ate in the cruiser, their food steaming in recycled containers on their laps.

"Coffee still tastes like shit," Ruthers said, lowering his cup.

"Joseph, I don't know why you order it over and over then. Repetition of an asinine act doesn't speak well of the repeater."

"I'm sorry, Sheriff, I guess it's convenience."

"We can stop anywhere else you'd like, as long as you quit complaining about coffee."

"Yes sir." Ruthers ate another bite of his mashed potatoes, bits of gravy and meat falling from his fork, before squinting at his container. "So could I ask you what you think?"

"About what, Joseph? Life in general or something more particular?"

"Well, what happened at the house, your theory?"

"Theory is a dangerous thing, Joseph. Theory can wreck a man if he begins to believe too closely in the way he thinks things are. Things are never the way a person thinks they are."

"What do you mean?"

"I mean, the only thing you need to remember about law enforcement is what our real job is."

Gray took several bites of his sandwich and chewed, glancing across the street they were parked on. Ruthers nodded, drinking some more of his coffee before holding up a finger.

"And what is that?"

"Our real job?"

"Yes."

Gray looked at the deputy and then away. "The truth, Joseph, we find the truth. The truth can be hidden, disguised as something else, but never dissolved. It's always there, you just have to know where and how to look."

Ruthers frowned and licked his lips.

"Is that why you left the city? The truth was too hard to find?"

Gray paused, his water halfway to his mouth. "No, I found too much of it."

Ruthers took in the blank look behind the sheriff's eyes and shook his head. "I didn't mean to overstep my bounds."

"You didn't at all, I know what you meant." He was quiet for a time and then said, more to himself than anything, "Maybe the wolves aren't all gone."

"What do you mean?"

"Never mind. Let's finish up, shall we? Death awaits us."

"Sir?"

"I guess I should rephrase, death's reports await us." Gray slid the cruiser into drive and pulled away from the curb. Ruthers nodded once and finished the last swallow of his coffee, grimacing at the taste.

the man was eviscerated after receiving these." She touched the gouges on the corpse's thighs and sides with the pointer.

"He was still alive when those happened?" Gray asked.

"Yes. It looks like a minor gash was made across his chest initially, but the cut wasn't very deep."

"A warning."

"That's what I'm thinking."

Gray worked his jaw up and down several times, wishing he'd brought a pack of gum. "How about the other two?"

Tilly rounded the table and approached the next in line holding Teri Jacobs's body. "Mrs. Jacobs died of severe trauma to the brachial tube. It's been severed in half a dozen places causing her to drown in her own blood. Here you can see the same gouges on her thighs and there are more on her back."

"Tilly, what do those wounds look like to you?" Gray asked, lifting his head from the carnage. The smell in the room was getting to him, death mixed with formaldehyde, a cocktail that churned his stomach.

"Why don't you tell me, Sheriff? It appears you have an idea."

"They look like bite marks."

Tilly nodded. "They are."

"From what?"

"I'm not sure yet, something large, a big dog maybe? The depth of the wounds indicate a wide snout, Rottweiler or Great Dane perhaps. We'll know for sure after a swabbing to determine saliva type. On the other hand the amount of flesh removed is too much for a single bite, which is what we're looking at here."

Gray paused, taking in the words. "One bite for each wound?"

"That's right."

"Is all the removed tissue accounted for?"

Something flashed across the medical examiner's eyes, there and gone, a shadow of disgust. "No."

The room fell silent again until Ruthers shuffled closer, still not within touching distance of any of the tables. "Are you saying that the animal that did this, ate parts of them?"

Silence fell again until the door to the room swung open, jerking them all from their thoughts. A petite brunette woman wearing a smart pair of dress slacks and a yellow blouse that hugged her pregnant stomach entered the room. She carried a batch of files under one arm. Her hazel eyes scanned them all and found Ruthers last. A smile. Ruthers returned it, the skin around his eyes crinkling.

"Well hello, Siri, how're you feeling?" Gray said.

"Hi, Sheriff Gray. Good, and big, but good. Hi, Joe."

"Hi, Siri," Ruthers said, stepping out of her way. Siri smiled again and made her way toward Tilly. Gray watched Ruthers watch Siri pass, the younger man's eyes those of a puppy beneath his hat. When Ruthers saw Gray looking at him, he bit his lower lip and began to examine the blank wall beside him.

"I brought the initial ballistic reports along with the crime scene photos," Siri said, setting the files down on a desk.

"Thank you, Siri, I appreciate it," Tilly said, stripping off her wet gloves.

"While you're here, Siri, do you mind answering a few questions for us?" Gray asked.

"Sure, Sheriff. Um, did you okay it with Sheriff Enson already?"

"My questions? Oh, Mitchel knows I like to ask questions. I've even tried to get him interested in doing the same but it hasn't taken yet."

Siri smiled and Tilly raised her eyebrows once.

"Do we know the succession of events last night?"

"We're pretty sure that they came in through the back door," Siri said, her eyes shooting to the tables and then away. "There was no sign of forced entry and the front door was still locked. We think there was two, possibly three assailants. After that it's a little sketchy. Do you want my opinion?"

"Please."

"It looks to me like one went upstairs and the other went directly to Devi's room, and maybe Dr. Swenson can reinforce this, but from looking at the scene it appears that they tortured Mr. Jacobs first and made his wife watch." Siri turned her head toward Tilly.

Tilly nodded. "That concurs with what I've found so far along with times of death."

"Sick bastards," Ruthers said under his breath.

"And what about Devi?" Gray asked, his eyes flitting to the table that held what remained of the pretty girl he'd seen picking beans with her mother in their garden from time to time.

"No signs of rape or semen, but she was definitely killed last. There's no bite marks on her body, but the amount of lacerations are innumerable," Tilly said.

"Any guess at how many?" Gray asked.

Tilly sighed, glancing at the sundered flesh of a girl that should've graduated the next year. "A hundred, maybe more."

Gray nodded, rubbing his fingers across his forehead, smoothing the wrinkles that were trying to embed themselves there. A faint promise of a headache began to pulse in the back of his skull. "Tilly, you did the autopsies on the Olsons last month, right?"

"Yes, why?"

"Was there anything unusual about the bodies?"

"Like this? Mac, those two poor people burned at more than eight hundred degrees Fahrenheit. There were barely bones left to look at. Besides, the two couldn't be related, not with the state of these bodies."

"Yeah," Gray said.

"Mac, what are you trying to do here?"

Gray took a deep breath in and then let it filter out between his teeth. "My job."

"Look, whoever did this is deeply disturbed, I'll give you that, but it must've been a one time, fluke thing. A couple people, maybe drifters, decided to rob the Jacobses and they got carried away. Maybe the Jacobses resisted and they retaliated."

"And they brought a bloodthirsty dog along just in case?" Gray said, tipping his head a little to one side.

Tilly's face hardened. "All I'm saying is there's no evidence that the two are connected except for the fire, and if they are then it was a crime of passion, anger and rage."

Gray glanced at the door, checking the digital clock above it. "Yeah, definitely."

"Gray," Tilly lowered her voice as though to keep Siri and Ruthers from hearing even though they were only steps away. "You're going down a dead end road. We need to find whoever did this before they skip town."

Gray nodded once. "Thank you, doctor. Siri." Gray tapped the bill of his cap and turned on his heel.

"I'll send over the full report when I'm through," Tilly called after them as they moved toward the door. Ruthers looked back and nodded, smiling tightly. He gave a little wave at Siri and followed Gray out of the room.

Chapter 5

Gray urged the cruiser down the road splitting two fields of golden wheat.

The sun glowed within the tipping crops, illuminating them beyond anything natural. Ruthers shifted in his seat, the squeak of his duty belt loud in the quiet confines.

"Hotter'n shit," Ruthers finally said.

"That it is."

"Think it'll rain?"

"Yep, late tonight. Might stave off the fire that's been waiting to start."

"Think so?"

"Nope."

A bit of static came across the radio and then fell silent again. The wheat rolled like a tide under the breeze.

"Sir, what—"

"Have you ever had real vegetables, Joseph?"

"Sir?"

"I mean not from the store, but from a garden?"

"Sure, my mom used to grow her own beets and potatoes."

"But you got those seeds from the store, right?"

"Yes, I suppose so."

Gray nodded. "You're off at five tonight and Thueson's on alone until nine, right?"

"Yes sir."

"Then you'll have dinner with me tonight, Joseph, if it's okay with you."

Ruthers just stared at the side of Gray's face for a while, not moving, then found his voice. "Okay, sir. I thought all of us would be on tonight, working on the case."

"Thueson and Monty will be able to handle things and I know what you're thinking, but if I'm wrong, the people that did that to the Jacobses are long gone, miles outside of our county right now."

"And if you're right?"

"If I'm right, well, I don't really want to think about that."

"Okay. Should I bring anything?"

"Just yourself, and those questions you've been trying to ask me all day." Gray gave him a half smile.

The radio barked to life, their dispatcher and office manager, Mary Jo's voice filling up the car.

"Sheriff?"

"Go ahead, Mary Jo." The display of the radio recognizing his voice pattern before sending back his response.

"There's a bit of an issue down at Harrington's."

"What kind of issue?"

"It seems that David Baron is having some sort of fit down there and won't leave."

"What kind of fit, Mary Jo?"

"I'm not sure but Clark called it in, says the kid won't leave."

"Thank you, Mary Jo."

The radio clicked once and then went quiet. Gray pressed the pedal down harder and the cruiser picked up speed, automatically sinking lower to the blacktop. Ruthers touched a black screen mounted in the console and when it lit up, he tapped a single icon that set the cruiser's lights in motion as well as the siren. Its wail muted but still audible in the interior, Gray knew anyone within a half mile was getting an earful.

"You always have to ask yourself, Joseph, what's next?"

~

The hardware store stood beside the café they'd left only hours before. Its walls were a bleached brown that looked like dried skin too long in the sun. A few cars were parked along the street before the storefront, their glass reflecting the beating sun in flashing arcs that hurt the eyes. Several people strolled on the sidewalk, some holding hands, some not. Signs proclaiming the coming city festival hung from doors and windows, the garish announcements promising fun for the entire family.

Gray took it all in as he coasted the cruiser into a parking spot, dousing the lights and siren with a touch of his finger.

"You think he's dangerous, Sir?"

"Davey Baron? Anyone can be dangerous, Joseph, but I don't think we have to worry about him."

They climbed from the vehicle and moved through the heat, a solid curtain that beaded sweat before they entered the air-conditioned store.

The building was large with cardboard displays of farming implements too big to house within the space, but could be ordered at the front desk. Racks of work clothes stood in aisles beside lawn mowers and chainsaws. Hunting and fishing equipment hung in locked racks before glass cases containing assortments of knives. A line of cashiers sat off to the left, the men and women manning the tills turned toward the rear of the store where Clark Redy stood, his rounded shoulders draped in the customary blue of a Harrington's uniform shirt. Gray could see from a distance that Redy's normally crimson neck was nearly purple. Not a good sign. Redy was gesticulating and saying something, his words lost in the echo from the high ceiling.

Gray crossed the store, nearing the storeowner just as he finished a tirade and glanced over one ham-hock shoulder.

"It's about time," Redy said, rounding on Gray as he approached. Gray stood a bit over six feet and weighed a solid two hundred twenty pounds, but Redy loomed over him, a hill of angry flesh and bone. Redy's face was the same color as his neck, eyes beginning to bulge with sweaty hair matted to his broad forehead.

24

"What's the problem, Clark?" Gray said.

"The problem is that little lunatic broke one of my displays and now he's got ahold of a clipper blade and won't let anyone near him. He won't leave!" Redy said the last sentence as if he didn't truly believe it himself.

"Let's take it easy, Clark, and we'll sort it out."

"Sort it out? Tase the little bastard and get his skinny ass out of my store. I'm losing business."

"Clark?" Gray put a hand on the other man's massive bicep. "We'll handle it." Without waiting for a reply, Gray walked around the proprietor and stepped into the aisle the large man had been shouting down.

David Baron sat on the edge of a shelf, his narrow torso hunched over his knees. He had a shock of red hair that Gray had never seen in any semblance of order. His pale face hung toward the floor, freckles dotting his long nose. An image of his father.

David turned his head toward Gray as he came down the aisle and shifted, revealing the sixteen inches of sharpened steel in his left hand. The clipper blade shone under the bright lights of the store, its edge meant for high RPMs and reed grass, now looked only a little menacing in the hand of the boy. Tear tracks ran in salty streams down both his cheeks and he made no movement to wipe them away.

"Stop." The boy's voice croaked. He'd been yelling.

Gray paused and turned to sit on a shelf across the aisle, its contents now covering the floor. "How you doing, Davy?"

The boy sniffed, his eyes turning toward the head of the row they sat in, faces peering back at them. "Go away."

"I just came here to chat, Davy, I'm not going to hurt you or make you leave before you mean to."

The hand holding the clipper blade lowered a little. "I don't wanna talk."

"That's fine," Gray said, crossing one leg over the other, getting comfortable. "Anyone can tell you I talk more than enough for two people." Gray smiled. "You're on the baseball team this year, aren't you?"

David glanced up the aisle again, then back to Gray, nodded.

"I thought I saw you out playing last week. You're shortstop, aren't you?"

David opened his mouth and then shut it. Finally said, "And first base sometimes."

"Really? That's interesting. You're playing two positions that complement one another. More hits go to shortstop than any other position, you know that?"

"Yeah."

"Coach must think well of your abilities to put you there."

"Maybe."

Gray imagined his next words as placing a foot on a tightrope, except they were already out there, weren't they? "Your dad used to play shortstop, you know?"

David's jaw tightened and the muscles in his left arm flexed. Gray shifted his eyes to the far end of the aisle over David's shoulder where Ruthers waited,

Chapter 6

The cruiser door thunked shut and David Baron gave them a wave before walking toward the two-story farmhouse, its paint ignited a dazzling white in the late afternoon sun.

Gray and Ruthers watched him until he climbed the steps onto the front porch and disappeared inside before pulling away in the turnaround that led back to the barren country road. The sun cut across the field clover to their right, a few head of cattle grazing behind an electrified fence. Dust kicked up behind the cruiser in a cloud, an occasional stone snapping against its undercarriage.

"That was a nice thing you did back there, sir."

"Why thank you, Joseph."

"I think Redy wanted to skin him alive."

"That's Clark Redy's solution to most problems."

"Yeah." Ruthers glanced out the window down a narrow road that shot off to their right, there and gone as they flew by. "You think he's alive somewhere, sir?"

"Who? Miles Baron? I'm not sure. There's always a chance."

"But you don't think so."

"I knew Miles from middle school on. He was one of the most kind, caring, responsible men I've ever known. He would not shirk his family or his farm for any kind of offer and if there was a way to get back to the two people in that house, he would. So no, Joseph, I don't think he is."

"It's just so strange for someone to vanish without notice. No vehicle, no body, no contact if he did run off."

"Mysteries, Deputy Ruthers, we're in the business of mysteries."

They finished the drive back to Shillings in silence. Farms passing by, then more trees, a dried river bottom, cracked and wishing for rain. The dirt beneath the cruiser's wheels became pavement, humming like a trapped hornet. Gray guided the vehicle down a side street, behind a row of homes set so close to one another a man would have to walk sideways between them. They parked in the long shadow of a two story, brick building. An American flag wilted on a shining pole. Breeze falling into nothing with the coming evening.

"Can you handle the necessaries for me, Joseph?"

"Sure can, sir."

"If you don't get it all done by quitting time, leave the simple things to Thueson. You remember where I live, I assume?"

"Yes sir."

"Good, I've got a couple things I want to check. I'll see you later."

Ruthers exited the car and strode toward the sheriff's office. Gray idled the cruiser out of the building's shadow and drove a slow path down Main Street. He watched the people he could see, how they moved, how they talked, where they were going. He looked at the way they held their hands and if they noticed him, if there was a reaction there, fear. Gray accelerated past the final business in town and took a left onto a patched asphalt road that led into the sun's full glare. He put his sunglasses back on, letting his mind coast with the scenery outside the car.

He made turns without knowing where he was going, and knowing the whole while.

The cruiser's tires crunched across the Jacobses' drive and Gray stopped short of the flapping tape strung several yards in front of the charred porch. He shut the cruiser off, rolling his window down to listen. Birds sang in the surrounding woods, the melody speaking of rain. He hadn't heard a bird in over a month, not since the last downpour. A squirrel chittered and jumped across a branch, its tail long, catching the sun in gaps of foliage. Gray inhaled, smelling the air. It would rain tonight.

He climbed from the vehicle, bending under the tape before stopping at the foot of the burnt stairs. He knelt, running his hand across the treads, feeling the fire's dust coat his fingers. The air still smelled like smoke this close to the house. Gray stood and walked around the side of the building, looking at the ground, the siding, the woods. The Jacobses' dog was gone now, an empty length of chain trailing to its house

Gray opened the backdoor and stepped inside, closing it behind him. He waited again, reliving the morning. He walked through the kitchen, stopping at the sink with the previous night's dishes within. Moving to the table, he sat in one of the kitchen chairs, staring down the hall toward the foyer, the front door beyond. The house quiet save for an antique ticking clock near the stairway.

Gray stood, moved down the hall and paused before the front door. He only spared a glance at Devi's room before turning back to the stairway.

The second floor had only two areas, a guest room and the master bedroom. The floor of the master still had blotchy patches of dried blood coating its surface but everywhere else was devoid of dust having been vacuumed by the forensic team. The bed sheets were gone along with the drapes. He studied the floor's blackening patterns until they became sickening depictions of torture.

He crossed the room to the bare window, the fading light barely dappling the sill. A massive oak grew close enough to climb down outside, a child's dream of escape come true. Through the branches the forest solidified in a seamless aura of green although most of the higher leaves were beginning to wilt.

Gray stood framed in the window, watching the afternoon creep toward evening when a new sensation pressed against him like a physical hand.

He was being watched.

He pretended not to notice, standing in fuller view while his eyes began to comb the trees, searching for an outline amongst the foliage. His hand slid to the Colt's grip. Nothing in the trees. The pushing touch of eyes relented, faded, disappeared.

Gray dropped his gaze to the windowsill, its surface cleaner than it had been since being installed he was sure. He shifted, his feet scraping across a heating grate in the floor, the hollow sound strumming like an unturned harp. A glint of something caught his eyes between the grate's slats. A shine of silver then gone as he moved.

Gray drew out his pocketknife and touched a button to release the spring loaded, six-inch blade. Kneeling, he placed the tip of the knife in the screw slit and turned it out. After doing the same to the other side, he set the knife on the floor and pulled the grate from its recess.

The duct below held a handful of dirt and clumped hair. A tarnished earing, its back missing rested amidst the grime, but that wasn't what he'd seen through the grate.

A shining, silver screw sat apart from the rest of the detritus, its threads pointed up.

Gray grasped it in his fingertips and drew it out into the light. The screw had a star pattern slot for tightening and was only a half-inch long. It looked brand new.

"What are you doing down there?" Gray said to the empty room that smelled of old copper.

Chapter 7

Gray took off his hat and set it in the seat as he rounded one of the last bends before his home.

The sunlight was almost gone, shadows stretching to unnatural lengths on the ground. Gravel kicked up beneath the cruiser's tires, a plume of dust marking its passage. Ancient trees lined the private drive, a county road in itself yet devoid of any habitable dwellings save one. Miles of woods stretched to either side of the car with only the occasional splash of field and the abandoned, overgrown driveway to break the feeling of complete wilderness.

The road narrowed, turned once more and then opened into a massive clearing. Gray sighed without meaning to.

His house stood in the center of the space, a high two-story with narrow windows set in its upper half. Long gables hung from the roof on all sides and a two-door garage sat beside it, squat when compared to the tall structure. A deck wrapped around from the north side to the rear of the house and two wind chimes hung from its rails, still now without the nudging hand of breeze.

Gray touched the console screen and tapped a button. The left garage door slid up and out of sight as he pulled beneath it, touching the button once more before he climbed out of the car and left the garage.

Gray glanced across the back yard as he walked to the house, the little stone bridge arching over a stream that was nearly dry. *Carah's stream.*

He grimaced, slapped his hat against his thigh once and continued toward the door.

A grinding roar began to build from the direction of the road and he paused, wondering why Joseph was so early. When the nose of the SUV came into view he licked his lips, smoothed his hair once, and donned his hat again. The blue Chevy stopped within feet of the garage and he waited as the woman behind the steering wheel fidgeted with something before climbing out. *Still acts like she lives here,* he thought, taking in the smooth line of her jeans, hugging her legs beneath, a well-worn tank top clinging in the heat to her flat stomach. Dark hair he'd run his fingers through tossed to one side, held by an elastic band.

"Glad I caught you," Lynn said coming closer. Her eyes were still hidden behind reflective shades that gave him nothing.

"You caught me. How are you?"

"Great, and you?"

"Fair to middling."

"Yeah?"

"Yeah. Long day."

"The days are long, especially now." She glanced at the sky. "I just need my last box, Mac."

"Thought you got everything last time."

31

"I was looking for mom's watch today and realized it wasn't there. I think I left a jewelry box in the foyer under the table."

"I put it in the garage."

Lynn shifted, her black boots scratching the dirt. "Is it open?"

"Yeah, should be on the bench near the door."

He watched her turn and move to the garage, disappear inside. She came out carrying the luridly colored jewelry box beneath her arm, guarding it. He reached out to put a hand on the doorknob and realized he wasn't anywhere near the house anymore. Lynn walked toward the SUV, not looking back.

"Lynn."

She stopped, hair dancing over her shoulder as she looked at him. So pretty in the evening light.

"Did you need anything else?"

"No."

"You drove all the way out here to get jewelry?"

"Yes."

"That's not logical."

She pivoted back toward him, anger beginning to speak in her stance. "What would you know about logic, Mac?"

Gray rubbed his forehead and took a tentative step toward her, the day still too hot. "I didn't mean anything, Lynn, I'm just trying to talk."

"You have funny timing, Mac Gray." No vehemence in her voice, nothing left.

"Didn't I always?"

"I can't do this now, Gray, I've got to be somewhere." She turned toward the SUV, pulled open the back door to set the box inside. Gray stared at the ground, right where she'd dug her boots in. He could see the design from the bottom of her soles.

"Date?" He didn't have to look up.

"Let me rephrase, I'm not going to do this now, don't have the time or patience." Her driver's door clicked open and he almost took more steps, but didn't. "Let me know if you find anything else."

He nodded at the dirt. "I will."

He waited to look up until she'd turned around and headed out, caught the glint of her red taillights before the SUV glided behind the trees. Then he made his way to the house, the yard quiet once again.

The interior always made him look up when he entered. It was open construction, Timber Frame style. The square beams set in the heated and cooled concrete floor rose high before arching to meet one another in the center of the house. Gray glanced at the loft, half expecting Lynn to be standing there, leaning over it with her easy grace, a smile on her lips to see him home on time.

Gray set his hat on the kitchen bar that opened to the living room before going to the fridge. He pulled out a protein drink tasting of vanilla chalk and pounded half of it down, the corners of his mouth pulling back.

"Out of fucking chocolate, whoever heard of such a thing?" He asked the house before taking one last swallow.

Unbuttoning his shirt, he moved past the deep living room toward a doorway leading to his office. A conglomeration of steel grips were mounted into the solid wood above the door, each facing a different angle. Setting his shirt down, Gray leapt into the air and grasped the two closest handles and began to chin-up. He stopped at sixty, having to struggle for the last three reps, then dropped to the floor, immediately going into a pushup position. He counted to one hundred and then leapt for the bars overhead again.

Gray repeated his workout four times and then stalked upstairs, snagging his shirt as he went. His breathing was back to normal when he reached the bedroom and by the time he stripped the rest of his clothes off and stepped into the shower, his heart beat at the slow, solid rhythm that he heard every night before drifting off to sleep.

After showering, he dressed in a pair of loose shorts and a threadbare T-shirt and returned to the kitchen, taking a pound of hamburger from the fridge. He salted and peppered the meat after making patties, the whole time staring out of the window above the sink, his eyes glazed.

Just as he was lighting the gas grill on the deck, he heard the unmistakable grinding of tires coming down the road and a minute later, Ruthers's late-model pickup glided to a stop before the garage. Gray went back through the house and washed his hands in the sink before walking to the door. When he opened it, Ruthers had his hand raised as if about to knock.

"Joseph, welcome. Come in."

"Thank you, sir."

"There'll be none of that 'sir' bullshit in my house. You call me Gray or Mac in this place, okay?"

"Yes s—Gray."

"That's better. Want a beer, Joseph?"

"That'd be great."

Gray made his way into the kitchen and pulled two frosted bottles out of the fridge, snapping them both open before returning to the living room where the deputy waited. Ruthers's eyes were tracing the lines of the room, the high ceilings, the long regal windows.

"Your house is unbelievable, s—Gray."

"Thank you, forgot you've never stepped inside before," he said, handing the younger man a beer.

"Who did the construction?"

"I did."

A surprised look crossed the deputy's face. "Really?"

"What, you don't think I'm capable of doing things other than talking?"

"No, not at all."

"I'm joking, Joseph, drink that beer and loosen up." Gray motioned to follow and Ruthers walked behind him through the kitchen and out onto the deck. "My father was a carpenter, modeled himself after Jesus right down to his profession and his shoes."

"Your father was a prophet?"

Gray barked laughter. "Nice one, Joseph. No, he was a God-fearing man and wore sandals most days. He built these types of homes as his specialty. For a long time people would have him come hundreds of miles to construct something like this, something that wasn't like the newer models."

"You mean low and efficient."

"That's exactly what I mean, Joseph. I picked up the trade from him, but not the religion."

"You're not a God-fearing man?"

"There's more things on earth to fear than God."

They walked to the edge of the deck and took in the panoramic view of the back yard. The stream trickled and the notes of birds drifted to them from far back in the woods.

"So that's your garden?" Ruthers said, pointing at a twenty-by-twenty-foot square of tilled dirt several yards from the bank of the stream.

"It is, and you don't sound impressed."

"No, it's not that, it's just that most people's are so much bigger."

"I don't have garden envy, Joseph."

"No, I didn't mean—"

"Joking, drink that beer."

A gust of wind began to caress the trees, bending their tops gently before releasing them. The wind chimes jangled in a tune that always reminded Gray of fall.

"My garden's smaller because all those plants down there are organic."

Ruthers' eyebrows drew down. "Organic? Like really organic?"

"Yep, not like the G-Mods that grow everywhere else. That's why my garden looks like it's taking a beating compared to all the other crops; it doesn't have the genetics to deal with a long-term drought. No matter how much I water it, it's drying out under the sun every day."

"Wow. I've never eaten anything organic that I can think of."

"Well, you will tonight," Gray said, moving to the grill.

"Is that a propane grill?"

"It is. Found it in an antique store a few years ago. Had to have a friend cobble a regulator together, but I got it working." Gray drained the rest of his beer and slapped the burgers onto the grill. The meat hissed and began to smoke, the smell making Gray's stomach ache.

"Another beer, Joseph?"

Ruthers tipped his brew, seeing that it was only half gone. "Uh, sure."

Gray nodded and disappeared into the house, appearing again with two fresh bottles. He drained half of his in the first drink and leaned on the railing again before reaching into his pocket.

"I went back to the Jacobses' farm tonight and found this," Gray said, placing the screw, now encased in a small plastic bag, on the railing beside the deputy's elbow. Ruthers picked it up, turning it over several times before putting it down.

"You think it's something important?"

"I do. I found it in the heating vent, forensics missed it somehow, but that's technology for you, Joseph, it's like people, you can't always trust it."

"You going to check it for DNA?"

"I am. I'm also going to have a friend who's versed in metals look at it. He might be able to figure out if it has unique properties."

"The same one that cobbled together your regulator?"

Gray smiled. "The same."

"Sheriff, shit, I mean, Gray, what was that all about at the medical examiner's lab today?"

"You mean with the way you couldn't keep your eyes off Siri? I was about to ask you the same thing," Gray said over his shoulder as he went to flip the burgers.

"Ah, well, you know, I think she's really nice."

"Siri's very nice and from what I understand her husband was a deadbeat that left as soon as he got her pregnant. Have you made an effort to speak to her outside of a professional capacity?"

"Sir? I mean—"

"Oh for fuck's sake, Joseph, call me whatever you want, I guess."

Ruthers couldn't help the laugh that slipped out. "Okay sir. No, I haven't, not really, but I should."

"Damn right you should. Next time you see that girl, ask her on a date, she'll say yes."

"You think so?"

"Joseph, she looked at you the same way you looked at her."

Ruthers's face became a bit pinker and he glanced away as he drank more beer. Gray brought out a plate and piled on the burgers before setting the patio table with condiments, a bowl of assorted vegetables, and two more beers.

"You didn't answer me, sir," Ruthers said as they sat down on either side of the table.

"I need some food in me, and another beer before we get into that."

"Yes sir."

They ate in silence with only the passing breeze fluttering the leaves along with the chime's voice to break it. The sky became a patchwork quilt, turning from a pale cobalt to purple with edges of black bleeding into stars. Two porch lights came on automatically with the falling dusk. When they'd finished eating, Gray cleared the table and placed another two beers between them before sitting down to stare into the deepening night.

"My father named me for the war," he said after a while.

"The war, sir?"

Gray glanced at his deputy and sat back in his chair. "The war that never came."

"I'm not following."

"MacArthur, it was the name of a famous general in the second world war. Does it ring a bell?"

"Not especially I guess, but history wasn't my strongest subject."

Gray smiled. "I love history, but not in the way historians love it. Historians keep the past like a display, something to look at but never touch." Gray sipped at his beer. "My father was a realist, he worked hard every day and read every night. He watched the way things were going, the tide of time you might call it. He knew over forty years ago that something had to give in the world. The pollution was only then getting addressed and crops were dying in droves. The veil of society was getting thin. All forward progress was stilted and people were getting closer and closer to an edge."

"A war."

Gray nodded. "That's like a release valve for the human race, sick as it sounds, it's a necessity, or an inevitability, not sure there's a difference. War is a forest fire. When the woods become too cluttered to grow new trees, a fire starts, cleanses the ground along with much of the mature forest, but it's essential. When it's over, things begin anew. The ash from life breeds new growth, a fresh start. As ugly as it is, that's the truth. Every end is harsh before a beginning." Gray looked down at his lap and spun an empty bottle in place. "So my father thought there was no way I wouldn't be involved in the next war, I'd have been just the right age, so he named me what he did. I suppose he thought it would give me confidence or be a talisman against getting killed, I'm not sure. Instead of war we got innovation." Gray motioned to the sky. "The cleaners up above burning some crystal ore mined from Mars, belching out pure oxygen into the atmosphere. We have cures for cancer, Alzheimer's, and diabetes. We got plants that stay green without water and can stand gallons of pesticides but are doing God knows what to our insides, and we have a nice assurance that goes even further back that no psychopaths will be stalking our streets at night."

Ruthers swallowed a mouthful of beer and stared at the sheriff. "You mean FV5?"

Gray nodded. "Your parents I'm sure weren't able to dodge the mandatory jabs for their kids, just like mine, right." Gray pulled up the sleeve of his T-shirt to expose the orange line of five dots running straight down his shoulder, each no larger than a pencil eraser. Ruthers slid his sleeve up, exposing the exact same formation. Gray let his hand drop back to the table. "Anyway, why should they be afraid of something that's guaranteed to keep their son or daughter from becoming a crazed murderer?"

"Are you against the jabs, sir?"

"No, I can't say that I am since there hasn't been a recorded serial killer in the last forty years. All those potential victims are safe, lived out their lives without ever imagining that they could've been the target of something monstrous. Just by turning off one tiny gene inside each person born, you assure everyone that they couldn't possibly be a sociopath or progress into a psychopath." Gray drummed his fingers on the tabletop. "What bothers me is that gene is there with every birth. The possibility of becoming something evil," Gray tapped his chest once, "is right here inside all of us."

The yard was quiet except for the trickle of the choking stream. The birds were silent, gone back to their roosts to wait for the rain that Gray could smell coming from the west.

"So you think the Olson murders and the Jacobses were—"

"I'm not saying anything yet, Joseph, and I'm well aware that plain old murder still happens every day, I saw enough of it in the cities to last a lifetime." Gray finished his beer and looked his deputy in the eyes. "But, something doesn't match up here, something is off. A month ago the Olsons burn up in a fire started by someone else. No suspects or arrests, not that I'd expect any from Mitchel and his county. Last night the Jacobses are slaughtered, and then their killers try to set the house on fire."

"To cover their tracks." The deputy's eyes were wide in the faint glow of the porch lights.

"Maybe."

"But that would mean someone would've had to have hidden their kids away from the start, had them at home, never brought them into town, no one could see they didn't have the Line on their shoulders, otherwise they'd be persecuted, run out of town."

"And then," Gray continued, sitting forward, "The chances of them being a full blown psychopath would be infinitesimal."

"Exactly, so…"

"So that leaves us with one of two options, Joseph. One, someone did just that, kept their children hidden from the system, kept them from getting the jabs and those kids just by chance became monsters or, two, the shot didn't work on them like it did everyone else."

"But, sir, I read about FV5, it was mandatory for the service. They tested a variation of it for thirty years on known serial killers, there was a one hundred percent success rate at nulling the gene before they ever brought it to public awareness."

"I know, but if I've learned anything from history it's this: life is not static. It moves, changes, adapts. We think we're smarter than nature, but we're not. Every step we take in fighting it is a step in the wrong direction. We come closer to the cliff, Joseph, not farther away." Gray sighed. "But the most obvious answer is normally the correct one so—"

"So that leaves us with—"

"Option one." Gray leaned forward, placing his elbows on his knees before staring into the darkness. "If I'm right, Joseph, the people who killed the Olsons and the Jacobses not only don't have the Line, they're the first serial killers America has seen in over forty years."

~

The rain woke him a little past two in the morning. It wasn't a violent crashing of thunder or even a staccato pulse of lightning that brought him up out of a dream where he'd been running from something massive that blotted out the sun. It was the soft tapping of raindrops against the window.

Gray turned his head toward the sound, the room so dark even the stormy night outside looked bright. He waited, blinking at the clarity of awareness, his

37

breathing, in and out, the softness of cool sheets over his body, the drumming rain. Alone.

He stood from the bed and crossed to the window, his own formless shadow appearing as a reflection in the glass. A thin wall of clouds moved across the sky, already broken in some places, their mass filtering through to the stars beyond. He watched the rain fall, trying to believe that it would make a difference, that tomorrow's heat would be lessened, the drying riverbeds quenched.

He went to the adjoining bathroom and drank straight from the tap, sucking down mouthfuls of water to wash away the stale taste of beer. He paused at the foot of the bed as he walked back into the room, looking at the sheets as if they might wrap around him, constrict his breathing until he struggled no more. Changing directions, he moved into the hall overlooking the rest of the house, feet silent on the wood floor, patters of rain above him. The door appeared to his left and he finally looked at it. Normally he hurried past it in the mornings and looked the opposite way at night when he went to bed, choosing to not see it.

He stood before it now, taking in the decorative oak panels. His fingers traced the flared grooves of trim and settled on the two screw holes, their edges small but sharp, always catching his skin. Gray reached down and held the doorknob for a moment, waiting for what had moved him here to turn him away again, back to bed to dream of the crushing mountain falling down upon him. He opened the door.

Cool light filtered in through the one window taking up most of the east wall. The carpet beneath his feet shushed with each step until he stood in the center of the room. His hands found the edge of the crib, the wood so smooth. It creaked a little, it was the only thing he hadn't made in the room, his work schedule over a year ago too heavy to allow him the time to do one justice. A toy box stood beside the crib, the colorful letters he'd carved and painted were indefinable dark shapes. The little changing table was after that and he found himself standing over it. The smell of baby powder, faint but there, hung above it. The sign with two screws backed out of its front lay on its surface, catching what little light came in through the rain-slicked window.

Gray traced the name with a finger, ran in the grooves created by his tools, made to hang on the outside of the door proclaiming someone who would never sleep in the room again.

He pulled his hand back, let it fall to his side before turning away. Without a look, he walked from the room, pulling the door shut behind him with a sound like that of a baby's breath.

Chapter 8

Ryan was in a boat, half full of water, barely floating.

The lake lapped against its sides, its iron-gray surface trying to get in, to pull the boat down, and he wished that it would float. He wished it would glide on, somehow draining itself of the weight of all the gallons. He had an idea that he could feel the water sloshing within his own stomach, too much to hold and still be alive, but there it was. The edge of the lake was a silver border cutting against rocks and sand alike. He knew if he took one step forward, he'd fall, fall and drown beneath the waves, his insides already full of water, he wouldn't have to go much farther to inhale a bit more. He would sink into the blackened depths and reach toward the surface of a place he didn't know anymore, didn't care to know.

But the boat, the boat was sad how it barely floated and he wished it would sit higher in the water. He wanted to bail it out, but that wouldn't do since he was full of water himself. And now the water was in his nose, coming out of his mouth, he choked on it, spluttered, sat up—

—and awoke to someone standing over his bed.

He didn't cry out, not because he didn't want to, but because he recognized the shape; the humped shoulders, the rounded head looking down at him. Only a sliver of light fell into the room from the hall, but it was enough to see the grin on Adam's face.

"I just had a dream and had to tell you about it," Adam said, the smile never leaving.

"Okay," Ryan said, his voice clogged with sleep, his own nightmare flattening out into a gray sheet of memory, the water flowing away into nothing.

"There was a spider the size of a cat eating me," Adam said, rubbing his stomach. "Right here. She was huge and black and had really sharp teeth. She tore into me so deep I thought she was going to eat right through me, and the pain was so nice, like right after you come, like that."

Ryan sat up a little, tried not to slide away from his brother. "You should go back to your room, Adam."

"Not done yet. Then she quit eating and came out of my stomach and looked at me, and I felt warm, but I was sad that she was leaving." Adam leaned down a little and Ryan braced himself. "But she wasn't leaving at all, Ryan, the warmth was her giving her babies to me in my belly, and I knew she loved me then and so would her babies."

Ryan's lower lip trembled but he nodded. "That's a good dream."

"Uh huh." Adam didn't move, his expression the same, still smiling.

Ryan was about to try to get past him, get out from under the glazed stare when the slat of light from the hall grew, the door opening more.

Darrin stood there, an outline, not moving. "The fuck are you two doing?"

Adam leaned back and Ryan managed to sit up all the way. "Just tellin' him a dream," Adam said.

"Yeah, I got that. What if Dad had heard you? What would he think?"

Adam shrugged. "Nothin'."

Darrin moved into the room, smooth, without sound. "Not 'nothin',' dumbshit, hearing you talk like that he would've had you locked up and on meds before the sun rose."

Adam slumped a little. "Sorry."

Darrin stopped and sat in a chair beside Ryan's bed, his face half shrouded in shadow. "You have to be careful, never know who's listening." Adam nodded and looked at his feet, shuffling them a little. "What?"

"I went back there," Adam said.

Darrin's head tilted, an eagle watching a mouse. "You what?"

"I went back there, to the house we were at the other night."

"Why?"

"I was missing a screw from clackers. I think it fell out in the house somewhere."

Darrin dropped his forehead into his hand, rubbed it. "And what happened?"

"The sheriff was there."

Darrin froze. He looked like The Thinker statue Ryan had seen in a textbook once.

"Did he see you?"

Adam shook his head.

"I can't hear you shaking your head," Darrin said, his face fully coming into view in the cold light. His features were sharp stone, eyes cutting.

"No, he didn't."

"You're sure? I don't really trust your judgment after you went back there."

Adam's head shook harder. "No, I was standing behind a tree in the brush. He didn't see me."

Darrin nodded. "If you ever do something like that again without talking to me first, you'll wake up being gutted, understand?"

"Yes."

"You're sure you lost the screw there, not in the van or somewhere here?"

"Not sure, but I think so."

Darrin stood and moved closer to them. "We allow ourselves these little pleasures because it's what makes it fun, it's the whole purpose to what we do, who we are." He shifted his gaze between the two of them. "But if we mess up, one step out of line, everything comes down."

"What do we do if they find the screw?" Adam asked.

"We don't do anything. That screw could've come from anywhere, plus we were all wearing gloves."

"What about the sheriff?" Ryan asked.

Darrin's eyes found him in the semi-dark. "Are you scared of him, Ry?"

"I'm scared he'll figure it out."

Darrin leaned closer, the same smell coming off of him as the night before. "He's not going to figure anything out, he's a dumbfuck county sheriff. He'll think the same as everyone else."

"He used to be an investigator in Minneapolis, he's not stupid."

Darrin sneered, pulling up the sleeve of his T-shirt to expose the line of dots running down his shoulder. "This means we're safe, little brother, and we have the medical records to back it up."

"But the house didn't burn," Ryan said, his voice quavering a little.

Darrin looked like he might strike him. Ryan waited, wondering where the blow would land that their father wouldn't see. "That doesn't matter, they'll think it was someone robbing the place, just like we set it up to look like," Darrin said finally. He smiled and it was like a knife blade in the darkness. "We're fine, boys. Don't worry, and don't do anything stupid." He looked back and forth again until they both nodded. "Good."

Darrin moved toward the door, stopping before he entered the hallway. His head turned over his shoulder, and he stared at them with an eye they couldn't see. "He came tonight."

There was a drawn out silence taut as a high wire.

"Already?" Ryan asked, the incredulous sound of his voice making him wince.

Darrin turned back to them, now a silhouette again. "You don't sound excited, Ry-Ry."

"It's not that, it's just so soon."

"You're right, it is."

"Why didn't you come get us?" Adam asked.

"Because I didn't expect him this quickly either."

"What'd he say?" Adam asked, stepping closer to Darrin, a hushed awe to his voice.

Darrin smiled again. Ryan could see the way it crinkled his face in wicked lines that belied all humor. "He's got big things planned for us, boys, very big things."

Chapter 9

Gray ran through the morning sunlight that cut between the trees in flashing blades.

His breathing came easy, a normal rhythm in time with the crunch of his shoes on the dirt drive. After a mile he crested a rise that overlooked a pasture, once housing a small herd of cattle long since departed. The sun was beginning to peek over the trees, its orange head angry at the moisture dotting leaves and blades of grass alike. It rose higher, leaching the ground of the night's rain. Drying. Dry.

Gray turned and ran back the way he'd come, not seeing anything on the jog home but the road before him, long and dusty. A layer of grimy sweat covered his body when he stopped before the door to the house. He took a deep breath in, held it, let it out. The scent of smoke hung in the air, but not smoke, it was the frying of the land giving up any and all water that it tried to hide from the burning orb in the sky.

He ate a light breakfast, showered, and poured a travel mug full of steaming coffee before leaving the house. He sat in the cruiser, watched the door to the garage close in front of his bumper and called the station.

"Morning, Sheriff," Mary Jo answered.

"Hey, Mary Jo, any calls last night?"

"A few came in with concerns to the automated system, but the service didn't hear any distress in the callers' voices, so none woke me up."

"Restful night."

"Not really."

"Anything new on the radar?"

"Nothing yet, Thueson and Monty didn't have anything this morning. Monty said he patrolled past the Jacobses' farm several times and scoped the place, but there was nothing."

"All right."

"You coming in this morning?"

"Not right away. Tell Joseph to do his usual patrols, and I'll call him when I'm in."

"Will do, Sheriff."

Gray ended the call and tapped his thigh once, noting the little bulge where the screw sat, still encased in its plastic bag. After taking a long swallow of coffee, he put the cruiser into gear and drove down the road slowly as to not raise too much dust.

Two hours later he slowed the vehicle to a crawl along the baking tar road heading north out of Shillings. The wind came in gasps and sputters that rocked the cruiser on its springs, the open field of bleached weeds rolling like a brown tide on his left. To the right a dense patch of forest swayed in time. The very ends of the leaves turning an alarming yellow, the roots without even a taste of the night's rain.

Gray inched along the deserted road, heat mirages swirling before and behind the car. The drive he looked for was so well hidden, he sometimes still rolled by it on accident, only seeing the sign after he'd passed. A bit of interlaced brush opened on the right and a small sign, suspended over a narrow trail, swung in the gusts. The *M* in *metallurgist* was almost worn away, he'd have to tell Danzig that it wouldn't do to have a steel sign proclaiming his own profession fading with time.

Gray spun the wheel and drove through a tunnel of trees, their branches interlocked so well only fleeting shafts of light fell on the trail. The road rose and fell before curving past and over a streambed holding nothing but stones and dried sticks abandoned by the water that carried them there. A bit of grass hissed against the undercarriage and then the car rose out of a dip and rolled past a three story house set in an enormous clearing. The house had a haunted look with rounded windows and a turret gracing one corner that rose a story higher than the rest of the roof and ended in an observatory. Three steel buildings stood in a line past the home, their sides a stale green. A stack of steel billets sat beneath the first building's long overhang where the nonexistent rain couldn't reach. The lawn looked recently mowed.

Nothing moved.

Gray parked the cruiser between the first steel building and the house before climbing out into the rising heat of the day. The clack of dry branches and hush of dying leaves were the only sounds. As he approached the building a wide man-door opened and a shadow filled the other side, blocking the glow of high-powered lights.

"Did you bring any booze with you?" The shadow said.

Gray stopped, cocked his head toward the tree line where the sun still hid. "Did I somehow lose about six hours of time, or is it still before noon?"

Danzig Sheppard stepped out of the building, instinctually ducking his head even though the door had been cut to fit his bulk.

The man was a mountain of muscle.

His shoulders were barely concealed beneath a sweat-stained T-shirt, holes gaping where a hot spark had landed. A leather apron hung down his front, its length doing nothing to hide the massive twin pectorals beneath it. He wore a pair of faded cargo shorts on his lower half, stained with grease and burn marks above black, steel-toed boots. His face was clean shaven save a trimmed goatee the same color as his dark, tightly cropped hair. A pair of welding goggles were pushed up onto his forehead, an outline of grime around his eyes where they'd sat.

"The only time you show up here before nine in the morning is when some terrible shit has happened, and I don't want to hear about it unless you have something to drink."

Gray sighed and looked down at his feet. Kicked a rock.

"Shit, it is bad, isn't it?" Danzig said.

"Yeah."

"Well, guess we'll have to do without the booze. Come on in."

43

Danzig disappeared into the building, moving with a grace not normally found in a man so large. Gray followed him inside and shut the door.

The air stank of oxide and grease within the workshop. Its walls were lined with shelves and pegs hung with tools of all shapes and sizes. A steel mallet, its head the size of a car tire, rested on a workbench, pitted and gouged but clean of any debris. The concrete floor looked cool, and for a moment Gray had to restrain himself from just sitting down to soak it in. Danzig crossed to a nearby desk and returned holding an iron chair. He set it down with a clank and then jumped to a sitting position on the top of the worktable, casually shoving aside the immense hammer with one hand.

"Let's hear it," Danzig said.

Gray began to speak, pausing only to take a breath or watch Danzig for his reaction. He left nothing out except his theory, and when he was done he sat and stared at the far wall, a slow drip of water filling the silence where his voice had been.

Danzig's head had dropped and his eyes were closed. He was motionless for a long time. "I fixed a beater bar on Stan's combine two weeks ago. He paid me more than I asked."

Gray nodded. "He was a good man."

"His wife was just as kind as he was and I don't know if I've ever seen a girl prettier that their daughter." Danzig raised his head and now there was a watery film that covered the huge man's eyes. "Who in their right mind would do that to them?"

"No one."

Danzig met Gray's gaze and then looked away. "So you think it's finally happened."

"Yeah."

"And the Olsons were the first?"

"Nope, I can't get myself to believe that they were. I think something has been going on for a long time and no one's caught wind of it until now."

"But no one has caught wind of it, have they?"

"No one but me."

"And what did our good friend Bitchel have to say?"

Gray huffed a small laugh at Danzig's refusal to call the neighboring county's sheriff by anything other than his high-school nickname. "Oh, you know him, always a team player."

"Bullshit."

"Yeah, bullshit is right."

Danzig studied Gray in the harsh light. "They're going to crucify you, you know that, right?"

Gray sat forward in his chair and rubbed one of his boots across the rough floor. "They may."

"If you can't prove it you'll be out of a job at the very least."

"Oh yeah, more like run out of town."

"You could come live with me."

"Fuck that, you snore too loud."

Danzig burst out laughing and Gray chuckled a little until the big man began to cough. The harsh racking filled the building as Danzig doubled over, steadying himself on the table as he slid off onto the floor. Gray stood and stepped forward to try and brace him, but Danzig waved him off, reaching for an immunizer containing a glass vial in its compressed chamber.

"Just get me the poke over there," he said between coughs. Gray grabbed the pneumatic deliverer and placed it in his friend's outstretched hand. Without pausing, Danzig pressed the immunizer to his bicep and triggered the device.

A short bark came from the steel pistol and the glass vial inside became cloudy. Danzig coughed two more times and then quieted, breathing in three deep inhalations.

"Forgot to take one yesterday, dry weather makes me feel better than I am." He wheezed. "Fucking luck, right?"

"Fucking luck." Gray repeated the mantra and watched his friend.

"I'm just glad you didn't go with me that day, otherwise you would've sucked down that pesticide from the air too, and we'd both be giants from the 'roids," Danzig said, tapping the immunizer once against the steel tabletop.

"We couldn't both have been this big, how the hell would we ride anywhere together?"

Danzig let out a laugh that coalesced into a dry cough before finally quieting.

"Sorry," Gray said.

"Don't be, laughter's good for the soul. Maybe it prolongs life too, give me more than the five years the doctors did the other day."

Gray scowled at the floor, shaking his head once. "They'll figure something out."

Danzig sighed and then slapped Gray roughly on the shoulder. "Enough of my pity party, let me see that screw."

Gray pulled out the baggie containing the silver screw and handed it to his friend.

"Am I going to contaminate anything?"

"Nope, I had it analyzed for DNA this morning. Nothing on it but a smudge."

Danzig strode across his shop to another workbench that lined the wall. Although neatly organized, the bench's top was covered with many different apparatus including a digital scale, a row of stainless steel tongs, several curved magnets, and a wide-mouthed crucible.

Danzig set the screw down and pulled a small bottle of clear solution away from the wall and unscrewed the top revealing an eyedropper. With a practiced twitch of his hand, he let one tear of the fluid fall onto the screw.

Nothing happened.

"Well, looks like it's plain stainless steel. The nitric acid would've smoked it otherwise," Danzig said, tweezing the screw up and holding it beneath a stream of water at a sink a few feet away. After it was washed, he brought the screw under a magnifying glass, turning it several different ways before handing it back to Gray. "Yeah, nothing special about it, you could get it in any hardware store from here to Mexico."

"Shit," Gray said, returning it to the plastic baggie.

"Sorry."

"No problem. Fucking luck."

"Yeah." Danzig leaned on his forearms and stared at Gray. "What's next?"

"You know what I'm going to ask you."

Danzig shifted a little. "I don't know anyone that would do something like that."

"But you do know some who don't have the Line, right?" Gray said.

"I have customers."

"Dan, people are dead and more to follow if I don't find the ones who did this."

Danzig stood and grimaced, looking at the wall for a moment before answering. "Terry Yantz and his family are way off in the boonies, south on sixty-three about five miles. You'll see a dried up swamp on the right and then a trail narrower than mine running straight in. Follow it to the end and you'll find them, but I can tell you right now, Terry didn't do it. He's got a family, he's an intelligent man but they live simply. They stay out of the way of most people. Shit, I wouldn't know him myself if he didn't need hand tools repaired every so often."

"No one knows anyone fully."

"So you say."

"So I know."

Danzig's posture relaxed and he rubbed the spot where he'd given himself the shot. "Besides interrogating an innocent man, what's your next move?"

"I think about it all, it's what I do best."

"What you do best is talk."

"Can't argue with that."

"Seen Lynn lately?"

Gray blinked and nodded once, the question blindsiding him. "Yesterday. Came by to pick up a jewelry box. She was headed out on a date."

"Yeah, I was going to mention I saw her with someone in town last week when I stopped in for supplies."

"Who?"

"Does it matter?"

"Yes."

Danzig rubbed his forehead, pushing the goggles off completely. "Mark Sheldon."

"You're sure?"

"Yeah, hate to say it but they looked pretty cozy at the café having lunch."

Gray shook his head, looking at the floor. "The fucking DA."

"Yeah."

"That just fits, doesn't it?"

"Why, because you hate the guy already?"

"Pretty much."

Danzig stood to his full height and grabbed a piece of cable off of the wall, turning it over in his big hands. "You know, it's surprising, but with the new technology springing up every year, people still rely on things like this for all different kinds of reasons. This steel is an alloy, it's made from a high content of iron and a low percentage of carbon. Now if there's too much carbon, or not enough, the alloy becomes too soft or too brittle. Put stress on it and it'll break, either way. The art of metallurgy is a continual exercise in balance. Without balance, things don't work."

Danzig pulled hard on the cable. It creaked, growing taut between his fists, but held.

"You're terrible at metaphors," Gray said. Danzig hung the wire back on the wall, shrugged. "But thank you." Gray looked at a clock above the workbench. "I need to get going."

"Before you do, I have a couple things to show you," Danzig said, motioning to follow him.

The two men walked the length of the building to a doorway leading to a smaller room tucked into one corner. The room held sets of steel drums, their gleaming hides reflecting light from overhead. Some of the barrels were misshapen, bulged out and pocked with internal distortions as if someone had taken a hammer to their insides. On the wall hung what looked like a shiny, black sweater, its sleeves and back catching the light. As Gray leaned closer to it Danzig pulled the odd garment off the wall and stuffed it into a nearby cabinet. The sweater made an odd clanging as he put it away.

"What was that?"

"Top secret. Not ready yet."

Gray didn't press him further and followed as the huge man proceeded deeper into the room.

Danzig stopped before a table holding a hardness tester. On the machine's small platform was a large ball bearing, compressed by a pointed indentor. The machine's gauge read all zeros.

"This is something new I've been working on for over a year. It's an alloy of stainless steel and M-Core."

Gray squinted at the sphere. "You alloyed the stuff from Mars?"

Danzig's smile creased his entire face. "Yep. Took me a bit to get the mixture and temperature right, but I think I've perfected it."

"Looks delicate," Gray said, motioning to the zeros on the hardness tester.

Danzig raised his dark eyebrows. "It's zeroed out because it maxed the machine."

"You're joking."

"Nope, and watch this, this is the real treat." Danzig decompressed the ball bearing and held it out to Gray. It felt like a polished egg in his hands. There were no markings visible on its surface to indicate the extreme pressure it had been under moments ago. "Now step over here and put it in that funnel system."

Gray walked to where Danzig indicated and traced a steel tube that ran in a descending arc, then shot straight down into one of the sealed barrels. Gray placed the bearing into the tube and watched it roll out of sight. The sound of the sphere traveling was like a fly buzzing inside a light fixture. Then there was a gap of silence before a quiet ting.

The barrel's sides expanded with a bang so loud Gray put his hands to his ears and flinched halfway across the room. Numerous bulges appeared in the drum's sides and the ticking of steel re-settling filled the air.

"What in God's name was that?" Gray asked, glancing wide-eyed at his friend.

Danzig's deep laughter overtook the clicking metal. "I call that a Tin-Snipper. It's completely stable under constant applied pressure, but if dropped above a distance of five feet onto a hard surface—" Danzig cupped his fists together and then sprung his fingers apart. "Boom."

"That's unbelievable."

"Like I said, it took me a year to perfect. It's got the same explosive power of a standard grenade but three times the shrapnel."

"You're a mad scientist and you're going to blow off a hand someday."

"Yes mother." Danzig laughed and guided Gray over to the far corner of the room. "Almost forgot, I have something for you." The huge man picked up a smooth-handled knife from a shelf and handed it to Gray. The weapon looked almost exactly like the one he carried, the blade hidden inside the handle itself. Gray made to push the release button on the back and felt Danzig grip his wrist.

"Hold on, let me tell you about that. First off, it's made mostly from meteor nickel with a dash of tungsten carbide."

Gray glanced up from the knife. "How the hell did you get your hands on a meteorite?"

"Got a contact in Texas, a star hunter. Found one last spring a few hundred feet off the coast of Corpus Christi. Now what makes this unique is the cooling factor the nickel underwent upon impact. It hardened the molecules perfectly, so perfectly it took me three months to figure out a way to superheat it and bind it with the carbide. I wore out sixteen diamond files shaping the blade too."

Gray looked down at the knife and triggered the button.

A seven-inch bit of slender steel shot from the handle so hard it nearly recoiled out of his hand.

"Holy shit," Gray said, studying the blade. Its color reminded him of oil pooled on water in the right light.

"Gas deployed, good for a hundred and fifty openings, then you have to have it recharged, which I can do for you. That alloy is hard enough to cut through a quarter inch of stainless steel and you could still shave with it on the other side."

"What if the damn thing goes off in my pocket?"

"It won't, the button can only depress if the grip is pinched on either side, almost impossible to deploy otherwise."

Gray pushed the button again and the blade retracted soundlessly into the handle.

"Thanks Frankenstein."

"Only the best for your birthday."

Gray paused before sliding the knife into his pocket.

"You forgot, didn't you?" Danzig said.

Gray nodded. "I thought about it last week, but with everything in the past couple days…" He shrugged. "Doesn't matter, but thank you for remembering."

Danzig put a hand on his shoulder and stared down at him from his towering height. "One other thing before you go—if you need me on this in any way, I'm more than willing to help. Those people didn't deserve to die that way and I'd have no qualms doing what needs to be done to whoever's responsible."

Gray squeezed his friend's hand once. "One thing's for sure, either I'll find them, or they'll find me."

Chapter 10

When Gray pulled up to the station his stomach sank as he saw the car parked in his spot.

He shook his head, sighed once, and got out of the cruiser.

The air conditioning inside the building wasn't working properly. The temperature seemed the same, if not higher than outside. Sweat sealed Gray's dark shirt to his body and he pulled off his baseball cap as he entered, smoothing his hair back. Mary Jo sat behind the station's main desk, an array of monitors surrounding her. A headset rested in her auburn and graying hair, her skinny fingers danced over a multifunction screen on the desk. She looked up at him as he entered.

"He's in your office."

"You let him wait in my office?"

"No, I did no such thing, he went in himself, blew past me before I had words out of my mouth."

Gray rapped his knuckles once on the desktop.

"I hope that wasn't directed at me," Mary Jo said, her fading eyebrows rising.

"No ma'am, just like the sound it makes."

Gray stepped away from the desk and walked down the narrow hall, hot air pushing at his head from an overhead vent. The bathroom door on the left stood open, a smell of old urine and disinfectant leaking out. On the right a window looked into a small office, a large desk standing in its middle, top covered in stacked papers. A man in a dark suit sat in the chair facing the opposite wall, greased hair plastered down to his head in a style resembling lawyers Gray had seen in the cities years ago. When he walked through the door, the man glanced at him.

Mark Sheldon had an overly handsome face with eyes light blue and a nose that you could cut a straight line with. His even teeth flashed white, once as he stood, more sneer than smile.

"Sheriff, how are you this morning?" The district attorney extended a hand that Gray shook quickly, not wanting to think about if it had touched Lynn, or where.

"Busy, what can I do for you?" Gray settled in behind the desk as Sheldon did the same across from him.

"Just stopped by to see how things were going with the Jacobs case."

"It's going. We're exploring a few different aspects at this point."

"Which are?"

"Gathering leads in the form of suspects."

"And those are?"

Gray blinked once at the other man. "We're compiling them this morning."

Sheldon nodded, his eyes closed, fingers steepled. "Gotcha, and the coroner's report?"

"Should be on my computer before noon unless Tilly ran into something."

"Tilly?"

"Dr. Swenson."

"Ah."

The seconds ticked by and Sheldon smiled, nodding to the silence.

"Is there something I can do for you?" Gray finally asked.

"Yes, there most certainly is," Sheldon said, sitting forward. "You can remember who the one person is that can remove you from your elected job, Sheriff. And that's me."

"Well, I very much appreciate you stopping in to refresh my memory, though I think you're speaking out of turn since the county board has that right, but I have a case to work on."

"Oh yes, you do," Sheldon said, still smiling. "You have this case to work on, this very normal, very average breaking and entering gone wrong. Mitchel explained to me some of the hints you've made in the past and let me tell you, Sheriff, fairy tales like the ones you've got in your head will do nothing but hurt this town and its people."

Gray unclenched his jaw before a tooth cracked. "With all due respect, Mark, get the fuck out of my office unless you're prepared to handle this case yourself."

Sheldon's smile flickered and then died under Gray's stare. He stood from his chair, brushing his suit pants of nonexistent wrinkles. "I know why you came back to your hometown, I know your theories weren't popular in Minneapolis either. But if you think you can shove your deranged fantasies onto a smaller town like Shillings, you're dead wrong. This place will eat you up and spit you out if you try peddling that shit to the public. You'd be out of this office with hell on your heels before you could say 'boo'."

"The door is what you walk through to leave." Gray pointed before turning to wake his monitor. He heard Sheldon's dress shoes snap across the floor and pause at the entry.

"Enjoy your last term in office, Gray, and I'll enjoy Lynn later tonight."

Gray looked down at his feet below the desk and counted to one hundred, listened to Sheldon's car start outside before he glanced up. The first thing he saw was the digital temp control mounted on the wall. It read 86 degrees.

Gray stood and put his fist through the screen.

The plastic smashed into spider-webbed lines and plaster cracked around the control's base. Mary Jo's voice came through the small speaker on the side of his monitor. "Are you all right? Did you fall down?"

Gray sat in the chair, gave his knuckles a look and leaned back. "Peachy. Send Joseph in when he gets back, we have work to do."

Chapter 11

"Are you feeling okay, son?"

Ryan jerked out of his trance, the plate holding his bagel before him coming into focus. He looked up at his father who held his coffee cup below his chin, blowing away the steam, his eyes soft and beseeching.

"I'm fine," Ryan said, reaching for his breakfast. His stomach flipped at the thought of eating anything.

"You look a little pale. Did you sleep okay?"

"Yeah, great." Ryan summoned a smile.

His father nodded, sipped his coffee, his sandy hair catching the morning light. "You know, I was thinking it would be nice to go to the lake over in Semingford when I have a stretch off. Maybe rent a cabin there and spend a weekend like we used to. What do you think?"

"Yeah, we should, definitely."

His father set his coffee down. "What's wrong, son, you can tell me."

Ryan almost laughed. "Nothing, Dad, I'm fine. Maybe I am a little under the weather."

"Want to come into work with me, I can fit you in right away this morning."

"No, that's fine. I'll just rest."

"Okay." His father glanced at his watch and stood, pouring the remainder of his coffee down the kitchen sink's drain. "Gotta go, I should be done sometime early tonight unless the ER is shorthanded today, then it might be later."

"Sounds good."

"And tell your brothers that it's their turn to clean the house today, you've been doing it more than your fair share."

"Sure, thanks, Dad."

"Love you," his father called over his shoulder as he left the kitchen and disappeared through the entryway.

Ryan listened to his father's BMW start in a muffled hum inside the garage and then pull out, the rattle and clank of the garage door shutting again.

"Love you too," Ryan whispered.

"Talking to yourself again?"

Darrin's voice startled him so much he spilled the half-full glass of orange juice across the table. The liquid pattered on the floor, the dripping reminding him of something else.

"Jumpy," Darrin said, moving to the fridge. Ryan stood and began to mop the juice up with a towel. Darrin pulled out a premade protein shake and leaned against the counter drinking straight from the bottle, his eyes on Ryan the entire time.

"What's going on tonight?" Ryan asked, his head still down.

Darrin finished drinking. "A little jaunt that he wants Adam and me to do while Dad's at work."

"What is it?"

"That's our business, little brother." Darrin gave him a long stare. "How long's it been since you did your chores?"

Ryan swallowed and finished wiping up the juice. "A couple days."

"You know he won't let you in on everything until you're finished, you know that, right?"

Ryan stood and paced to the sink where he deposited the sticky towel. "Yeah, I know."

Darrin stepped closer to him, the fetid stink of morning breath mixed with sweet protein drink washing over him. "Do it tonight, while we're gone and Dad's at work. You don't have it done when we get back, I can't guarantee what he'll tell me to do with you."

Ryan nodded, his eyes averted, staring out at the morning light, a mockery of hope. "I'll do it."

Darrin put the drink back in the fridge and slapped Ryan on the bicep, hard. "Good. You'll enjoy it, little brother, you'll see." Ryan nodded and waited until Darrin turned away and climbed the stairs out of sight before sinking down into a chair, his eyes locked on the window and the world beyond. A bird flew past, a streak of yellow. There and gone.

The morning ached with heat when he stepped outside. Small puffs of dust kicked up beneath his feet as he transitioned from the paved drive running before their three-story house, to the packed dirt turnaround that wound to the open fields. The corn stretched toward the sun, the unnatural green of the plants enhanced by the meager rain the night before. Ryan walked past an immense storage shed where their Churner sat, the machine scheduled for a bit of maintenance before it would be rented out again to another farmer needing to expose the rich phosphate sixty or more feet down in the ground. The shadow of the towering silo spilled onto the heated dirt and Ryan walked into its embrace, the air changing only a little in temperature. He readjusted his grip on the peanut butter sandwich wrapped in plastic as well as the glass bottle of cool water, already beginning to sweat beneath his fingers.

The dirt track led around the side of the silo and turned right before petering out in the cornfield's emerald mass. Ryan left the path and threaded his way between several maple trees, their leaves' dry clicking filling up the morning air. A high stand of reed grass, trampled in places, stood past the trees and Ryan pushed his way through it until he felt his feet land on smooth concrete.

A row of stairs cut into the earth.

Their short steps numbering half a dozen, led down to a steel door set within a poured concrete enclosure, its top even with the rest of the ground. Grass grew in matted clumps from a layer of earth upon it, a hard fall for anyone who didn't know it was there.

Ryan climbed down the steps, not looking at the dirty, five-gallon pail filled with rusted instruments, their bladed smiles gleaming beneath clumps of matter gone dark with age. The memory of the pail's handle in his palm nearly overwhelmed him and he rubbed his hand on his jeans to assure himself he wasn't actually holding it.

A sliding block of iron graced the front of the door, a shining padlock securing its end. Ryan set the food down and dug a single key from his pocket. The key shook and jittered against the lock's cylinder face before sliding inside.

He pulled the lock free and set it on the ground. He slid the shaft to the left, the rasping scrape of steel on steel grating against his eardrums. Picking up the food, he pulled on the door, letting the bright light of the day spill inside.

The root cellar was only seven feet wide but over twenty feet long. Its smooth walls were dry and powder-white, helping the light from outside stretch farther in. The smell hit him as soon as he stepped inside and even though he braced himself, he couldn't help the gag that spasmed in the back of his throat. The scent was a mixture of human waste along with body odor laced with fear. The latter was sharp in the close air.

A tinkle of chains came from the far end of the cellar and Ryan waited for his eyes to adjust before he took several steps inside.

A man lay on his side near the furthest wall, one arm tucked beneath his head, the other ran down to his hip where it ended in an ugly stump that oozed blood and pus through a soiled wrapping of gauze. He wore only a brown pair of underwear, once white, that barely hung on his emaciated frame. Scars, old and new, covered his legs and torso in archaic etchings of pain, their puckered mouths speaking silent agonies. Chains ran down from deep-set anchors sunk in the wall to a dozen oversized fishhooks that were embedded in the flesh of the man's back and buttocks, their tips catching the light in evil glints.

The man's eyes were twin reflections of terror, their shine that of a beaten animal past the point of breaking. He shifted and tried to scramble back against the wall, but the hooks twisted in their fleshy moorings and he made a choked sound before lying once again on the floor, urine flooding the front of his underwear. The formerly vivid shock of red hair on his head was a matted maroon, looking like strands of old blood.

Ryan cleared his throat and moved closer, trying not to vomit from the smell of fresh feces that lingered in the air.

"I brought you a sandwich, Mr. Baron."

Chapter 12

"We're looking for a dried up swamp, Joseph."

Ruthers glanced at Gray as the cruiser lifted slightly over a hump in the road and then settled again, the car feeling like an airplane instead of a vehicle.

"Sir, if you don't think this man is the one we're looking for, why are we going out to talk to him?"

"Links of a chain, Joseph, links of a chain."

"Sir?"

Gray looked at the deputy. "It's something my mentor, James Dempsey, taught me when I was training in Minneapolis. An investigation is finding a chain. Even with all our fancy gadgets and technology, what we're looking for will always be the same. People are links in the chain, objects are links, even hunches can be links. If you find a link, and it doesn't have to be the first link but usually it is, you follow it to the next one, and the next one. Sometimes it dead ends and you have to backtrack until you know where to start again, but mostly you find whatever's tied to the other end."

"You don't think this is a dead end?"

"Hard to say. Maybe."

Ruthers rubbed a finger against each temple and closed his eyes. Gray smiled a little. "Beer wreaking havoc on your brain pan, Joseph?"

"Yes sir."

"There's a bottle of pain killers in the glove compartment."

"Thanks." Ruthers fumbled the small pill bottle out and deposited two caps in his palm before dry swallowing them.

"You didn't get any coffee this morning," Gray said.

"I'm quitting."

"Altogether?"

"Yes sir."

"It all doesn't taste like the stuff from the café, you know?"

"I know, just thought it would be better for me. Your vegetables got me thinking about things."

"That sounded dirty, Joseph." Ruthers busted out laughing and Gray smiled again. "How long have you been drinking coffee?"

"Five years or so."

Gray whistled low as he slowed the car, a bleached, withering swamp approaching on their right. "That headache's going to get a lot worse, Joseph."

A hacked hole in the thick brush appeared where the swamp's wasted reach ended. The trail leading into the woods looked cavern-like, hewn by a machete or hatchet but not near large enough to accommodate the cruiser. Gray pulled onto the side of the road and shut the vehicle down.

"We walk from here, Joseph, prepare to leave the map."

"Really?"

"Links of the chain, Joseph, links of the chain."

The heat buffeted them in layers, each warmer than the last as the sun crawled toward noon overhead. They left the quiet highway for the dense thicket, sounds of the drying forest pressing in on all sides. Gray could hear it speaking to him, calling out for the teasing taste of water from the night before.

"Is Minneapolis as big as people say?" Ruthers asked after a while.

"Bigger. Some people are like flies, and the biggest cities are just heaping piles of technological shit."

"Can I ask you something, sir?"

"Joseph, when have you ever not asked me something?"

"How many cases did you work on there?"

"Too many. That's why I came back here. The homeland calls the blood no matter where you go."

The trail continued straight for nearly a mile and then made a sharp turn to the left. Daylight shone through the trees in bigger quantities, signaling a clearing was coming up. A hint of wood smoke rode the breeze to them and Ruthers placed his hand on his sidearm.

"Easy Joseph," Gray said, and stepped into the clearing.

A sturdy house made from rough-hewn timbers stood at one end of the open ground, its roof a lashing of tin and shingles. A chicken coop sat next to a small shed that looked barely large enough to house the goat that poked its head through the doorless opening, its mouth chewing lazily. A fire ring in the center of the small yard smoked a yellowish haze into the air that quickly dissipated. A man wearing a sweat-stained set of coveralls knelt near the fire ring, poking at its contents.

"What do you want?" the man said without raising his head from his work.

"Just to talk to you," Gray said. "We don't mean any harm."

"Get walking in the other direction and I won't mean you any either."

"Terry, do two things for me; turn around and face me fully, and tell your boy off the trail there to put down his gun, it's shaking pretty bad and I don't want him to accidentally shoot me or my deputy."

Terry Yantz stood and turned toward them. He had long, blond hair that hung nearly to his shoulders. A solid chin jutted forward and his eyes, so light blue they were almost colorless, inspected them with a sharp clarity.

Terry waved his hand once at the left side of the trail and a boy no older than fourteen with his father's shade of hair tucked behind two ears that stuck out like open car doors, moved into view. He held a lever action rifle that looked much too large for him, but his eyes never left Gray and Ruthers as he moved to his father's side.

"Good eyes, Sheriff, I'll give you that, but my boy's aim is steadier than the earth."

Gray smiled. "You're right, I was more worried about him pulling the trigger intentionally than not. Is that a Winchester model ninety-four?" Terry nodded. "Beautiful gun, although the bore isn't as appealing from this angle."

Terry nudged his son who dropped the weapon's muzzle toward the ground. "What do you need, Sheriff?"

56

"Information, that's all."

"About?"

"I'm guessing you heard about the Jacobses?"

"I've heard rumors by sources I don't entirely trust."

"Well then, you've heard enough. You didn't know the Jacobses, did you?"

"Not from Adam."

"But you haven't had the FV5, am I correct?"

"Nope. Don't believe in messing with nature that way."

"By ensuring children don't ever become sociopaths?"

Terry glanced over his shoulder as the door to the house opened and a woman with chestnut hair came out to stand on the porch. A pudgy-faced baby holding an aluminum rattle that looked like Danzig's handiwork, perched on one of her hips.

"I'm raising my children right, sir, that's the way you ensure that they don't become sociopaths."

Gray nodded once and looked at the ground. "You wouldn't happen to know of anyone else with your frame of thinking on the subject? Someone who avoided the Line too?"

Terry didn't move for nearly a minute and then shook his head. "Not presently. It's not very common if you didn't notice. My wife's had the shots but none of our boys have." He seemed to mull something over for a moment. "The last instance I heard about in the area was a friend of my father's who didn't have his son inoculated, but he died while the boy was young and my father told me later that the family who adopted him got him the jabs thereafter. I remember visiting them a couple times when I was young, but that's it." Terry shrugged. "Can't think of anyone else offhand."

"I appreciate the information and taking time out of your day," Gray said. "But I do have to say, you know there's a burning ban right now, don't you?"

Terry glanced at the small fire. "I'm boiling sugar sap down to make rock candy for my kids, it's the only treat they get. I mind the fire well."

Gray stared at the other man for a second and then nodded once. "Have a nice day."

Gray walked away from the clearing and the watching family with Ruthers a length behind. They didn't speak until well out of earshot of the house and its residents.

"Sir, with all due respect, can we really just let him keep that fire going when it's so dry?"

"Joseph, everything that man cares about is in that clearing. He would no more let the fire get out of control than I would let you drive my cruiser."

After walking another hundred yards Gray stopped and pulled out his wallet. He drew out a hundred-dollar bill and placed it on the ground, securing the edge with a small rock.

"What are you doing?" Ruthers asked as they resumed walking.

"You didn't see the other boy behind the shed holding another rifle bead on us?"

"What?"

"He was there, and no doubt he and his little brother are following us right now to make sure we leave. They're paranoid and right to be since they would be cast out as monsters when all they want to do is live naturally. They have three children to feed and next to no money to do so, Joseph. The cash's just a thank you for talking with us."

Ruthers nodded as he kept abreast of Gray. "Dead end."

"It appears that way, but let's keep this link in mind, you never know when a dead end will become a highway."

~

Gray slid the cruiser into his parking spot behind the station and shut the engine off. As soon as the air conditioning ceased, the heat crept in through the windshield, the unforgiving sun pushing its gaze into the car.

"I could try looking up medical records for the county, start back about forty years ago and work my way forward. See if we can find a match between births in the hospital and an absence of FV5 from the records for the children?"

Gray stared ahead at the individual bricks lining the wall before them. "That's a good idea, but it would take forever, even in a little town like Shillings."

"I could feed the info into a program, run it to look just for that occurrence, I don't think it would take more than a day or so."

"I don't doubt you could, you're way more suited to the computers than I am, but I think we would find nothing, or that if you found a match, the person would have moved away and got the shot eventually anyway."

"So what do we do?"

"You know how I said you start at the first link?"

Ruthers nodded.

"What would you say the first link is if we're traveling under the guise of my little premise?"

Ruthers thought for a moment. "I would have to say the Olsons burning up in their home."

Gray shifted his eyes to the deputy. "What if it wasn't?"

"You mean another murder that was disguised?"

"Maybe, or how about a simple disappearance?"

"Like a missing person?"

"Yep."

"But wouldn't there be evidence of foul play in a situation like that, something that says a person was taken?"

Gray opened his door to the full heat of the day. "Not if the circumstances were right and whoever took them was careful."

They went inside the building and Gray sighed as the promise of respite from the heat was denied.

"Mary Jo, can we please put in a call to have the air conditioning fixed?" Gray said, wiping his brow. "And the thermostat needs to be replaced in my office also."

"Called twice to city hall, Sheriff, nothing back yet."

"What do you mean you called city hall?"

"Didn't you read the memo from last week?"

"Apparently not, enlighten me."

"All expenditures, including repairs, must be run through the tasking clerk at city hall as of last Tuesday."

Gray shook his head. "Tell me some good news, Mary Jo, please."

The older woman tore her eyes away from one of the screens on the desk. "Greg Taylor asked me to the city dance."

"Congratulations," Gray said, putting his hat back on.

"I turned him down flat," Mary Jo said, bringing her attention back to the screens.

"Congratulations," Ruthers said with a smirk.

"Thank you," Mary Jo said. "The man has an unsightly mole with hairs growing from the center of it in the middle of his forehead. If he'd like to date me he needs to start with taking care of his own hygiene."

Ruthers laughed and shrugged as Gray shifted his gaze from him to Mary Jo. "My God you two."

"You asked," Mary Jo said.

Gray shook his head. "Mary Jo, can you look up every missing-person report we've gotten in say, the last seven years?"

Mary Jo's hands flew over two different screens. "Male, female, adult, child?"

"All of the above."

The clicking of the dispatcher's fingernails became the loudest sound in the room. "There are forty-two coming up over the last seven years."

"Narrow that by those that weren't resolved."

More tapping.

"Twenty-six left."

"Narrow that by those that were changed to an ENS file."

Mary Jo raised one eyebrow. "That leaves only one, happened just six months before you took office and Sheriff Enson left for Wheaton."

"Why would it get changed to evidence not supported?" Ruthers asked, coming closer to the desk.

"It would be on the sheriff's orders," Gray said. "If it doesn't look like the person is actually missing, the officer in charge can close it and re-label the final file."

"Which is exactly what Enson did," Mary Jo said.

"What's the name and address?" Gray asked.

"Joslyn Worth. Twenty-nine ninety-five Second Street, Briton Addition."

Gray leaned away from the counter, his eyes narrowing beneath his hat. "Widow Town."

Chapter 13

Gray flew west from Shillings, the cruiser's tires buzzing beneath him, endless rows of corn to either side.

He tapped the screw in his pocket with an index finger, trying to keep time with the small bumps in the road. The land slowly changed from flat to hilly, trees dotting the edges of fields, sentries standing watch. The road leveled again and the crops ended in a jagged cut of ground that became scrub weed. The area looked like an atomic test site, the earth flat and featureless, cleared of everything save the indomitable weeds that grew to over five feet high in some places. A single sunflower held its wilting head above the rest of the field, its color browned by the sun.

A side road approached on the left and Gray swung into it, past the sign reading "Briton Addition," and below that "Transon Inc Mining, site #5471." Another fiberboard sign had fallen in the last year beneath the weather's pressing hand, its proclamation faded beyond reading. Gray drove up the narrow street until the houses began to appear.

There were four rows of them in all, eight in each line. White clapboard siding that was actually single pieces stapled to the four walls. All the roofs slanted the same way, the front doors stood inside modest porches, flanked by two windows that looked unto yards long devoid of any green grass.

Gray idled down the first street, gazing at the attached garages, a dancing napkin fluttered in the breeze like a broken-winged bird. Some of the house's windows were shattered, their gaping mouths ringed with teeth of glass. Hastily scrawled graffiti covered a few garage doors, the profanity laced messages nearly meaningless idioms of hate. Gray shook his head and turned the corner at the end of the street, cruised up the next until he came even with a house on the right, identical to its neighbors on either side.

The breeze was hot breath on the back of his neck when he stepped outside and surveyed the empty street. He expected a tumbleweed to roll out of the field but didn't wait to see if one would.

He walked up the drive to the covered porch, paint peeling like the tips of cracked skis. A nest of beetles undulated in one corner near the front door, their black bodies crawling over one another until they looked like one animal writhing in pain. Gray peered in through the door's windows, relatively clean carpet and linoleum butted together under garish orange walls.

Gray tried the door and entered when the knob turned in his hand. The smell of dust and mold came to him and he listened to the silence of the house, the breeze coursing past the windows, the creak of the floor heating in the sun.

The heat intensified in the closed air as he walked through the single level home, noting how clean the house was. Two bedrooms, one bath, a well-arranged kitchen minus appliances. The backyard was a postage stamp running parallel with the two houses on either side. A little oak tree grew in its center, its branches bare save for three brown leaves at its top.

Gray glanced to the right as movement caught his eye. A plastic beach ball rolled across the yard and bumped into a multicolored play set, its swing swaying back and forth, apocalyptically empty.

When he stepped outside he smelled cigarette smoke and saw that a young woman stood on the porch next door. She was pretty in a weary way with blond hair tied back in a ponytail. She held one of her arms across her stomach, tucked beneath her opposite elbow, a long cigarette perched between her first two fingers like a delicate bird.

"Good afternoon," Gray said, shutting the door behind him.

"What's good about it?"

"The sun's shining."

The woman squinted and inhaled a deep drag. "You're the sheriff."

"Yes ma'am."

"What are you doing in Joslyn's house?"

Gray moved down off the porch and walked into the woman's front yard, stopping before her steps. "Just looking around."

"Cops don't just 'look around'."

Gray smiled. "No, they don't." He studied the woman as she took another puff from her cigarette. "You're Rachel Simmons."

Only a flutter of surprise in her eyes. "That's right, what do you want?"

"I'd like to come inside and talk, if that would be okay with you?"

"What's this about?"

"It's about you calling in a missing-person report on Joslyn Worth."

Rachel looked down and stubbed out her cigarette on the porch railing, adding to a grouping of innumerable black circles. "Come on in then."

She turned away and Gray went up the steps, following the young woman inside. The sounds of cartoons floated to him from another room as he walked into the house and a bout of déjà vu assaulted him at seeing the exact same interior as the gutted house next door, only this home looked lived in. Three paintings of the same yellow flower hung in the entry hall and a vase containing dried reeds sat on a chest of drawers near the door.

Rachel motioned for him to follow her. "You don't have to take off your shoes, I was going to sweep and mop the floors anyway later this afternoon." She disappeared around the corner at the end of the hall, which Gray knew led to the kitchen. "Coffee, Sheriff?"

"Please," Gray said, moving farther into the house after checking to make sure his shoes were clean. When he came even with the living room he saw the television lit with colorful figures dancing in a circle, their cartoon faces overburdened with glee. The song they sang was familiar and for a moment he felt the floor drop away from his feet as the memory of where he'd last heard it overcame him, the toy in his hands emitting the same song he heard now, its colors pleasing to the eye.

"He likes taking his naps there," Rachel said, pulling him back to the present. Gray glanced at her and then at where she looked in the living room.

A small boy no older than a year sat in a reclined bouncy chair, his skin the color of coffee with cream. He had dark hair that curled in ringlets above his ears. A tiny runner of drool leaked from one corner of his mouth.

"What's his name?" Gray asked.

"Kenneth." Rachel blinked once and then smiled tightly. "For his father."

Rachel led him into the kitchen and he sat at a round table overlooking the backyard. After a minute she brought two steaming cups of coffee and set one in front of him.

"Seems almost wrong to drink something so hot when the weather's like this," Rachel said before sipping at her mug.

"It's nice and cool in here. Makes it a little easier."

She smiled but it barely lifted the ends of her mouth. "So what is it you'd like to know?"

"What can you tell me about Joslyn?"

"What's this all about?" Rachel said, reiterating the words she'd spoken outside.

"It's concerning an ongoing investigation."

She studied him, her brown eyes sharp and clear. "I reported Joslyn missing well over a year ago, did you find something?" A twitch of her lips. "A body?"

"No, nothing like that," Gray said. "I read the file on your call, but I wanted to speak to you personally, see if there was anything else you could tell me."

Rachel cupped her hands closer around her mug. "I told everything to that other sheriff."

"Well I'd like to hear it," Gray said, easing his voice down a notch lower into what he hoped was a soothing tone. Rachel shot him a long look and then dropped her eyes back to her coffee.

"We came here at the same time, I mean within the same hour. Joslyn and Tony were moving in next door, unloading some terrible looking furniture from a trailer when Ken and I pulled up in our truck. You saw the inside of their house, the orange walls? Joslyn loved bright colors like that, she was always wearing something neon. We helped each other unpack and right away I could tell we were all going to be friends." Rachel looked up at Gray. "You know how that is? When you meet somebody and you have that good feeling that you're going to have someone new to care about?"

"Yes I do."

Rachel nodded. "It was like that with Joslyn and me. She was already three months pregnant when they moved in. You should have seen her, so happy, always rubbing her belly and smiling. This place was a new start for her, just like it was for all of us. When Transom Inc. called, Ken almost jumped for joy. He'd been out of work for a while and there wasn't much call for an ordnance expert back in Wisconsin where we're from, there just isn't that many companies still using explosives to mine. But Ken was good even though he wasn't versed in mining Lithium. It turned out the system they were using here was similar to what he'd done before, so it was a fit. And with housing provided along with a company car to each family, it was hard to turn down.

"So Joslyn and I started visiting each other when Ken and Tony were on shift. Typically they worked at night with a crew of twenty other guys, so we'd sit up and watch movies, play games, cook, anything to pass the time." Rachel paused and her brow dipped as she swallowed. "We worried, I won't lie, that's what part of our friendship was based on. People think it's a safe profession, but being a miner's wife is a waiting game. You watch them leave for shift and breathe a sigh of relief when the door opens and they come through it again."

Rachel wiped at one eye where a tear tried to slide free, but she caught it and whisked it away, her voice steady. "I can still feel that rumble under my feet, Sheriff, and sometimes I wonder if I'm going crazy. Joslyn was over that night and I'd just told her I was pregnant, and I'd only told Ken an hour before he went off to work. God, he was so excited." Tears tried to overwhelm her eyes again but she blinked them back. "Then we felt it. The whole house shook for a second and then came the quiet except for the car alarms starting up all through the neighborhood from the vibration. We just sat there, paralyzed until Joslyn finally got up and went to the phone to call the office near the site. When no one answered, we knew. We wouldn't say it out loud, but we both knew we wouldn't ever see our husbands again."

Rachel fell silent and let her shoulders round as she finished her coffee, deflating into an even more diminutive figure.

"I'm very sorry," Gray said, putting his hand on her forearm.

She smiled into her cup. "Not as sorry as I am."

"Did most of the families move away after the cave-in?"

"Some stayed. Well, you know as well as anyone that they shut the project down, not because of the accident but because the latest surveys from underground showed less than optimal conditions for the Lithium content. I'm not sure if their reports were wrong to begin with or what, but it's insult to injury that my husband and all the rest died trying to work a project that was doomed from the beginning." Rachel laughed and it was a bitter sound in the close area of the kitchen. "I hate them a little, you know, the families that didn't have loved ones on shift that night. They came by the house when Joslyn and I were trying to make sense of our worlds being flipped upside down, and I wanted to scream at them. I knew what they were thinking, that Ken was in charge of the blasting and that's what caused the accident, but there must've been something else wrong because he was excellent at his job, so careful." Rachel rubbed the table with a fingertip. "Mostly we just didn't want to see their faces, the pity in their eyes."

"But you and Joslyn decided to stay."

She looked up at him and for the first time Gray realized how young the woman truly was. "We didn't have anywhere to go. Transom signed over the mortgages as part of the settlement and at the time Joslyn and I had no jobs, so yes, we stayed. And don't think that I don't know what they call this place. There was thirty-two families here before the explosion and seventeen widows afterward, eight of them had infants or were expecting. All eight stayed because as sick as it was to stay at the site where our husbands died, it was the most financially secure for us."

"I don't think anyone blames you for staying," Gray said.

"I don't think anyone has an idea what we lost." The venom in Rachel's voice cut the air but Gray held her gaze until she dropped it to the tabletop. "I'm sorry."

"You don't need to be." He let her have a moment of silence before asking, "When did Joslyn disappear?"

"Two months after the accident. She was fit to burst, her due date was in a week. We had a get together the evening before, the remaining women of the neighborhood try to gather once a week, let our kids play, catch up with one another. Joslyn left the little park at the end of the block where we were all sitting around nine in the evening and waddled home. I remember someone saying she looked like a penguin walking away." Rachel smiled her sad smile again. The expression fell from her face like a mask being drawn away. "In the morning I went next door to ask her if she wanted to go into town to grocery shop and she didn't answer. I knocked and knocked and then I called her cell before I took the key out of her hiding place under the first patio block and let myself in."

"The door was definitely locked?" Gray said.

"Definitely, I remember trying it."

"And what did you see when you went inside?"

"Nothing out of the ordinary. There were no windows broken and nothing spilled on the floor. Most of her clothes were gone along with her jewelry and a suitcase. Some of the kitchen stuff was taken too like the toaster and microwave."

Gray nodded. "But you called in a missing-person report anyway."

"Of course. Sheriff, Joslyn was almost ready to give birth. You don't run off in the middle of the night when you're that close."

"You don't think that's why she left? To go to a different town to give birth, start a new life?"

Rachel leveled her eyes on his and shook her head. "She would've told me, I was her best friend and she was mine. We talked about everything. If she was going to leave, she would've wanted me to come with. Besides, she had nowhere to go. She was an orphan and Tony's parents wanted nothing to do with her after he died, kind of broke her heart." Rachel glanced away from him to the window. "That little oak that's dead or dying in the backyard? Tony planted that for his son before the cave-in. Said he would be able to hang a swing from it when he was old enough. Joslyn went out and watered that tree every day after he died, she was determined to keep it alive for her child. She wouldn't have left that tree behind." Rachel sniffed once and shook her head. "I told all this to that other sheriff and he assured me he'd look into it."

"Do you feel that he did?"

"Hell no. He walked around her house for a while, had a guy come scan for prints but I heard them talking through an open window. They thought she split town, finally had enough of the pity in the community and went somewhere new."

64

Gray finished his coffee and swirled the dregs around in the bottom. "Is there anything else you can remember?"

Rachel reached over to a nearly empty cigarette pack and pulled one of its long contents out, rolled it between her fingers. "Yeah, but I told the last sheriff and he almost laughed at me."

Gray leaned forward and touched the young woman's hand with the tips of his fingers. "Rachel, he and I are two very different people. You can tell me."

He thought she might cry again, but instead she clenched the cigarette in one fist, crushing it in her grip. "There was a smell in the house when I went in there that day. At first it didn't register fully, but after I came outside and went back in to make sure, I knew."

"Knew what?"

Rachel released the broken cigarette and let it fall to the table in pieces of paper and tobacco. "That there had been someone else in the house with Joslyn the night before, and the only way I know that is they had on the same cologne Ken used to wear."

Chapter 14

"Do you think she was telling the truth?" Ruthers said.

The deputy sat in the chair Mark Sheldon occupied that morning, his face creased with thought, one leg crossed over the other.

"I do," Gray said, tapping the digital keyboard to bring his computer screen to life. His shirt was a wet skin over his own, the heat in the office almost unbearable. He glanced at the immovable pane of glass in the wall and wished once again he could open it, at least to gain some moving air through the office.

"So someone came and took Joslyn from her home in the middle of the night and carried out all her belongings too?"

"That's what it appears like, Joseph, and the one thing that makes me think that's the way it happened is because Mitchel was headed in the opposite direction. The difference between wise men and fools is that fools learn from their own mistakes and wise men learn from other people's."

"Do you want to take a scanner out there and comb the whole place again, see if we can pick anything up?"

Gray shook his head. "No. If they were careful enough to make the whole thing look like she left under her own accord, they wouldn't leave anything behind. Technology is wonderful, Joseph, but it'll never rival an inquisitive mind." Gray tapped his temple once. "So now that we've established an idea of how, we ask why."

Ruthers frowned and rubbed a scuff on the toe of his boot. "There'd be no one to ransom but maybe she had a bunch of money stored away from the settlement or life insurance from her husband?"

"Possible," Gray said, bringing up his email. "But I saw in the report that her beneficiaries were her in-laws. Just two months ago they had her declared legally dead. Why don't you give them a call and see if her accounts were transferred to them also."

"Okay. Did the coroner's report come through yet?"

"It did and I'm looking at it right now."

"Anything?"

"All three victims died of lacerations to various parts of their bodies but we already knew that. No fingerprints, no traces of saliva or sweat other than the victim's." Gray reread the last part of the paragraph, his brow drawing down. "Bite marks appear to be nonorganic."

Ruthers sat forward. "What?"

"Bite marks found on two out of three victims were not concurrent with any known organic bite pattern, nor was there any animal saliva found within the wounds. Digital rendering of the wounds show nearly perfect symmetrical configuration of teeth marks."

"Sir, what the hell does that mean?"

Gray read the passage again. "It means an animal probably didn't do it. It was something manmade." He glanced across the desk at Ruthers and watched disgust darken his features.

"Like a machine to take bites out of someone?"

"Something like that."

Ruthers sat back in his chair. "My God, what the hell are we dealing with here, sir?"

"I'm not sure yet, but we need to bring this to light somehow. If Joslyn's disappearance is connected to these murders, we have something big on our hands here that stretches back years." Gray drummed his fingers on the desk and then looked at Ruthers. "Are you sure you're with me on this, Joseph?"

Ruthers had a shell-shocked quality to his features, but his eyes cleared after a moment. "With you?"

"Yes, this theory could lose me my job and you yours if we pursue it. We'll be ostracized and possibly face charges of some sort if it doesn't pan out. If you have any second thoughts, let me know and I won't involve you from this point forward, you can go on patrol and pretend we never talked last night or today."

Barely a second passed before Ruthers answered. "Our job is to find the truth, right?"

Gray smiled. "Yes it is."

"Then I'm with you."

"Good. Make those calls and I'll see if I can get someone else on our team here," Gray said picking up the phone.

~

Gray sipped his bourbon and watched the sun begin to slide behind the tree line to the west. The restaurant's deck was mostly empty considering the dying day's heat. Bits of music and conversation filtered to him as a door opened and closed nearby, the clink of glasses and silverware against fine plates. Gray's fresh dress shirt was beginning to dampen at his chest and stomach and he pulled the light fabric away not wanting to look completely soiled. The cool shower he'd taken a fading memory.

The afternoon had slid away in a wash of paperwork and regular calls coming in. Several were from concerned citizens who'd finally caught wind of the murders. Mary Jo fielded most of them, assuring the callers that all measures were being taken to ensure the safety of the town.

Gray finished his drink and pressed the sensor on the table that signaled a waiter inside the restaurant. When he heard the door open and close, he didn't look up.

"I'll take another."

"Rough day I'm guessing."

Gray looked up and saw Tilly standing beside the table. She looked prettier than he'd ever saw her before, her white and green scrubs traded for a black blouse and a short skirt. She wore viciously pointed high heels on her feet.

"Sorry, I thought you were the waiter," Gray said, standing to pull out her chair.

"I waited tables when I was a teenager, it didn't stick."

"You look very nice."

"Thanks, so do you."

Gray sat again on his side of the table and smiled at her. "Thanks for coming."

Tilly nodded once, her eyelashes long in the failing light. "To be honest your call caught me off guard."

"Sorry."

"Don't be, I haven't been someplace this nice in years."

"That's a shame."

Tilly gave him a smile and a little light glinted in her eyes. "Yes it is."

Their waiter hurried out of the door of the restaurant and took their drink orders in a rush before returning to the air conditioning at a half run.

"No one likes the heat," Tilly said, fanning herself with a menu.

"I can't say I'm partial to it."

"I don't mind it, it's better than the cold that's coming in a few months."

"See, we're opposites. I like the fall best of all the seasons. The cool air helps keep the peace. Heat enrages people."

"Excites others," Tilly said, crossing her legs. She adjusted her skirt and Gray managed to keep his eyes above the table as their waiter came back with their drinks, leaving as soon he'd placed them on the table. Gray sipped from his glass and looked off toward the setting sun, an open furnace behind the trees.

"It was never this hot when my father was a kid," he said after a time.

"No, my mother still complains about the heat and mentions the cooler summers when she was young."

"Too many things have changed, the earth's heating up because of it."

"The last study said they had global warming under control."

"I'm not talking about global warming, I'm talking about the rage and the angst mixed in with the technology that won't stop coming. We think we're controlling everything, but we're not." Gray shook his head. "We're burning up."

"You think that's what caused the Jacobses' murders?" Tilly asked.

"I don't think the heat had anything to do with it."

"I hope I wasn't reading you right the other day in the morgue."

"What did you read?"

Tilly lowered her voice even though there was no one in earshot of their table. "It sounded to me like you were insinuating that the Olsons' and the Jacobses' murders were connected in a way other than coincidence."

Gray smiled into his glass. "I wouldn't go that far."

"No, it wouldn't be smart if you did."

"Because that would raise questions about my own position."

"Yes, it would."

Gray finished his drink in a long swallow. "What do you think?"

"About the murders or your questions?"

"The murders."

Tilly sighed. "I think there's a possibility that they were done by the same people, but," she said, raising one finger off the table toward him. "If they were, we're dealing with very desperate individuals that are in a great need of money."

"There was cash left at the Jacobses' home."

"They panicked seeing what they'd done and left in a hurry."

"But took enough time to use a machine to take bites out of them?"

Tilly's eyes shifted around Gray to the other people on the deck. "This really isn't the place, Mac."

"I know it's not, but I need you to tell me in your professional opinion if the Line could ever fail."

Tilly sat back as if slapped. "What do you mean, the Line fail?"

Gray pressed on, tumbling down a slope. "Could it ever work in the opposite way or, change someone somehow?"

"Mac, FV5 shuts the murder gene off, end of story. There is no changing someone into a psychopath once it's done. It would be like trying to fire a gun without cartridges."

"Yes, but what if there was a reaction that we're not aware of?" he plunged on, unable to slow now. "What if there was a way that science hadn't predicted?"

Tilly stared at him, her expression hardening, becoming poisonous in the deepening evening. "You sonofabitch. That's why you asked me here, to try and get me to back up your little theory."

"You saw the bodies yourself, Tilly, my God, you saw what was done to those people."

Tilly shook her head, her body no longer relaxed in the chair. She finished her drink and stood, her purse gripped in one white-knuckled hand. "I should've known better, but I thought—" She shook her head. "Goodbye Gray, have a lovely dinner."

He opened his mouth to say something else, to apologize, to stop her from leaving. Instead he looked away and listened for the sound of the door as he sipped at the stinging ice melt in his glass.

Chapter 15

"We're leaving, little brother."

Darrin's words snapped Ryan from his trance, his eyes focusing on his brother's face instead of the television's blank screen across the room. Darrin and Adam stood side by side near the kitchen doorway; both dressed in black clothes, brand new black gloves dangling from their fingertips.

"Okay," Ryan managed, his throat raspy from not speaking for most of the day.

"Go wait for me in the van," Darrin said to Adam without looking at him. Adam lumbered off, his large shadow following him across the floor and out of sight. Darrin waited until he heard the front door shut and then grinned. "You ready?"

Ryan tried not to hesitate. "Yes."

Darrin rounded the large couch and sat beside him, his eyes alight with frenetic intensity. Ryan could only hold his gaze for a few seconds.

"I know you're nervous, little brother, but it's fine, this is all part of the plan. Once it's done, you're in the fold. He'll come to you more often and then you'll know the true shape of what we're doing."

"Does Adam know?"

"He knows but I'm not sure he understands."

Ryan nodded. "I'll do it."

Darrin put a hand on his shoulder. "This is who we are, Ryan. We're bigger than everything else, more special. We're some of the few, maybe the only ones in the world. Doesn't that feel good?"

"Yes."

"It's been too long since the balance has been tipped. We're part of the way the world used to be. Every system has its kind, something that trims populations down, hunts, feeds. Without us, there is no order, no fear, only a blind rushing onward of life without consequence." Darrin squeezed his shoulder once and stood, hovering over him. "Without fear there's no beauty. We're the consequence, little brother. We carry the fear."

Without another word, Darrin left the room and a minute later the roar of the van rumbled away into the night. Ryan stared at the black screen across the room for a time and then stood, moving like an automaton, his motions stilted and unnatural. He paused at the kitchen sink and drew a glass of water, drinking it all down without stopping. He set the glass aside and looked at it, marveling at how different things would be when he washed it later. Just a passage of time and everything would change.

He barely made it outside before vomiting.

The water he'd just drank came up lukewarm and washed with acid. He gagged again, his stomach clenching to the point of pain before relenting. When he was able to stand straight again his eyes immediately went upward, hooking on the sky above.

It was a cloudless night, still warm to the point of discomfort. Stars spread across the sky like the universe was nothing but a patched quilt hung over the world, pinpoints glinting through its seams like gaps into something beyond.

Ryan lowered his gaze and moved away from the house, its glow no longer a comfort as a cold sweat broke out over his body. His shoes crunched in the darkness, one after another, taking him closer and closer. The silo looked down on him in the starlight, its rounded cap a brilliant white against the night sky. Soon he stopped and turned right, pushing through the weeds until his feet scuffed against concrete.

Down the steps, his legs wanting to furl beneath him.

A tomb stood before him, its shadow an open mouth waiting for him to step inside. Ryan's stomach churned and he wondered if he would be sick again. But the nausea receded leaving a tight wire of his insides. The bucket stood to his right and he found it in the dark corner of the concrete wall, his hands fumbling over handles until he found the thickest one.

He drew out the machete, its blade singing against its brethren before sliding free. Dark pockets of rust were black boils on its steel in the faint light. He ran his fingertips against the roughness for a while, reading the story of agony in each braille-like bump.

Ryan turned and strode to the steel door, taking care not to trip and fall on the wicked edge of the machete. His hand raked the darkness until it met the small switch box. With a flip of his thumb, a thin band of light flashed on beneath the door's bottom edge, its yellow glow painting the area around his feet gold. He dug in his pocket for the key and pulled it out, not giving himself time to pause before sliding it into the lock.

"It will be quick," he whispered, opening the lock and dropping it to the ground. He hefted the machete once, wrapping its handle deep within his palm before throwing back the slide with a shriek.

The door exploded outward and slammed into the side of his face.

Ryan stumbled back, flashes of light showering his vision. His feet tangled and he fell onto his ass, the machete clanging to the concrete somewhere beside him. The steel door traveled the full range of its hinges, opening wide, cutting the ground with light as a skeleton with red hair staggered out of the root cellar.

Miles Baron's face was shrouded in shadow but Ryan could see his mouth hung open, unhinged, air gasping in and out of his lungs in noisy hitches. His arms were bent at his sides, remaining hand and stump near his chest as if waiting for a blow. Blood pattered down on the concrete from the fresh wounds on his back and buttocks where he'd ripped the hooks free.

Miles turned his head toward the place where Ryan sat and Ryan stared up at his former science teacher as his own blood ran from the gash in his cheek.

Everything was still for a moment, a frozen painting of horror and decision before Miles's feet skidded on the floor as he lunged toward the stairs and ran up them. He stumbled once near the top before pelting away into the night.

"No," Ryan heard himself whisper. "No!" he yelled and reached out, his hand skittering over dirt and empty space until it closed on the machete's handle. Then his feet were under him, pulling him up the stairs as a caged animal struggled to release itself from his chest.

The moon hung over the trees at the edge of the cornfield, throwing the stalks into a strange aquatic light, their tassled heads like broken hands stretching toward the silver orb. Ryan tried to calm his breathing as he wiped away the flowing blood from his cheek, feeling flayed skin beneath his fingers. The rows of corn stood motionless but over the noise of his raging heart he heard the padded falls of feet in dry soil.

The open alley between where the crops began and the brush ended was a straight line only yards across, and it was down this that the hunched figure of Miles ran. Ryan caught sight of his gangly, naked form as he entered the softer dirt of the field. His legs, still acting on their own accord, carried him toward the fleeing figure while the thrum of adrenaline coursed through his entire body making him feel as if he were holding onto a livewire. Ryan pushed forward harder, dirt flying up behind his feet, arms pumping, the machete's long blade sawing the air beside his head as he flew down the narrow alley. Miles didn't pause to look over his shoulder but merely ran, his stick-thin legs and bare feet carrying him faster than Ryan assumed the man could run.

He shortened the distance between them, but not fast enough.

The end of the field came to meet them in a tangle of overgrown weeds and low bushes, dried to the point of brittleness, before the forest began in earnest. Miles piled into the brush without stopping, twigs snapping and breaking in a sudden rush of noise. Ryan met the boundary seconds later and plunged in after the older man, hacking once at a small sapling with the machete. The land dropped away through the scrub and opened unto the trees, mostly deciduous with wilting leaves that hung down in shadows of mourning.

Ryan followed the sound of his teacher's progress, the moonlight flickering between outstretched branches. His eyes began to adjust and he saw a flash of red hair through the trees, the pale body struggling beneath it. Ryan ran after him, pointing the blade off to the side in case he tripped. He ducked under low branches and leapt over a fallen tree before the ground dipped again and he slid downward into a dried streambed.

With all the water gone, the stream's bottom was hardened mud, dotted with rocks and uneven tables of fine sand. A corridor of moonbeams coursed through several wide openings in the trees, transforming the streambed into a stage of milky light. Ryan came to a stop and breathed through his mouth, listening over the sound of blood pounding in his ears. The trees were silent curtains on either side.

Nothing moved.

Ryan walked forward, searching the shadows of the banks, prying into their murky depths for the scarecrow form. Panic rose up then and tried to seize him. He'd lost Mr. Baron. Lost him somehow in the transition between the woods and the dead river. The teacher was hiding, waiting for him to pass by in the dark.

"Mr. Baron?" Ryan called, as he stalked forward, head swiveling like an owl. "I was, I was coming to let you out." His eyes combed the riverbank. Jutting roots became arms and fingers, a sloped rock became a face. Ryan moved closer, straining his eyes at the dancing shapes that wouldn't still.

Nothing there.

"Mr. Baron, I'm sorry." He moved farther down the streambed, his eyes beginning to water, throat closing up. His chest hitched and tears began to run down his face, mingling with the smeared blood. "I'm so sorry for everything." Even as he spoke, he gripped the machete tighter, his fingers beginning to ache.

A short bend in the hollow came to meet him and Ryan made to move around a stand of grass when he stopped, something halting his progress. He glanced to his right, wiping away the stinging tears and sniffled. An overwhelming tingling rolled through him and he turned his head the other way, pulling in another breath, tasting it.

The air smelled of waste and fear.

"Mr. Baron?"

Miles exploded up from where he lay in the scrub grass.

The sudden movement so close made Ryan flinch and his hand nearly released the blade. The science teacher ran straight down the stream's corridor, his movements jerky and painful. Without thinking, Ryan drew back his arm and flung the machete end over end.

The blade made a strange fanning noise as it flew, cutting the air. At once Ryan knew he'd made a mistake, he'd thrown too low. But as he watched and prepared to run, the machete stuttered once on the ground behind Miles, jumped and tangled in the man's bare legs.

Miles fell to his stomach gasping, as the wind shot from his lungs. Ryan ran forward, his heart beating so hard he thought he could hear it echoing off the trees. He scooped the machete from the sand it lay in, its edge scraping on a rock, a song of steel. The moon's light sculpted the blade into blue fire and Ryan teetered on the brink of fainting, his head too heavy to hold up any longer. Miles crawled forward, two new gashes on his legs where he'd tripped over the machete, oozed blood. The teacher made an animalistic sound in the back of his throat and Ryan raised the weapon over his head, focusing on the back of the prone man's neck.

"I'm so sorry," Ryan whispered, tensing his arms.

Miles rolled over and sat up, whipping his arm around in a quick arc.

Ryan saw the heavy rock leave the teacher's hand and tried to step sideways but a burning agony detonated in his left kneecap. His leg held him for a moment and then folded. He fell to his side, a breathless moan escaping him as the pain ratcheted up into something he'd never known before.

He rolled on the ground in agony, trying to bring his knee up to check that the rest of his leg was still there, but it would barely bend. Through bleary eyes, he watched Miles scramble to his feet and limp away, up the streambed's bank, and into the blanketing dark of the forest. Ryan tried to push himself up but his knee was a pulsing bowling ball, growing each second with poisonous swelling.

"No," he whispered through the pain. He searched the darkness but the teacher was gone, swallowed by the night. "No, no, no, no."

Ryan rolled onto his side and vomited a string of bile, hacking up what tasted like acidic soil as he listened to the fading sounds of his life running away through the woods.

Chapter 16

Darrin watched their long driveway unwind before the van's headlights.

He dug slowly beneath his right thumbnail with the tip of his knife, gouging out the specks of dirt there, pushing deeper, deeper, until the thrill of pain became too much.

"She's pretty," Adam said from the driver's seat.

"Got your eye on this one, brother?"

Adam looked almost embarrassed. "If he lets me."

Darrin smiled. "He'll let you, that's what all this is about."

"Yeah."

"But you can't do what you did to the other ones, you know that, right? That's not what she's for."

"I know." Adam frowned at the windshield. "When can we do that again?"

"We'll have to wait awhile, let things settle down some."

"Okay."

"I need you to promise you won't hurt them, Adam," Darrin said, glancing over at his brother. "He'll be very upset if you do."

"I promise."

"Good." Darrin went back to digging beneath his nails. A bump in the road shoved the blade in deep and he hissed with pleasure. The van moved up a small grade and he knew they were back in the yard but he couldn't keep his eyes off the blood that welled from beneath his thumbnail.

"What's Ryan got in his mouth?"

Darrin looked up, squinting into the bright outdoor lights mounted above the house's entry. Ryan sat on the steps, one leg straight out and the other bent, his heels resting on the ground. He held their father's antique revolver in both hands, the barrel propped in his open mouth pointing up past his teeth.

"Fuck," Darrin said.

"What's he got that gun for?"

"Listen to me, I want you to drop me off by the door and then you go around back to the storage shed and put all her stuff inside it, we'll bury it tomorrow, then bring them in, okay?"

Adam nodded as the van neared the house, his eyes never leaving Ryan on the steps. Adam stopped the van near the attached garage and Darrin climbed out, slamming the door behind him.

"Whatcha doing, little brother?"

Ryan's eyes watered above the stainless-steel gun barrel. They followed the progress of the van as Adam pulled away and then jumped back to Darrin as he approached. Darrin was like a piece of the night, still dressed in his black clothes, his new gloves now gone. Ryan watched him approach and then cocked the hammer of the pistol back with a forefinger, the clicking sound loud in the empty yard.

"Hey, hey, hey, let's talk about this, you don't need to panic. I felt a little scared after my first time too, it's natural." Darrin stopped several feet from the steps, his handsome features sharpened by the bright light.

Ryan sobbed around the gun barrel, the steel chattering against his teeth.

"I'm gonna sit, okay?" Darrin said, lowering himself to the ground. "By the way, what happened to your face?"

Ryan closed his eyes and re-gripped the gun, placed his thumb against the trigger.

"Whoa, just relax, little brother, calm down. Why don't you take that old thunderclunker out of your mouth and talk to me. Then, if you really want to you can blow your brains out, I won't stop you. It's not my right to keep you from your business."

Ryan opened his eyes and stared at Darrin, his breath fogging the steel in his mouth. Gradually he withdrew the barrel, the sight hooking on his front teeth before it came free. He didn't lower the gun but instead placed it under his chin, keeping a finger on the trigger.

They sat that way for long minutes, Darrin waiting, blinking lazily. Ryan's breath began to hitch in his chest and new tears streamed down his face.

"He's gone," Ryan finally managed to choke out.

Darrin nodded. "So you did it?"

Ryan strained to breathe through the panic that gripped him. "No, he got away."

Darrin's face froze. His gaze as sharp as the knife he carried. "What do you mean?"

"He was ready when I went out there," Ryan cried, the dam inside him crumbling. "He pulled the hooks free and was waiting when I opened the door. He knocked me down and ran away and I chased him into the streambed past the field. I tripped him up with the machete but he hit me in the knee with a rock and I couldn't chase him anymore, Darrin, I couldn't. I'm sorry, Darrin, I'm sorry."

Darrin waited, watching him blubber. He didn't blink. "He went east?"

Ryan sniffled. "Yes."

"That land runs over two miles before it hits even a dirt road. The only other place close by is crazy Hudson's, and he won't find any help there. He's bleeding, disoriented, and hasn't had any food or water in two days, he won't make it anywhere. We'll go out and look for him in a while."

Ryan pushed the barrel harder underneath his chin and bleated out another sob, shaking his head.

"What?" Darrin asked.

"I fed him this morning."

"This morning?"

"Yes, I didn't think he'd last much longer, Darrin, he was getting so thin. So I brought him a sandwich and a bottle of water."

"Did I tell you to feed him?"

"N-n-no."

Darrin sighed, dropping his face toward his lap. "Well, that makes things a little more complicated."

Darrin moved like a cobra, springing forward in one smooth motion. His hand snatched the revolver away from Ryan's chin and spun it around. Ryan cried out and leaned away but Darrin kept coming, his free hand finding the gash on his brother's cheek. He forced his thumbnail into the clotted wound. Ryan squawked and tried to roll to the side but his swollen knee and the grip Darrin had on his face held him like stone.

"You little fuck," Darrin breathed into his face. "You soft little follower. I should end you right now. Open your mouth." Darrin pressed the barrel against Ryan's lips, pushing them hard against his teeth. Ryan tried to squirm again but Darrin applied more pressure to the cut on his face. Ryan opened his mouth with a moan and Darrin jammed the barrel inside.

"Taste that oil, it's sweet, isn't it? Tastes like forever. I've had it on my tongue before and let me tell you, it stayed there for days."

Darrin pressed the barrel farther into his brother's mouth and felt it touch the back of his throat. Ryan gagged.

"Don't you be sick now, Ry-Ry. You'd choke on your own vomit." Ryan convulsed, froth beginning to form at the corners of his mouth. "I thought you wanted this, little brother? I thought you wanted out? Funny, now it doesn't seem the case. What a change in a matter of seconds. Everyone wants to live, Ry, even the ones that think they want to die really don't. See, I'm free that way, I love life but if I go, I go. No regrets, no worries, just a little hop-skip into the nether."

Ryan spasmed, coughing against the gun barrel. Darrin pressed harder, his finger tightening on the trigger, and then pulled the gun away, letting Ryan roll onto his side, spluttering and choking.

Darrin pivoted and sat beside him, putting a hand on his back. "Don't worry, Ry, we'll fix this. Things always have a way of working out."

Ryan tried to sit up and Darrin helped him. Gradually his coughing ceased and he sat there silent, rubbing at his throat.

"I'm sorry," Ryan said. He sounded as if he were speaking through a layer of garbage.

"Quit saying that. Just listen to me. You're going to make this right. We're going to find Mr. Baron and bring him back here and you're going to do what you should've done tonight."

Ryan nodded, still massaging his Adam's apple. "Okay."

Darrin looked up at the flawless sky sprinkled with stars. "And Ryan? If you ever disobey me or put everyone in jeopardy again, I'll peel off your skin, one layer at a time. I'll use my knife and a pair of pliers. It'll take days to do it, to make sure I get it right." He glanced at his brother, starlight glinting in eyes colder than space.

"Okay," Ryan said.

Darrin smiled, his face cracking. "Good. Let's get you inside, get some of Dad's cooling gel on that knee, it looks like shit."

He helped Ryan to his feet and supported him until they made it inside. As Ryan settled himself into a chair at the kitchen table, wincing at the flaring pain in his knee, sounds came from the rear of the house and a moment later two figures appeared in the dining room.

One was Adam, carrying what looked like a sleeping child over his shoulder. The baby boy's dark hair shone in the light, his eyes closed, fist near his mouth. The other was a woman, waif thin with blond hair. She was pretty but Ryan could see tear tracks tracing lines on her pale face. Her forearms were locked in a set of steel binders, clamping her elbows together before her so that she stood like some sallow mantis. Her eyes shot around the room, looking, searching, until they lit on Ryan's face and jumped to Darrin as he returned to the kitchen with a bottle of cooling gel.

"Oh good, our guests have arrived," Darrin said, his smile climbing on his face again like a spider. "Ryan I'd like you to meet these two, they'll be staying with us for a while. This is Rachel and her son Ken."

Chapter 17

An electronic chime sang in the back of the store as Gray shut the front door behind him.

He gazed around the small shop, its space made to look like a farmhouse from years ago. The wood floors were tarnished with nail heads painted on in uneven rows. The walls were a soft beige trimmed with a border of chickens pecking in a yard, sitting on eggs in a coop, and huddling close in a winter scene. Crystal figurines graced shelves, their actions frozen in mid-stride. An antique grandfather clock ticked in a corner, and hand-carved picture frames holding digital screens stood in rows along the front counter. 'Memories' was painted in stylish letters, faded to look vintage on the far wall.

Gray made it to the cash register before Lynn emerged from the back room. She stopped mid-stride, her dark hair pulled up and folded the way she wore it so many times at home, before.

"Good morning," he said, trying a careful smile.

Lynn continued walking toward the cash register. "What do you want, Mac?"

"Was passing by and thought I'd stop in."

"So what do you need?"

"Just to say hi."

"Hi."

"Hi."

She sighed and walked away, carrying two oblong globes with sparkling rocks suspended within a viscous fluid. Gray followed her across the store, keeping his distance.

"Are those selling well?"

Lynn placed the globes on a shelf, kept her back to him. "As good as everything else."

"I always liked those."

"I know."

"Business has been okay?"

"Not great, but I'm getting by."

"Good. People still coming in despite the heat?"

"Yeah, mostly because of the air conditioning though."

"You should start charging for that."

She turned to face him and tucked an errant strand of hair behind her ear. "What are you doing, Mac?"

"Breaking ice, isn't it obvious?" He tried the smile again. Lynn's face remained impassive.

"Mac, do you know how ironic it is that you're trying to talk now?"

"Listen, I know, but—"

"No, I'm not doing this again, we've been over things too many times." Lynn pushed past him and made her way back toward the counter.

"But we haven't, we really haven't and that's what's wrong."

She wheeled on him, her pointer finger poking out from a clenched fist. "No, you will not do this to me today, I'm through with your blame-shifting shit, Mac. You had ample time to talk to me when we were married and you didn't. When you came home from work you'd be so self-involved I'd be lucky to get a 'goodnight' out of you before bed."

"That was Minneapolis, why do you think I suggested we move back here? I wanted to slow things down, I wanted a life with you where I wasn't burnt at the end of the day."

"But it didn't change when we came here, Mac, don't you see? You just shifted your energy from a grueling and painful schedule to becoming the sheriff, and after you accomplished that you were busy getting things organized."

"I was home way more than you're giving me credit for."

"You were home, but you weren't with me," Lynn said, tapping her chest. "You haven't been with me in a long time."

Gray shifted his eyes down to the floor. "You're right, I know you're right, and I'm sorry."

Lynn shook her head. "It's not enough, Mac, too little too late."

Gray opened his mouth to speak and struggled for a moment before shutting it. He shrugged, looking at the floor again.

Lynn pursed her lips and moved behind the counter. "Listen, I have to haul in some more boxes from the back."

Gray nodded and began walking toward the front door. He stopped halfway there and turned back to her. "The town celebration is tomorrow."

"I've seen the signs."

"Are you going?"

Lynn shifted her gaze to him. "Yes."

"With him?"

If she was surprised he knew, she didn't show it. "If you have to know, yes, with Mark."

Gray dropped his eyes to the floor, dipped his head once. "Hope he's a better dancer than I am."

He turned toward the door again and stopped, running his hand over the wood before dropping it to the handle. "I was finally able to go in there the other night."

The silence of the shop became so loud his ears rang with it. Lynn took in a slow breath.

"Mac—"

"I just wanted to tell you that. I hadn't set foot in there in over eight months, but I managed to do it. I wanted you to know."

Without looking back he pulled the door open and stepped into the building heat of the morning, the electronic chime the only farewell he received.

The street was nearly deserted, the hour too early for most businesses to be open. The sun shone in spangles of light too bright to look into. Every inch of glass was a mirror speaking in blinding tones. A car glided by, its engine ticking beneath its hood.

Gray made his way to the cruiser and dropped inside, reaching for an iced coffee that was already warming on the dash. The bark of the radio startled him and a drop of coffee fell to his thigh.

"Sheriff, you there?" Mary Jo's voice came through the speakers so loud he winced.

"Go ahead, Mary Jo."

"Sheriff, I just got a call from Wheaton Medical and you're going to want to get over there right away."

"Okay," he said, starting the engine while he stowed away the coffee. "What's going on?"

"A transport driver found a man out on East Six early this morning in a ditch."

"Okay?"

"Sheriff, they think it's Miles Baron."

Chapter 18

Gray turned the last corner on the third floor of Wheaton Medical and spotted the door he was looking for.

A tall doctor in a white coat stood at the end of the corridor, his hands shoved into his pockets. He had sandy hair, swept to the side and wore an expression of concentration on his long face. His eyes moved back and forth between a Wheaton sheriff's deputy and the bulky form of Sheriff Enson himself. Gray made his way toward them and Enson turned just as he stopped before the closed door beside the group.

"Gray, glad you could make it."

"I bet."

"We were just speaking with Dr. Barder about his findings."

"Well, I appreciate the help, Mitchel, but I'll be fine from here on out."

Enson grimaced and glanced over his shoulder at the doctor. Barder looked between the three men and nodded once. "I'll be inside whenever you gentlemen are ready to continue." When the door shut behind him, Enson turned a gaze full of anger on Gray.

"What the hell's the matter with you, Gray?"

"Nothing, actually I feel fine, although hospitals do make me antsy at times. Nothing good except babies come out of places like this."

"Quit fucking around, you know what I mean."

"I know exactly what you mean, Mitchel, that's why I'm saying thank you to you and this strapping young lad here for securing the door for me until I arrived. Now you can leave."

The deputy shrugged his shoulders and threw out his considerable chest as color began to creep up from Enson's neckline in a border of red that advanced like an invading army. "You don't have the right."

"Actually I do, Mitchel, you see Miles was taken from my county and was also found there, so the jurisdiction is mine."

"I meant you don't have the right to order me around, this is my county hospital. And he was not *taken*," Enson said, spitting the last word.

Gray cocked his head. "I'm sorry, was he on vacation in the woods for the last month?"

"I looked at the man's wounds, he was attacked by an animal of some sort."

"Thank you, doctor, but I'll wait until the medical evaluation comes in."

"You're a sonofabitch, Gray, you know that?"

"If I say I do, will it make you leave faster?"

The deputy stepped forward and put one thick finger in the middle of Gray's shirt. "You should watch your mouth."

"And you should watch where you put your hands if you want to keep them attached," Gray said, looking down at the deputy's finger. He waited another beat and then looked up at the young man who couldn't have been older than twenty-two. Gray smiled. "Son, I've had two days full of shit and I'm not about to take any of yours."

"Terrel, stop," Enson said. The deputy sneered at Gray and then stepped back to a comfortable distance. "I'm warning you, Gray, no bullshit without backing it up."

"I'd like to have one of my deputies stationed outside his door at all times," Gray said, ignoring Enson's words as he glanced at the room number.

"No, there isn't any need for that."

"Are you deaf as well as stupid, Mitchel? Someone was holding that man somewhere and torturing him, the driver who brought him in said it looked like he was in a week-long knife fight."

"The guy was shook up, that's all. I'll bet my paycheck that he was attacked by an animal and got lost in the woods. Nothing more."

Gray stepped nearer to the other sheriff. "There will be a guard outside this man's door, Mitchel." The hulking deputy reached for Gray but Gray caught his arm at the wrist and squeezed, feeling the movement of the small bones there. The deputy grunted in surprise and tried to lunge forward but Enson stepped in the way.

"Stop it, let him go, Gray!"

Gray smiled and released his grip. The deputy tried to maintain a calm demeanor but couldn't resist rubbing his wrist with the opposite hand.

"I'll put a guard here since this is my county," Enson said, pushing his deputy back a few more inches. "That's the best you'll get, Gray."

Gray sighed and clenched his jaw once before nodding. "Okay, but whoever it is stays on this door night and day. No leaving for the john, no going home before he's relieved."

"Fine."

"Where's the driver who brought Miles in?"

"He's downstairs in a meeting room."

"Good. It's been a pleasure, truly," Gray said, looking at Enson before tipping a wink at the glaring deputy. Gray turned away from the two men and opened the door to the hospital room.

It took a moment for his eyes to adjust in the sudden shift of light. The room was spacious with an upright bureau to hold clothes standing near the only window, its shade tucking the sunlight out. A small bathroom opened to the left and a wide medical bed sat near the middle of the space with a headboard made completely of wires, blinking lights, and switches. Several of the hoses snaked down to the figure occupying the bed beneath a layer of heavy blankets.

Gray moved to the bedside and nodded to the doctor who made an attempt at a smile and continued examining a digital chart in one hand, touching icons with the tip of his finger. Gray's breath caught in his throat and he blinked, taking in the man who lay before him.

In school, Miles had been an athlete, well built but a little gangly. Gray had been able to keep up with him on longer runs, but in the sprints, no one was faster than Miles Baron. The man who breathed slowly in and out in the bed now was at least forty pounds less than the last time he'd seen him. His hair was a dirty red, matted in some places with what could only be dried blood. Miles was bare chested, his skin blistered and raw around numerous lacerations that coated him like a rash. Some Gray could tell were deep while others were shallow and long, barely cutting through the uppermost layers of skin. Gray traced the pallid lines of his friend's face down to the missing left hand ending in a freshly bandaged wad of gauze.

"My God," Gray said, his eyes never leaving the massacred flesh. "He's cut to ribbons."

"Yes, he's suffering from multiple lacerations and gouges on over eighty percent of his body," Barder said, setting his chart down. "He's extremely malnourished and dehydrated. His left hand has been amputated as you can see with a sharp object, but not so sharp to do a good job. It was basically hacked off. I'm amazed that he isn't consumed with infection."

Gray reached out and put a hand on his friend's shrunken shoulder. The skin was cool and overly soft. "Was he awake when he was brought in?"

"Semiconscious but unresponsive. We gave him a sedative to help him relax and we're infusing him with a calorie concentrate along with saline."

"Will he make it?"

The doctor sighed and came closer to the bed, his intense eyes now filled with compassion. "This man has suffered more trauma than anyone I've ever seen in my twenty years as a physician, but he's strong. His pulse is steady and I don't see any signs of head injury." Barder looked up at Gray and smiled. "I think he's going to be okay."

Gray released Miles's shoulder and straightened. "Doctor, what caused these injuries?"

"I won't really be able to say until the digital analysis comes back along with the blood work."

"In your opinion, I won't hold you to it."

"My opinion? Someone did this to him, most likely with knives or hooked instruments."

"So you don't think it was an animal?"

"Like the sheriff was insisting upon?"

Gray squinted at the other man. "Is that what he was telling you to say?"

"He was suggesting it in so many words."

"And you don't think so?"

"Absolutely not. These wounds couldn't have come from an animal; the lines are completely uniform in keeping with an edged object. An animal bite or claw marks would have tears; the trauma would be ragged, unkempt."

Gray lowered his gaze, his eyes unfocused. "Thank you, doctor."

"You're welcome. I'll be his primary physician while he's here with us, so if you have any questions, please let me know. I'll be sending over the lab results to your office as soon as they come in and I'll notify you with any changes." Barder moved around the end of the bed and stood next to Gray. "You know, what scares me is not only that someone was insane enough to do this to him, but that he was found less than ten miles from my home."

Gray glanced at him. "You live near Shillings?"

"About fifteen miles northeast. They said he was found on East Six, correct?"

"Yes."

The doctor's eyes glazed over. "Makes you wonder."

Gray regarded the other man for a moment. "Don't worry, doctor, we'll find whoever is responsible for this."

"I hope you do," Barder said before quietly leaving the room.

Gray turned back to Miles and sighed, watching his friend's face twitch in the drug-induced sleep.

"You're safe now, Miles, no one's going to hurt you anymore. Renna and Davey are on their way, they'll be here soon." Gray waited for any acknowledgment from the prone man. None came. "I'll get them," he said in a lower voice. "I'll find them for you. They won't go free."

Miles's right hand flew up from the bed and latched around Gray's forearm. He jerked in surprise but managed to keep the yell behind his teeth. Miles's eyes sprung open, two traps of bloodshot veins that stared at the ceiling above the bed. Gray tried to pry his friend's grip from his arm but he held fast.

"Dark," Miles whispered at the ceiling tiles, his broken voice drawing out the vowel. His hand relaxed and dropped away from Gray, settling on the bed once again. His eyes drifted shut, disappearing behind bruised lids.

"Miles?" Gray said. "Miles, can you hear me?"

Nothing. The other man breathed deep and exhaled, his thin chest rising and falling.

Gray stepped back from the bed, watching for any more movement. Miles lay still. He steadied the tremble in his fingers before reaching the door and moved into the hallway. The first thing he saw were two people moving toward him down the corridor, a skinny boy with red hair leading a slender woman, swaying like a reed on the bottom of the sea. Gray tried to smile as they approached.

Davey's face was lit from within by a cautious smile, his eyes shining. "Is it him, Sheriff Gray? Is it Dad?"

Gray put a hand on the boy's shoulder. "Yes it is, Davey, it's him."

The restrained tears dropped down the boy's cheeks and he didn't attempt to wipe them away.

"You're sure?" Renna Baron said. Her voice startled Gray and he looked at her fully for the first time.

She had aged in the last three weeks since he'd seen her, her hair growing gray roots at the temples, eyes sunken in folds of worry lines that had no business being on a woman's face that had yet to turn forty.

"I'm sure, Renna."

"Because I couldn't take it not being him, not now. I won't let myself believe it until I see him."

Davey tried to move past Gray, towing his mother with him, but Gray stopped him with a gentle hand on his chest.

"Wait just a second, son, I need to say something to both of you." He paused, looking from one face to the other. One so aged, damaged by despair, the other young enough to still hope. "I want to warn you, Miles is in pretty bad shape."

"He was in an accident, right? That's what they told us at the front desk," Davey said, trying to look over Gray's shoulder at the door behind him.

"We're not sure yet, but he doesn't look like the last time you saw him, so I want you to be prepared, okay?" Davey blinked several times and then nodded. Renna stared. "I'll have the doctor sent in right away and he can speak with you both."

Gray released Davey and stepped aside for them to pass. Davey opened the door like a present on Christmas, flinging it away to get inside, his mother a weightless waif towed behind him.

Gray readjusted his hat and began to walk away but not fast enough to drown out the muffled cries of intermingled joy and horror that came from behind the closed door.

Chapter 19

"Joseph, bring that map you're always going on about into my office."

Gray released the intercom button on his computer and waited, the seconds ticking off inside his head loud enough to drown out all other noises. He didn't move as he sat behind his desk, his eyes beginning to dry in the hot air. Soon he heard the deputy moving down the hall and a moment later the younger man entered the room and strode to his desk, setting down what looked like a folded square of leather.

"I'm surprised you remembered we had this, Sheriff."

"Don't get cheeky with me, Joseph."

"No sir."

"What did you turn up with the calls to Joslyn's in-laws?"

"They were a little cagey with me but said that they did receive the account balances in full, all the money was there."

"Well we figured as much."

"Yes sir."

Ruthers unfolded the map one layer at a time until it covered over half of the desk. Its surface was opaque with several round symbols sealed beneath a clear, protective cover. Gray ran his fingers across the map.

"It looks like a miniature Twister game," Gray said.

"A what?"

"Am I the only one who likes classic games in this town?"

"What sort of game is it?"

"It has a larger mat like this with differently colored circles to put your hands and feet on. Two people get on there and someone else calls out colors and whose hands and feet to go where."

Ruthers stared at him.

"The two people get twisted up with one another. Twister."

"Hmm."

"The hell with it. How do you turn this damn thing on?"

Ruthers squeezed the map once at its corner and the entire surface lit up from within, its face brightening with lines signifying roads and a scattering of blocks in the center. The words 'Shillings County' hovered at the top of the map.

"Well that is handy, isn't it?" Gray said, bending over the desk.

"Yes sir," Ruthers said, rubbing his forehead.

"Headache still bothering you?"

"Yes sir."

"Caffeine withdrawal is a bastard."

"I'll say."

"Maybe you should go get a coffee."

"No, I'll just suffer."

Gray chuckled. "Okay, let's find East Six."

Ruthers touched the pliant mat and slid his finger across its surface, dragging the digital view with it. He stopped and placed his other pointer finger on the map and pulled his hands away from one another. The map zoomed in, the small squiggles of roads expanding into clearer definition, several lakes and plots taking up most of its area.

"This is East Six," Ruthers said pointing to a relatively straight line running through the center of the view.

Gray studied the intersecting lines and then touched a spot on the upper right side of the map. A little dot of green light appeared where he'd tapped it. "This is where the transport driver found Miles, about a mile from where Six hits Northbound."

"Is he still in custody over in Wheaton?"

"No, I released him. He's from Massachusetts, just passing through on a delivery. All his background checked out. Poor guy was still shaken up when I interviewed him." Gray studied the map for a while, his eyes tracing different features before returning to the point he'd marked. "Make me a concentric circle around that point, Joseph, twenty miles in diameter."

Ruthers touched the mark twice and then drew a line away from it. A circle appeared and grew on the map, a barrage of decimal-pointed numbers racing along its outer edge until Ruthers paused, stopping the circle at a ten mile radius.

"Good, now can you show current homesteads on here?"

"Sure can." Ruthers touched the edge of the map. A line of symbols appeared. After tapping one of them a grid materialized, overlaying the current view. Over a dozen rectangular shapes lit in borders of orange. Miniscule print floated within each of them.

"The labels are the names and addresses of each plot registered in the county," Ruthers said. "The map gets updated each month through the courthouse's files."

"Okay, here's where things get tricky because we'll have to rely on logic," Gray said. "Stop me anytime you think I'm wrong, Joseph. In my opinion, Miles escaped sometime yesterday, I'm willing to bet in the evening or early morning. Now with his injuries and seeing how frail he is, it's unlikely he would travel more than ten miles in the space of twelve hours." Gray glanced at his deputy.

"I'm with you so far."

"Good. Now normally I would cut our search down considerably with Wilson Creek running parallel to Six since it would carry even a strong man away when the water's high, but with no rain that stream would be dry as a bone allowing someone to either cross it or walk down it." Gray leaned closer to the map. "Which poses a problem for us because most of the residences are on the north side of the creek."

"Which side of Six was he found on?"

"The north side."

"So he most likely came from that direction."

"If we're still treading water in logic, yes." Gray peered at the map for a full minute without speaking before straightening up. "Joseph, I want you to call

Dodger and get him and Tex out to the spot where Miles was found, see if that dog's nose can pick up a trail. The heat might've burnt away any scent but it's worth a shot. And bring a scanner with you out there, I don't think it'll be any use with how dry it is but you never know."

"Sure thing."

"Can you send a snapshot of that map to my cruiser's readout?"

"Yes sir."

"Do it. I'm going to make a few house calls and meet up with you later this afternoon."

Ruthers nodded and folded the map in half and then half again. "So the town celebration is tomorrow."

"Joseph, I'm not easy if you're asking me to the dance."

Ruthers laughed and shook his head. "No, but I wanted to thank you for the urging the other night. I finally got up the nerve to ask Siri out."

Gray surveyed the younger man from beneath the bill of his hat. "Well by God, Joseph, you're growing up on me."

A hint of scarlet flushed the deputy's cheeks and he nodded once, a small smile on his lips. "It surprised me she said yes."

"Joseph, that girl is just as smitten with you as you are with her. I would've bet on that before the rain any day."

"Thanks, Sheriff."

"You're welcome. Now get your ass moving, we have some serious ends to tie up here."

"Yes sir." Ruthers headed for the doorway and stopped shy of the hall. "Sheriff, you think it's all connected don't you? Even Miles's disappearance?"

Gray glanced out of the window. The shimmering heat shifted on the street in tangent layers. Not a soul occupied the sidewalks. "Yes," he said, bringing his gaze back to the young man in the doorway. "But I honestly hope I'm wrong."

~

Gray eased the cruiser off the highway and into an overgrown driveway. Weeds slid against the doors and undercarriage, a snake's hiss that drowned out the quiet music coming from the speakers. He switched the radio off and peered through the windshield as a fallen tree came into view, blocking the narrow drive. Gray slowed the cruiser and put it in park, sat looking at the obstruction and the surrounding woods.

The heat soaked into him as he stepped from the car and approached the fallen tree. It was an oak, snapped off several feet from the ground but still attached to its stump. Gray walked its length and studied its dead branches that stretched into the forest. A black line near the upper branches caught his eye and he knelt to examine it. A small steel latch was embedded in the tree's trunk and crossed the narrow line that looked like a cut. The latch was painted a grayish brown to match the tree's bark. Gray fingered the latch and flipped it up.

The tree pivoted toward him, the cut opening like a jaw.

89

"Sonofabitch," Gray said.

With a slight pull, the tree swung like a gate, leaving its upper branches where they were and opened clear of the driveway. Gray inspected the stump closer and saw a pinion driven through the trunk that allowed the tree to swing.

He returned to the cruiser and pulled past the gate, not bothering to shut it behind him. Ahead the driveway rose and a narrow clearing opened up. A single story, brick house appeared on the right, its solitary window opaque. The structure was small and square, a single bedroom home at most. A larger building stood behind a row of trees, its front obscured by their wilting leaves.

Gray parked and got out, watching the woods for movement. A bird flitted between branches, the wind gusted and then fell.

Quiet.

His hand on the butt of the Colt, he approached the door, the sensation of reaching toward a high-RPM blade as he knocked. The sound echoed in the clearing as well as inside the house. He waited, moving closer to the side of the door and away from the window.

"Sheriff's department," he said in a raised voice. No response.

Sliding closer to the window, he glanced inside. Dirt covered the hardwood floor in piles. A scarred table stood to one side of the room and a mound of clothes that might've doubled for a bed took up the rest of the space. Several gallon jugs lay interspersed on the floor. He imagined he could smell the refuse from where he stood.

Gray moved away from the house and around back. There was only the front door, no other way out. A creaking filled the yard with the breeze and he made his way past the stand of trees toward the other structure.

It was a leaning barn, two stories tall, its boards bleached and dull as old bones. It had no windows that he could see, only a single door that hung partially open, a rusty hinge protesting the wind. Gray moved toward it, his hand still on the Colt, tightening. He stopped beside the door, waited for a draft that pushed it open.

A smell wafted to him, the harsh bite of chemicals, acrid in the hot air.

"Sheriff's department," he called again. No answer, no sound of movement. Gray nudged the door open with his foot and stepped inside.

Hazy light slanted through a hundred cracks in the walls and roof, the beams catching motes of dancing dust. A matted covering of old straw lined the floor. Several stanchions stood empty to the left but the bulk of the room was occupied by a long bench covered with plastic tubing, glass beakers, and an industrial heating element. Stacks of plastic bags rested beneath the bench along with a pallet of what looked like red bricks wrapped in cellophane. A plastic drum in the corner held a black ichor that bubbled continuously.

Gray approached the lab and pulled up his shirt collar to cover his mouth and nose. The chemical bite in the air became so strong near the bench it watered his eyes. Slowly, he backed away, drawing his handgun. He glanced upward into the vacant loft and turned toward the rear of the barn.

The light waned the farther back he went, his feet padding on the crushed straw the only sound. An ancient motorcycle leaned on a bent kickstand, a layer of dust covering its black seat. Another short stanchion grew from the opposite wall and when Gray rounded its boards he pulled up short, taking in the sight.

A five gallon pail full of long knives and hatchets sat off to one side, their blades speckled with dark stains. A multi-legged chain hung from a solid beam mounted in back of the stanchion, half a dozen glinting hooks dangling from its ends. The hook's polished steel was marred with blackened crimson, beads of it dried in suspended drips. On the floor lay a pair of soiled, men's underwear, their edges frayed and torn.

In the distance a dog barked.

The door to the barn flew open and something hit the back wall above his head. Gray ducked and swung the Colt up, centering its sight on the door. A hissing whine came from his left and when he looked down he saw a canister the size of a coffee cup, white smoke issuing from one end. Catching a whiff of it, he coughed, the smoke singeing the insides of his mouth and throat.

The door opened again and another canister flew through the air, landing a half dozen steps from the lab. The white smoke spurted from its end and obscured the only exit in the building. The door slammed shut again.

Gray coughed and moved away from the first gas bomb, shielding his nose and mouth as he'd done earlier. He kept the pistol aimed at the door he couldn't see anymore and turned in a circle. The boards lining the walls faced him on both sides, the smoke creeping toward him at an even pace. He lunged to the right, flinging his foot out at a particularly rotted board. It cracked and a piece flew free, dragging his foot with it. Sunlight poured inside, making the growing clouds of smoke even brighter. The dog barked again, sounding closer than before. Hurried footsteps approached the hole he'd made and Gray yanked his leg inside just as a thick-bladed axe slammed into the wood where his flesh had been moments before.

With a deep breath that stung to the bottom of his lungs, he inhaled and held the tainted air as he barreled forward in the direction of the door. His head spun and all was blinding whiteness, a blizzard indoors.

There was nothing but the fray of movement and cataract air until at last his shoulder met with solid wood. There was a snapping shriek as old nails and boards gave way, and then he was outside, falling on the hot, dry grass, its touch more welcome than any other he'd ever known. Gray hacked, sucking in the clean breaths that tasted like velvet honey on his tongue. The air bubbled with black spots and he blinked, trying to clear his vision.

The dog yapped somewhere nearby but the sound shifted, melding with the wind nuzzling his face as a bearded man carrying an axe rounded the corner of the barn. Gray had a half second to register the manic flicker in the man's eyes as well as the open sores on his face before he raised the axe over one shoulder and charged.

Gray brought the Colt up and fired.

A red spatter appeared on the barn wall behind the other man's head. The sound of the pistol shot was detached and came a moment later, thunder beneath the clear sky.

The man jerked once and pitched forward, the axe coming down. Gray rolled to the side as the blade bit into the ground where he'd been. The man's weight landed on his legs, no movement from him, just heaviness. Gray kicked him once, rolling the body away before collapsing into a fit of coughing so deep, his entire core ached with it. His lungs were on fire, burning with each breath. The oxygen was fueling it.

The dog barked, closer, very close.

He heaved and vomited into the dry grass. The falling night at the corners of his vision became deeper as the sun winked out in a supernova of darkness.

Chapter 20

Gray opened his eyes to a white ceiling he didn't know.

He blinked, letting his mind spool back, the memories unwinding like a Celtic knot coming undone. He tried breathing deeply and encountered the sensation of a cement block resting on his chest. He wheezed.

"Sheriff?"

Gray turned his head to see Ruthers rise from a chair beside the bed he lay in.

"Joseph, good to see you." His voice cracked just above a whisper.

Ruthers laughed and gripped the bed's railing. "Holy shit, sir, I thought we'd lost you."

"Can't have my job yet, Joseph." He swallowed broken glass, winced. "Water?"

Ruthers nodded and picked up a plastic cup with a straw poking from its top. "Don't want the job, it's all yours." The deputy's grin seemed to fill up his entire face. He bent the straw toward Gray's mouth. The water was cold ecstasy sliding down.

"You got him, sir, you got the killer."

Gray finished drinking and Ruthers took the cup away. "It was him?" Gray asked, his voice stronger.

"It sure looks that way. Dodger and I started out with Tex right where you told us and Tex caught a scent immediately. We started following it and it was leading toward that property you were on. Right before we heard you shoot, Tex tried to pull off to the left toward Wilson Creek but by then we were almost in the yard. It only must've been thirty seconds after you passed out that we found you."

Gray closed his eyes and then opened them in a long blink. "How long have I been out?"

"Only four hours or so."

"Get me sitting up, Joseph."

Ruthers fumbled with the bed's controls and began to adjust the mattress, raising Gray's upper body into a sitting position.

"What do we know so far?" he said, suppressing a cough.

"The guy's name was Donald Hudson. He'd been in the system a couple times for minor assault and public intoxication, but nothing major. His property belonged to an uncle that got passed down to him about five years back. Well, and you can see what he decided to do there."

"He was brewing Red Rock."

Ruthers nodded. "We hauled out two hundred pounds of the stuff. Enough to get every person in the county high twice with some left over."

"He was using too, I saw the sores on his face."

"I'm sure you're right, although there wasn't much left of his face after you shot him. Dr. Swenson's doing the autopsy as we speak, she'll be able to tell us for sure."

"Have the knives and hooks been analyzed that were in the back of the barn?"

"Yes sir. They came back with a positive match to Miles along with the Jacobses. There's some unidentified DNA that the lab is still working on, Dr. Swenson could tell you better than I could. We also found what appears to be the money taken from the Jacobses' place."

Gray tried to breathe deeply again and failed, his chest inflating without the satisfying rush of air.

"What the hell did he use on me?"

Ruthers opened his mouth to reply but at that moment the door to the room opened and Dr. Barder walked inside carrying a small box in his hand.

"Ah, good, you're awake," Barder said, walking to Gray's other side.

"I know you told me what he inhaled, doctor, but could you repeat it so I don't get it wrong?" Ruthers said.

"It was a clever mixture of vaporized formaldehyde and another highly noxious gas called diborane. Whatever else that man was, he was fairly gifted when it came to chemistry."

"Glad you're thoroughly impressed with him, doc, but it feels like I can't take a full breath here," Gray said.

"That's normal. The compound you inhaled was designed to literally burn the cilia in your lungs away and scar the tissue beneath so that you couldn't absorb oxygen. Fortunately you inhaled very little of the gas, only enough to do some minor damage to your brachial tube and the upper area of your lungs. One more full breath and your lungs would be smooth as glass. Here," Barder said, holding out a canister he pulled from the box. "This is a nebulizer that will soothe the airways and speed up your recovery. We gave you a shot when you arrived to neutralize the toxins and flush them from your system."

Gray took the inhaler and placed it between his lips before triggering the medicine. An icy wave tasting of peppermint coated the back of his tongue and he coughed once but when he inhaled the air seemed to travel farther into his chest than before.

"Thanks doc."

"You're welcome. Now, you have to use that every few hours, whether you feel like you need it or not, otherwise the healing will slow."

"Got it."

"I'll have a nurse come in and give you something else for the pain."

"No need, I've got things to do." Gray hoisted himself up farther and swung his legs over the side of the bed.

"Hold on, Sheriff, you can't go anywhere, you've had major trauma to your upper respiratory system."

"I appreciate the concern but I'm feeling better. I'll give this thing a pull every so often like you said. I like the taste of it anyway, might hit you up for a few month's supply."

Barder's frown was almost comical and after a moment he shook his head and laughed. Ruthers stepped forward and gripped Gray's upper arm, steadying him as he stood.

"I'll keep an eye on him, doc," Ruthers said.

"Yeah, Joseph here has me on a tight leash."

Barder laughed again and tilted his head. "Okay, if you're able to move under your own power I'm not going to stop you from leaving."

"Good man."

"There is one thing I wanted to ask you though," Barder said, glancing at the closed door. "The man that attacked you, you think he's the one that killed the others?"

"We're not sure of anything yet," Gray said, throwing a look at Ruthers.

Barder nodded. "I understand, it's just scary since he lived so close to me and my sons. If he was the one responsible, I'm glad you did what you did."

Barder reached out a hand and Gray shook it. "I'm sure there'll be more information soon, doctor. By the way, how's Miles doing?"

"The same as this morning, catatonic. We've cleaned all his wounds and we're keeping him sedated to help him rest. Other than that we'll have to wait and see."

"There's a guard outside his door?"

"Yes there is."

"Good."

"I'll leave you gentlemen to your business," Barder said and moved into the hallway shutting the door behind him.

"Thank you for waiting here with me, Joseph. I'm beginning to think you have a crush on me."

Ruthers laughed. "You're welcome, sir. But I wasn't your only visitor."

"Really?"

"Nope. Lynn came to see you as soon as she got word."

Gray sighed, leaning on the bed. "I forgot to change my emergency contacts. I'm assuming she left as soon as she saw you were here with me?"

"No, she asked me to step outside for a bit. I, ah—" Ruthers made an uncomfortable movement with his hands. "I heard her talking to you through the door."

"Great. The one time the woman actually speaks to me and I'm unconscious."

"Sorry, Sheriff."

"For what?"

"I don't know, all this?"

"It's not your fault, Joseph. Don't go taking blame for things you didn't do, we crucified the last man that did that."

"Yes sir."

Gray stood away from the bed and swayed, dizziness reeling him on his feet.

"Sheriff, you sure you're up to leaving so soon?" Ruthers said, handing Gray a bag containing his clothes after he'd steadied himself.

Gray took another pull from the nebulizer and smiled. "We're not going far, Joseph, just to the basement to see our killer."

Chapter 21

The morgue smelled of fresh blood and old disinfectant.

Gray made his way inside, his breathing feeling almost normal one second and strangled the next. When the door shut behind them, Tilly looked up from where she stooped over an examination table.

"Sure keeping you busy, Tilly," Gray called as he walked as steady as he could to the far end of the room. Tilly gave him a long stare behind her protective glasses and then stood, pulling down the mask she wore over her mouth.

"You're one lucky bastard, Mac."

"You see Joseph, no one ever gives me credit for anything. It's always luck."

Tilly shook her head and moved closer to them. "Seriously, what the hell are you doing out of bed. This sicko hit you with some nasty stuff."

Gray waggled the inhaler at her. "Got some magic peppermint, I'm all better."

Tilly made an exasperated sound and turned back to the table. "What do you want, Mac?"

"Seems like people are always asking me that. I'm beginning to feel needy."

Tilly only looked at him.

"Well, I'd like to start with what you've found out about our friend here."

Tilly regarded the partially dissected body on the table. "Male, age forty-six. Toxicology report came back with extremely high levels of Phenocartal."

"Red Rock," Gray said.

"Yes, Red Rock. The guy was in the late stages of addiction from what I can tell. His circulatory system looks like a series of rusty culverts and the upper dermis was decaying nicely."

"Is decaying nicely," Gray said.

Tilly gave him a withering look. "He may have not even known who you were."

"He knew he wanted to kill me."

"Oh, I have no doubt about that. The aggression and delusions associated with Phenocartal is well documented. I'm guessing that's what drove him to do what he did to the Jacobses and to Miles."

Gray's jaw hardened. His eyes slid over the corpse, the open chest cavity, internal organs removed, face collapsed inward like a sinkhole, the back of the skull a jagged line of shattered bone.

"This isn't right," Gray said finally, bringing his eyes up to meet Tilly's.

"What do you mean?"

"Him, he doesn't fit." Gray saw Ruthers move closer to his side but he didn't turn to look at the deputy. "This guy, his brain addled by Rock, goes to the Olsons', robs them, kills them, burns their place down, then a month later storms into the Jacobses' place, robs and tortures them, tries to burn their house down. And sometime in there he captures Miles for unknown reasons and chains him up in his barn and tortures him." Gray looked from Ruthers to Tilly. "That make any sense to you guys?"

"He was an addict, making sense went out the window a long time ago for him," Tilly said. "He obviously needed money for more supplies, that was his motive and as the drug took over more and more of his mind, he became violent and murderous as well as desperate. He had the murder weapons, Mac. He threaded hooks through Miles's flesh like a worm. Your own deputy walked Miles's trail that led right to the guy's place."

"I thought we were in agreement that there was most likely more than one person responsible."

"One person was definitely capable of the crimes, especially given the evidence."

"Look, I'm not denying the evidence, but this guy didn't have the smarts or the capability to murder those people and cover his tracks.

"He had the smarts to get the upper hand on you."

"Yep," Gray said, pointing at the ruined remains on the table. "It sure worked out well for him too."

"The bottom line is he was crazy enough to commit the crimes, his mind was gone and he was running on enough drugs to kill a bull."

"Damn it, Tilly, you're basing your thinking on one thing," Gray said, stepping forward to jab a finger into the dead man's cold shoulder at the line of orange dots. "This. You can't get past the idea that the Line might not be foolproof."

"And you can't get past that it is!" Tilly said, her voice peaking short of a yell. "You don't want it to be him, Mac, you want it to be someone else so you can prove your theories. This isn't the past, no matter how much you want it to be."

"You can learn a lot from the past, Tilly, it has a way of repeating itself."

She stood like a statue for a long time and then adjusted her mask back into place, covering the grim line of her mouth. "I have work to do, I'll send over the rest of the reports as soon as they're available."

Without another look at either of them, she went back to her task, the whirring of a pneumatic bone saw began shrieking off the tiled walls. Gray turned and made his way past the empty tables until he and Ruthers stood in the vacant hallway outside the morgue. Gray leaned against the wall, the burning in his lungs from the argument sapping the strength in his limbs. Glancing at his deputy's face, he drew out the nebulizer and inhaled another blast.

"Go ahead, Joseph, I know you have questions."

Ruthers frowned. "I'm confused, sir. I thought this was pretty cut and dried."

"Then let me hear it. Tell me a story."

"Well, Dr. Swenson is right, the guy's mind was gone so that would allow him to kill time and time again without being an actual psychopath."

"Go on."

"And we did match the weapons as well as the blood to the victims."

"Continue."

"And we tracked Miles's trail to his property, so I would have to say the simplest answer is the right one."

Gray took in Ruthers's apologetic look and chuckled a little. "You don't need to be sorry for deducing, Joseph. You're right on all accounts."

"Then what makes you think that he's not our man?"

Gray started walking down the hall and placed the inhaler in his pocket. "Remember when I told you about links in the chain?"

"Yes."

"What I didn't get to is that when a case is closed, the chain becomes a full circle without any loose ends. Loose ends mean reasonable doubt, not only in the courtroom but also in the minds of those who catch the criminals."

"I guess I'm not following a hundred percent, sir," Ruthers said, keeping pace with him as they reached the stairway leading up to the main floor.

Gray paused on the first step and turned to the younger man. "There's a loose end in our case, Joseph, and her name is Joslyn Worth."

Chapter 22

Gray guided the cruiser into the center of Widow Town.

The sun slanted in hot rays against the buildings, washing the streets with a baking amber light. A small child played in the shade of a dying tree in a yard, his mother watching him from the corner of their porch, one of her hands fanning herself with a paper plate.

"If it was Donald Hudson behind all this, there's a good chance Rachel would've seen him around the neighborhood before Joslyn was taken," Gray said. He glided the car to the curb in front of Rachel's home and shut the engine off.

"But wouldn't she have mentioned seeing someone like him before when you questioned her?" Ruthers asked, opening his door to let the heat pour in.

"She most likely would have, but maybe we can jumpstart her memory. We'll give her a description of the pickup that was registered to Hudson a year ago, maybe she'll remember seeing it."

"But you don't think so."

"No, but right now I'd rather exhaust the possibilities of what we have, not what we don't," Gray said, stepping from the car.

They moved across the wilted lawn to the porch and stopped before the door. Gray knocked once and waited. Ruthers scanned the street behind him and readjusted his duty belt. Gray knocked again, his eyes beginning to narrow.

"Joseph, go look in the windows of the garage and tell me what you see." Ruthers said nothing and left the porch. Gray kept watching for movement inside the house, saw only the ticking hands of an old clock on the wall.

"Garage is empty, sir. She has a vehicle?"

"She does."

"Maybe she went shopping."

"Maybe." Gray put his hand on the doorknob and turned it. It opened. "Rachel?"

He waited, listening for a full minute before he pushed the door all the way in and stepped across the threshold. Gray glanced at the floor and walked toward the living room. Ruthers followed a few paces behind.

Toys littered the floor. A colorful book sat at the edge of the large couch. Shadows gathered near the toy basket in the corner. Gray turned and walked out of the living room and through the kitchen. There were dishes beside the sink, clean ones on the right, dirty on the left. The smell of cigarette smoke hung heavy here. Over a dozen butts covered the bottom of the glass tray on the table. A wine glass with a sip left at its bottom rested beside a cup with a straw hanging from its side.

Gray moved into the narrow hallway, pushing open a door to a room painted in yellows and blues. He stepped inside and opened and shut several drawers on a low dresser using the bottom of his shirt to cover his fingers. His gaze traced the room, the walls, the ceiling, the floor. A hanging mobile featuring grinning monkeys turned slowly in the still air above the crib.

The next room was the master. A queen bed took up most of the space. A picture of a lake dotted with slender-necked geese hung above the headboard and a small bathroom led off to the right. Gray walked to the closet and peered in through the open doors. Kneeling, he scanned the area beneath the hanging clothes. He stood and moved to the bathroom, opened the four drawers in the vanity before stopping to stare at his reflection in the mirror.

"Sir?" Ruthers asked from the bedroom doorway. Gray moved back into the room.

"They're gone, Joseph," he said, glancing out the window. "They were taken."

"What? How do you know?"

"There's nothing in any of the drawers in the bathroom but only a few empty hangers in the closet." Gray motioned to the closet. "There's three pairs of shoes on the floor, but none in the front entry."

Gray walked toward the hallway and sidled by Ruthers. "And this," he said, entering the living room to point at the little chair he'd seen Ken sleeping in on his first visit. "She told me her son loves to sleep in this chair. Even if she left in a hurry, a mother wouldn't forget something like this." He paused, the image of the hand-carved sign at his house along with the smell of baby powder overwhelming him for a moment.

The smell.

"Cigarettes," Gray said, stepping into the kitchen. He sat in the chair before the mostly empty glass of wine. "She wouldn't smoke inside the house with her son."

"Looks like she had something to drink," Ruthers said, walking toward the garbage can in the corner of the kitchen. He popped the lid. "The empty bottle's in here, Sheriff."

Gray didn't turn in his seat. Instead he leaned forward, staring at the full ashtray. With one hand he began to mimic stabbing the butts out in the glass bowl.

"They wanted it to look like she was unstable, ready to do something rash. Smell the sink, Joseph."

"What?"

"Put your head in the sink and take a whiff. See if you can smell anything near the drain."

Ruthers moved to the sink and bent over it, pushing his face down close to the drain.

"I'll be damned."

"You smell wine, don't you?"

"I do. It's faint but it's there."

"They poured it down the drain after they made her drink this glass." Gray studied the wine glass, the light catching the ghostly marks of a lower lip on its rim. "And look at the cigarettes, they're stabbed out in different ways, like the person smoking was standing up and moving around instead of sitting in one place drinking a full bottle of wine."

"I'll call for forensics," Ruthers said, walking out of the room.

Gray gazed at the backyard, bathed in strong afternoon sunshine. His eyes gradually unfocused until they saw only blurred shapes and colors, the brown death of life under the constant heat.

"They won't find a thing," he said to the empty kitchen.

Chapter 23

"Wake up, little brother."

Ryan opened his eyes and stared into Darrin's cold pupils less than six inches away. His fetid breath hung in the air between them and Ryan had to resist from shoving his older brother away in revulsion.

"You've been sleeping all afternoon, champ. Time to rise and shine, you've got a busy night ahead."

Darrin moved away from Ryan's bed as he sat up and swung his feet over the edge. His head ached and there was a broken spring above his shoulders where his neck had been. When he stood, his knee throbbed but bent normally and didn't seem near as swollen as the night before.

"Knee looks better, gel does the trick, doesn't it?" Darrin asked as he watched Ryan gain his bearings.

"Yeah, it's not so bad today."

"The plan worked, Ry-Ry. Crazy Hudson is dead."

Ryan froze. "He is?"

Darrin nodded. "Yep."

"What happened?"

"They used a dog, just like I thought they would, so I dragged your project's undies on the ground from where he was found to Hudson's property. Our good sheriff was canvassing the area and Hudson's place was the first he went to. Hudson tried to kill him with some gas and the sheriff shot him." Darrin laughed, a sound like a rusty hinge. "They found everything, the blades, the chains, the hooks. Not to mention Hudson's lab." Darrin held his hands like a book before him and then slammed them together. "Open and shut, little brother. Didn't even have to call it in like I was going to."

Ryan sighed. "I wasn't sure it would work."

"Always the doubter."

"But what if they find that lady's car?"

"We dumped it in one of the abandoned mine pits where they were digging for lithium. Even with no rain there's still sixty feet of water at the bottom. No trace, Ry-Ry."

Ryan put his forehead in his palm. "God my head hurts."

"Take a couple pain killers, you need to be ready to move when it gets dark." Darrin came toward him and dropped something in his lap. Ryan picked up the square, hard piece of plastic with a key-ring hole in one corner.

"He left that for you this afternoon. It'll get you in the rear maintenance entrance. From there you take the stairs up. There's a switch on the inside of the stairwell on the landing. Flip it off and it'll kill the lights on that end of the hall. The camera will be blind. First door on the left."

"Is Dad—"

"He's working again tonight. He came home this afternoon, got some sleep and then went back in. You can't let him see you or everything's fucked. Got it?"

"Yeah."

"Don't worry, it'll be fine. You can still make it right. Here." Darrin reached behind his back and drew out a long knife with a gracefully curved blade. It was one piece, its handle forged out of the same steel as the edge. When Darrin dropped it in his hand, its heft surprised him.

"My other one was in the bucket with the rest of the toys I left in Hudson's barn. This is my new one, so don't lose it."

"I won't."

Darrin appraised him, his eyes two dead spots in his face. "There's no other chances past this one, little brother. You fuck this up ..." Darrin shrugged. "You're done."

Ryan tried to nod but didn't know if he actually managed to or not. Darrin left the room, swirls of dust twisting in the evening light like miniscule tornados. Ryan swallowed and looked at the blade in his hand. His reflection gazed back at him from the polished steel.

Chapter 24

Danzig was sitting on the tailgate of his ancient pickup next to Gray's house when he drove into the yard. His friend smiled at him as he pulled even with the truck and shut the cruiser's engine off.

"I always said you were too stubborn to die," Danzig said when he stepped out of the car.

"So far," Gray said, stepping up to the back of the pickup. "I expected you to be at my bedside when I woke up this afternoon."

"Didn't hear a peep of it until an hour ago. Happened to run into Monty at the gas station. He filled me in." Danzig's paused. "You okay?"

"Yeah, just fine. Got this to cure me," Gray said and held out the inhaler. He took a pull off of it and felt the now familiar cool blast coat his throat.

"You interested in something stronger?" Danzig turned and pulled a bottle of Harbinger Whiskey out from the bed of the truck.

Gray smiled. "Have I ever told you that I love you?"

"Nope, and let's keep it that way," Danzig said, hopping down. The truck's springs squealed as its bed rose four inches.

They sat on the deck behind the house. A warm breeze pushed against the trees that barely concealed the sun's outline, now sinking like a wounded ship below the horizon. Their glasses beaded with condensation and pooled about their bottoms in interlocking rings. A woodpecker rattled against an oak at the edge of the yard.

"Quiet," Danzig said.

"Yep."

"So you gonna tell me?"

"Tell you what?"

"About your dreams. What do you think, Mac? About how you almost got yourself snuffed out today."

Gray sipped the whiskey. It stung in a blaze of honey to roots of his stomach. He wondered if the doctor would approve of him drinking and then cast the thought aside.

"For your information I didn't attempt to get myself killed, it was the axe-wielding maniac with a drug-addled mind that tried to perform said duty."

"Smartass."

Gray shrugged and drank. He set his glass down, turned it in a circle. He could feel Danzig waiting. "I don't think it was him," he said finally.

"You think he was a fall guy?"

"Something like that. If he wasn't, there were others in on it with him. There are just too many things that don't add up." Gray tapped his glass once against the tabletop. "It was a package too neatly tied. Like I was meant to find everything." He glanced at Danzig and then shook his head.

105

"Do you think, and don't take this the wrong way, that you're wanting it to be someone else?"

"Now you sound like Tilly."

"Mmm, how is my Tilly?"

"As stubborn and thickheaded as ever."

"Gotta love her."

"I don't, but you can. Why, after all these years have you not asked her on a date?"

The big man shifted in his seat. "She and I are two very different people. Wouldn't work, that's all."

"Never know until you try. What was that metaphor about alloys you were trying to sell me?"

Danzig grunted. "So the doctors said you're going to make it?"

"Yeah, just have to keep sucking on this nebulizer for a few more days."

"You should take a day for yourself, rest up."

"I can't, Dan, not with everything that's going on."

"But don't you see, nothing's going on now that you shot that guy. Everyone involved thinks it's over, that you got your man."

"Joseph is still with me."

"Okay, you've got a young, impressionable deputy on your side. Bitchel and your good friend Mark the DA will hang a solid case on this Hudson and unless another murder crops up with the same MO, it's finished, my friend."

"Maybe. But if and when Miles wakes up, he can either confirm or deny that Hudson was the guy holding him hostage."

"You said it, Mac, 'if'."

"Miles will wake up. He's the one person that can blow this thing wide open. And if he identifies Hudson, then I'm wrong. I can live with that. In fact I'd be more than comfortable with it."

"Still, until then, you're shut down."

"I know, I know, but there's something bigger going on here, Dan. The woman over in Widow Town who called in a missing-person report on her friend is gone now too. Her and her son. Zip, gone, vanished in the middle of the night. No witnesses, no evidence, nothing."

"Maybe she got tired of the view over there."

Gray stared down at the boards beneath his feet. "History's more than just facts and dates. It's a pattern, a circle of events, and it's everywhere. We're history right now, every second that ticks by. That woman and her son were stuck, Dan. They were mired in the days since her husband and all those other men got blown to pieces by a faulty explosive. Every moment she stayed, there was another chain, she'd made her decision." Gray emptied his glass. "She didn't leave under her own will. She couldn't."

The yard became dimmer, a blanket of evening drew closer from the east. Danzig finally sat forward and tipped the bottle over Gray's glass, filling it once more.

"Going to the celebration tomorrow?" Gray asked. His head swam a bit but he took a long pull from the amber-full glass.

Danzig laughed, topping off his own tumbler. "When's the last time you saw me at the town festival?"

"Twenty years ago."

"If that."

"Tilly might be there."

"I'm un-temptable, you know that."

"You're incorrigible is what you are."

"I'm assuming you're going?"

Gray tapped the badge hanging from the breast of his shirt. "Have to make an appearance."

"Wouldn't have anything to do with Lynn being there on Mark's arm?"

"Not at all." Gray sipped more whiskey, waited. "She stopped by the hospital today while I was out."

"Really?"

"That's what Joseph said. I guess she spoke to me. I wish I knew what she said."

"I could hypnotize you."

"You could pour me more booze."

Danzig chuckled and drizzled more alcohol into his glass. The bottle was over half empty.

"I've never not been able to fix something so simple. For such a long time my eyes were stuck on the job. Lynn said I wasn't there emotionally. Sometimes I wonder if I'm the sociopath, killing the ones I love with neglect." Gray said, his eyes half lidded, looking at the streambed. It was arid and cracked into a thousand fissures.

"You're not a sociopath, you're an asshole."

Gray huffed a laugh and shrugged.

"And you think a relationship is simple? My God, Mac, I took you for an educated man," Danzig said.

"Educate me."

The giant remained quiet for a while. Stars began to stitch themselves into the sky as the sun's bloodshot eye dropped fully below the horizon.

"You talk about history, you always have. There's a lot there to learn, more than I ever wanted to know. Applying it to the future is important, it's how we avoid mistakes of the past, but we can't forget what tomorrow is, what it really is."

"What is it?"

"It's nothing. It's blank, waiting to be filled in. We're history, you said so yourself. But tomorrow is different. Tomorrow we *write* it."

Gray opened his mouth to speak but poured whiskey into it instead, drowning out the words.

Chapter 25

Ryan keyed the van's engine off and gazed through the trees at the parking lot lights.

He gripped the steering wheel once, making the synthetic gloves creak with the pressure. When he released his hold his fingers were numb, like the rest of him. He gazed at the lights for another minute and then climbed out of the vehicle.

The walk through the woods was short. Arid twigs snapped beneath his feet, arteries of the forest gone dry. The cornfields spoke somewhere to his right, the parched language sounding like dead whispers in the night. Soon he came to a long clearing that expanded from the edge of the trees, ending at a paved parking lot large enough to hold several thousand vehicles, although at this time of night there were only a few hundred.

Wheaton Medical waited beyond it.

Ryan stood there, dressed in black, part of the night against the woods. His hand strayed to his belt where Darrin's knife hung in a composite sheath. He fingered the pommel for a second, his eyes glazing before setting off again.

He circumnavigated the parking lot and its lights without problem. Only once a blazing ambulance flew by him on the service road, its flashers throwing reds and strobes of white toward him as he ducked down, the scrub grass hissing beneath his weight. When it passed he continued until he reached the rear entrance to the hospital. A dark loading dock waited empty like a corpse's open mouth. One of the lights flickered on the building, shadows vanishing and reappearing in its faulty glow. Ryan waited, watching the door for movement but there was nothing. No sound except for his pulse slamming constantly in his eardrums.

Springing from his hiding place, he ran, crossing the space between the brush and the building in quiet strides. He drew the electronic key from his pocket and flashed it across the small eye built into the side of the door. The lock clicked, the light flipping from red to green. He stepped inside.

The drop in temperature chilled him and he shivered. The door shut behind him and he waited, listening for footfalls or telltale voices. A bank of stairs ran up and turned ahead of him. A similar set went down into the subbasement. Ryan set off up the stairs, counting each step without thinking about it. Sweat crawled over his skin like something alive and he swallowed the sick that kept trying to rise in the back of his throat.

A door opened somewhere above him and he froze, the clang of feet coming toward him the loudest sound in the world. He glanced to his right, his eyes those of a rabbit hearing the baying of a dog nearby. An alcove sat to his left, its cleft in the wall full of darkness. He swung into it, just as a man in a green jumpsuit rounded the landing above him. The janitor wore wireless earphones and bopped his head to the music only he could hear, his fingers clamping an unlit cigarette. He was there and then gone in Ryan's line of sight, close enough to reach out and touch. Close enough to slit open.

The janitor's passage echoed in the stairwell and then two stories below, the outside door opened and shut. Silence returned.

Ryan slid out of the niche in the wall and placed a hand on his chest, his heart hammering harder than it ever had before. An unquellible nausea rose and receded like an acidic, internal tide and he clenched his jaw several times before continuing up the stairway. He stopped outside the third story landing and found the bank of light switches. None were marked. His hand trembled as he touched the last one in the row and flipped it off. No lights went out in the stairwell. He found the doorknob and turned it, easing the solid steel door open.

A long hall stretched away, either side peppered with doors. The corridor was empty save a medical cart loaded with gauze and blue gowns. The first thirty feet of the hall was unlit, only a neon exit sign throwing any light onto the shining floor. Farther down the corridor the lights continued to glow.

Ryan eased out of the stairwell and turned to the first door on the left, his bowels threatening to give way. The door seemed to open on its own, and then he was in the room, a soft beep coming from a monitor above the bed. A single light in the ceiling set to its dimmest was the only illumination. The shades were drawn tight over the window and shadows covered the rest of the room in inky blankets.

Miles Baron lay in the bed's center, a skeleton of a man. His eyes were closed, sunken eyelids covering them. One shrunken arm curled near his stomach, protective in the way a pregnant woman might cover her swollen belly. His skin was yellow in the low light, parchment paper left to dry in the sun.

Ryan vibrated within his dark clothes, his hands struck tuning forks. He swallowed again as he stepped forward, blinking to keep the moisture from flooding his eyes. Miles's slow inhalations were the only sound in the room besides the man's electronic pulse that would be gone within minutes.

He readied himself, adrenaline pouring through his veins in a cold flood. Sweat dripped down his face and he wiped it on the sleeve of his shirt. The knife was in his hand, drawn from the sheath without him realizing it. The blade glimmered, almost asking to be used, bloodied, its curve made for sundering, nothing else. He stepped close to the bed, and brought the knife up, tears now streaking down his cheeks, his position the same as in the dried streambed except now there was nothing for the man before him to use as defense, no cranny or crevice in which to hide. The tip of the knife hovered over the prone man's chest.

Miles opened his eyes.

Ryan's arms jerked, the knife bobbing with his surprise before he yanked it back, his breath racing from his chest. Miles stared at him through a haze of drugs before recognition bloomed deep in his eyes. His mouth opened and a moan so quiet it was barely audible escaped his lips.

Ryan shook his head, the image of Darrin stepping on a partially crushed frog in their driveway when they were young. *He was suffering, Ry-Ry, did him a favor.*

"I'm so sorry," Ryan whispered as he stepped closer, bringing the blade up once again. His hands shook and the muscles in his arms tensed, preparing for the sickening sensation of steel sliding through flesh.

The unmistakable sound of footsteps came down the hall and neared the door, slowing, then stopping.

Ryan's head whipped around and he sidestepped away from the bed, sliding into the unlit bathroom as the door opened.

A skinny form sidled into the room and shut the door behind it before crossing to the bed. Ryan watched as David Baron stepped up to his father's side and reached out to grasp the older man's hand.

"Hi, Dad. Hey, you're awake! I snuck past the desk downstairs since it's not visiting hours. Had to come see you again. How ya doing?"

Ryan hovered in the black doorway, watching his former schoolteacher's face. His fingers squeezed the knife's handle. Miles's eyes jittered from his son to the bathroom and back, a grimace tearing at his mouth.

"Are you okay, Dad? You can hear me now, can't you?" David said, stooping closer. "You're here now, you're safe." The smile in the boy's voice was solid, palpable happiness. Ryan inched forward, his mouth open wide to mask the sound of his breathing.

"You don't have to worry, Dad, you're gonna be okay and you're going to get better, the doctor said so. Mom's so happy. After we left here this afternoon she baked three pies and made a turkey dinner. It's the first time she's been out of bed all day since you…" David struggled for words. "You were gone."

A tear slipped free of Miles's left eye and rolled down his cheek. His gaze glided from the knife in Ryan's hand to his son's face.

"It's okay, Dad, she's gonna be okay, we're all gonna be okay. Sheriff Gray got the…the bastard that did this to you. He killed him. It's justice. You told me that once, that justice gets served in this life or the next. Well he got his in this life, and I'm glad."

David wiped a hand beneath his nose and sniffled once. Miles's Adam's apple bobbed and clicked, more tears coursing down his cheeks.

"Don't cry, Dad. It's okay, everything's going to be okay now, you'll see. I took good care of the crops. The weeder's pinion seal went out but Sheriff Gray got Gary Klennert to come and put a patch on it that held. So, everything's ready for when you get back. But you can rest as long as you need to."

Ryan stepped back into the recesses of the small bathroom, melding to the blackness within. His teeth hurt from keeping his jaw open and his legs kept trying to buckle. With one hand he steadied himself on the wall and with the other he turned the blade around, placing the razor tip against his jugular. He could feel his own pulse through the steel, a solid thump of life waiting to be released. One little twitch of his wrist and it would be all done. He closed his eyes, holding his breath. The blade parted the first layer of skin and the pain made him jerk his hand away. David's voice floated to him across the few feet that separated them.

"We have a game coming up next week. Maybe you'll be well enough to come home by then and you'll be able to watch. Coach says I've got potential. He said he's going to put me on A-squad next season." David's head dipped as if in prayer. "You'll be home soon, Dad, before you know it and everything will go back to the way it was."

David swiped at his eyes and released his father's hand. Ryan stayed well in the darkness and prayed the boy wouldn't need to use the bathroom before he left.

"I'll let you rest now, Dad. Mom and I will be back in the morning." David moved past the bathroom and paused, his hand on the door handle. "Love you." The door swished open and then clicked shut after an eternity. Ryan listened to the boy's footfalls trail off into silence before stepping back into the room.

Miles watched him, his lips pulled back from his teeth in a rictus grin. His arm rose and fell sluggishly as his fingers tried to grasp the bed's railing. Ryan moved forward, wiping a speck of his own blood from the knife's tip.

"I wouldn't have killed him, Mr. Baron. I wouldn't have killed your son, I would've slit my own throat first."

Miles's lips came together, pressing themselves white. "Please," he whispered, his voice dry leaves rustling.

Ryan sobbed once, the hitching emotion breaking free of a larger piece in his chest. He shook his head. "I'm sorry, they'll kill me if I don't."

He raised the knife again and grasped it with both hands. His pulse filled the room. The world. The beats of one life ready to end another.

"Stop."

The voice came from the corner of the room near the window. Ryan turned so quickly he slammed his hip into a cupboard and fell into a chair, all the air rushing out of him. A man's silhouette detached itself from the clustered shadows and walked forward, his shoes clicking against the floor.

"You're here," Ryan said, his words nearly dying in his throat.

"I'm always here, Ryan. I'm always watching, you know that. You've done well even with your carelessness yesterday." The shadow stepped closer to the side of the bed and Miles moaned again, taking in his face. The man's eyes found the schoolteacher's and held them as he nodded once. "Mr. Baron. You've been quite the conundrum. Inconceivably so. I never would have guessed you would be. Your spirit is admirable."

Ryan watched as he drew something out of his pocket and grasped the I.V. hanging from a fiberglass stand attached to the bed.

"Your loyalties are confirmed, Ryan. There's no need for that knife now, it would ruin the ruse we have in place. Mr. Baron is going to suffer a tragic stroke tonight." The syringe's tip glinted once before it slid into the injection port on the I.V. With a quick plunging of his thumb, the man emptied the syringe and withdrew it.

Miles struggled on the bed, but his movements were weak, still hindered by the heavy drugs. His eyes rolled to each of them and then toward the ceiling.

"What was that?" Ryan heard himself ask.

"A mixture of fibrin and adrenaline. Untraceable within the body, something your father and the medical examiner will never notice." he said smiling.

Miles spasmed on the bed, his back arching with bone-breaking effort. He began to pant, his breathing sounding like a boiler overheating. The heart monitor near the bed picked up speed until it was almost a constant beep. The man leaned forward as Ryan watched, wide-eyed. He caressed Miles's cheek lovingly, like a father touching his sleeping son.

"It's beautiful. Wondrous in the way birth is." he said, his voice soft with awe. He seemed to come out of a trance and looked across the writhing man's form to where Ryan sat. "We'll need to leave now before the nurses are alerted by his monitor."

Ryan nodded and rose from the chair, his legs shaking with effort. He stowed the knife away as the man crossed the room and followed him out to the hallway. An agonized grunt came from Miles as he strained against the confines of his body, his eyes bulging at something only he could see. Ryan looked over his shoulder and saw Miles's remaining bony hand rake a row of scratches across his chest before the door shut to the room.

The man touched the side of Ryan's face in the darkness, almost the way he had done to Miles, and Ryan couldn't contain the shudder that coursed through him.

"You're within the fold now, Ryan. Welcome to the rebirth."

Chapter 26

Gray woke to the first strands of daylight seeping in through his window.

His dream followed him up through sleep and he lay there, immersed in its embrace. There had been rain, a downpour that washed the fields in silver sheets. It was gentle but steady, unyielding in a natural and graceful way that only summer storms possess. The cracked ground had become solid once again, the green coming back to the trees and bushes almost at once. He had watched it all from inside his house, watched the water gather and begin to flow in the channel. He had watched his daughter play in the puddles, her small feet splashing each one with yellow boots, a hat pulled down over her head. Flashes of her smile beneath the hat's brim. Lynn's smile.

Gray stood and made his way downstairs to the kitchen. He prepared coffee, listening to the pot chuckle as he looked out at the dry streambed. No water, no life, no laughter.

His phone jittered on the counter and he picked it up, glanced at the number and answered.

"Monty, it's too early for shenanigans." Gray listened to his deputy speak and slowly leaned on the counter. A long sigh escaped him. "I'll be there as soon as I can." He set the phone down and stared at a blank spot on the wall. With a sudden batting motion he knocked his empty coffee cup off the counter and into the far wall where it shattered, spraying shards of porcelain in every direction. He watched a spinning piece dance on the floor and then fall still before he left the room to dress.

~

When he rounded the corner on the third floor a sense of déjà vu swept over him. Dr. Barder stood outside Miles's door along with the much shorter form of Monty Wells. A man no older than twenty-five leaned against the wall, his eyes focused on the phone in his hand. He wore a dark blue uniform with a golden patch in the form of an eagle sewn to its shoulder and left breast. Gray walked past him and nodded once as he neared Monty and Barder.

"Morning, Sheriff," Monty said, his paunchy face drawn tight beneath his hat.

"I'm so glad you didn't say 'good' before that, Monty," Gray said, stopping near the doorway. Muted sobs came from within the room, lamentations of a soul that has broken.

"Dr. Barder," Gray said, extending a hand.

Barder shook it. There were deep lines around the doctor's eyes. "Sheriff. Sorry to see you so soon again."

"Likewise. What happened to him?"

113

Barder shook his head. "I'm not entirely sure of the cause yet but late last night Mr. Baron had a massive stroke as well as a coronary hematoma. It was very violent in nature. I checked on him during my rounds an hour or so before and he was resting peacefully."

Gray turned his head toward the door as a louder wail rose and then fell. "What could have caused it?"

"It may have been a number of things but most likely it was due to some trauma that he underwent while he was being held captive. A blood clot could have formed somewhere in his system that our initial scans didn't pick up. Even with the advanced technology we have at our disposal the body still can keep its secrets if it wants to. It appears he had some sort of seizure which dislocated the clot and then pumped it to a vital area such as the brain, causing almost immediate death."

"Sonofabitch," Gray said.

"I thought you should know so I called the department and deputy Wells here said he would contact you."

"Thank you, doctor. Miles was a friend." Gray rubbed his eyes, mashing the fatigue from them. "How long have they been in there?"

"A half hour or so," Barder said, lowering his gaze to the floor. "You never get used to hearing that sound. But I'm sure you gentlemen know all about that."

"Yes sir, we do," Monty said.

The man in the blue uniform approached their group and pocketed his phone. He chewed a piece of gum and the powerful odor of mint hung around him like a cloud.

"So am I good to go, yet?" the man asked.

"I would assume so, but I'll let the sheriff decide that," Barder answered. "This is Justin Hawkins from Spire Security. He was supposed to be on duty for this morning's shift."

Gray began to turn to the younger man but stopped. "You mean he was relieving the other guard that was on duty overnight, right?" Gray said, looking first at the doctor and then at the security officer.

"No one was on duty overnight," Justin said, snapping his gum with a loud crack.

"What do you mean, no one was on duty?" Gray asked, rounding fully on him.

"Just what I said. We were contracted for shifts from seven a.m. to seven p.m. That's it."

Gray inhaled a long breath. "Sheriff Enson hired your company?"

"Yep, far as I know."

Gray closed his eyes and shook his head. "Damn him."

"So are we good, or—"

"Yeah, we're good," Gray said, his voice taking on an acidic edge. "Get out of here."

The younger man nodded and walked away, checking his phone again as he rounded the corner out of sight.

"He hired a fucking rent-a-cop instead of placing one of his own deputies here," Gray said to Monty and Barder as he turned back to them. "And he didn't even pay them to stay overnight."

"Well, to be honest, Sheriff, it didn't matter in this case, correct? I mean, the man who was responsible is dead and Mr. Baron died of natural causes," Barder said.

Gray looked down at the floor and then brought his gaze back to the doctor. "Could anyone have done this to him? Caused it somehow?"

"The blood clot?"

"Yes."

"Not that I'm aware of. The body naturally forms clots but usually they aren't released into the blood stream. There are a few chemical agents that could form clots but their effects would kill a person much faster than the clot they cause." Barder ran a hand through his light hair and blinked. "I'm very sorry, gentlemen, but I've been on shift way too long. I need some sleep."

"Thank you, doctor," Gray said.

"You're welcome, and I'm sorry for your loss, I didn't know Mr. Baron personally but he seemed to have many people who cared about him."

"He was a good man," Monty said.

"Yes he was," Gray said.

"By the way, how're the lungs feeling, Sheriff?"

"Better, I'm keeping up with the inhaler."

"Good deal. Please call me with any other questions."

"We will," Gray said. He watched the lanky physician proceed down the hall and turn at the corridor junction. A black orb mounted in the ceiling snagged Gray's attention and he turned, looking at Miles's door.

"Well, I guess that's that, as they say, Sheriff," Monty said, tugging at his duty belt to fit it higher over his round stomach.

Gray turned back to look at the camera in the ceiling. "Who the hell are 'they,' Monty?"

"Not sure."

Gray started down the hall, his eyes dead beneath his hat. "I'm not either."

~

The video room wasn't much more than a glorified broom closet. Gray looked around it as he entered behind the slender IT coordinator, whose name he thought was Delly. One wall held a thin viewing strip above a keyboard. The technology was completely wireless so the room had a disused look, the desk blank except for a finger pad and a stale cup of coffee. The viewing strip was segmented into dozens of smaller videos, all showing rooms or corridors in the hospital.

"You were concerned about the west third floor hallway?" Delly asked. She had long red hair that hung above her waistline in a tight braid.

"That's right," Gray said, trying to turn in the small space to accommodate Monty's presence. After a few attempts by Monty to struggle past him, Gray shook his head.

"It won't do, Monty, just wait outside for now. There's not enough air in here for the three of us anyway."

"Sorry, the room was an afterthought when they built the building since all of the technology service is hosted offsite. This is just a control center and no one thought we needed a large room for that," Delly said, turning back to the viewing wall.

"Feels like a bomb shelter."

"A what?"

"Never mind. How far back does the recording go?"

"From when the service was turned on. We could go back to day one."

"Good. Can we see last night from the time the guard left Mr. Baron's door to this morning when I arrived?"

"Sure thing." Delly's long fingers flicked across the finger pad. The screen before them changed, one square in the upper corner filling up the bulk of the video. The picture contained a view from the ceiling of the third floor hallway. A nurse pushed a patient on a rolling cart, the man's eyes closed to the harsh light. The scene flickered and changed. A man in an identical uniform as the guard from earlier walked toward the camera and disappeared from view.

"Here we go," Delly said. "Would you like to spool through it in real time or a different speed?"

"You can go faster, just so that we can see if someone goes in or out of that room on the end." Gray tapped the screen where Miles's door sat. It was definable but small even with the enlargement. Motions became hurried on the video. Nurses, doctors, and patients all passed through the viewing area at quadruple their actual speed. Sunshine angled into the hall through a window and moved in a smooth arc as the evening passed into night. Gray recognized Dr. Barder making his rounds and then exiting the scene. Headlights from the parking lot swung across the hallway several times, blazing and then gone. After that the video seemed to still with no movement for a short time and then a rush of activity filled the screen.

A line of nurses rushed down the hallway to Miles's room and flooded inside. A moment later two ran back the way they'd come before reentering the picture rolling a narrow cart between them. Barder followed close behind and all was still for several seconds, then the activity began again with various hospital personal hurrying to and fro, their movements frenetic, the looks on their faces harried then gone.

Gray watched the screen, his eyes never leaving Miles's door. The hunched form of Renna supported by David moved down the corridor, their motions choppy and stunted before they vanished inside the room. At last the video calmed and the uniformed guard strode into view, his movements lazy even in fast forward.

"That's enough, thank you, Delly."

"Sure thing. Can I ask what you were looking for?"

"Anything, but I didn't see it."

"Well, let me know if you need any more help," she gestured to the close walls. "This is my kingdom."

Gray smiled. "Thank you, I may be in touch."

He exited the confined space and adjusted his hat. Sunlight streamed in through a bank of high windows above a stairway at the end of the hall. Monty waited for him near a drinking fountain, watching nurses pass by. He straightened up as Gray neared and cleared his throat.

"Got what you needed, Sheriff?"

"No."

"Oh. Uh, well what're we—"

"You can go home, Joseph will be coming on in fifteen. Appreciate you calling me this morning."

"No problem. What's on your agenda today?"

Gray walked toward the stairway, the sun too bright on the floor. "Have to get my chores done before the ball or wicked stepmother won't let me go."

Monty shook his head, his face scrunching up before he followed Gray down the sunlit stairs.

Chapter 27

Rachel woke in a panic, realizing only as she rose from the depths of sleep that she hadn't managed to stay awake.

She sat up on the narrow bed, stretching her legs in a flare of pain as the feeling came back to them. The air was cool but not cold, the subtle odor of wet concrete invading her nose. Her eyes flew to the transparent wall across from the bed and found the sleeping form of Ken lying half on and half off the mattress situated on the floor of the next cell.

A sob slipped from her mouth as she stood and moved to the composite glass that separated them. She placed a hand against the barrier, reaching out to him while steadying herself at the same time, tears running down her cheeks. His little knees were on the hard concrete while his upper body rested on the mattress. No blanket covered him and as she watched, he turned his head in his sleep, tucking his bare arms beneath him. He was cold.

Rachel sobbed again and looked around the room. The simple bed against the wall, a water fountain in the corner, a toilet next to it, the steel door without a handle set in the concrete. Nothing else. A scream welled up inside her and she clamped her mouth shut against it. She didn't want to wake Ken up, now that he'd calmed down and wasn't crying anymore.

The door to Ken's cell squeaked and then swung open.

Rachel pressed herself against the glass, her hands balled into fists. A man came into Ken's room, not bothering to shut the door behind him. His eyes found hers and he smiled as he approached her son and gently moved his lower half onto the bed.

"Don't you touch him! Don't you dare hurt him!" Rachel yelled.

He looked up at her, the constant cold smile on his face. He turned and sat on the bed near Ken's head and began to stroke his dark hair.

"He's finally sleeping," the man said, his voice filtering into her room through several vents in the ceiling.

"I'll kill you, I'll kill you if you hurt him," Rachel said through the tears that threatened to choke off her voice.

"I don't doubt you would, Rachel, but seeing that you're in there and I'm in here, there's not a whole lot you can do."

"What do you want?"

The smile again. A snake's grin. "I want the natural order of things to be restored, Rachel. The balance is off and the world knows it. There must be equality in all things, don't you agree?"

"I don't know what you're talking about."

"I know you don't, but someday you will."

"Let us go, please. I won't tell anyone about what happened. We'll leave town and never come back."

The man laughed. "Oh Rachel, let's not be banal. You know that would never work. You would call the police the moment you were free, we both know that, so let's dispense with the pleas for freedom, you're wasting your breath."

"Please, just don't hurt us."

The man stroked Ken's hair one last time, tenderly rubbing his forehead with a thumb before he stood and walked closer to the glass. "This is what I'm talking about. Your groveling is nauseating. Your weakness surrounds you like a filthy cloud. You *stink* of it."

"I'll do anything, anything," she said, the strength slowly seeping from her legs. She slid down the glass to her knees, her hands still pressed to the barrier.

"Yes, you will. Sometime soon one of the men who took you from your house will come to you. You'll do whatever he wants or your son dies while you watch. Do you understand?"

Rachel's breath stuttered out of her in short blasts. "Yes."

"If you try to escape, your son dies. If you refuse to eat or drink, he dies. It's all very simple, yes?"

"Yes."

"Good, I'm glad we have an understanding. You'll find the more cooperative you are the better things will be. Ken will not be harmed if you behave, his salvation lies in you."

His last words must have struck him funny for the man began to chuckle, a grating sound that echoed in flat tones through the vents. Rachel shook, her entire body trembling with barely contained violence.

"I know you want to kill me," he said. "And that's good, it gives me hope for the future."

She said nothing, only stared at her captor.

"I'll let you rest now, you've both been through an ordeal but you'll get used to it here; the routine, the way life flows. It will all become normal soon enough. When faced with something day in and day out, anything can become normal."

The man turned away, graceful in his movements, fluid like floating death. He stopped at the door and pivoted back around for a last look into the cell. Rachel watched him, the tremors ceasing in her and giving way to a coating of sweat.

"I almost forgot," he said. "I announced your arrival here this morning and I have a message for you." He waited, the silence between them stretching out.

"Yes?" Her voice barely cleared her mouth.

"Joslyn says 'hello'."

The man smiled one last time and shut the door, its lock snapping home loud in the sea of quiet.

Chapter 28

Gray stopped the cruiser before Hudson's low brick house and shut the engine off.

He stepped outside into the punishing heat, its touch lancing beneath his shirt, pulling sweat from his pores. He walked toward the house, its door now cordoned off with strips of plastic tape. He pulled these aside and opened the door.

The house stunk of unwashed flesh and mold. Hazy light filled the room and left shadows discarded beneath a single table in the corner. Gray stood in the doorway, his eyes passing over everything within the single-roomed residence. Dust was smudged here and there where the forensics team had scoured the surfaces with their scanners and vacuums. All of the man's meager possessions were stacked near the hump of clothes that once served as a bed. Gray kicked an empty plastic jug and left the house, shutting the door behind him.

He made his way through the long grass, its touch dry and brittle beneath his boots. The barn loomed ahead, its eyeless face and open-mouthed door waiting for him. Inside the pallets of drugs and the materials to make them were gone. The cooking equipment had been removed also. The filthy space was barren. Rotted and broken boards lay in the dirt. The acrid smell of the poisonous smoke still lingered; a taste of death in the air. A fly lay on its back in the dirt, buzzing its wings in futility.

Gray walked to the rear of the barn and knelt in the furthest stanchion. The torture bucket's outline was still traced in the dirt. He touched the circle with his finger and stood, walking to where the chains and their hooks had hung.

The wooden beam was rough and several splinters tried to stand up and invade his skin as he ran a hand over it. He leaned in closer, straining his eyes against the feeble light. The wood was almost unblemished save for one place where Miles's chain hung earlier. He stared at the spot and then rubbed it with his thumb, feeling the slight groove. He turned and knelt in the dirt, spreading his arms out wide. His hands fell against the stanchion's sides. He sat there for a long time looking at the ground and boards around him. Slowly he rose and shook his head.

"Nope."

Gray walked out of the barn and kicked the door partly closed behind him. He went to his right, around the barn's decaying side and within five strides was in the thicket that lined the overgrown yard. The trees' bony shadows didn't throw enough shade to cover his passage fully and the sun became an X-ray strobing through the dying leaves.

The land sloped away with tangled nettles and wilting Hackberry. There was no respite from the heat beneath the broken canopy and Gray stopped to trigger the nebulizer, the mint cooling his burning lungs. The ground gradually leveled out and then dropped again in an abrupt dip. He stopped on the lip of the dried stream, looking at the naked rocks. The sand bottom was mostly undisturbed; a small animal track the only sign life existed in the woods.

Gray moved along the bank, his feet crackling in fallen leaves. He imagined the sound the water normally made within the rough channel. Its voice was calm, the words it spoke rushing with its passage. Its urgency to reunite with the sea muted by the forest around it.

A flash of clothing through the trees stopped him mid-stride and he waited, listening to the footfalls coming closer around the bend in the streambed. A teenager appeared, head down, eyes combing the ground as if he'd lost something. Gray watched his progress until he was within a stone's throw of his position.

"Good morning," Gray said.

The boy flinched like someone had taken a swing at him, his eyes flying to where Gray's voice had come from. Gray moved into full view.

"Didn't mean to scare you."

"That's okay, I didn't expect anyone to be down here."

"MacArthur Gray," he said, extending his hand as he walked closer. The boy had an ugly gash on the left side of his face, a blossomed bruise around its edges. The teenager shook his hand, his grip feeble and quick.

"Ryan Barder."

"Barder? You wouldn't be Dr. Barder's son, would you?"

"Yes, I am."

"Small world. Your dad fixed me up yesterday after the incident with your neighbor," Gray said, nodding his head back toward Hudson's property.

"I heard about that," Ryan said, rubbing the back of his neck.

"Unfortunate. You never noticed anything strange?"

"About Mr. Hudson?"

"Yeah, or anything around his land?"

"Not that I can think of. He was a pretty quiet guy. He looked scary but always kept to himself." Ryan shifted his weight from foot to foot.

"I see. Never heard any strange sounds coming from his place?"

"Not that I remember."

Gray nodded and glanced around the streambed. "Beautiful out here. I forgot how nice it is, even without the water."

Ryan looked at the ground. "Yeah, it's been dry."

"Sure has. Well, I'm just on a little hike, taking a peek around. You doing the same?"

"Uh, yeah. Our place is just a mile or so that way," Ryan said, jerking a thumb over his shoulder.

"Were you looking for something?"

"No, just walking."

"How'd you hurt your face?"

Ryan's hand went up to his cheek. "Tripped the other day and hit the kitchen cabinet."

"Ah. It looks like it hurts."

"Dad took a look at it, it's not so bad today."

A gust of wind tunneled through the overhanging limbs and made the leaves whisper to one another. Ryan met Gray's eyes and then dropped them to the ground once again. Gray stared at the boy for a span before smiling. "I'll leave you to your walk, Ryan." Gray put his hand out again and Ryan shook it. "Very nice to meet you."

"You too," Ryan said, turning in the opposite direction.

Gray watched him go and then began to make his way back toward Hudson's property. As he entered the weed-choked yard his cell rang.

"Hello."

"Sheriff, I just heard about Miles. I'm very sorry," Ruthers said.

"Thank you, Joseph, he was a good friend."

"Monty said it was a stroke of some kind."

"Something like that."

"You think that it wasn't?"

Gray reached his cruiser and climbed inside. "I'm not sure what I think, Joseph. I haven't committed to anything yet."

"Where are you now?"

"Out at Hudson's poking around."

"Find anything interesting?"

Gray paused, wiping the accumulated sweat from his brow. "Maybe. We'll have to wait and see."

~

Ryan waited until he could see the cornstalks of the field before he began to sprint. He made it three steps before a hand snagged his arm and yanked him around. A short yell came from him and he knew that when he turned it would be the sheriff standing there, dressed in his black clothes, his hat pulled down over those hard, questioning eyes.

Instead it was Darrin's face that pressed close to his own.

"What was that all about?" Darrin asked giving Ryan a shake that sent a throb of pain through his head.

"It was nothing."

"The fucking sheriff was poking around on the edge of our property, dipshit, and I saw you talking to him. Now what did he say?"

"Nothing, he was out for a walk. He was checking out Hudson's."

"And what the hell were you doing down there?"

"I wanted to make sure all the footprints and blood was gone from where Mr. Ba—where he fell."

Darrin's gaze was a vice that wouldn't relent. His dark eyes contained a coiling violence that built like a storm front.

"We swept the prints and raked the blood under already, Ry-Ry."

"I know, I'm just paranoid."

Darrin studied him for another second before releasing the painful grip on his arm.

"Don't go down there again, little brother."

"I won't."

"I'm watching you, Ry, always. Remember that."

Ryan nodded and began to walk away.

"Dad's off tonight and he wants us all to go to the festival."

"Okay," Ryan said, and kept walking.

"Cheer up, little brother, we'll have some fun tonight."

Ryan said nothing and continued past the corn. Their leaves swayed and fluttered with the wind as the sun climbed an azure ladder in the sky.

Chapter 29

The lights strung over Main Street were like low hanging stars.

Gray looked up at the jeweled wires crisscrossed from the buildings into the night sky beyond but couldn't see the real thing for light pollution. He ambled down the sidewalk, nearing the festivities, the sounds of a dozen songs filtered out through the doors of the open businesses.

The street had been cleared of cars and was now lined with benches and chairs. People roamed between the buildings, most dressed well, kids running around their feet in circles of excitement, long glowing wands held in their hands. The air smelled of popped corn and brown sugar, frying grease and coffee. A wide tent was set up at the far end of the street, dozens of people passing through its pinned flaps for the cold beer being doled out within. The tunings of a twelve-person band came from the corner of the last block, their instruments not yet harmonious but alien and ugly in their discordant singularity.

He breathed it in and looked at the front of Lynn's store. A girl in her early twenties stood behind the counter in Lynn's customary spot. She was smiling at a group of adults who all held wares from the shelves. The people flowed like water across the street and several of them raised a hand in his direction. He tried to smile and nod at each of them.

"Evening, Sheriff."

Gray turned to find Ruthers and Siri, arm in arm, moving toward him. Siri wore a light blue dress that hugged her pregnant belly and brought out her eyes. Ruthers wore a pair of light slacks, a dark dress shirt, and a smile.

"Well by God, look at the two of you. Puzzle pieces if I ever saw them."

Siri smiled and blushed while Ruthers grinned harder.

"Or is this boy actually bothering you, Siri? I can have him hauled off in the blink of an eye."

"No, Sheriff, he's behaving so far." Her hand went to Ruthers's arm and then dropped away.

"Good. Beautiful night to have the festival."

"Yeah, no rain," Ruthers said looking at the sky.

"Yeah, no rain," Gray said. "Well I won't hold you two up, I'm throwing off how dapper you both look just by standing next to you."

Ruthers laughed and held out his hand. Gray shook it. "Have a good night, sir."

"You do the same."

He watched them move into the crowd, how Ruthers supported her as she walked, making sure she wouldn't trip over any of the power cords that stranded the street, how Siri held onto him in return.

"They were just waiting for each other weren't they?"

Gray glanced to his left and saw Tilly approaching, her hair tied back and a red floral dress sweeping down just below her knees.

"I believe they were," he said as she stopped and watched the milling townspeople.

"I hope they make it."

"They will, for a time anyhow. Everything ends eventually."

"Well you're full of sunshine tonight."

He smiled. "I'm sorry for the other day, I didn't mean to get so vehement."

"Was that just an apology from the great Mac Gray?"

"I suppose so."

"Well I'm sorry too. You were almost killed and I should've been a little more patient."

"Being almost gassed to death didn't put those ideas in my head, you know."

Tilly sighed. "Yes, I know, Mac. But have you listened to yourself lately? The things you're suggesting are out there."

"I'm just paddling upstream, that's all."

"Did you ever consider that upstream might be the wrong direction?"

"I consider everything."

Tilly shook her head. "You're one aggravating individual."

"But you knew that in grade school, Tilly. I'm having a hard time figuring out why you're so surprised at this point."

She laughed, a low and sad sound and looked out across the milling people before turning her gaze back to him.

"Did you ever think that maybe what you and Lynn went through, what you're still going through, is having an effect on you?"

He stiffened, his spine straightening. "My judgment is my own, Tilly. There's grief and there's reason. I like to keep the two separated."

"Most people think they do."

"It's okay if you believe I'm wrong, but don't tell me I'm off because I can't handle my emotions."

"Mac, I didn't mean—"

"Have a nice evening, doctor."

Gray moved away down the sidewalk, not looking back, his eyes flowing over the crowd, not seeing any of them. The street was empty save for him, the clack of his shoes. He walked past Lynn's store and continued on, the glowing lights nearing and then receding as he passed across a vacant lot, dust puffing beneath his feet. Rocks that hadn't been collected yet he kicked out of his way, the night closing in.

The town pond had been filled during the last week in preparation of the town event. A gushing pipe, now underwater, continued to pump in hundreds of precious gallons a minute to keep the level up as the earth sucked at the artificial spring, pulling it down into the unquenchable dirt. There was no moon but waterproof lights were lit in its depths, their bulbs down in the dark like glowing fish that have never seen the sun.

He walked to the railing that looked out over the pond, its surface flat calm, only a handful of scattered trees growing here in the center of town. The week before, children had played tag in the pond's dusty depression, their heads well below that of street level as they ran. He stopped and leaned on the rail, its touch lukewarm even in the night. So quiet.

A little sound came far down from his right and he looked, seeing a figure there wrapped in the darkness, but even from the distance he knew it. He walked the railing, his hand grazing it now and then, the brittle grass breaking as he moved. He cleared his throat when he got nearer, not wanting to surprise her.

Lynn's face turned toward him in the dark and just the faintest light from town coated her features.

"Evening," he said.

She wiped errantly at her eye and looked out over the water. "Hello."

"Didn't think I'd catch you standing in the dark. Thought you'd be dancing."

"I'm tired, needed a rest."

"Beautiful night."

"Yes it is."

He paused, placing his forearms against the railing. A pair of ducks paddled across the pond, soundless and smooth feathers.

"Thanks for coming to see me at the hospital."

Lynn didn't move. "That deputy of yours can't keep his mouth shut."

"He's my deputy."

"I came to make sure you were okay."

"Thank you."

"It wasn't entirely for you, you know. I didn't want you to die without saying a few things."

"Did you get to say them?"

"Yes."

"I suppose you wouldn't want to repeat them?"

She sighed and her head drooped. "God, Gray, will you leave it alone?"

"If you wanted it left alone you would've never come to the hospital."

"There's a difference between compassion and love, you know that, right?"

"Just as long as it's compassion and not pity."

Lynn pushed away from the rail and began to walk past him. "You're impossible."

He followed her. "I'm trying to talk to you."

"No, you're trying to make jokes. It's what you've always done. While I face things, you shield yourself and put up a front that you think holds everything back. You don't realize that you leave everyone else on the outside. I'm the one that took things head on, and all I needed from you was a little support, that's it, but you couldn't even bring yourself to do that."

"Please Lynn, stop." He grasped her arm, slowing her. She turned just enough for her face to be outlined against the lit town. "I'm sorry. I should've said that years ago. I'm sorry for the late nights and the early mornings and how I was. It's a character defect not being able to open up. Believe it or not I tried over the years and I failed each and every time. I would go to tell you something that was on my mind or try to comfort you and a joke would come out, or something sarcastic. But for a while you seemed to be okay with that."

He let her go and she stayed where she was, still not looking fully at him.

"I loved you, what else could I do?" she said.

"Nothing, I wouldn't let you. You think I don't know these things? I haven't just been thinking about it for months. I've known it for years. I wondered how to make myself better, how to be good to you."

"You were good to me, you just never let me in."

He sighed and rubbed his sweating palms against his pants. "We never talked about it. About Carah."

Lynn turned her head toward Main Street but she didn't walk away.

"There's nothing to say."

"There's everything to say. She deserves that."

She spun toward him, her hands grasping his shirt, strong. "Don't you tell me what she deserves MacArthur, don't you dare!"

"I didn't want to face it, not after that morning. I couldn't."

"Don't," she said, her grip loosening.

"I always checked on her before work, you know that," he continued, his mouth dry as the soil. "I would be late sometimes because I'd watch her sleep and lose track of time. Her little hands, that's what I remember the most. How small her fingers were, and always balled into fists, like she was ready to fight the world."

"Please, stop," Lynn said, her voice airy.

"But that morning they were open, unclenched and spread out. She looked like she was still sleeping and I didn't know, Lynn, I didn't know for over a minute that she wasn't breathing."

"Damn you, damn you to hell." She hit his chest once and a sob slipped out, something broken, irreparable.

Now his own tears were sliding like gentle rain down his face. "I tried, I tried to save her but I couldn't, honey, I couldn't, and I couldn't talk about it even though I knew that's the only thing you needed from me. You're that strong, the strongest person I know, and all you needed from me was to say a few words. I fought all these years against what I thought was wrong and something as fragile as a baby girl broke me when she left."

Lynn leaned her head against his breastbone and struck him again, lighter this time. He put a hand on the back of her head and stroked her hair. A gust of wind came up and curled around them. The dead grass talked and the band began to play.

"I won't bother you anymore, but I had to say it. I'm just so sorry it's too late."

She clutched his shoulder and breathed deeply before letting it out. She pushed him away, not unkindly, and swiped once at her eyes.

"She would've been beautiful," Lynn said.

"Just like her momma."

He didn't realize until then that he was holding her hand. He let it go and made his way around her back toward the lights.

When he stepped onto the street a group of men were sipping frosted glasses of beer. They turned as one as he moved out of the dark and he frowned.

"Well, Sheriff! I've been meaning to come by and see how you were doing," the closest man said. He was shaped like a pear, the belt of his pants seemed to go on forever. His face was red beneath the light and the little hair he had waved in the air as he moved to shake Gray's hand.

"John, how are you?"

"Good, good. How're you feeling?"

"Never better."

"Still taking the nebulizer?" Vincent Barder said stepping forward. Gray nodded and shook his outstretched hand.

"Sure am, doc."

Mark Sheldon appeared at the doctor's shoulder. "I was just telling the Mayor the details about your impressive dispatching of Mr. Hudson, our local scourge. Our sheriff here did some very fine detective work and stopped him cold before he could hurt anyone else." The DA gave him a frigid smile and Gray didn't return it.

"You're quite the shot with that antique," the rotund mayor said, bouncing on the balls of his feet like a much lighter man.

"I'm lucky, that's about the extent of it," Gray said, still eyeing the DA. Gray saw Mark's vision shift over his shoulder and when he looked back he spotted Lynn striding out of the darkened lot, her skin contrasted with the black dress she wore that he hadn't been able to make out near the pond. A cloud passed over Mark's face and Gray let the smallest of smiles twitch at his lips. Lynn started to approach the group and then motioned to Mark, tipping her head toward the beer tent.

"Excuse me gentlemen," he said, winking at Gray.

"Yes, by all means don't keep the lady waiting," the mayor called. He let out a loud guffaw and drank down more of his beer.

"Great job on the festival this year, John," Vincent said, gesturing to the lights. "Beautiful turnout."

"Well with the damn weather not cooperating we couldn't have the fireworks the city purchased early in the year. Disappointed the hell out of the council and me, to say the least. But we couldn't have a forest fire just on account of some pretty lights in the sky." The mayor laughed again and finished his beer in one giant gulp.

"I think it turned out wonderful. I always enjoy this time of year, always makes me think of my wife."

"How long's it been now, Vincent, if you don't mind me asking?" The mayor said, reaching out to touch his arm.

"Not at all. She's been gone eighteen years this fall. My youngest son's birthday is always a tough time for us. She passed away giving birth to him," Vincent said to Gray.

"Very sorry to hear that."

"Thank you, Sheriff, I appreciate it. She was one of a kind. And hey, speak of the devils themselves!" The doctor gestured toward the end of the street and Gray turned to see three young men walking toward them. The first was well built and handsome, with dark hair and piercing eyes. The next was very large, broad shouldered with a thick forehead and a continuous eyebrow. The last Gray knew from their meeting earlier that afternoon. Ryan Barder's face was downturned, watching the heels of his brothers' feet as they walked.

"My boys," Vincent said and smiled as they came nearer. "Gentlemen, let me introduce you to my sons. This is Darrin, Adam, and Ryan. Boys, I think you know Mayor John Wilkens and this is Sheriff MacArthur Gray. The younger men shook hands all around. Darrin's grip was strong when he took Gray's hand and his gaze confident. Adam didn't meet his eyes and barely squeezed his fingers before letting go.

"And we had the pleasure of meeting more than once today," Gray said, shaking with Ryan. The doctor looked between Gray and his son.

"I was taking a walk down in the streambed this afternoon and ran into Sheriff Gray," Ryan said, glancing at his father.

"He was kind enough to answer a few questions about Mr. Hudson, your neighbor," Gray said.

"Ah, I see. Gives me the chills that that man was living so close to us. I can't believe the destruction some people can cause. I understand he was deeply addicted to Phenocartal?"

"It appears that way."

"Terrible drug," the mayor said, waving his empty mug. "Who would've thought, something like that right here in our little town. We should really sit down soon and go over a plan to look into the challenge against the drug problems our community faces, don't you think, Sheriff?"

"Absolutely John."

"Excellent, I'll tell Evelyn to set up a meeting with the council next month. Anyone else thirsty, I'm heading to the tent."

"I'll join you," the doctor said and turned to shake Gray's hand one more time. "Keep that nebulizer going, Sheriff."

"Will do."

"Good to meet you," Darrin said before turning away into the crowd. Adam followed his older brother and Ryan trailed after them both, head down, shoulders slumped.

Gray watched them go and then saw Mark and Lynn heading toward the end of the street where the band wailed away beneath the brightest lights. Their fingers were intertwined and as he watched, the DA slipped an arm around his ex-wife's waist.

Gray looked down at the street, scuffing his boot once as the crowd slowly flowed toward the music.

"Well, I guess you deserve that," he said, and began to walk the opposite way to his cruiser.

~

Darrin carried a pitcher of beer up the darkened stairs that led to the side entrance of city hall and sat on the cool marble of the first landing next to Adam and Ryan. He handed Adam a stack of plastic cups and began to pour golden streams of beer into each one.

"Here's to the night, boys," Darrin said, raising his glass. Adam giggled and sipped his beer while Ryan held his cup near his stomach, not moving. The band started a contemporary tune and dozens more people flooded onto the makeshift dance floor that had been constructed in the center of the intersection. The night was filled with clapping hands and stomping feet. Whirls of scented hair and flashing smiles under the lights.

Ryan closed his eyes, his stomach tightening.

"What's the matter, little brother?" Darrin asked, nudging his elbow.

"Nothing, just tired."

"You're always tired," Adam said, slurping his beer.

"Ryan here is a delicate soul. He walks the tender path and loves in silence."

"I'm not delicate," Ryan said, sipping at his cup. The beer was briny and flat.

"You're getting less so. He told me how you were going to end our good teacher before he intervened. I'm impressed, Ry-Ry."

Ryan said nothing.

"Not that I didn't think you had it in you, but I didn't think you had it in you."

Adam grunted laughter and guzzled the last of his beer down, reaching for the pitcher.

"I would've done it," Ryan finally said.

"Hey, hey, lighten up, little brother. I'm just giving you a hard time. Plus, this is a night for celebration."

"You think the sheriff knows anything?" Ryan asked.

"He's as ignorant as the rest of the cattle," Darrin said. "It looks like he likes Dad, he'll like us too. No need for suspicion, or concern. Yet." He glanced at Ryan as he spoke.

Darrin stood and drained his glass, throwing it to the other end of the landing before he walked to the edge of the stairs. He stood there for a long time, gazing down at the throngs of people dancing to the thudding beat.

"There she is," Darrin said.

"Who?" Adam said, rising.

"Siri Godfry, the one in the blue dress."

"Oh. She's pretty."

"Yeah."

Ryan rose from his seat and stood behind his brothers, their shoulders blocking his view for a moment before he spotted the woman they spoke of. Siri danced slowly with a good-looking, tall man in a dark dress shirt. She was smiling up at him as he held her hands and though they weren't dancing in time with the song, they moved gracefully together, as if they were hearing music no one else could.

"Who's she dancin' with?" Adam asked.

"Joe Ruthers. He's a deputy, but I went to school with him. He ratted me out in eighth grade for stealing the class hamster, remember?"

"Oh yeah."

Darrin stared at the couple. Ryan saw the flame begin to burn brighter in his brother's eyes.

"She's the next one, boys. She's the one I want."

Chapter 30

She came to him in the middle of the night.

Her skin glowed moon-like, pale and soft in the dark beside the bed. Gray watched her, traced the points on her flesh he used to touch, caress. Where he would again. She slid in between the covers, close to him, her hands finding him in the dark, their bodies old friends, reacquainting themselves. She moaned and he drew her closer to him, hard against his thigh until she pulled herself astride him, taking him in with a long gasp. She rocked in liquid motions, the tide building within him as she stared down at him and that's when he saw her eyes were not her own. They were black and depthless, deeper than any mineshaft. They traveled into and through him and he shoved at her even as he felt himself hurtling toward a climax. She grabbed his wrists with iron claws, immovable.

"I'm dead, Mac. You killed me."

He opened his mouth to scream and jerked his arms away. His hands met wood and he realized he was standing in Carah's room. Lightning flashed outside in dry, heat pulses and he saw his fingers grasping the side of her crib. There was something inside beneath her blankets, moving.

His head shook as the lightning faded, leaving the room in complete darkness. A whisper, so quiet he couldn't discern the words, came from close by and the strobing light returned. The thing in her crib moved again, the blankets rising a little, then falling.

Whisper. A word.

He reached inside, the light there then fluttering down to nothing as his fingers grazed the fabric. Again the sky flashed and he gripped the edge of the blanket, pulling it away.

Hudson's broken head lay in the crib, its hacked stump of a neck still trickling dark blood. Its remaining eye looked at him and it was black like Lynn's had been.

Fool, it whispered.

Gray sat up in bed, his mouth open, gasping for breath. His throat burned and his lungs were two singed plastic bags. He stared around the room, waiting for something to rush at him from the darkened corners but everything was still. He found the nebulizer on the bedside table and triggered a blast of mint down his throat. The relief was immediate and tangible, like a weight being released from within him. He breathed deep and let it out, the last vestiges of the dream echoing through his mind.

He lay back and settled into the pillow before rolling onto his side. The window was a blackened rectangle. He watched it, waiting for a flash of lightning but none came. He was still watching it when dawn crept into the sky and sleep didn't reclaim him until the sun crested the trees in the east.

~

The steel door creaked and Rachel tensed, coming out of the half sleep she'd been in.

Her attempts at staying awake to watch Ken had worked until he'd fallen asleep again after crying for nearly an hour, his small face pressed against the barrier that separated them, her own hands rubbing the glass, tears streaming down her cheeks. Helpless. When he'd finally nodded off, his face turned away from her on the bed, she'd searched the room, looking for a camera. The ceiling was seamless concrete but for the small vents. The floor was smooth, nothing but dust. The three walls that weren't glass had no openings and no fissures that could hide even the smallest camera. Her bedding was one piece, the frame bolted to the floor. The door had no holes or glass eyelets. She'd even checked the toilet.

The room seemed to be unwatched.

So she'd waited in the corner closest to the door, her knees locked straight to hold her up. She'd drifted, not sleeping, not awake, between the two, hovering like a ghost. But the squeal of the door opening brought her fully out of rest.

When the door came all the way open she readied herself, her breath held, heart slamming so loud she knew it would be audible to anyone nearby. Her hands were talons at her sides, every muscle strained to the point of tearing.

Adam stepped into the room, swaying a little like a tall tree in a breeze. She waited a beat as he looked around the room, a glaze of puzzlement coating his rounded features. A second too late he realized his error.

Rachel stepped forward and jabbed her hand toward his face.

Her fingernails skidded up his cheek and tore into his left eye. Blood welled out and dropped onto the floor as Adam released a screech and stumbled away. One of his fists came out automatically and cuffed the side of her head. Her vision doubled, tripled and then came back to normal.

"Oh bitch! You bitch!"

He turned in her direction but she was already moving. Through the doorway and into the dimly lit hall. She grasped the steel and spun, whipping the door shut. Adam was there, his arm outstretched but his reflexes were slowed by pain and the lack of sight on his left side. The door came shut on the meaty part of his hand. Rachel threw her weight against it and Adam howled on the opposite side, but didn't pull his hand away. He began to push back.

She pressed her shoulder against the door, digging with her bare feet against the smooth floor, sliding. She shoved harder, her teeth gritted to points of pain, tears pouring from her eyes. Her feet skidded more and she saw her only chance.

Rachel leaned forward and bit down on Adam's exposed fingers.

The pressure from the other side of the door disappeared and he screamed as she bit through skin and muscle, her teeth stopping against bone. He yanked his hand away, peeling back the layers of flesh as it went. Blood flowed into her mouth and she gagged but pushed hard one last time and heard the door click home, an electronic lock engaging near the handle.

She sagged, spitting blood, as her muscles turned from stone to liquid in between breaths. Before she could fall, she pulled herself upright and hobbled down the corridor. Adam pounded against the door, his screams and exertions muffled to an almost imperceptible level. When she came to Ken's cell, she stopped, her hand triggering the door handle over and over. It flopped bonelessly down and up. She stepped back, searching for an external locking mechanism, but there was nothing but a card reading slot and a small, oblong hole.

"No," she said, her voice scratching out along the hall.

Behind the door, Ken began to cry.

"No, no, no," she moaned. Her fingers scrabbled along the door's edge and back down to the lock.

"You're dead, bitch! So's your son!" Adam yelled.

She started down the hallway again, glancing at the ceiling. There were more doors lining both sides of the passage, all of them closed. There were no windows. She ran, her feet slapping the floor as the cells flew past. The end of the corridor approached with another sealed door. She pulled on its handle before turning back the way she'd come.

She jogged past Ken's door, past her own where Adam railed on, shouting threats in a nonstop flow. The hall turned left in a ninety-degree angle and a door with a small porthole stood at its end. The porthole was a circle of light amidst the dingy gray steel. She walked toward it, squinting against the brightness. She neared it and reached out to the door handle. It flopped uselessly like all the others. A sob broke free of her throat and she pushed hard against the barrier. It didn't move. Bringing her face up to the porthole, she looked in.

And froze.

The sight caught her so off guard, she didn't hear the soft footsteps behind her.

A sharp jab of pain landed between her shoulder blades and she cried out, trying to turn. But her legs wouldn't hold her and she fell, crumpling into a heap, a rope pooling in on itself. The back of her head rapped off the door and her eyelids flickered, flashes of film on a high-speed movie, the man coming toward her, holding a tubular, black device. A smell in the air, so familiar and warm, she almost smiled as she inhaled, the hallway narrowing and then expanding. The man came closer, kneeling before her and his features taking on definition. This time she recognized his face, the familiarity of before solidifying into memory.

"I know you," she said, trying to raise a hand.

"No," he said. "You only think you do."

The light in the hall diminished and then snuffed out altogether.

Chapter 31

Gray sat on the wooden bench outside the building.

The shade provided by the sheriff's department crept closer to where he sat, a hard line of light that was already heating the air into something barely breathable. He triggered the nebulizer into his mouth and then exchanged it for one of the two cups of coffee beside him.

A cruiser rounded the corner up the street and glided to a stop at the curb. Ruthers climbed out from inside and came striding up the front walk.

"Morning Joseph."

"Good morning, sir."

"Just morning will do."

"Yes sir." Ruthers sat down beside him, glancing at the extra steaming cup of dark liquid. "Why are you out here and not in your office?"

"That building is just one big brick oven. You know what they used to cook pizzas in?"

"No, but I can guess."

"I don't know how Mary Jo can stand it. She's not even sweating in there."

"She was sweating last night dancing with old Greg Taylor, mole and all."

Gray glanced at the deputy and chuckled. "Well that's two happy couples tallied up."

Ruthers dropped his eyes to the brown grass, a small smile pulling at his lips. "It was a nice night."

"I'm glad you had fun. Going to see one another again?"

"Tomorrow evening. A movie, I think."

"That's good."

"Yep."

"That coffee's for you."

"I just got over my headache, Sheriff, I can't drink that."

"Whatever you say."

"Is that the report from Hudson's autopsy?" Ruthers said, motioning to a slim file beneath the full cup.

"Sure is."

"Mind if I take a peek?"

"Peek away."

Ruthers opened the folder and read for ten minutes in silence as Gray sipped his coffee. A car rolled by, the morning sun bright on its windows.

Ruthers set the file back on the bench. "No surprises there."

"Nope."

"I assume the DA will be wanting this closed out?"

"You assume right, the necessary files came through this morning."

"So what can we do?"

135

Gray stood, slinging the last dregs of his coffee onto the dead lawn. "We keep our eyes open. Other than that, nothing."

"Do you think there's a possibility that Hudson did take Joslyn and Rachel along with her son? Maybe buried them somewhere on his property?"

"Do you?" Gray said, peering out from beneath the bill of his hat.

Ruthers chewed on the inside of his lip. "No."

"We could dig until Judgment Trump, Joseph, and not find a thing out there, and that's because of one reason and one reason only, the man didn't do it. He might've had more Red Rock in his brainpan than anything else, but he didn't kill anyone. At least no one we know of."

"But if we're right, then he or they are still out there. They could do it again anytime they want."

"Yes they could, but you have to pick and choose your battles. If we made a ruckus now we'd look like fools. And if we pushed hard enough we'd be unemployed fools. I like the DA a bit less than I do our friend Mitchel, but they're right as far as how the community would react to us shouting about serial killers running amok."

Gray turned and stared down the street to the vacant lot. The pond would be drying up now without the constant water flow hydrating it.

"We've done all we can right now. Until they surface again, and they may not, we have to wait. If they do, they'll make a mistake and we'll be ready."

"That's infuriating."

"That's police work." Gray faced the deputy again. "Did you know the first Sonic-Rail they built, crashed on its initial run?"

"No sir."

"It did. Killed a hundred thirteen people when its magnets went out. Careened right off the track and hit a bus that was traveling on the highway below it."

"That's terrible."

Gray nodded. "The real tragedy was it could've been prevented. The story came out later that one of the designers wanted to hold up on the commercial run because he was worried about the exact problem that occurred. But he was overridden and as a result those people lost their lives."

Ruthers nodded slowly, looking across the street.

"Here, I wanted you to have this." Gray stepped forward and pulled his old knife from his pocket.

"Sheriff, I can't take this, it's your knife."

"I got a new one given to me and I don't need two of the damn things."

"You're sure?"

"Joseph, if you don't take it I'm going to throw it at you."

"Thank you, sir."

"You're welcome. My father gave me a knife when I was ten. I still have it. It's not an auto or anything like the one you've got there, just a folder, probably seventy years old or more. Its blade is worn down almost to nothing from how many times it was sharpened, but it'll still cut as well as the day it was made."

"I'll keep it on me at all times."

"Good. Now, Mary Jo mentioned that a dog got hit over on third. You mind going over and getting it off the road?"

"Will do."

Gray started moving toward the building, the file and the coffee cups in his hand.

"Sheriff, which are we? The ones that pushed the Sonic-Rail ahead or the man who tried to postpone it?"

Gray paused but didn't look back over his shoulder.

"Neither. We're the people on the bus."

~

Rachel rose up through a jellied sleep. The vividness of the dream she'd been having dissolved into a blur of Picasso images, the clarity of the words and sounds slurring into babble. She opened her eyes to the featureless ceiling above the cot.

The memories returned on their own. Her escape. The taste of blood in her mouth. Running. The lit porthole. Ken.

She turned her head to the side and tried to sit up. Her hands and feet moved only inches then stopped. Blinking through the fog that plagued the boundaries of her vision, she saw that her wrists were locked in wide manacles attached to the bedframe. Her feet felt as if they were in the same position though she couldn't gather the strength to raise her head far enough to see for certain. The cot swayed beneath her as if she were on a ship.

"Rachel, are you awake?"

The man stood on the other side of the glass within Ken's cell. Her eyes found his somber face and she yanked on the shackles hard enough to draw blood from both wrists.

Ken sat in a highchair facing the glass.

He was buckled in tight across the chest and legs though his arms were free to swing, which he did, looking around the room with cautious eyes.

"Don hurt 'im," Rachel said, her tongue swollen three sizes.

"I'm disappointed, Rachel. I thought we had an agreement?" The man began to pace behind Ken's chair. "I told you not to try to escape, and what do you do?"

Rachel tried swallowing but her mouth was a desert, gritted with sand. She pulled again at the bindings and her wrists began to ache.

"I wouldn't struggle, those manacles are iron plated and lined with ratcheting mechanisms that tighten whenever you move too much. It'll eventually cut the circulation off to your wrists and ankles, and the tissue in your hands and feet will die over time."

"P-please."

"Oh the time for begging is long past I'm afraid, Rachel. You knew the consequences before you injured Adam and tried to run away. What did I tell you would happen if you did that?"

"I'm s-sorry, please, don't hurt him."

The man stopped pacing and looked at the back of Ken's head. He drew out a pistol.

"No! Anything! I'll do anything you want! I won't try to get out again, I promise!"

"But Rachel, how can I trust you?"

"I won't, I won't, I promise, don't hurt my baby. Please, please, please." Her voice gave way to sobbing. The man sighed and tapped the pistol against his thigh. Slowly he brought the barrel up and aimed it at Ken's back.

"No!"

The gun clicked once as he pulled the trigger.

Empty.

Ken laughed and banged his hands against the tray before him.

Rachel dissolved into soft weeping, her body going slack.

"This is your last chance, Rachel. The next time there will be rounds in the gun. I'll execute him in front of you after gluing your eyes open. Do you understand?"

She could only nod. Her tears trailed in hot streaks across her face. The man holstered the weapon and knelt next to Ken's chair.

"Okay little man. Now you have to watch mommy, okay?" He held Ken's small hand in his own and tapped against the glass three times. Ken giggled and reached for the partition.

The door to her cell opened and Adam walked in. His face was bandaged on the left side, hiding his damaged eye. The other one stared at her, muted rage burning in its center. His mouth was a straight slash at the bottom of his face.

"You watch mommy, watch close now."

Adam sneered and unbuckled his belt.

"No, please," Rachel said, staring down her own length at the approaching man. Only then did she realize that she wore a loose nightgown that trailed to her knees. Adam's smile widened.

"I'm gonna make you sorry," Adam said, dropping his pants to his ankles. He wore stained underwear that once might've been white. "So sorry."

"Please, don't make him watch." Rachel turned her eyes to the man kneeling by Ken. "Please don't."

Adam stripped away his underwear and climbed onto the cot, pushing up her gown as he did. His face was huge like the moon, pitted with acne scars that could have been lunar craters. His remaining eye was a cavern of darkness.

Rachel tried to hold back the scream but it slipped out as she turned her face away from her son.

"So sorry," Adam grunted. "So sorry."

Chapter 32

Gray drove for hours.

No calls came through on the radio. It sat as quiet as a stone in the dash. He watched it and when it didn't speak he gazed out at the rolling fields of too-green corn. He drove to the Olson farm, stopping in the empty yard. All that was left of the house was blackened rubble caved into the hollow basement. Boards singed and ash covered floor. The ground crackled beneath his boots as he walked the old home's border, kicking a rock into the hole now and then. The birds lamented unseen in the trees. The corn spoke.

He left the Olson's and wandered the back roads until the Jacobses' driveway came into view. A fox, its white and orange tail twitching, slipped from the edge of the field and disappeared into the drying forest. Gray pulled even with its trail but it was already gone.

The scorched farmhouse stood silent and still. An old homemade swing swayed from the strong arm of an oak. The garden, untended, withered beneath the sun. Gray walked across the lawn to the doghouse and looked at its empty hole for a long time.

Inside he sat down at the kitchen table, turning one of the placemats beneath his hand. Turning, turning, turning. A fly buzzed and knocked against a window somewhere. He flung the placemat across the room in a violent motion. It banged into a cabinet and fell to the floor, settling like a tiny rug.

"Come on," he said. "Come on."

He locked the door on his way out and went back to the cruiser, climbing inside. Checked the radio. Nothing. He drove into town, ten miles under the speed limit, his eyes blank on the road, the cracks clicking beneath the wheels.

When he pulled down Main Street he kept rolling past the station, past Lynn's store, past the vacant lot, and turned, coasting toward the pond's depression.

It was a muddied hole now. The water was gone, leaving a brownish muck that was cracking at its edges, drying inward toward a puddle no wider that a man's reach at its middle. Deep footprints marked the places where the underwater lights had been retrieved.

Gray parked the cruiser and got out, walking down the path to stand at the same spot as Lynn had the night before. A candy wrapper fluttered toward him and skidded away, scratching at the ground. To the right, the path followed the pond's edge into a small park dotted with hearty bushes and evergreens that had yet to lose their color to the leeching sun. Next to the path was a steel bench, ornately carved wood on its seat and backrest. Ryan Barder sat upon it.

Gray walked down the trail, losing sight of the boy as it first wound away and then came back toward the parched dip. As Gray neared the bench, he saw Ryan held a small chain in his fingers and a bag of groceries sat near his feet.

"Afternoon," Gray said.

Ryan jerked a little and his eyes widened. "Afternoon, Sheriff."

"Sorry I keep startling you."

"It's okay, I was just thinking."

"Looked like it. Mind if I sit?"

Ryan gazed at the spot beside him for a moment and then scooted down, pulling his grocery bag with him. Gray sat, stretching his legs out. A massive pine shaded the bench, its shadow stretching much past its true length.

"You working anywhere this summer, Ryan?"

"No sir."

"Just on your farm there?"

"Yeah, but we don't do a whole lot. Dad has a crew come in every fall and harvest for us."

"You have your own equipment?"

"Yes sir."

"How many acres?"

"Around five hundred."

Gray whistled low. "That's a lot of crops."

"Yes sir."

"How old are you, Ryan?"

"Seventeen. I'll be eighteen in a few months."

"Gotcha, fall boy. Not too far from mine. I just turned forty this week. You wouldn't have known Devi Jacobs, would you?"

"No sir."

"You're about her age, would've been in the same grade at least, right?"

Ryan nodded. "She was in my class, but I didn't know her."

Gray looked out over the vanished pond. "Such a shame. Pretty girl, so much life ahead of her. Was she popular at school?"

"I don't know, maybe." Ryan grasped the grocery bag handles and began to stand. "I really should be getting home, Sheriff."

"Sure, sure. I just saw you sitting here and thought I'd say hello. Not too often you see a young man like yourself alone looking so thoughtful."

Ryan stared down at his hands that worried at the chain.

"Was that your mother's?"

Ryan glanced at him and frowned before looking back at the ground. "How'd you know that?"

"I surmised. The chain's delicate, too small for a man's taste, and your father mentioned that you lost your mom on your birthday."

"Yeah, it was hers."

"Your birthday must be kind of tough each year."

Ryan shrugged. "I never knew her. It's worse for my dad."

"I suppose it is." Gray stared at the boy for a long time until he met his gaze. "Are you all right, Ryan?"

"Yes sir."

"It seems there's something bothering you."

"No, I'm tired. I didn't sleep well last night."

"Your face is healing up nicely. How'd you get that again?"

"I fell, in the kitchen."

"That's right."

"I really have to go, sir."

"I do too," Gray said, rising from the seat. "Hotter than hell in July around here. A man can't sit still too long, he'll turn to ash. I'll walk with you if you don't mind."

They moved down the path together. Ryan kept his focus on the ground and Gray looked ahead.

"I like history, Ryan, didn't know if I mentioned that."

"No sir."

"I do, always have. My father enjoyed it and passed it down to me. I even like natural history, scientific history, things like that. Do you know how long our sun has been around?" Gray said, motioning to the blinding sky.

"A couple billion years?"

"Four point six billion, approximately. That time itself is something to ponder, isn't it? The amount of life and events that have occurred in that span, it boggles the mind. The only problem with the sun is it's like everything else, it's finite. Someday it will end, in fact I read recently that it's nearing its halfway point of life. Middle aged, like me." Gray chuckled. "But we'll never see it burn out, humankind I mean. You see, the sun's getting brighter, and personally I think it's already getting hotter. In another billion years or so it will be too hot to keep the water from evaporating into space. It'll all just dry up and blow away into the dark."

They reached Gray's cruiser and he paused, watching Ryan who stopped several feet away.

"I don't understand," Ryan finally said.

Gray laughed again. "I'm glad in some ways you don't, it's a harrowing thought to say the least. What I mean by it is this: there are things to worry about and things that can be let go. In the end everything you see around you will be gone. Everything anyone's ever worked for, the steps we or any other life has taken will be erased like they never were. Now, I don't tell you these things to depress you, I'm trying to give you the one thing that I got from thinking on all this."

"What's that?"

"Perspective."

Gray watched Ryan for a beat from beneath the bill of his hat, then nodded and climbed into the car. Ryan looked after the receding cruiser and tried not to let his legs tremble until the sheriff was out of sight. When he knew he could walk without stumbling, he set off for his own car parked on the baking street.

~

Gray stopped the cruiser before the farmhouse and studied the young man seated on its front porch. His red hair was in disarray and his forehead was propped in one palm. Gray let out a long breath and opened the door. Davey didn't look up as he approached and placed one foot on the lowermost stair.

141

"Afternoon Davey."

"Hello."

"May I have a seat in the shade?"

"Sure."

Gray climbed the steps and sat in an open chair beside the boy. Everything was still, not a breeze moved the drooping leaves. The house popped with the heat.

"I didn't get to say how sorry I am," Gray said. "Your father was a good man. Good friend."

Davey nodded into his hand and finally sat up. His face was as red as his hair, but dry.

"He was strong and he passed that on to you, I can see it. There's nothing I can say to comfort you, son. No words ease suffering like this, only time does. The memories that are painful now will become different as the days pass. They'll change from bitter and hurtful to something else, something mellow and good. The memories will be a comfort, you'll see."

Davey stared at him, through him, his eyes lifeless. After a time, he blinked and licked his lips.

"I wanted to thank you, Sheriff."

"For what?"

"For killing that man who hurt him. He deserved worse than he got but I appreciate you ending him."

"You know it was self-defense, right, Davey? I had no choice. If it had been any other way, I would've brought that man in alive."

"I know, but I'm glad you didn't, especially now." Davey turned and looked out across the field that spanned in a rolling green sea beyond the yard. "It's a joke isn't it?"

"What's that, son?"

"Life. It has to be. It couldn't be anything else after he went missing and then we got him back only to lose him for good."

"Sometimes it seems that way."

"Like how you lost your daughter."

Gray's jaw clenched. "Yes, that's right."

Davey studied Gray's face for a while before looking at his hands. "Are the memories better about her now?"

He opened his mouth to reply and closed it again before rubbing the heel of his boot across the parched decking.

"Not yet."

"But you think they will."

"I have to believe so."

"Otherwise life's not worth living, right?"

Gray dipped his chin once.

"Everyone tells me there's a heaven and a God that's watching out for us, and that Dad's with him now, but I want to ask, why wasn't he with him when he was taken from us? Where was he then? The only comfort I get from that is if there is a heaven, there must be a hell, and that's where Hudson is now."

A cicada began its slow, buzzing drone and the sun beat down. They sat without speaking for a long time.

"How is your mother holding up," Gray finally said.

Davey shook his head. "She hasn't come out of her room since last night, hasn't eaten anything."

"Would you like me to talk with her?"

"You can try."

Davey rose and Gray followed him into the house. It smelled like dust and old flowers inside. The sun fell on the wood floors in oblong shapes, motes dancing like things alive.

"Their...her room is at the back through the kitchen." Davey slumped into a chair that had one of Miles's old work shirts hanging from its back.

Gray moved through the house, his boots clicking on the floor. A hallway led off of the tidy kitchen and at its end was a closed door painted white. Sunshine burned in a line beneath its edge. He knocked once and waited for a response. When none came he leaned his head toward the door.

"Renna? It's Mac, can I come in?"

Silence.

"I just want to talk to you for a minute, then I'll go." He looked over his shoulder through the house to where Davey sat and lowered his voice. "Renna, I know this is hard, but there's a young man out here that's depending on you. You're all he has left."

Something creaked in the room and he waited. When the knob remained motionless he grasped it and turned, hoping it wasn't locked. It wasn't. He pushed the door open a few inches and started to look inside when it bumped into something. He shoved on the handle and the door moved with resistance and he was able to squeeze through the opening.

Renna hung from a hook in the ceiling, a wide leather belt cinched tight around her neck.

Gray let out a groan as the corpse spun, Renna's bloodshot eyes, glazed and bulging. Her tongue, ashen and swollen, hung from the side of her mouth. The chair she'd stood on lay on its side beneath her dangling feet and her shadow pirouetted on the wall.

Footsteps came down the hall and he pushed the door fully closed.

"Don't come in here, son." He looked up at the hanging woman and then squeezed his eyes shut. "Don't come in."

Chapter 33

The morning sunlight slanted into Gray's office and made his eyes sting.

He rubbed his face, the unshaven whiskers scratching against his palm. He poured his third cup of coffee and sipped at the lukewarm brew before returning to the article he'd been reading. Someone approached his office and when he looked up, Ruthers stood in the doorway.

"Morning, Sheriff."

"Morning, Joseph."

"You look tired."

"Why thank you. With a silver tongue like that I can see why Siri agreed to date you."

Ruthers laughed and sat in the chair across the desk. "Sorry."

"Didn't get much sleep."

"What time did everything finally get taken care of last night?"

"Around eleven. Davey's nearest relatives are Miles's second cousins that live in Wisconsin. They arrived near dark and agreed to stay with him until everything was settled. Not that I know the meaning of the word anymore."

"What a thing, to lose your father and mother in the same week."

"The boy's strong but I had a word with one of the cousins to keep a close watch on him. Grief's a powerful drug, never know what he might do."

"When are the funerals?"

"This afternoon."

"This afternoon?"

"Yep. Both Miles and Renna wanted to be cremated and since everything was cut and dried as far as Renna's death went, Davey decided he wanted them both taken care of on the same day. Can't say I blame him. Who the hell wants to go through that twice if you don't have to?"

Ruthers shook his head and took off his hat. "It's like madness, isn't it? Like a stone rolling down a hill that just gets bigger and bigger as it goes."

"That seems to be an appropriate analogy, Joseph," Gray said, turning to look out the window. "You ever heard of Apollo Silva?"

"No sir."

"He was the last psychopath on record in the country, never had the Line. He was apprehended in 2074 on a tip given to the local authorities from a next-door neighbor of his. She was an older woman who was at home a lot and from what I can gather, a bit nosy. She saw Silva coming and going at odd hours of the night and always noticed his garbage smelled worse than anyone's on their street. Turns out Silva was abducting women both young and old, he'd taken five that they eventually linked him to. He was divorced and his first victim was his ex-wife who'd moved three states away. He'd taken her from her home and driven back to his house before tying her up to their old bed. He then proceeded to roast her feet and legs with a butane torch and eat them while she was still alive. He did this to all of his victims and when they eventually perished from blood loss and sheer trauma, he'd dissect them and put the pieces in the trash bin in front of his home. He did it for two years before the old lady living next to him called in his suspicious behavior."

"My God, Sheriff. That's about the worst thing I've ever heard."

"I'll agree there. But what raised the hair on my neck is that no one knew he was doing it. Not his boss, not his extended family, and definitely not the investigators that were working on the cases. No one could see him for the monster he was."

Gray fell silent and they sat not speaking until the intercom clicked and Mary Jo's voice came through the speaker, startling them both. "Sheriff?"

"Yes?"

"I just received a call from a Sam Griner up near Emberton."

"Okay?"

"He owns a Churner and was contracted to work a field for a new landowner. Well he went and started working this morning and he found something he thought we should take a look at."

"What is it, Mary Jo?"

"He said he dug up a bunch of bones."

~

Gray guided the cruiser beneath a towering oak and found the overgrown access road shooting off from the highway. Two enormous ruts were carved into the land and he drove in between them, taking in the surroundings. Fields of browning clover and alfalfa spanned the horizon and beyond without a single house in sight. A row of trees lined the edge of the dying grassland. The sky was an ocean of blue above without any skiffs of cloud to mar its surface. The trail curved and traveled over a hill. The remains of a homestead scrolled by on the right, the house's carcass sunken and blackened, time's mouthfuls taken from the collapsing roof and missing siding. What might have been a barn lay flat with broken boards sticking up like teeth from the ground. They drove on for another mile before the hulking machine came into view that had made the tracks they followed.

The Churner was a hill of steel. Its boxy sides rose forty feet in the air where a glass cab perched in the center of the mass. Iron wheels covered by tracks a foot thick stood almost a story high. Its gouging blade was retracted from beneath its bulk and soared above everything like a shining castle wall. The soil behind the machine was the color of old blood, uneven and broken in a swath the width of the implement. A middle-aged man wearing jeans and a blue work-shirt stained with sweat at the armpits and neck, was climbing down the Churner's side ladder. Gray stopped the cruiser a dozen yards from the machine and shut it off.

"Quite a location for a graveyard." Ruthers said from the passenger seat.

"That it is."

They climbed out of the car and strode through the heat to the Churner just as the man stepped from the ladder to the ground.

"Sam?" Gray asked.

"That's me," the man said putting out a hand for each of them to shake. He had dark hair flecked with gray and a wide, tanned face. "Appreciate you coming out so fast, it's a little drive up from your neck of the woods."

"No problem," Gray said. "Tell us what happened here, Sam."

The operator started walking along the machine's side. "Well, it's the damndest thing. I got a call from a fella named Oyster, yeah, like the shellfish, and he had just bought this three hundred acres we're standin' on now. Said he wanted the whole thing flipped so he could grow barley. Barley of all things! I told him corn was what moved in the market but he wouldn't have none of it so I just kept my business my business, you know? What do I care of some fool from the cities wants to lose himself a hundred grand? So I came out here this morning to start, figured it'd take a good two days to churn the whole field up. I got going over there where you can see and was making good time until I came upon this patch here."

The air was moist and heady near the open ground but already the dirt was beginning to dry, the hearty red becoming pale. They stopped behind the implement's left track and Sam pointed toward the fresh soil.

"Now I seen some things, gentlemen, but never anything like this."

Bones protruded from the ground in stark contrasts of white and mottled gray. The entire swath made by the machine was filled with their jagged ends and rounded tops. Nearest to the untouched ground, a full spinal column was attached to a broken skull that looked skyward with its remaining socket. A crescent moon shape with clustered teeth still clinging to it, was half buried close the center, the sunlight shining off of a titanium filling.

"My God," Ruthers said panning the scene.

"That's about what I said when I looked at the screen that shows where I've driven," Sam said, putting his hands on his hips before spitting onto the ground.

Gray walked along the edge of the disturbed soil and knelt. A small group of bones were strewn in a circle along with a smattering of shards like that of broken pottery.

"How deep were you digging when you saw them?" Gray said.

"Oh I was just getting going since I'd made a turn. Probably twelve feet, give or take an inch. Actually it's lucky too since the spinners on the blade there hadn't really gotten up to full RPM, otherwise they would've been dust." Sam paused to spit again. "I guess it's lucky for you fellas, not for them."

Gray stood and moved around the open ground as Ruthers followed, the younger man's hand on his phone case.

"What's your idea, Joseph," Gray said, stopping on the opposite side of the mass grave.

"I don't know, sir. Definitely not an ancient burial site."

"Not unless they were filling people's teeth a thousand years ago."

"So I would say this is recent."

"How recent?"

"Fifty years for sure."

146

"I would say closer to twenty."

"How many do you think are here?"

"I counted four different sets of backbones and pelvises, but there's no telling until we exhume this entire area."

"You guys think it's an old graveyard? Unmarked and whatnot?" Sam called from the other side.

"Could be," Gray said and then motioned to Ruthers as he turned away from the bones. "Why isn't this an unmarked cemetery, Joseph?" he said in a lower voice.

"Because there's no debris from any caskets, no stone markers either."

"Thatta boy."

"So what is this, Sheriff?"

"A dumping ground."

Gray made his way back around the bare earth and stopped beside the Churner's track.

"Sam, I'd like you to pull away from this spot nice and easy and then go ahead and take your equipment home."

"I can't finish the job?"

"Not today."

"So what do I tell Oyster?"

"You tell him whatever you see fit and if he has a problem, direct his calls to my office."

Sam wiped his brow and then shrugged. "If that's the way it is."

"It is."

Gray led the way to the cruiser and opened the door. He looked out over the burned land. Dead and dying. Bones glowing in the sun, the rich earth offering them up like a sacrifice.

"Joseph, call this in and request extra personnel for the forensics team."

"Yes sir."

"And Joseph?"

"Yeah?"

"Tell them to bring a lot of evidence bags."

~

When he turned onto his drive it was fully evening.

The light was red behind the trees, burning out into a purple horizon. Dust blocked the view behind him and he rubbed his eyes. An SUV sat before the garage when he turned the last bend. It was her spot anyway, the vehicle looked right there. Gray parked next to it in case she was only stopping for something else she'd forgotten and got out.

He found Lynn watching the last rays course through the trees. She stood beside the barren stream, shadow the only thing that flowed between its banks. He stopped beside her and she didn't look at him. She stared at the broken skin of the ground, its fissures pleading for water.

"You said this was going to be hers once," Lynn finally said.

147

"Yes, I did."

"What did you mean?"

"What anything means when you give it to someone."

"She was supposed to have it."

"I know. I hate seeing it so dry like this. There should be water here."

"She should be here."

"Yes, she should."

"You weren't at the funerals today."

"I wanted to be. Something came up that I couldn't let go."

"You couldn't ever let anything go, Mac."

He didn't say anything to that.

"Davey did so well, you should've seen him. He even spoke. I couldn't have done it."

"He's a special kid."

"I would say he's a man now."

He looked at her, watched her not look at him.

"I'm sorry for the other night," Gray said. "Not sorry for what I said, but because it hurt you."

Lynn was quiet for a long time.

"You were wrong."

"About what?"

"About me being strong. I was being hypocritical saying you hide from everything. I'm not strong, I fake it."

"You can't fake strength."

"You'd be surprised."

The sun fell away and a blue twilight seeped into the sky. The air cooled only a little, but it was enough. They stood by the dry streambed until it was almost full dark, the air humming with insects. Heat lightning began to pulse on the horizon, striding threads of light, there and gone without a sound.

Without a word, Lynn began to walk toward her vehicle. He followed.

"Didn't you forget anything this time?" He asked.

"Like what?"

"Like anything you might need to come in for?"

She paused near the door of the house, looking up at its height. She was only a shape in the falling dark.

"It isn't what I've forgotten, it's what I haven't."

He went to her and didn't stop until they were inches apart. He reached to pull her close as she brought a hand up and he braced for the slap he knew would come. But it didn't. Her hand found the back of his neck and guided his face to hers. Their lips met without hesitation, old paths traveled by blind eyes. He pressed himself close to her and she slid her hand through his hair, gripping it, not letting go.

He got the door open but they only made it to the kitchen floor. Their clothes came free as if cut from their bodies. Hands sliding over buttons and snaps until there was nothing between them. The lightning strobed and they moved, sinuous against one another until she gripped him, guided him into her.

148

The dream came back to him then but it was there and gone as she flowed over him, beginning to say his name, slowly at first and then quicker. She chanted and moved above him while he caught glimpses of her in the throbbing light, and the light was inside him and then it was in her. Over and over until it faded with the deafening quiet rushing like a palpable tide into sound.

They lay there on the floor, holding one another. The tears came without warning, unbidden as they flowed down his face. She kissed him on the cheek and said his name again, quiet.

Chapter 34

Ruthers parked his truck in front of Siri's brick two-story and turned the radio lower.

The night had dropped over everything like a curtain while they'd been in the movie theater, and now the only illumination in the cab was from the green glow of the dashboard. Siri's face was half-lit. She looked at him from where she sat, the portion of her lips in the light was curved up in a smile.

"That was really nice, I haven't been to a movie in over a year," she said.

"Yeah, it was. Sorry we missed the one you wanted to see."

"I think we both had a pretty good excuse."

"You can say that again." Ruthers frowned and looked at the headlights splashed across the yard. Stars glittered from the moonless sky. A black desert of glinting sand.

"You think he's right, don't you?" Siri asked.

Ruthers looked at her again. "I do."

"So you don't believe Hudson was responsible for all those bodies in the ground or any of the other killings?"

"Sheriff Gray doesn't think so."

"I didn't ask you what the sheriff thinks."

Ruthers sat for a moment and traced the circle of the steering wheel with a finger.

"I didn't believe it for a while, or didn't want to believe it I guess. But the more I saw, the more it made sense."

"What about the Line?" Siri asked, reaching out to touch his shoulder. A wave of gooseflesh flowed outward from the spot.

"Nothing's perfect."

"Tilly thinks he's still grieving for his little girl."

"I would say she's right, but he's a brilliant man, smarter than anyone I've ever met."

"Grief doesn't care how smart you are."

"And instincts outstrip reason sometimes."

"You're very loyal to him."

"I am, but he's earned it."

"I hope you're both wrong."

Ruthers sighed. "Me too."

They were quiet for a long time. Only the night sounds filtering in from outside the cooled vehicle and the low tune of a song coming from the speakers.

"Why did you ask me to the festival, Joe?"

He blinked at her in the low light. "What do you mean?"

"I mean, why? There's a hundred other women our age that aren't pregnant that you could've asked."

"I didn't want to take a hundred other women, I wanted to take you." His voice was soft and he hoped she didn't hear the tremble in it.

"If you feel sorry for me, don't. I made a mistake, not in getting pregnant but with who I chose for the father. I've made my peace with that and I'm ready to raise this baby alone, so if pity is pushing you to date me we can just shake hands and go our separate ways. I don't need pity."

"The only person I pity is the man who left you, and I dislike him enough on principal to get past that."

He watched the half of her face he could see and when she smiled again he leaned toward her. Her perfume smelled like warm honey and a fresh flower; daisies. Then her lips were against his, pliant and unlike he'd dreamed they would be. Better. She touched the side of his face, running her fingertips down the skin he'd shaved only hours ago. Then her lips were gone, but her hand remained where it was.

"Thank you," she said.

He put his hand over hers. "Thank you."

"I should go, it's late and there's a lot of work to do tomorrow."

"I'll walk you up."

"I'm fine," she said, grabbing her purse from the floor. "I'm sure I'll see you tomorrow."

"You can count on it," he said, watching her ease out of the door and make her way to the house. He waited until she unlocked the door and waved before turning around to pull down the short drive that met the county road.

As he guided the truck toward town, he looked up at the stars again and smiled.

~

Siri shut the door behind her and leaned against it, one hand on her stomach in the spot the baby usually kicked.

"What do you think, honey?" she said aloud, rubbing her belly. "He might be something, huh?"

She slid off her flat shoes and flipped on several lights. Pausing in the doorway to the kitchen, she frowned. The air smelled of something. She sniffed, inhaling the scent. It was like old sweat or faint body odor. The hair on the back of her neck stiffened as a sound came from the living room, quiet, almost indistinguishable, but there.

Breathing.

She spun and let out a short cry as two hands grasped her upper arms, the fingers digging into her flesh.

"Hello Siri, have a nice date?"

~

Ruthers pulled to a stop at the first light in town and considered grabbing a six-pack. He could almost taste the beer on his tongue. The liquor store was right and his house was left. He glanced down the well-lit street and checked the clock. If he hurried he could still make it before closing time. He was about to spin the wheel when his eyes fell on a dark rectangle on the passenger floorboard. Keeping his foot on the brake, he leaned to the side and picked it up.

Siri's phone.

Holding it, he thumbed the display on as the time ticked over to the next hour.

"Probably too late anyway," he said.

With a last look down the street, he cranked the wheel and headed back the direction he'd come.

~

Darrin threw Siri across her bedroom. Her legs slammed into the bedframe and she fell onto the mattress, the air rushing out of her lungs.

"You just lay there for a second while I show you something," Darrin said, walking closer. Ryan entered the room behind his brother carrying a sleek pistol in one hand.

"What are you doing?" Siri said. "I know your father, I work with him." Her eyes went from Darrin's cold stare to Ryan. The younger boy's features were slack and he was pale. "Please, just don't hurt me and I won't tell anyone you were here."

Darrin laughed as his hand went into his pocket and came out holding a round steel cylinder. One of its ends was flat and smooth while the other narrowed to a short, needled point. He smiled at her as he stopped at the side of the bed and knelt down so that they were at eye level.

"Do you know what this is?" Darrin asked.

Siri looked at the instrument in his hand and shook her head.

"It's a deseminator. They use these in abortion clinics. See, this little needle here is inserted right through a woman's stomach wall into her uterus." Darrin squeezed the handle and the short needle slid out nearly a foot with a clicking sound. "Then once it's been maneuvered into the perfect position by a qualified medical professional, such as my father, this other button is pushed."

He squeezed the cylinder again and the last four inches of the needle split apart into six individual pieces, like an umbrella opening in reverse. Siri's eyes widened as Darrin brought the splayed edges of the needle closer to her face.

"These barbs tear the fetus apart. Barbaric, isn't it? I mean, we put men on Mars but we can't find a better way to kill babies?" Darrin laughed, the sound like screeching vehicle brakes. "Anyway, this model's a bit large, normally used for livestock with abnormal pregnancies." He moved closer to her, thrusting the deseminator into her face. "You make a move that I don't like, try to run, scream, anything, I'm going to have my brothers hold you down and I'm going to shove this into your stomach and hit the trigger. You'll feel your baby die inside you, then we'll watch you bleed out. Do we understand each other?"

Siri drew in a shuddering breath. "Yes."

"Good girl. Now where do you keep your suitcase?"

152

"In the closet on the floor."

Darrin stood and retracted the needle into the deseminator's handle.

"Keep that on her in case she decides to be stupid," Darrin said to Ryan as he passed him. Ryan swallowed and raised the pistol, leveling it at Siri as she sat up on the bed. His hand trembled.

"Why are you doing this?" Siri asked.

Ryan swallowed and blinked. It looked like he was going to pass out. Darrin emerged from the closet carrying her black, rolling travel suitcase.

"Isn't that the question of the hour? Why? Why? Why? Everyone wants to know that." Darrin stalked to the clothes dresser beside the bed and dropped the suitcase. With a snap of his hand he snagged her hair in his fist and pulled her toward him as he bent over. His breath was rotten on her face and his handsome features were pulled into something demonic.

"I'll give you an answer, darling: because, that's why." He released her hair and opened the top drawer of the dresser. He chucked handfuls of her underwear and socks into the suitcase and then moved on to the next drawer. Ryan watched him work, flinching every time he slammed a drawer shut.

The barrel of the gun wavered.

Ryan stared at the back of Darrin's head, his eyes shooting once to Siri and then to Darrin again. Slowly, the pistol dropped a fraction of an inch, lining up with Darrin's skull. Ryan shook, the sights sliding on and off of his brother's head.

Siri watched Ryan's eyes lock on his brother's task and eased her hand over to where the dresser met the bedframe. Her fingers brushed the grip of the handgun that was stowed there and she tensed her body, taking in a deep breath before releasing it.

Siri jerked the gun free of its holster and swung it up. Darrin yelled something unintelligible and reached for her. The pistol bucked in her hand and blood flew from Darrin's shoulder in a fine spray. Ryan fired, his finger reflexing on the trigger and three rounds burst from the barrel, burying themselves in the floor. Siri rolled across the bed, falling from its top to the space near the wall. With one hand she covered her stomach while she threaded the gun up over her head and then under the bed.

"Fuck!" Darrin screamed, and fell to the floor as he skittered backward. "Shoot that bitch! Shoot her!" A shot came from beneath the bed and punched a hole in the wall near the doorway at foot level. Ryan ducked and ran into the upstairs hall as Darrin floundered after him.

"Are you hit?" Darrin asked, grabbing Ryan's arm for support.

"I don't think so."

"What the fuck, where'd that gun come from?"

"I don't know."

"Cover the fucking door in case she comes out." Darrin staggered to the head of the stairs and examined his shoulder in the light. A crater large enough to put his thumb in was gouged in his arm. Blood oozed out of the hole and began to soak his shirtsleeve, turning it a darker black.

"What do we do, Darrin?" Ryan asked, his eyes locked on the bedroom door, the gun vibrating in his grip.

"Shut up," Darrin hissed. "I have to get this bleeding stopped. Don't move and shoot her if she comes out. She can't get out that window, it's a fourteen-foot drop."

Darrin made his way down the stairs, blood dropping from his fingertips. He found a towel in one of the kitchen drawers and looped it around the wound but couldn't tie it with only one hand. As he walked toward the stairs again a knock came from the front door and it began to swing open. He stopped, frozen where he stood as a hand appeared and then a face.

Ruthers stepped into the entry holding a cell phone in one hand.

"Siri? The door was open and—" His words cinched off in his throat as he saw Darrin standing in the kitchen doorway, blood slowly soaking through the starch-white towel.

"What the fuck are you doing here?" Ruthers said taking another step into the house.

Darrin reached with his good hand into his pocket and drew out the steel cylinder. Ruthers began to move backward as his eyes shot toward the stairway.

"Don't move, police!"

Darrin nodded once and something hit the back of Ruthers's neck hard and the lights tipped to the side as he fell.

~

Siri blinked away the tears that kept forming as she aimed at the doorway. Sobs tried to build up inside her but she swallowed them down each time. The baby kicked, a watery, sliding motion that made her clench her jaw each time. She heard the Barder boys talking in the hall. She'd hit one of them but she didn't know which. Blood lay in a triangular spray on the white carpet, an arrow that pointed directly at her.

Footsteps receded down the stairs but there was still heavy breathing in the hall. She tried to calculate where it was and if she could send a shot through the wall. Tears again, blurring her vision. She wiped them away and glanced at the window beside her and then back at the door.

Voices came from downstairs, muddled and indistinct. Then a yell that made her gasp.

Joe was downstairs.

"Joe! Get help! There's two of them!"

Silence except for the breathing in the hallway.

"Darrin? You okay?" Ryan called.

"Yeah, we're good."

Siri waited, her stomach roiling in time with the baby's movements. Vomit tried to make a run for the back of her throat but she gagged and managed to hold it down.

"Siri, you're going to put that gun down and come out of your room in ten seconds, you hear me?" Darrin said from what sounded like the bottom of the stairs.

Siri licked her arid lips. "Joe?"

"He's right here, and if you don't come out of the room unarmed I'm going to slit his throat."

"You're lying."

There was a sliding thump and then a moan.

"Tell her to drop the gun," Darrin said.

A pause and then Joe's voice, weak and groggy came up the stairway. "Don't do it, Siri, don't—"

Joe cried out and there was a scuffle followed by a gagged groan of pain.

"Don't hurt him!" Siri yelled, her arms trembling from holding the gun so tightly.

"You do what I say and you both live. You don't, he dies first, slow, and then we burn the house down with you inside. Your choice, Siri, we've got all night."

She waited, the baby kicked.

With another look at the window, she stood, the blood flowing back to her legs in painful ebbs that coalesced into tingling needles. She crossed the room as quietly as she could and stopped at the door.

"I'm coming out, don't shoot."

"Lay the gun on the floor of the hall," Darrin said.

She bent over and tossed the pistol through the doorway.

"Good girl. Now come out, nice and slow and no one dies."

She stepped into the hallway. Darrin and Ryan stood at the base of the stairs. Adam, the huge middle brother, held Joe with one massive forearm pressed to his neck from behind. Joe's lip was swollen and seeping blood. Darrin had the deseminator poised below Joe's chin and he watched her over one shoulder, his dark eyes gleaming. Ryan held an unsteady bead on her with the pistol.

"Let him go."

"Come down the stairs first, then we'll talk. Make any sudden moves and I'll shish-kebob his fuckin' brain."

Siri took a step as Joe gurgled something and shook his head. Darrin gouged the soft skin of Joe's neck and a small runner of blood appeared that slid out of sight into the collar of his shirt.

"Stop, I'm coming, don't hurt him." She stumbled down the last several stairs and Ryan caught her arm, breaking her fall.

"Take her, Adam," Darrin said.

Adam released Ruthers who sagged as Darrin clutched the back of his shirt, moving the weapon from his neck to his lower back.

"You know, I've never been shot before, but it wasn't like I thought it would be. More like a bee sting."

"Let her go," Ruthers wheezed.

Darrin ground the sharp end of the instrument into his back. "Shut up, Joey. You always were a pain in the ass."

"Stop," Siri said. Tears finally broke free of her eyes and slid down her face.

"Does our good sheriff suspect anything about us?" Darrin said, shaking Ruthers by the collar.

Ruthers stared into Siri's eyes, his jaw tight.

"Always the hard-ass. Well, probably couldn't believe anything you'd tell us anyway. What's the world coming to when law enforcement can't be trusted?" Darrin let out his screeching laughter again.

"Darrin, we have to go," Ryan said, looking out the front windows.

Darrin didn't seem to hear him.

"It's thrilling, isn't it? What we're experiencing now? We're on the edge of something beautiful, predator and prey locked in the dance." Darrin gripped Ruthers harder, drawing him close. "You'd do anything to save her, wouldn't you?" he whispered into Ruthers's ear. "What's it feel like to know you can't?"

He triggered the deseminator.

There was the same metallic click and Ruthers stiffened, his eyes flying wide. Darrin held him fast and pressed the second button. There was a hollow thunk that came from inside Ruthers's stomach and his legs dropped from beneath him.

"No!" Siri screamed, trying to lunge forward but Adam grasped her by the hair and yanked her back. Darrin pulled the instrument free as Ruthers fell, its end one piece again. Crimson coated its length and ran from the needled tip. Ruthers crumpled to the floor, a whoosh of air coming from his chest, the sound of a balloon deflating in one blast. Siri sobbed and Adam twisted her hair, holding her tighter. Ryan stared at the fallen deputy.

"Oh shit! That worked great!" Darrin yelled, stepping back from Ruthers to look at him. "Must've cut a nerve to his legs along with his liver. Damn, he pissed himself, look at that!"

"We should go," Ryan said, his eyes locked on Ruthers as he shuddered against the floor.

"You're a fucking coward, Ry-Ry, and for that you get the duty of hauling our fine deputy out of here."

"We're taking him with us?"

"Can't leave a body here. They'd be able to ID him even after the fire."

Siri cried out again and tried to lunge at Darrin.

"Will you shut her up, Adam?"

Adam nodded and pulled a small plastic tube from his pocket. One end was slim and pointed and he jammed this into Siri's left nostril as he wrenched her head back. Her eyes fluttered and she gagged before slumping forward. Adam held her upright easily and dragged her across the living room toward the front door.

"Nice thing about this is almost all the bleeding is internal. No messy cleanup," Darrin said, gazing at the weapon in his hand. "Although I kind of like the mess." He motioned to Ryan. "Go ahead and drag him to the door, we'll load him in the van from there."

Darrin moved toward the front of the house while Ryan swayed and took a step forward, tucking the pistol in the back of his pants. Ruthers gasped in a hitching breath, a ratcheting sound coming from deep in his chest, and his eyes found Ryan's as he approached. He tried pushing himself along the floor with his arms but he barely moved an inch. Finally he lay still, bringing his hands to his sides as Ryan bent over him to grasp his ankles.

Ruthers fumbled with something and then slowly lifted his hand up, half sitting as he did so. Ryan glanced at him, thinking that the dying deputy was reaching to him for help. When he looked up, the other man's hand was in front of his face. There was something in Ruthers's palm, something metallic.

The six-inch blade shot from the end of the knife and slid into Ryan's right eye.

For a moment he remained where he was, holding Ruthers's ankles and then his body convulsed, snapping him upright as his hands came instinctually to the injury. Ruthers lost his grip on the knife and it went with Ryan as he stood, its handle jutting from his ruined eye socket. There was a beat of quiet stillness as Ryan's jittering fingers found the blade, his jaw dropping loose, and Ruthers watched him through the fading that was filling up his vision. Then the younger man's legs unhinged and he slammed to his knees before tipping forward. He landed on his face, driving the knife even deeper into his skull just as Darrin stepped back into the room.

"What the fuck?"

Darrin latched onto Ryan's shoulder and rolled him over. Blood poured out around the knife's haft and expanded in a dark pool on the floor. Ryan's body shuddered once and fell still.

Darrin let go of his brother and stood to his full height, teeth gritted, eyes aflame.

"You sonofabitch," he said, stooping over Ruthers as he drew out the deseminator again. He was about to thrust it into the deputy's chest when he noticed the glaze coating the prone man's eyes.

"Hey Darrin, how many cans of gas should I bring in?" Adam said, stepping into the room. He stopped, taking in the scene before him. "What happened to Ryan?"

Darrin's breath came and went in labored puffs. He wound up a kick and delivered it to Ruthers's side. He kicked the body again and again, grunting deep in his chest each time. Finally he stood still, breathing hard through his nose.

"What're we going to do?" Adam asked, still staring at the knife-handle protruding from Ryan's eye.

Darrin kept his gaze on the deputy's slack face for a long time before he put the deseminator back in his pocket.

"Bring in the gas, Adam. All of it."

Chapter 35

Gray stopped the cruiser behind Mitchel's shining SUV and climbed out.

The sun was a disc of ash on the horizon, a negative of what it would become later in the day. The early morning hung muggy and thick, cloistering as he made his way up the drive toward the smoking ruins of the two-story brick house.

The roof was gone, wilted inward in a spine-broken way, small flames chuckling amongst the tiles. The windows were black holes with laughing shadows from the fire inside. A fire unit idled a dozen yards away from the house, its personnel doing final checks of the scene, one automated hose attached to a mobile crane extinguishing the sputtering embers. Mitchel leaned against the hood of a deputy's car speaking with one of his men, his round form shaking with laughter at a joke Gray had just missed.

"Good morning, Mitchel," he said, stopping a dozen paces from the building's husk.

"What are you doing here?" Mitchel said, standing up.

"I'm being courteous, let's play nice, shall we?"

"The county line's two miles in that direction," Mitchel said, pointing the way Gray had come. "I'd suggest you check your boundaries when you get back to your office."

"Is Siri okay?"

Mitchel sighed. "Are you deaf, Mac? Do you want me to have you removed, is that it?"

"I'm merely checking on a friend, Mitchel. Courteous, remember?"

"We're not sure at this time."

"Not sure if she's a friend of mine or if she's okay?"

"Fuck you, Mac."

"So where is she?"

"We don't know. Her vehicle is gone."

Gray turned his head to look at the other sheriff.

"She's missing?"

"No, she's not here, there's a difference. You leave your house from time to time, right Mac? She's just gone somewhere, I'm sure. It is the weekend, people travel, it's in their nature."

"What started the fire?"

"It began in the kitchen near the stove, other than that the crew hasn't been able to determine anything else."

"Why?"

"Because the fire was extremely hot. It burned the center of the house all the way out as you can see. We're just lucky it was one of the older homes in the area and made of brick, it kept the fire somewhat contained. That and the neighbors called it in shortly after it was started."

158

"Have you questioned them yet?"

"About?"

"About their feelings on this year's election. About the fire, Mitchel, what else."

"I just told you they called it in. They saw flames in the early morning hours and alerted the department."

"That's it?"

"That's it."

"So where's the forensic team?"

"Why in hell would we need a forensic team, Mac?" Mitchel took a step forward, close enough for Gray to smell sweat and not enough bad cologne to cover it up. "This isn't a crime scene."

"The homeowner is missing, her house is gutted, and you don't think that's strange?"

"I'll thank you to find your way back to your cruiser, Mac," Mitchel said, spinning on his heel. "Or I can have one of my men escort you if you've forgotten the way."

"I suppose you have plenty of manpower since you hire out rent-a-cops whenever you can."

"What's that supposed to mean?"

"You know damn well what I mean. You said you'd have a man on Miles's door round the clock."

"Baron died of natural causes. Are you losing it, Mac?"

"I don't believe so."

"Get off this property, now."

"Mitchel, was there a defining moment when you knew for sure you were a full-blown asshole?"

Enson paused in mid-step but shook his head and kept going, waving his hand at a deputy who was beginning to make his way toward Gray.

Gray studied the house again. The smoke drifted in pale wreaths toward the lightening sky, ghosts leaving a carcass. He inhaled and spit once on the ground before walking back to his car.

~

"Mary Jo, has Joseph called back yet?"

The intercom was quiet for a beat and then the dispatcher's voice drifted out of its speaker.

"No, Sheriff, he hasn't. It is his day off, you know."

"I do. When I went past his home this morning his truck wasn't there and he's yet to answer his phone. Uncharacteristic of our Joseph."

"I suppose it is. Maybe he went for a drive."

"Maybe."

"He had a date with Siri last night, didn't he?"

"I believe so."

"And that's why you're concerned."

"I'm like a book to you, Mary Jo."

"There were no bodies in the house."

"No there weren't."

"You think it's still going on, don't you?"

"I don't know what to think anymore." Gray flicked the pad of his computer and watched the pointer fly across the screen. "Anything on the schedule this morning?"

"No, but the reports for the landowner history you asked for came back just now."

"And?"

"Before the current owner, Mister, um, Oyster, purchased it there was only one other listed. A Mister Clarence Drucker who is now deceased. Before that it was state land used for commercial pesticide testing."

Gray rubbed his temples and closed his eyes.

"When did Drucker die?"

"December seventeenth, 2075."

"Forty years ago."

"Yes sir."

"Thank you, Mary Jo."

"You're welcome. And Sheriff?"

"Yes?"

"I'm sure Joseph is fine."

The intercom clicked off and he stared at the wall, the empty chair on the other side of the desk. His cell phone buzzed against his hip and he dug for it, studied the number for a moment before answering.

"Good morning."

"Hi," Lynn said.

"How did you sleep?"

"Good until you left, then not so good."

"I'm sorry."

"It wasn't your fault, it was just—"

"Being in the house?"

"Yeah."

Gray stood from the desk and shut the door to the office.

"Last night," he started, then stopped.

"Let's not talk about it," Lynn said.

"Why? Because it'll cheapen it or you want to forget it?"

"I'm not sure yet."

"Well when you figure it out, let me know."

Lynn fell quiet for a long time. He could hear some of the background music she played in the store tinkling away.

"I turned on the water pump for the stream, hope you don't mind," she said finally.

"Not at all. I was going to do it today."

"I couldn't bear to see it so dry."

"It's supposed to rain in a few days."

160

"So they say."

"Yeah. Lynn, can we—"

"Just leave it alone, Mac. It was what it was."

"I'd like to see you."

"I need some space, will you give it to me?"

"If that's what you want."

"It is."

He paused, licking his lips that were dry, so dry.

"I never stopped—"

"I have to go, Mac," she said. "I have customers."

"All right."

"Goodbye."

"Goodbye," he said, but she'd already hung up.

He was still holding the phone, scrutinizing it, when a knock came from the door and Mary Jo stepped into the room.

"Sheriff, a call just came in from Vincent Barder. He says his son, Ryan, is missing. He wondered if you'd stop out as soon as you could."

"I'll go presently," Gray said, adjusting his hat. "Anyone respond as far as getting our air fixed?"

"Not yet," Mary Jo said, making her way back down the hall.

"It is a Godforsaken oven in here, Mary Jo. How are you not sweating?"

"Women don't sweat, Sheriff, they glow," she said over her shoulder.

Gray shook his head and turned to the right, stepping out the back door to where his cruiser was parked. The concrete baked and steel ticked under the fist of sun hanging in the mocking blue sky. He was almost to the door of the cruiser when Mark Sheldon rounded the corner of the building. The DA's shoulders were thrown back and he squinted against the glare. They narrowed further as he spotted Gray by the car.

"Hold up, Sheriff."

"I'm on a call, Mark, I need to get going."

"This will only take a minute."

"It never takes a minute with you Mark."

The other man stopped a short distance away and glared at him.

"You didn't take my advice."

"I didn't know you gave me any."

"Mitchel called me this morning and said you were out of jurisdiction, trying to undermine his authority."

"Now I'm just a commoner, Mark, and those were a lot of big words."

"Quit fucking around, Gray. You and I both know why you went out there."

"I heard about the fire at Siri's and wanted to make sure she was okay."

"You wanted to keep your weird little fantasy going by making problems where there aren't any."

Gray took a step forward, closing the distance between them.

"I want to find the truth, whether it's comforting or not."

"The truth is you're delusional and not fit to hold office."

"You can tell that to the people who elected me," Gray said, turning away.

"I intend to," Mark said, following him to the car.

"Good."

"Oh, and I don't know what ideas you have concerning Lynn, but forget them. She's moved on."

"Thanks for the tip."

"She told me herself the night of the celebration." The DA paused as he placed one hand against the cruiser's hood. "Right after I fucked her."

Gray hit him in the mouth just as he began to say something else, his fist cutting off the words before they were fully formed.

Mark fell to his ass and rolled onto his back, his polished shoes flying up in the air. Gray caught himself stepping over the fallen man to deliver another blow, and stopped. He moved back, passing a hand over his throbbing knuckles. The DA's lips were both split in their centers, blood painting his chin in a crimson goatee. Mark looked up at him, cobwebs of pain and shock covering his face.

"If you'll excuse me, I have a call to go to. And if you get a chance, send someone over here to fix our fucking air conditioning," Gray said before climbing into the cruiser. He backed out of the parking space and sped away, throwing a last glance at the fallen man who was trying unsuccessfully to sit up.

Chapter 36

"Would you like something to drink, Sheriff? Coffee, iced tea?"

Dr. Barder stood by his refrigerator, scanning its shelves as if it had something to hide.

"A cup of coffee would be great, thanks," Gray said, settling into a chair near the kitchen table. While Barder made the coffee Gray studied the rest of the house, his eyes traveling over each surface, every object. When the doctor set the cup down in front of him, he smiled and brought it to his lips, blowing the steam away.

"I know I really shouldn't be this worried, but I am," Barder said, interlacing and then pulling his fingers apart over and over. "He's seventeen and active, I'm guessing he's at a friend's house but I've already called everyone I can think of."

"When did you last see him?"

"Last night. I worked a shift at the hospital until around eight and then came home. All the boys were here. We had a quick bite to eat and then watched TV for an hour or so. I was beat so I went to bed shortly after that. I took the next three days off since we were planning on going camping. When we got up this morning, Ryan wasn't here."

"And his vehicle is gone, I'm assuming?" Gray asked, sipping his coffee.

The doctor nodded. "Yes. Adam and Darrin said they all went to bed around eleven and didn't hear him leave."

"Does he have a girlfriend?"

"Not that I know of."

"How has he seemed to you lately?"

Barder squinted. "Seemed?"

"Overall. Disturbed, troubled, quiet, depressed?"

"Well, I guess he has been pretty quiet the last few weeks. But I spoke to him and he said he was having trouble sleeping."

"Anything in particular that could've been bothering him?"

"I don't think so. He's a gentle boy, kind and thoughtful. His birthday is coming up and he usually recedes a little from everyone around then."

"Because of how your wife passed away?"

"Yes. I get the feeling that he still feels it's his fault, even though I've assured him there was nothing that could've been done." Barder swallowed once. "I was the one that delivered him and tried to save her, but there wasn't—" He pressed his lips together and shook his head. "I'm sorry."

"That's okay. Does he have any places that he likes to go to think? I met him down in your hollow and saw him sitting on a park bench near the town pond."

"Not that I know of other than the two spots you just mentioned. I used to take him fishing in both places." The doctor looked out of the window at the yard.

"I suppose that's why he goes back there. We were going to do some fishing today."

Gray reached out and squeezed the other man's arm.

"I can't file a missing person on him until twenty-four hours have passed, but I'm sure he'll turn up soon, most likely of his own accord. Now, would you mind if I spoke to your other boys?"

Barder met his gaze again. His face was slack and he blinked several times before answering.

"Of course, let me get them."

He stood and moved to the stairway leading out of the kitchen and called up it. A moment later footsteps padded overhead and then traipsed down the stairs. Darrin appeared first followed by his hulking younger brother. Gray took in the large Band-Aid below Adam's eye as well as the wrappings on his fingers.

"Good morning, gentlemen," Gray said, standing and shaking both their hands.

"Morning, Sheriff," Darrin said.

"I'm going to go out to the garage and get some things packed just in case Ryan comes back. Then we'll be ready to go." Barder said, moving toward the door. "Thank you for coming, Sheriff."

"It's no problem at all."

The doctor left the room and Gray waited until he heard the door close in the entry before looking at the two boys seated across from him. He shifted his gaze between Darrin and Adam until the younger of the two finally looked down at the floor.

"So tell me about last night," Gray said.

Darrin stared at him from across the table and then sat back in his chair.

"Dad got home a little after eight. Ryan, Adam, and I were all here. We had dinner and watched some TV. Dad went to bed and we stayed up a little later then went to bed too. This morning Ryan was gone."

"That right, Adam?"

Adam raised his eyes to meet Gray's and then dropped them again, nodding slowly.

"That looks painful," Gray said, motioning to Adam's face. "What happened?"

"We were wrestling, goofing around, and I scratched him on accident," Darrin said. Adam nodded again.

"And your hand?"

"Shut it in a barn door," Adam said, looking past Gray's shoulder toward the far wall.

"Wow, you boys sure are accident prone around here. I mean, just a few days ago Ryan told me he fell and hit his face on a kitchen cabinet. You wouldn't know which one he hit, would you, Darrin?"

"Can't say that I do, sir."

"Hmm. Well, I suppose injuries do happen on a farm and whatnot. I'm guessing you boys stay busy working around here."

"We sure do, it's a full-time job," Darrin said.

"Is that your plans, to take over the farming?"

"I guess I don't see what this has to do with Ryan going missing," Darrin said, sitting forward. He placed his hand on the table near a butter knife that was resting on a plate. Gray shifted his eyes down to it and back up.

"Oh, just trying to paint a picture here. You must be what, twenty-three?"

"Twenty-four."

"Gotcha. About the same age as my deputy, Joseph Ruthers. You wouldn't have known him in school, would you?"

"Didn't know him but we were in the same grade together."

Gray smiled and adjusted his hat.

"Yeah, he's a good man. Reliable. On time. Always can count on him."

Gray let the silence hang in the kitchen and glanced at Darrin's fingers, a half inch closer now to the knife.

"Anyway, you boys don't have any ideas on where your brother may have went?"

"Not off the top of my head, no."

"How about you, Adam?"

"No sir."

"Well, I wouldn't worry, he'll turn up soon. Things have a way of revealing themselves most times. All you have to do is watch for them."

Gray rapped his knuckles twice on the table, hard, and Adam flinched but Darrin didn't move. He stood and smiled at the two seated boys before heading through the door to the heat outside.

When the door shut behind him Darrin relaxed and drew his hand away from the butter knife.

"He knows," Adam whispered.

"No he doesn't. He thinks he knows which is almost as bad but not quite."

"He'll know what to do about the sheriff, right, Darrin? He can tell us what's next when he comes again."

"We don't need to wait for him to tell us."

"What are we gonna do then?"

Darrin stood and walked to the window. The sheriff was shaking hands with his father. He gave the house a final glance and then headed for his waiting cruiser.

"What else? We're going to kill him."

~

Gray drove the hot road.

His tires wailed lamented hums and the ashen blacktop cracked like dead skin beneath the furious light. His eyes watched everything and nothing. The crops the only color in the fading world, their waving those of a death parade issuing forever goodbyes. He ran through all the events during the last few days, shuffling past each one on the screen of his mind until they became a jumbled collage. On the highway something glinted. It flashed there and gone as he came closer, the sun repeating its signal over and over.

Over and over.

Gray blinked and reached out to the dashboard, punching a button.

The radio flashed to life and Mary Jo's voice came through as clear as if she were sitting in the passenger seat.

"Yeah, Sheriff?"

"Mary Jo, the head of IT over at Wheaton Medical is named Delly. Please patch me through to her."

"Sure thing."

The speakers hummed for almost a minute and then a woman's voice streamed through them.

"This is Delly."

"Delly, this is Mac Gray."

"Hello, Sheriff, what can I do for you?"

"You wouldn't be in your cozy little office there, would you?"

"I am actually."

"Can you do something for me? Scroll through that same span of time that we scanned the other day and tell me what you notice about the headlights that swung through the corridor in the middle of the night before Mr. Baron's death."

There was a long pause. "Okay. It'll take me a second."

Gray waited, coasting the cruiser to the side of the road. He closed his eyes and listened to the faint sounds coming through the speakers. There was a short intake of breath and then Delly's voice filled the cab.

"They're the same. The path of the lights on the wall is exactly the same all four times. I just checked the outdoor cameras at that time and there's only one vehicle coming and leaving. Sheriff, I don't...what the hell?"

"What is it, Delly?"

"It's been looped. The surveillance in the hallway, it's been looped over itself. That's why the lights are the same each time."

Gray sat, tapping his thigh with one finger, faster and faster.

"Someone covered up a span of time is what you're telling me?"

"As far as I can tell, yes."

"Who has access to the video files besides you?"

"The twelve members of the board, the four heads of staff, the maintenance department which is at least ten, a few other IT personnel that are part time."

"Are the video files accessible only through your office?"

"No, they aren't."

"Let me guess, since most everything is hosted offsite someone could have looped the video from somewhere remote."

"You got it, Sheriff. All they would've needed was a decent computer and the password."

Gray pulled his hat off, rubbed the grime of sweat away from his forehead. "Damn it."

"Why would someone do this, Sheriff? I mean, Mr. Baron died from a stroke if I'm not mistaken, so what would be the point of looping over the footage of the hallway right before it happened?"

166

Gray ignored the question and studied the row upon row of corn out the passenger window.

"I appreciate your help, Delly. Keep me posted if anything else comes up."

"Okay, but—"

"If I have any more questions I'll let you know."

Gray ended the call and sat in the silence of the car. There was a beep and Mary Jo's voice came from the radio.

"Everything okay, Sheriff?"

"Dandy."

"What did you find out at the Barders'?"

"Nothing we didn't already know. Anything else come in?"

"The first reports from forensics on the bodies from the field."

"Good, what'd they say?"

"There were a total of eight full skeletons and two skulls that were unearthed. Two of them were identified by dental records already."

"Who were they?"

"A Dennis Letchin and a Geraldine Smith. Both were reported missing twenty-two years ago this fall. They were from up north in Ellis County."

"And they were called in missing around the same time? Were they related?"

"Doesn't look like it."

"Shit. Cause of death?"

"Trauma was found on the cervical vertebra most likely from an edged weapon."

"Their throats were cut. Hard."

"It appears so."

"And the others?"

"That's all I have so far, Sheriff. Tilly said she'd have the rest over before morning."

"Okay. Anything else?"

"The mayor called twice."

"Great. What did you tell him?"

"That you were out on a call. He wants you to come by his office the first chance you get."

"Wonderful."

"He sounded angry."

"Good."

"What did you do?"

"Nothing that didn't need doing. If you could phone him back and let him know I'll be there directly, I'd appreciate it. Also, can you start putting the files for all the recent cases in my shared drop box so I can access it from home?"

"I sure can, but why?"

"Just in case I'm no longer welcome at the office."

"Sheriff, what do you mean?"

167

"I'll talk to you later, Mary Jo, and if Ruthers calls in, please let me know."

"I will do."

"Thank you."

Gray checked the vacant road behind him, stretching away into a hill that joined the sky. The thought of spinning the cruiser around and just driving away floated through his mind. He could drive and see if the sky ever did touch the earth like it appeared to. And if it didn't, he could keep going.

Instead he pulled back onto the highway and headed toward town.

Chapter 37

City hall was as cool as his office was hot.

Black marble veined with twisting lines of green made up the floors and half the walls. The ceilings were high, the white banistered stairways and landings open to the third floor where he stood, waiting with his back to the Mayor's secretary.

"He'll see you now, Sheriff," the woman said at the desk without raising her eyes from the computer screen in front of her.

"Obliged."

"What?"

"Nothing."

He moved past her to the mahogany door and stepped inside the office. The mayor sat behind his desk, a wireless tucked inside his ear. His face was red above a blue tie that was the color of the sky, his bald pate shining. Gray shut the door behind him and waited, meeting the other man's eyes.

"Come sit down, Mac."

Gray came closer but only rested his hands on the back of a chair.

"Think I'll stand if you don't mind."

The mayor studied him for a moment and then shook his head, looking out the window instead.

"You're a damn mystery, Mac, a true enigma embodied."

"Here I thought I was cut and dried."

"I was unaware until recently that you hold certain beliefs. I'm disappointed."

"I'm sorry that I'm not sorry, John."

"For God's sake, Mac, you hit my district attorney in the mouth!"

"You just told me I was a mystery but I'd say that's pretty straight forward."

The mayor launched to his feet and planted his hands on the desk.

"Damn it, Mac! What in the hell do you think you're doing?" He lowered his voice to a hiss. "Mark told me about your insinuations concerning the Line."

"Open your eyes, John, there's something going on here that's beyond the Line, beyond what we understand."

"Hudson is dead, those cases are closed."

"Hudson didn't kill those people, he didn't kill anyone. The man was a ruse, nothing more. The ones that are responsible for this are still out there."

The mayor threw his hands up in the air and let out a breath that sounded like an overheated boiler.

"Do you hear yourself? You're unstable, Mac. All of the evidence shows that Hudson was responsible."

"What about the bodies in the field? You're telling me Hudson killed them too? Drove half an hour from where he tortured those people and then buried them all in the same spot? And what about the fire at Siri Godfry's? Two other murder scenes had the same MO."

"First of all, the Olsons were never confirmed as murder victims. Secondly, there's no proof that Siri's been murdered either."

Gray leaned forward, putting his full weight on the back of the chair, his fingers digging into the material.

"Then where the hell is she, mayor? And where is my deputy?"

"That's actually something I'd like to know too."

Gray turned toward the new voice coming from the doorway to find Mitchel Enson standing there with Mark Sheldon a step behind him. Mark's lips were purple and crusted with dried blood. He glared at Gray for a moment before motioning to the mayor's secretary who stood from her desk and walked briskly down the hall and out of sight. The neighboring sheriff and the DA moved into the room and shut the door behind them.

"What is this?" Gray said, eyeing the newcomers before returning his attention to the mayor.

"Mitchel here has had a new development and wanted to ask you some questions," the mayor said, slowly seating his bulk into his protesting chair.

"About what?" Gray said, glancing at Mitchel who moved to the right side of the mayor's desk and propped himself upon it like a giant toad squatting on a stone.

"Have you had any contact with Joseph Ruthers today?" Mitchel asked.

"No, why?"

"Well, it just so happens that we had several witnesses say they saw Miss Godfry and Ruthers at a late movie last night."

"My God, Mitchel, you've finally found your calling. You are Sherlock Holmes in spirit if not in stature. Joseph told everyone that would listen that he was taking Siri to that movie, it wasn't a secret."

Mitchel sneered but there was an evil triumph to his smile.

"Then maybe you can explain how his blood got on her front stoop?"

A silence fell over the office and the room became a cold tomb of granite.

"You found his blood there? How? You didn't even have forensics on the scene."

Mitchel frowned. "Come now, Sheriff. It's standard procedure to have a basic forensics sweep of any fire where the cause isn't apparent."

Gray huffed laughter and shook his head once as Mark sidled up to the windows and leaned casually against them.

"You're something, Mitchel, I'll give you that. I'm guessing someone else spotted the blood and you stepped in to take credit."

"It doesn't matter who discovered it, the fact is we have DNA evidence putting your deputy at a crime scene," Mark said, his words somewhat slurred due to the swelling of his lips.

"Now it's a crime scene?" Gray said.

"A large amount of gasoline was the accelerant used in the fire," Mitchel said.

"So what are you implying here? That Joseph started dating Siri just so he could kidnap her and burn her house down?"

"I don't pretend to understand all the motivations of violent criminals, I just catch them," Mitchel said.

Gray laughed again, louder this time.

"You couldn't catch the clap from a five-dollar hooker, Mitchel."

"Gentlemen, this has gone far enough," the mayor said from behind his desk. "The matter remains to be seen if Deputy Ruthers is fully involved in Miss Godfry's disappearance or if there is another explanation."

"Yeah, there's another explanation; you bastards are all blind to what's happening here. There are at least two, if not more, violent sociopaths at work in our community right now, and one of them has been active for more than two decades. They've been here, killing and kidnapping and torturing people right under your noses, and you're turning your collective back to it because of this."

Gray yanked up the sleeve of his dark T-shirt exposing the line of orange dots.

"This is not an assurance of safety, this is a mockery of nature. We live our lives in an age of guarantees brought about by our egotistical intelligence, but this is not one of them. The Line has failed and if you don't open your eyes, so have you."

Gray dropped his sleeve and stared around at the other men. Mark watched him coldly while Mitchel shook his head and slowly stood from the desk. The mayor merely twirled a pen in his fingers and gazed blankly at him.

"I'm afraid the events in your recent past have clouded your judgment, Mac. We're all very sorry for your loss, but the community needs and demands a competent sheriff. I'm relieving you of duty until the board can convene."

"This has nothing to do with losing my daughter, John, and you know it."

"You can drop off the cruiser tomorrow but I'm going to need your badge and your gun now," the mayor said in a quiet voice. "Otherwise Mark has said he'll press charges for battery."

Gray looked at all three men again and then pulled his wallet out to reveal the iridescent, digital card displaying a rotating gold star along with his name and picture as well as an ID number. He then yanked the badge from his chest and slapped them both down on the mayor's desk, making a Mars rock jump from its place as a paperweight. The digital display on the card winked out.

"You can have your badge back but this gun was my father's and his father's before him. I'll lie dead on the floor before you take it from me."

He turned from the desk and walked toward the door, metering his steps, each stride stoking the anger within him like a bellows.

"Get a grip on yourself, Gray, you're losing it," Mark said behind him.

"With all due respect, get fucked, Mark," Gray said without slowing.

"Lots of people lose kids, you're not special in the least."

Gray froze as he pushed the door open, his eyes meeting Lynn's who stood several feet beyond the threshold. Her mouth began to work as her hand came to her throat. Gray closed his eyes and turned back to face the DA.

"You're right, I'm not special. But she was."

He left the room, walking past Lynn without another look. A second passed and then footsteps followed his own toward the stairway.

"Mac, wait."

He stopped at the head of the stairs. Lynn's hand slid beneath his arm as she turned him toward her.

"What happened?"

"They fired me, I'm done."

"For what?"

"For telling the truth."

The door to the mayor's office opened and Mark strode out, his eyes first latching onto Lynn and then the point where her hand still rested on Gray's arm.

"Lynn, let's go."

"I'm not going to dinner, Mark," Lynn said without looking at him. "Come on, Mac."

Without a look back they went down the stairs, their footsteps the only sound in the quiet building. They pushed through the front doors and into the heat. A breeze was blowing, throwing dust up in its wake, an arid breath from an unseen and forgotten god.

"Where'd you park?" she asked as they walked into the smoldering lot. He motioned to the opposite side of the building and they made their way to his cruiser, climbing inside before he looked at her.

"What were you doing up there?" he asked.

"Meeting Mark for dinner."

Gray nodded and looked the opposite way out of the window.

"I was going to end it with him, Mac."

"Why?"

"You know why."

"I thought you needed space."

"I did, just not from the person I intended."

Gray smiled a little. "Darlin', you jumped from one sinking ship onto another."

"I don't care if you're not sheriff anymore, Mac."

"It's not about that." The edge in his voice made her flinch. "People are dying." He held her gaze for a moment and then shifted it to the darkened dashboard. "Joseph's dead."

"What? How?"

"They must have got him when they took Siri, just like they took Joslyn and Rachel."

"Who?"

"The women that disappeared from Widow Town."

"They were taken?"

"Yes."

"Why?"

Gray shook his head. "I'm not sure."

"How do you know?" Lynn asked.

"I just do. Vincent Barder's youngest boy is missing and the other two know something, but they're either scared or in on it somehow."

"Why would you think that?"

"Number one because Darrin was itching to grab the butter knife that was on the table between us while I was asking him and Adam questions. I don't know if he was scared of me or wanted to gut me. And number two because I spoke to Ryan the other day in the park and I asked him if the farm was a lot of work. He told me they barely did anything, most of the labor was hired out. When I asked Darrin and Adam the same question, Darrin told me they were working constantly. Ryan seemed harried every time I spoke with him. It was almost like he wanted to tell me something but couldn't." Gray frowned. "Adam was banged up too, his hand was bandaged and someone had scratched his eye. Now either someone is threatening them, or they were the ones that ran into Joseph and had a go-around with him."

"But if that pit of bones up north is tied into this, they couldn't be involved, those people were killed a long time ago, way before those boys would've been old enough, right?"

"That's because there's someone else, someone older than them that's behind all this. He's a puppet master pulling strings, slipping in and out of the light. He's responsible for everything; the murders, the disappearances, even Miles's death." Gray said, finally turning on the vehicle. Cool air rushed out of the vents, chilling the sweat on his skin. "The problem is, it could be anyone."

"Are you sure about all this, Mac? Couldn't this be coincidences upon coincidences? Couldn't Siri and Joseph be somewhere safe together?"

"I'll never be one to say that I can't be wrong." He turned to look at her. "But I'm not wrong, not this time. I don't know who's responsible, but all this is not by chance."

Lynn studied his face and then nodded, her lips pressing together in a white line.

"So what do we do now?"

"*We* don't do anything. You need to go home and be somewhere safe until all this passes over. In fact you should get out of town and go stay with your aunt in Illinois."

"Mac?"

"Yeah?"

"I'm not going anywhere, so quit wasting your breath and shut the hell up."

He opened his mouth but then closed it, a smile forming at one corner of his mouth.

"Yes ma'am."

"That's better. Now what are we going to do?"

He sighed and looked at the afternoon sky. The barest wisp of cloud traveled across the cerulean, a pale scar cutting a path with the growing wind.

"When you run out of road, you double back."

"What if you're not even on the road anymore?"

Gray paused, his eyes growing distant. He threw the cruiser into gear.

173

"Then you make a new one."

~

They pulled to a stop on the side of the barren road. The swamp to their right dried and decaying in wafting fingers of gray moss, beckoning them in.

They left the cruiser parked to bake in the sun and cut into the woods beneath the canopy of skeletal branches, barely shading them. Gray led the way and Lynn stayed close to him, her hand brushing his occasionally. Eventually the clearing appeared ahead and Gray slowed, moving with deliberate noise, breaking branches and twigs beneath his feet that he could've avoided.

The little house stood silent without a shadow behind its windows. No gun barrels poked from any holes or rested on logs that he could see. He stopped and Lynn did the same, both of them waiting, staring at the front door of the house.

It opened after a minute and Terry Yantz stepped onto the porch, a rifle tucked in the crook of his arm.

"Sheriff."

"Evening Terry."

"Thought I'd had my share of visits from the law for the year but I guess I was wrong. If you have more questions concerning those deaths you better be packing a warrant for my arrest."

"Not at all. I do have a question but I can assure you, you aren't under suspicion."

Terry moved down the steps of his porch and stopped several paces away. He kept the rifle trained on the ground.

"Go ahead."

"You mentioned before that you used to know someone who opted not to have his son immunized, a friend of your father?"

"That's right."

"Do you remember his name?"

"My father's friend, or his son?"

"Either."

Terry pursed his lips and shifted the rifle to his opposite arm.

"They lived north, or used to, up by the county line on some fields," Terry said. He turned his eyes to the ground, shuffling one shoe in the arid grass. "Drucker, I believe his name was."

Gray nodded. "Could it have been Clarence Drucker?"

"That's him. Clarence. Hadn't thought of that name in ages."

"How about his son? What was his name?"

"Can't recall now. Lord, it's been years and we only played together a time or two."

Terry looked at the blackened fire pit where Gray had watched him cook down rock candy for his children.

"I'm sorry, I can't remember. I can barely remember what he looked like. Real slender kid with blond hair. But that was thirty-five or forty years ago if it was a day."

"That's okay, thank you for trying. You've been a help. We'll leave you be now."

Gray and Lynn walked back the way they'd come but Terry's voice stopped them before they entered the path.

"Sheriff, I wanted to thank you for what you left the other day. You didn't have to do that, but it was appreciated."

"You're welcome, Terry. Take good care of those children."

Terry bobbed his head once and then he was out of sight as they rounded the first bend.

"What was that about?" Lynn asked as they walked.

"You mean the name or what I left?"

"Both."

"Clarence Drucker was the landowner of the property where the body pit was found, and I left some money as a token of thanks the last time Joseph and I stopped out here."

"Isn't that a bribe?"

Gray smiled. "Not when you've already gotten the information."

"I see."

Back on the road a massive transport truck barreled by, peppering them with a hot gust of wind and stinging grit. The driver didn't look at them. Gray watched it go and then climbed inside, turning the cruiser on. He flicked the air conditioning to the highest setting and realized it was already there. After punching a button on the console, he waited and held up a finger to Lynn as she started to speak. Mary Jo's voice came out of the speaker, low and hushed.

"Sheriff's department."

"Hi, Mary Jo."

"Hello."

"You have company, I'm assuming."

"Yes, that's right."

"Mitchel and Mark?"

"Yes."

"Okay. I need you to do something for me. Research Clarence Drucker, the man that owned the land the bone pit was found on. Find out everything about him along with his son. From what I've been told his son wasn't inoculated with the Line until after he was adopted. He might be the missing piece in all of this. Can you do that for me?"

"Absolutely."

"Good." He paused. "It's been good working with you, Mary Jo, you do more than you know."

"Oh, I know."

Gray smiled. "Keep me posted."

"Yes sir."

He pushed the same button and the air quit humming with transmission in the cab. The cruiser's engine idled, barely vibrating.

"You really think the Barder boys killed all those people?" Lynn finally asked.

Gray rubbed his eyes, pushing his hat back from his forehead.

"I don't know, but they're hiding something. They might know who's doing this, or what happened to Joseph. I'll have to wait to hear back from Mary Jo to see if Clarence Drucker's son is a dead end or not."

"How could those boys be the ones? Their father being a doctor I'm sure they all have the Line. If they have the Line, then they can't be responsible."

"I think maybe we've come to new territory. The world isn't playing by the rules anymore because we aren't. We change things, there's a reaction. Ripples on a pond. I'm afraid we don't know what we've tinkered with."

Lynn sighed. "We should've never left the cities."

"The cities were killing us, you know that."

"Fast death compared to slow death, your choice."

He reached across the car and put a hand on her shoulder, her skin so hot beneath the thin fabric.

"We're not dead. Not yet."

She turned her eyes to his. "Are you sure?"

"Yes."

"Then take me home."

Chapter 38

They arrived at the house an hour before sunset.

The wind grew exponentially and it tossed the top of the trees, tearing crumpled leaves and scattering them to the ground like a careless child. He thawed steaks from the freezer and made them each a drink of whisky to sip on. Every so often he would glance at her sitting at the kitchen table, soaking in her profile, telling himself that she was really there.

When the steaks were ready they sat on the deck and he tended them over the fire, turning them with the high heat like his father had taught him. They ate at the table beneath the darkening sky, baked potatoes smothered in butter, salted green beans, and toasted bread. He kept his phone close, his eyes falling to it over and over again. She noticed after a time and pulled it away from him, squeezing his hand once.

"If she finds something, she'll call, you won't miss it."

The night deepened around them, flowering into a gusting dusk, the dried leaves clattering. No moon. She finished her drink and took his hand again. When she pulled him from his chair he followed. Down the steps and onto the lawn to the stream where they stopped, the small chasm barely visible in the growing gloom.

Water flowed between the banks, over a foot deep in most places.

"I forgot you turned the pump on," he said, slowly kneeling down.

"I know most would say it's a waste of water."

"It's not a waste."

"Don't ever let it go dry again. Okay, Mac?"

"I won't."

Her hand found his, intertwining fingers.

He stood and pulled her closer, feeling her length against him. So right, so true. He kissed her, her hair brushing his face as the wind pushed it. He drank her in and soon she ran her fingers through his hair, stroking lines through its coarseness.

She broke away and led him into the house, leaving their plates and glasses where they stood on the table, pausing only to hand him his phone. They climbed the stairs so familiar, her in front, her hand trailing back, guiding him up behind. Their room, theirs again now, not just his. Ambient light from the window coating her body as she undressed, quicker than him, lying on the bed waiting for him, skin pale and glowing in the dark.

He covered her with himself, cupped her close with everything he had, her breath in his ear, quick, quickening.

"I want a baby, Mac. Please, I want a baby."

He moaned above her as she thrust her hips up and pulled him down, pulsing inside, a trapped butterfly beating wings of ecstasy. No words, only shuddering release as he said her name, over and over again.

They lay, still intertwined, as the house creaked around them, the wind finding holes to tune its voice. He stroked her hair as she lay against him, her heat almost unbearable, making him want to walk outside to cool off and start what they had just finished all over again at the same time.

"Did you mean it?" he asked after a long time, almost sure she was sleeping.

"Yes," she answered. "Yes I did."

He hugged her closer, her body somehow more tangible than it ever had been before.

"Good."

She was quiet for a long time and then she shifted, looking up at him, her features defined with curves of shadow.

"It can't be the same."

"I know."

"Do you?"

"Yes."

She studied his face and then finally settled back into place beside him.

The wind threw aside all pretenses and began to howl. The night aged and Gray fell asleep, only hearing the woman beside him breathing.

~

A sound woke him later. His eyes flew open, looking through the darkness as his head came off the pillow. He waited for it to come again, either a nudging of something by the wind outside, or not.

A scrape of a footstep on tile in the kitchen.

He slid from bed still naked, removing Lynn's arm from around his waist, reaching for the gun belt that always hung from the bedside table. His hand met empty air. He'd taken it off in the kitchen, fastened it around the coatrack near the back door.

"Mac?"

"Shhh, there's someone in the house," he whispered. Lynn didn't reply. The wisp of sheets from her side of the bed.

Gray moved to the open door and peered down to the living room. Stillness, quiet but for the railing wind. Then a shadow, sidling against the far wall.

"Call for help," he whispered and lunged out of the room and down the stairs.

Gunfire erupted from the living room and he threw himself flat, the last three stairs smashing into his ribs as he tumbled down them. Lynn screamed his name and he rolled toward the kitchen, scrambling against the floor, the tile scraping his knees and drawing blood. Bullets zinged over his back, the bright pulse of muzzle flash lighting up the kitchen enough for him to see no one stood there. Footsteps pounded toward him across the living room and he leapt for the coat rack, his fingers snagging the gun belt as he fell.

He landed on his spine, in one motion pulling out the .45 as a shadow blotted out the doorway. He fired a wild shot that ripped plaster from the wall near the figure's head. It dove out of sight as the big pistol boomed again.

Gray's breath came in ragged gasps that he tried to control, listening over the base pounding in his ears. He glanced to the left to where the kitchen table rested beside the front door. It stood open to the windy night, air gusting into the room. He moved that way, low, knees bent, arms stretched out before him, the long barrel of the gun leading the way. A smell wafted to him with the breeze. Gasoline, sharply pungent with each draft that coursed through the door.

He came to the archway leading to the living room. The high ceilings cobwebbed with dark, the supporting pillars adversaries themselves. He swept the room with the gun, keeping his peripheral vision on the entryway to his left. A shape lunged up the stairs and he stood, firing but only getting off one shot before a spray of gunfire came from his office alcove.

There were two of them.

The hot passage of lead brushed his face and he fell to the living room floor, rolling behind one of the wooden columns. Lynn screamed again in the bedroom, this time without words, her cry cut off as abruptly as it began. He flew to his feet, swinging his arm around the pillar and firing in the general direction of the office.

"Sheriff, drop your gun!" The yell came from the top of the stairs and he aimed in that direction as the lights came on along the stairway.

A masked man stood on the landing, one arm clutched around Lynn's throat, the opposite hand pressing a snub-nosed auto-pistol to her temple. For a beat Gray kept a bead on the man's head above Lynn's shoulder and then slowly lowered the gun to his side.

"Mac, don't," Lynn choked out. The man holding her tightened his arm and her eyes bulged as she coughed.

"I'm the man with the gun, Sheriff, I'd listen to me."

A figure stepped out of the office hallway and Gray took in its much larger form, the face hidden beneath a similar hood, hands holding a short-stocked rifle.

"Drop the gun, Sheriff, last time I'll ask nice," the man on the landing said.

Gray stepped out from behind the support, keeping the Colt lowered but in his hand.

"You boys are out of your element here, way over your head," Gray said, shifting his gaze from the landing to the black eye of the rifle barrel pointed at him.

"I'd be tempted to say the same thing about you. Naked old man with only an ancient pistol to hide behind."

"How long have you been killing, Darrin?"

The man on the landing didn't move but Gray saw the larger figure on the main floor turn its head up the stairs.

Slowly the man holding Lynn reached up and drew the mask away, revealing his handsome features.

"Darrin, what are you doing?" the larger one asked.

"It's okay, Adam, he knows it's us. I have a feeling he knew for a while. Isn't that right, Sheriff?"

Gray nodded. "I had my suspicions. What did you do with Siri and Joseph?"

Darrin smiled. "Siri's safe. Joe, not so much. Now are you going to drop that gun or do I put three rounds through this pretty woman's head?"

Gray hesitated, flicking his eyes toward Adam who had also drawn off his hood and was staring dumbly at him. Darrin screwed the end of his pistol into Lynn's temple and she choked out another short scream.

"Okay, okay," Gray said, bending his knees. He lowered himself close to the floor and set the Colt down near his feet. With one heel he slid it to his left across the hardwood.

"That's a sport," Darrin said, and shoved Lynn down the stairs.

She fell and rolled, the sick sound of bones connecting with treads echoing through the house. Adam was there at the bottom and arrested her downward progress with one of his tree-trunk legs. Lynn moaned and blood ran from a gash on her scalp near her hairline. Gray started across the room but Adam raised his rifle again and shook his head.

"Don't you worry about her, Sheriff, she'll be safe where we're going," Darrin said, beginning to descend the stairs.

"What are you doing with them?" Gray asked, shifting his eyes from Lynn's unmoving form to Darrin's face. "With all the woman and children from Widow Town."

"Oh you caught that too? Aren't you something? I guess Ryan was right, you're not as dumb as you look. Well, I'd love to tell you but then I'd have to kill you." Darrin cracked a grin and snickered as he stepped over Lynn and past Adam.

"Who's the brains behind it all? It can't be you, even though you think you're smart enough to orchestrate this whole thing. Who's pulling your strings?"

Darrin walked close to him, the younger man stopping a pace away. He was three inches shorter than Gray and had to look up slightly to meet his eyes.

"And it's definitely not Adam over there, I'm guessing you still have to help him tie his shoes in the morning."

"Shut your mouth."

"Couldn't be Ryan either, that boy didn't have it in him to do real harm. I could see he didn't have a backbone the first time I met him."

Darrin whipped his arm around and slapped him with the pistol. Gray's head rocked to one side and his lip split against his teeth. Blood flooded his mouth and ran down his chin in a thin stream. Darrin's jaw was clenched, the muscles beneath his cheek bulging. Gray brought his hand up and wiped the blood away.

"Oh, I see. Ryan's dead, isn't he? That's why he's not here."

Something moved behind Darrin's eyes. There and gone.

"Joseph got him, didn't he?" Gray began to chuckle. "Good boy."

Darrin swung again and Gray was ready.

He ducked, the gun whistling an inch over his head, and pistoned his fist in an uppercut that connected with Darrin's chin. The younger man staggered back, fighting to remain upright and failing. He fell to his ass, skidding a foot before coming to a stop. Gray dove for the Colt and heard the crack of Adam's rifle.

There was a plunging ache in his side and all the strength went out of his arms as he landed near his gun. His face connected with the floor, his nose breaking in a dry crunch. The room spun and nausea crashed over him in a sickening tide. There was a baritone yell and then Lynn's voice beginning to sob words clouded by her crying. Gray reached out and fumbled with the grip of the pistol but then it was gone, kicked by a booted foot that sat level with his gaze. The boot reared back and then barreled at his face.

The pain was exquisite. It detonated and rolled out from his nose before coming back to the center of his head where it nestled itself in a cocoon of pain.

"You okay, Darrin?"

"Yeah, fucker surprised me."

"I got him. I got him while he was in the air. Did you see?"

"Yeah, I saw. Good shot."

Their voices slithered in through Gray's eardrums and he raised his head, opening his eyes to a mist of red that covered them.

Darrin and Adam stood over him and Lynn hung limply from Adam's arm, her legs buckled, her face a mask of spider-webbed blood.

"Mac?"

Her eyes sought his, trying to hold his gaze and he blinked, steeling his focus into an iron rail. The burning pain in his side came again in a lancing wave. He curled into it, sliding in blood that covered the floor. His blood. Darrin knelt beside him, grabbing a fist of his hair and turning his head up to face him.

"Nice shot, old man. I'll give you that. Won the battle, lost the war though. I'd love to carve you up, that's my specialty, it's what gets me hard. You saw my handiwork over at the Jacobses'. Cut them up so nice. But I don't have the time I'd like to spend on you, so we'll be going, but we're gonna take your pretty here. Hope you don't mind."

He leaned in close to him and even through the fog that threatened the edge of his vision, Gray could smell the younger man's fetid breath.

"I'm gonna fuck her, Sheriff. Gonna get her pregnant and she's going to bear my child, not yours. You couldn't keep the one you had alive anyway. I'll be doing her a favor, and with time, she'll prefer my cock over yours. I want you to think about that as you slip into the void."

Darrin released his hair and Gray reached out, trying to grab hold of him but he slapped his hand away.

"Adam, haul her out to the van and then bring me the gas. The good sheriff here needs a bath."

Lynn cried out again but she sounded far away, getting farther away each second. Gray pushed against the floor and managed to almost sit up. Blood pattered down from his nose, splashed in the growing pool around him. The hot pain in his side flared as he sat up further, and he slumped beneath the weight of it. The room carouselled, tipping and wavering before steadying. Footsteps came toward him again and he swiped at his eyes, clearing them of more blood.

Gasoline washed over his head, flowed into his nostrils and mouth. He gagged and choked, sliding down to an elbow as the gas burned into every cut and wound.

"There you go, Sheriff, nice hot bath," Darrin said. More gas drizzled over his legs and feet and then it was gone. He coughed and finally vomited, his stomach a cauldron filled with red coals. His vision blurred and then cleared, the blood washed free by the gas. Darrin was pouring a trail as he backed out of the house. A fuse. He shook the can as it emptied and then tossed it into the kitchen. Adam stepped inside behind him and threw a look at where Gray lay.

"She's all set, Darrin."

"Good. How much gas did you spill outside?"

"I don't know. Some."

"It smells like you tipped over a whole damn can out there. Pull the van away from the house and I'll light this."

"Okay."

Gray heaved himself up again and finally looked down at his stomach. A round hole, six inches to the right of his belly button, oozed blood. The wet shine of intestine rolled into and out of sight as he slid down to the floor again. Darrin walked into the living room holding a small, silver Arclighter in one hand. He knelt by Gray, balancing on the balls of his feet.

"Gotta run, Sheriff. You were fun to play with and I'm sure your ex will be too. You didn't know how close you were to this or how big it really is. Thing of beauty."

Darrin gave him another grin before standing and walking out the front door.

Gray flipped onto his stomach and began to crawl. It felt like a bear trap was closing over his right side every time he moved and blood kept rolling down his throat, a river that wouldn't stem. He spit and managed to get to his knees, the cloying smell of gas spinning his brain within the walls of his skull. There was a soft whump from the entryway and then light bloomed across the living room wall, the high windows reflecting an angry orange. He struggled to his feet and staggered to the hallway leading to his office, but stopped at the first door instead of continuing down the corridor. His hand found the doorknob as a line of fire raced into the living room and traced a path toward him, moving like liquid.

He spun the knob and tumbled down the open stairway to the basement.

The cool concrete at the bottom welcomed him by sending lightning across his vision, the dancing strikes mixing with the fire that leapt near the doorframe but didn't follow down the treads. He lay there listening to the gnashing mouth of flame eating his home above him as the dark of the basement tried to close in.

Gray slapped his smashed nose with a bloody palm and the darkness was swept away by a blinding white pain. He shuddered and vomited again as he rolled onto his hands and knees and crawled to his workbench. His legs held him when he pulled himself up, and through the blood that was hardening to a crust on his eyelids, he looked out the small window above him.

The outside was a world of twirling flames.

The ground crackled with heat and the air leapt with lashing tongues of fire. Smoke poured across the window, obscuring his view and the floor above leaked its first ember, a tiny comet trailing to the concrete before winking out.

He moved around the end of the bench and looked up the stairway. A solid wall of flames burned there, its face that of red and orange rage that twisted like a snake constricting itself. He sidled to the far end of the basement and stopped beneath the last window. An electronic water pump hummed on the floor beside the mop sink. He stared at the pump for a moment and then looked at the window again. There was no fire directly outside.

Without hesitating, he bent low, issuing a grunt of pain as he doubled over, and turned on both spigots. Water poured from the faucet and he sat in the sink, letting it wash over his head and down his back. He sat there, the agony pulsing across every inch of him, and sloshed water over his legs and feet until his body was soaked. Then he stood and flicked the water pump's control to high.

The heat from above became palpable. It pushed against the top of his head as he found a stool beside the bench and dragged it beneath the window, resting every few feet. Blood gouted from the bullet wound on his side every time he moved and dizziness assaulted him after each step. He positioned the stool below the window and heaved himself onto it, steadying a hand against the warm wall. His fingers fumbled with the latch and finally opened it, folding the glass upward to where it locked against the ceiling.

Hot air billowed into the basement followed by a stream of smoke. He coughed, the effort to stay upright on the stool making his legs shake. Gray placed his hands on the sill, gripping the edges until he thought his fingers might break, and counted to three in his head.

He launched himself up toward the window, pulling hard as his abdomen struck the frame. He screamed, the plastic casing biting into his belly, and it felt as if something were uncoiling from him, lengthening where it shouldn't. He shoved once, and tipped himself forward onto the waiting ground outside.

The heat struck him full force, pummeling his face, his back, his lungs. When he was able to rise to his knees he saw that the entire yard was alight, the fire running in lapping swaths that grew closer and closer to the trees as he watched. The wind fanned the flames, gusting them forward with billowing breaths as the waiting dryness offered itself to the inferno. The smell of gasoline was still on his skin and he searched through the cascading smoke for what he knew was there.

Carah's stream ran strong between the banks, the pump in the basement doing its work. The water was a rippling orange serpent reflecting the fire on its surface like molten glass scales. He made it to his feet and hobbled toward it, one hand clutching his side, waiting for his guts to roll out between his fingers. The fire was closer than he'd thought and as the flames reached toward the far bank, he flung himself down, the water coming up to meet him.

Its embrace was electrically cold. The water raced into his ears and eyes, his open mouth as he tried to gasp, and sent stinging needles into his flesh. He turned to his back and sucked in air, paddling as well as he could with one hand. The muddy bottom scraped his heels as he kicked feebly like a harpooned fish.

The bank passed by, the fire growing so fierce in one place, he submerged, holding his breath for as long as he could before returning to the flickering air. Even with his ears below the water the crackle of burning ground was still audible, the flames eating up the dry tinder that waited to give itself up in sacrifice.

He drifted to a bend where the stream left the yard and entered the woods in earnest, and dug shaking fingers into the bank, stopping his progress. He crawled up with one hand and managed to stand, swaying in the wind. The entire yard and house was engulfed. It burned, releasing greasy rings of smoke into the night sky where they became one.

Gray flanked the fire, crossing within a dozen yards of it and still the hairs on his chest and arms blazed away in singeing curls. He made his way to the garage, coming around its corner to see that his cruiser was still there, the driver's side within a stone's throw of the inferno. He limped across the distance and wrenched the passenger door open, clawed the glove compartment wide and drew out the first aid kit inside.

With the kit beneath his arm, he stumbled into the wind, sucking at the cleaner air until he could no longer feel the heat at his back. His legs gave out and he fell to the dry grass, the stars overhead mixing with the fluttering, white moth-spots in his vision.

When his breathing slowed he sat up and opened the kit, turning it over on the ground beside him. The pack he was looking for was inside a clear plastic bag that he tore through with his teeth, doing it again to the white, perforated strip at its top. He tipped the pack over on his palm and a silicate dust poured out. Without waiting, he pressed his hand against the wound on his side, hissing and tipping his head back until his skull nearly touched his shoulder blades. He held the powder there until he couldn't stand it anymore. When he looked down, the bullet hole was a mound of crystallized blood, black and speckled brown where the dust had done its work. The pain was less, numbed by the chemical agent in the powder. With a shaking hand he reached around his back, waiting for his fingertips to encounter a ragged exit wound, or worse yet, none at all.

Instead he felt a hole that matched the front almost exactly. He traced its edge, the stickiness of it beginning to clot. With a cough that sent runners of pain through his midsection, he laughed.

"Stupid bastards were using full-metal jackets."

He chuckled again and winced, pouring another handful from the pack before applying it to the hole in his back. When the bubbling pain eased he released his hold and turned himself so that he could see the house.

It held its shape wrapped in flames. The windows were gone, exploded outward, and fire licked out the holes and onto the roof. The walls were consumed and all that held the structure up were the large support beams that hadn't succumbed yet. The immolation of everything he had, there before him.

He stood, his legs barely holding his weight as he walked away from the fire. His head throbbed in time with his heart and his feet cut on the rough gravel of the drive. His head swam, lolling first to one side and then the other. He stumbled and managed not to fall. The air wavered in front of him. It shimmered, elasticizing and shrinking the landscape beyond. His eyes watered from trying to focus and he swiped at them.

Gray's feet touched grass and he saw that he'd wandered off the corner of his driveway to where the dried bramble and wilted grass took over. The slight decline caught him off guard and he fell, crumpling to his knees before rolling over and over. Branches and poking thorns tore at him before he came to a stop, the new wounds welling blood. He tried to rise again but his strength was gone, tapped out and dry as the ground he lay on.

He managed to raise his head one last time, thinking the moon had finally appeared since the night looked too bright. But then his eyes closed, and all he heard was the static hiss of fire.

Chapter 39

When he awoke, the sky beyond the trees was murky.

It hung like a mildewed sheet above him, blanketing the clouds and cataract sun in a yellow gloom. Gray swallowed, sand and shards of glass covering the inside of his mouth and throat. He tried to sit up and volcanic pain erupted in his side and he lay back down, breathing shallow breaths that tasted of smoke. A small sapling grew beside him and he used it to haul himself upright, blinking at his nakedness and the blood that streaked his abdomen and upper thigh. He swayed in the ditch beside his drive, letting his bearings return. Eventually they did.

He moved up the little rise and found the dirt drive crisscrossed with so many tire tracks it looked like an entire army had ground its way through his property. He gained momentum coming around the bend and caught sight of his house.

Or where it used to be.

The land past the drive was a smoldering ruin, the ground scorched a midnight black interspersed with burning piles of trees that had fallen over one another. His house was a sunken hole of wreckage. It smoked in a pit of burnt timbers and ash that once had been his basement. Beyond it lay a wasteland of monochromatic destruction. The flames had grown and stretched their legs to the east and west, devouring the dry underbrush before cutting down the majority of the trees. Some larger oaks and towering pines still stood, devoid of any leaves or branches, like used matchsticks twisted into the earth. The fire itself was miles away, enshrouded by a veil of smoke so heavy it looked like the world ended and a void began past its shadowed border.

He stared at the devastation for a time, only registering that a truck was parked before his untouched garage when a figure moved near its front, the titan-like shape walking toward the edge of the basement.

Danzig stopped with his back to him, a gas mask covering his mouth and nose, a long prodding bar held in one hand. He peered into the basement and shuffled through the slag, pausing to poke with the steel rod every few steps. Gray walked down the drive and made it within a dozen yards of where his friend stood before the giant heard him. Danzig's eyes widened above the seal of his mask and Gray leaned against the truck's tailgate for support.

"If you're looking for booze, I don't think any made it through," Gray said.

Danzig dropped the rod and rushed to the truck in time to steady him with a hand on his shoulder.

"My God, Mac, what the hell happened to you?"

"Hell of a party that got a little out of control, sorry I didn't call you."

Gray tried to smile and began to shiver, his muscles quaking beneath his skin.

"Holy shit, let's get you in the truck."

Danzig half supported, half carried him to the passenger seat and buckled him in. A moment later a rough blanket fell over him and then they were moving, bouncing over rough patches and potholes at high speed.

"I thought you were dead you stupid sonofabitch. An emergency broadcast was sent out to everyone in the county this morning warning about a possible forest fire. I tried to call you but there was no answer, so after a bit I called the station and Mary Jo told me you were let go yesterday. She'd been trying to get ahold of you too and when she said that, I came to find you. There were a dozen fire units in your drive when I got here, lights blazing, water spraying, and not even making a dent in the flames. It was something like I'd never seen before."

Gray shifted in his seat, reaching up to touch his broken nose.

"Do you have any water?"

"Yeah, here."

A cold, steel canister was thrust into his hand, the top already off. He tipped it up, the water so frigid it tingled on the way down. He drank until the container was dry and then set it on the truck's console.

"Thanks."

"What the hell happened, Mac?"

"The Barder boys, they're the killers. They showed up last night and put a round through me and took Lynn before giving me a gasoline shower."

"Holy shit."

"I barely made it out. Is the fire under control now?"

"Not even close. They brought in a bunch of the state's helicopters and dump-planes, but it doesn't look like they're going to contain it. It's headed straight for Shillings. The mayor's ordered an evacuation." Danzig paused. "From what I gathered before all the fire units left, they think you started the blaze."

"Wonderful. Let me see your phone."

Danzig placed the device in his hand and he dialed the station's number. An automated message played in his ear about the circuits being full but to try again later.

"Damn thing's busy." Gray erupted into a bout of coughing and doubled up against the seat restraint. They stopped at the paved road and Danzig began to turn right but Gray grasped the steering wheel.

"What are you doing?"

"Take me to your house."

"Are you crazy? You need to go to Wheaton Medical, have you seen yourself?"

"I never was pretty."

Danzig stared at him and tried to remove his hand from the wheel, but he held fast.

"I'll walk if I have to, Dan."

Danzig studied him for another span and then turned left, accelerating toward the veiling smog.

"You're a stubborn bastard, I ever tell you that?"

Gray closed his eyes.

~

He came awake as the truck halted in front of Danzig's shop.

"We have arrived," Danzig said, his words still muffled behind the gas mask. Gray sat up, holding a hand over the bullet wound. When he opened the door, the cloying air came rushing in that had been filtered out by the truck's ventilation. The smell of musky ozone hung thick in the yard and a tangible mist swirled between the trees. Gray held out his palm and saw that it was minute flakes of ash falling from the sky.

"It's the fucking fertilizers along with the drought," Danzig said, rounding the truck's bumper. "Like I said before, they didn't take into account the flammability of that shit during dry times. I saw a field of corn on the way to your place go up like it was hit with napalm."

"Yeah, this year's crop might be down a bit."

"I would say."

"How many guns do you have?"

"Two. My old pump shotgun and my dad's Taurus."

"Get them and meet me in the shop."

"You can't be serious about this, Mac. You're shot, your face is busted up, you've probably got smoke inhalation."

"Probably. Listen, they took Lynn and no one's going to go find her except me, now I need you to get me those guns."

Danzig stood motionless, the flakes of ash falling around him.

"Us," he said at last.

"What?"

"No one's going to go find her but us."

Gray smiled and then nodded toward the shop. "I'll be in there."

Ten minutes later, Danzig returned holding an archaic looking Remington shotgun and a box of shells along with a massive, shining revolver holstered in leather. A pair of boots and several pairs of socks were tucked beneath his arm. Gray had found some of Danzig's overalls and modified them to fit, tying the waist with a belt of electrical cord and trimming the sleeves and pant legs off. He reached for the handgun as Danzig swung it toward him.

"You look ridiculous."

"I was gonna say the gas mask is a great accessary for you."

"This is to save my lungs, asshole."

"This is to save my dignity," Gray said, pulling once at the oversized clothing.

"I would say that's long gone."

Gray tugged the Taurus from its holster, drawing the six-inch barrel out into the open. *Raging Bull* was lasered across it in dark lines.

"How many rounds do you have?"

Danzig handed him a box along with a speed loader. "Maybe twenty. Went targeting the other day and didn't get a chance to special order any more. Four-fifty-four is hard to come by."

Gray swung the belt around his waist and fastened it, the huge pistol's grip sticking up near his right side. The belt pinched his wound and he winced.

"You sure you aren't gut-shot?"

"Yeah. I'd be dead if I was," Gray said, bending over to pick up the boots Danzig had brought.

"These are a little big."

"Only two sizes, right? Put the socks on, they'll take up the extra room."

Gray layered the socks and tucked his feet inside the boots. They fit well enough to walk in. He shoved the box of shells and the speed loader into a pocket and then patted his thigh several times until he realized what he was doing and grimaced.

"What's wrong?"

"My knife. It was in the house."

Danzig's eyes twinkled above the gas mask and he reached into his back pocket, drawing out Gray's knife. The steel handle glimmered under the overhead lights, and other than a little soot marring one end, it appeared unharmed.

"How?" Gray asked, accepting the weapon.

"Spotted it while I was fishing around for your corpse in the wreckage."

Gray triggered the knife and the blade shot out like a spear, retreating inside the handle when he touched the button again.

"It's fine," Gray said in amazement.

"That little bastard is tempered at a thousand degrees Fahrenheit, a forest fire ain't got nothing on me."

"I thought the gas would explode inside it," Gray said, bending to tuck the knife, blade down, into the side of his boot.

"I thought so too, but the casing didn't fracture. What are you doing?"

"Don't want all my eggs in the same basket."

Gray rose and put his hand on the doorknob, his eyes trailing across the long bench. A padded tray holding four ball bearings the size of eggs sat on its surface. He reached out and grabbed the tray, placing two of the Tin-Snippers in his pocket and handed the others to Danzig.

"We might need these."

"Along with some luck."

"Fucking luck."

"Fucking luck."

Gray nodded once to his friend and they stepped out of the building into the steadily darkening day.

Chapter 40

Alien yellow light filled the air moted with scales of ash.

They drove through it along the road that would fade and reappear with the breeze. Gray looked up through the truck's window at the sky and saw that not only did the smoke coat the sun, but a layer of clouds had also formed, tumorous and thick.

He took Danzig's phone off the console again, thinking for a second before dialing a number. A man's voice answered on the second ring.

"Sheriff's department."

"Please connect me with Sheriff Enson."

"He's out of the office right now, can I please—"

"He damn well better be out of the office, there's a forest fire rampaging across the next county. This is Sheriff MacArthur Gray and you will put me through to him, son, if you enjoy being employed by the county."

"Yes sir, sorry sir. I'll patch you right through."

"Thank you."

There was a hesitation and short bark of static before the phone began to ring again on the other end.

"What is it?" Enson answered, his voice rough as if he'd been coughing.

"Well good afternoon to you too, Mitchel."

A blast of silence. "Gray, what the hell do you think you're doing?"

"Well at the moment I'm headed toward the Barder residence to arrest Darrin and Adam for murder, attempted murder, kidnapping, arson, breaking and entering, and anything else I can think of on the way."

"Are you insane? The Barder boys? Vincent's sons? They're who you're trying to pin the fire on?"

"Since they're the ones that started it, yes, I am, along with all the other things I mentioned before that."

"You've completely lost it, Gray. Everyone thinks you're dead."

"Mark Twain summed that up nicely about two hundred twenty years ago. In other words, I'm not."

"You need to turn yourself in, this fire isn't stopping, Gray. You have a lot to answer for."

"Are you not listening to me, Mitchel? Darrin and Adam are the killers, it's been them the whole time, them and someone else that's been planning this. They've been kidnapping women and children from Widow Town and now they've taken Lynn. I need you to send backup out to their farm. For once in your life, Mitchel, do the right thing and trust me."

"Don't go anywhere near the Barders' farm, Gray. You're delusional and you need help. Besides, the fire's headed in that direction, the whole area's turned into hell itself."

"Remember this conversation, Mitchel, because I'm going to recite it when I see you released from your position."

"Fuck yo—"

Gray ended the call and put the phone in his chest pocket.

"So it went well, I take it?" Danzig said, his eyes never leaving the road.

"One thing you can say about Mitchel, he's consistent."

"Consistently ignorant."

"Yeah."

"So we've got no cavalry coming?"

"None. He won't risk sending any of his deputies in front of the fire."

Danzig sighed, the sound mimicking the wind buffeting the truck.

They passed into the edges of town, the buildings obscure and hazy in the strange light. There were no other vehicles on the road, the streets parched veins devoid of flowing traffic and people. On the north side of the city limits they got their first glimpse of the fire.

It was a wall of flame shooting fifty feet in the air. Its lapping tongues twisted and turned in the wind as it rolled forward, stretching out in a wave of orange and black boiling smoke. The border of a cornfield ignited, fire branching out across its green stalks like a web. In less than a minute the entire field burned, coiling embers into the sky.

Gray pulled his eyes away from the devastation and drew out Danzig's phone again, dialing his own office one last time. A recording played in his ear, telling him to leave a message but he hung up before the tone.

"How long you think we have before that reaches the Barders'?" Danzig asked.

"Maybe an hour, not more than two."

"What's our escape route?"

"Take six west until we can circumvent it I suppose."

"We taking these boys alive?"

"We'll see."

Danzig guided the truck onto the county road, having to slow to a crawl to make sure it was the correct number. They drove in silence, flakes of ash sliding across the windshield. When the Barders' turn came into view, Danzig coasted into the drive and shut off the headlights.

"We going in through the front?"

"I think we have to. Hopefully the sick bastards haven't killed their father and we can get him out."

They cruised up the lane, the trees to either side cloaked in a thickening darkness as the day fell around them. The house came into view and movement caught Gray's attention near the garage door. Vincent hauled a large duffle to the back of his car and hoisted it into the trunk. His blond hair was in disarray and his movements were jerky and frenetic. A man in the grip of panic. The doctor's gaze fell upon them as they coasted to a stop and it almost looked like he was going to return to the house without addressing them, but he waited, his eyes flitting from Danzig's gas-masked face to Gray's bloodied appearance, then to the weapons they carried as they stepped out of the truck.

191

"Hello, doctor," Gray said.

"Sheriff, what's going on?"

"There's not a lot of time to discuss this. Are your sons inside?"

"No, they're closing up all the outbuildings and silo. We're getting ready to leave." The doctor's drawn face collapsed. "Is this about Ryan? Did you...did you find him?"

"No," Gray said, glancing across the stained air of the farmyard to the looming shapes of the barns and silo. Nothing moved but the dancing cornstalks in the field beyond.

"Then what's this about? We need to get moving, the fire is coming in this direction."

"Your sons started the fire," Gray said, fixing the other man with a stare.

Barder froze, all the frenzied movement of before leeched from him.

"What?"

"They came to my house last night and tried to kill me." Gray unzipped his coverall, showing the other man the blood-glazed hole in his side. "They took my ex-wife with them after dousing my home and yard in gas."

The doctor shook his head once, his mouth hanging open.

"No, that's impossible. They were home last night, they were here."

"I saw their faces, doctor, they were in my house. I'm sorry, but that's the truth."

"No. Why would they do that? They wouldn't hurt anyone, they're not killers."

"We need to get out of the open," Danzig said, cradling his shotgun as he surveyed the outbuildings.

"They're good boys, my sons. They wouldn't do that, it's not true."

"I'm sorry, doctor. I wouldn't ever make an accusation like that without knowing for sure."

"No, they're...they're my boys. They're not—"

The doctor paused and slowly stopped shaking his head. He blinked, frowning.

"What is it?" Gray asked.

"I...I heard something last night and I thought I was dreaming."

"What was it?"

"I thought I heard a...a woman scream." He looked up into Gray's face, the caving of belief sagging his features. "I thought I was dreaming," he repeated, his voice growing weak.

"Okay, it's okay. We'll work all this out. What I need now is to get Darrin and Adam to come in peacefully and we can talk about everything. There's no need for this to end in bloodshed."

Vincent's head bobbed but his eyes were blank, his lips moving as if he were silently reading something.

"Let's go," Gray said, putting a gentle hand on the doctor's shoulder.

They walked abreast down the center of the path between the outbuildings. Danzig drifted to the right, checking a shed door that was secured with a large padlock. Gray and Vincent moved left along the immense steel-shelled barn. The

192

wide sliding door was closed and locked, as was the man-door beside it. All was quiet except for the hushing whisper of the corn and the gusts of wind from the east bringing a subtle rumble that was more felt than heard. The air moved like something alive around them as they walked through it, seeing no more than a hundred yards in any direction.

The silo came closer as Danzig rejoined them, shaking his head when Gray looked at him. The towering structure stretched up into the choking atmosphere, a rounded obelisk obscured by the drifting smoke. The outlines of a steel door solidified and Gray approached it, placing his hand on the knob. It turned easily. He motioned to Danzig who raised the shotgun, positioning himself directly in front of the entry.

"Please, just be careful and don't hurt them. Please," Vincent whispered.

Gray considered the doctor for a moment and then tipped his head once before he shoved the door inward and paused, raising the pistol from his side. Danzig kept the barrel pointed into the silo and finally nodded. Gray swept inside, keeping low and tight to the wall.

The air smelled of grain above the stink of smoke. A deep, heady scent that seemed tangible enough to cut. A pile of wheat stretched from one side of the silo to the other but came barely past Gray's height in the center, the edges sloping down to bare concrete floor. The steel walls flew up to the cathedral ceiling six stories above, and an eyelet of sky winked through a small hole in the vaulted roof. The circular space was dark and still.

Gray waved one hand behind him, motioning the other two men inside, and began to move around the perimeter, his vision adjusting to the dimness. A long grain elevator and its chain leaned against the wall, running up to and ending at a paneled access door high on the silo's side. Cobwebs undulated in the drafts. Their footsteps echoed and crackled with the chaff beneath their boots. Gray kept the barrel of the gun moving as he walked, both hands on the grip. Glancing over his shoulder, he saw that Vincent was following Danzig in the opposite direction. The wind creaked against the building, the entire structure griping with the pressure. On the opposite side of the wheat, they met and stopped, Gray lowering the gun to his side.

"They're not here," he said, glancing at the doctor. "Where else could they be?"

Vincent shook his head. "I don't know. There's the old root cellar, but we haven't used that in years."

"Where is it?"

"Farther down the path, but there's no reason for them to go there, it's locked and below ground."

Danzig scanned the high walls and then nudged some wheat with his boot.

"They must've saw us coming and ran," Gray said. "Let's take a look at the root cellar and then we'll have to leave, there's no other choice."

Danzig nodded and began to walk away. Vincent followed as Gray threw a final look around the silo. He took one step, the sound of his boot clunking on wood very loud. He looked down at the wooden panel set in the floor, as wide and tall as a man. Its surface was painted the same color as the pale concrete, and it blended perfectly save for a finger hole drilled into one end. Gray stomped on the panel again, listening to the hollow thunk.

"Doctor, what's this?"

Vincent came back and studied the board.

"I think it's the main elevator motor housing. My workers usually handle all of the harvest, I just oversee from time to time."

Gray knelt and placed his index finger in the hole, lifting the panel up.

A steel door was set in the floor beneath it.

It resembled the hatch of a submarine, its riveted face and crank handle having the appearance to withstand vast pressures.

"What the hell is that?" Danzig asked, leveling the shotgun at the door.

"I don't...I don't know," the doctor said, bending to look at the horizontal entrance. "I've never seen this before." He tipped his head up and looked from Gray to Danzig and then back to the hatch. Slowly he stood and put a hand against the wall to steady himself. "I think I'm going to be sick."

"Have a seat, Vincent," Gray said, guiding the doctor to the floor where he sat with his knees bent, glassy eyes staring at the pile of wheat.

The shrill ring of Danzig's cell phone burst from Gray's pocket and they all jumped. Gray winced at the pain that radiated through his stomach with the tensing of his muscles and dug out the chirping phone. When he saw the number on the display he touched the answer button and put it to his ear.

"Mary Jo?"

"Who is this?" Mary Jo said, her voice sharper than he'd ever heard it before.

"It's Gray."

"Oh thank God you're okay. Everyone said that you died in the fire. I saw that Danzig had called a couple times and I hoped that he was calling to say he'd found you alive. The lines have been tied up with people panicking all day."

"Why in hell are you still at the office? The fire's coming right toward you."

"I know, I've got my car running outside the door, but I found out more about Clarence Drucker and his son."

"Okay." Gray looked around the quiet silo and turned to see Danzig kneeling by the hatch, his hands on the handle. The shotgun rested on the floor beside him. Vincent still sat catatonic against the wall.

"Clarence Drucker died when his son was ten years old and the boy went to live with a foster family that eventually adopted him. I had to dig and pry for a while but I eventually found his vaccination records. He was inoculated with the Line when he was eleven."

A short squawk came from the handle as Danzig turned it, pulling Gray's attention away from Mary Jo's voice.

"Dan, wait."

But the giant was already lifting the heavy door. It came up without a sound on oiled hinges and opened into darkness.

"What the hell," Danzig said, rising to his full height. Gray stepped up beside him and peered into the hole. A narrow set of stairs dropped down and out

194

of sight. A faint glow emanated from the very bottom, as if a light burned farther down below. Mary Jo's voice brought him back as she repeated herself, asking if he was listening.

"Sorry, Mary Jo, say that last part again."

"I said the boy's name was Vincent Drucker, and he took the last name Barder from the family that adopted him. Dr. Barder is Clarence Drucker's son, Sheriff."

Something fell inside Gray's chest with her words, a plummeting within that sent a chill racing across his skin. He dropped the phone and began to turn, but Vincent was already there, Danzig's shotgun leveled at the huge man's back.

The gun blast was deafening.

It reverberated through the silo in breakers of sound. The pellets peppered Danzig's back from less than six feet away, he flew forward, propelled by the force. He landed face down in the wheat chaff, his arms out to either side, fingers gripped into fists. His knees unhinged and he slid down, the gasmask peeling off his face before coming to a stop.

"No!" Gray yelled, bringing up the pistol, but Vincent was moving, his hand finding the barrel before Gray could aim. He pulled the trigger anyway. The gun bucked in his hand and the round tore past Vincent's body and out the wall, leaving a hole as big as a baby's fist in the steel. In one motion, Vincent yanked the pistol and kicked Gray in the stomach.

Pain exploded in his guts and he fell, the revolver coming free of his hand in a horrible instant that left him grasping at nothing. He tried to step back but there was only open air, and he was tumbling into it, down the open set of stairs, sharp treads biting into his spine. The light exchanged for darkness in a sickening pinwheel as he flipped over and fell into a rushing curtain of black that enveloped him completely.

Chapter 41

Bitter aching cold and stabbing light filtered through Gray's consciousness.

The pain slammed into him as if he'd fallen a dozen feet to the ground. The wracking throb of it ebbed and flowed through him, making his teeth grind against one another. His ribs were lines of agony in his back, the sensation of rending flesh and tissue with each breath. His brain was too large for his skull. It was pressing against the bone and seeping from his ears, he was sure of it. His side felt as if it were bleeding again, but when he tried to reach the wound, he found that his hands were bound together. Prying his eyelids farther open, he looked around.

He was in an operating room.

He sat in a straight-backed chair in its center. Smooth, stainless steel manacles were fastened to both his wrists, a thick piece of chain linking them together. His ankles were locked in similar fashion and a short length of chain attached the two bindings. He blinked and took in his surroundings.

Sterile whiteness everywhere. The room itself was circular with a portholed door to his right, and another, wider entrance straight ahead that was blocked by what looked like two elevator doors. Shelves and cabinets lined the walls and an operating table took up the center of the space. Electronic monitoring equipment stood around the bed like a group of mourners. The floor was tile and slanted in the center where it met a large drain. A tray of surgical tools rested on a wheeled cart several steps away. The instruments shone with clear purpose, their tips and saw teeth grinning.

Gray yanked on the shackles, straining until he was out of breath. There was no give whatsoever. He tried to stand but made it only inches before he realized he was bound at the waist to the chair. A strap gouged into his wound and he hissed with the burning that filled his midsection. As the pain abated he opened his eyes and noticed a small camera mounted in one corner of the room, its black pupil unmoving. He stared back at it for some time until he heard movement from behind the door to his right.

Vincent Barder strode into the room wearing a pair of blue operating scrubs. His unkempt hair had been smoothed to one side and a small smile rested on his lips.

"Ah good, you're awake," he said, approaching Gray.

"You sonofabitch."

"Yes, it's something, isn't it?" Barder kneeled down, balancing on the balls of his feet so that he was more on Gray's level. "I bet you're more than a little confused as well as banged up. I did do a preliminary exam of you while you were out. You have two cracked ribs, possible concussion, a broken nose, and your gunshot wound looks like it may be infected, but I'm only responsible for those first two." The doctor smiled and a predatory shine flashed across his eyes. Gray studied him for a moment and realized something was different. The entire set of the man's face had changed. The harried look the doctor always carried with him, as if he were constantly late, was gone. A strange relaxation had taken its place.

"Who are you?" Gray asked, his eyes still running over the other man's face.

"Now we're getting somewhere."

The doctor stood and walked to the tray holding the surgical instruments. He picked up a long curved blade with serrated edges at its end and came back, holding the tool beneath Gray's chin. With a flick of his wrist, Barder opened a shallow cut on his jaw and Gray jerked away, clenching his teeth.

"That is who I am, Sheriff. I am pain and pleasure, the constant need for satisfaction of the primal necessities. You pull away from the knife's touch because it is painful, the cutting of skin, tissue, bone. You do this because you require the comfort of having your body whole and untouched. Freud, he was a brilliant Austrian—"

"I know who Freud is."

"Ah, someone who enjoys history as much as I do, excellent. I'm so glad I shot your friend and not you, Sheriff."

"I'm going to kill you."

"I find that highly unlikely, and besides, we're getting off track with threats and whatnot. Moving on, Freud believed in something called the id. The id is what I just explained to you; our most basic desires and needs that are there from birth. Instant gratification. It is beautiful chaos that each one of us is born with. Inherent knowledge, right here." Barder tapped his temple once. Gray watched him as a drop of blood beaded and fell from his jaw to his thigh. Barder turned away and set the tool back onto the tray without bothering to wipe it off.

"That is what this has taken from us." The doctor pulled up his sleeve, revealing the line of orange dots on his shoulder. "What was almost taken from me."

"The Line turns off the murder gene, it doesn't rob us of anything except psychopaths such as yourself."

Barder chuckled. "It's an illusion, my friend. A false wall that society hides behind while they continue to murder, cheat, and lie. They tell themselves that they've defeated a great evil, yet they haven't. Man isn't in control of life any more than an ant is in control of the sun. Life will always find a route to circumvent man's attempts at control."

"And you're this miracle? Tell me how torturing and murdering people is some sort of wonderful phenomenon."

"It's balance, Sheriff. When people started getting injected with this poison, the world lost something crucial. There have always been hunters, since the dawn of time. Herod, Vlad the Impaler, Hitler, the list goes on and on. They were visionaries of their time, using their ids to better society as they saw fit."

"They were butchers."

"That may be, greatness does have its benefits. But my own aspiration is no less noble or ambitious."

"And what is that?"

Barder came close to him again, leaning down so that Gray could smell his cologne, something smoky mixed with citrus.

"I'm going to resurrect the psychopathic mind from extinction."

Gray lunged forward, trying to head butt the doctor in the face, but the restraint at his waist held him back. Barder stepped away nimbly and chuckled again.

"I'll hand it to you, Sheriff, you're tougher than some I've had the privilege of getting to know in rooms like this."

"Like those people buried in your father's field?"

"Ah yes, you found my depository. What a strange coincidence too. I knew someday they would be unearthed, but during your short reign as sheriff, how fortuitous for you, or unfortuitous, considering where you are now. Yes, I used that place when I was young, coming of age you might say, or *becoming,* in my case."

"What do you mean, becoming? You said you were this way from birth."

"I was, that being another dealing of fate. My father didn't believe in the Line. He thought much the same as I do, but his reservations about the inoculations were more naturalistic, simpler. He didn't think we should meddle with nature. So he kept me from getting the shots and only started to worry when he found me disemboweling our pet cat. Of course he was only concerned for about ten seconds before the heart attack took most of his attention away. All I had to do then was wait until he quit breathing to call the emergency services."

Gray shook his head and looked around the room.

"You don't even know how crazy you are, do you?"

"Insanity is an objective term, Sheriff, you know this. We wage wars and kill millions of people in the name of peace. We allow slavery, rape, and murder to transpire for extra money in bank accounts. I would put any of these under the label of insanity, but that's neither here nor there."

Barder paced across the room and looked out of the porthole in the door. He grinned and came back, his face slowly losing its cheer. His lips turned down at the ends and his eyes began to look not at Gray but through him.

"My adopted family wouldn't hear of me not having the Line. I'll never forget that day. I didn't know what would happen to me, the real me, when they gave me the shots. Because you see, I had my mask that all hunters wear and even then I knew I was special, maybe one of a kind. To my family I was the doting adopted son, upbeat, loving and thoughtful. So when I went into the hospital that day, I wasn't sure of my future. It turns out I needn't have worried. The id abided."

Barder came close to him again, staying out of range of another attack.

"Instead of dissolving who I truly was, I became two people, Sheriff. Two. The Line affected me differently and I'm still not sure if it was the late age at which I was injected or not. My persona, my mask, grew stronger. Who I truly was receded, almost into nothing. Violent thoughts were as close as I came to myself for years, and I was confused. I remember being and then un-being, if that makes sense? There was before the Line, and after."

Gray stared at him, transfixed in spite of himself.

"Your personality split."

The doctor seemed excited. "Precisely my thoughts, but I can't say for sure. All I know is that over the years I, the real me, emerged more and more. I'd find myself staring at the back of a boy's head in class and wonder what it would be like to crush his skull. To hear the bone break beneath something hard. It excited me. Soon I had my first, emergence, I'd call it. I became aware, completely and totally. I butchered the family dog that night. Led him into the woods behind our house and slit his throat. I played in the blood for hours."

Gray couldn't help but grimace, but held the other man's gaze.

"After that I began to plan and emerge more from inside the shell of my other personality. By then I was old enough to stay out later at night. I followed a woman for two weeks who walked home after her job ended at a grocery store. She was my first, and I made it last. I kept her alive for three days inside an abandoned factory."

Barder's gaze was reverent, a glossy stare of a child looking through a window at Christmas treasures. His eyes refocused and he moved to the hospital bed, rolling it backward until it was close to the wall along with the surrounding equipment.

"The differences between the real me and Dr. Vincent Barder are so defined and so real, my boys always knew who I was when I entered a room. Whether I was their loving, hardworking father, or—" Barder smiled. "Who you see now. They knew from a young age whom they could speak to freely and which would have run screaming from the house if they were to tell him what they did to the missing pets around the farm. I was always aware of my other side, the family man side, but he was never fully conscious of me. That rift opened wide when I dismembered that woman in the dusty factory. Her screams were the purest music I've ever heard."

Barder grinned again.

"After her, I knew what I needed to do. Are you familiar with the tabula rasa, Sheriff?"

Gray moved his feet around, the chains binding his ankles clinking together.

"It's the theory of the blank slate, that all human beings are born with a mind that's unwritten."

"Very eloquently put, Sheriff. If I didn't have other uses for you, I'd keep you around just to chat. Yes, you're correct. I researched the subject continuously after I graduated high school and believed in it wholeheartedly. I still do. The notion that every child is born without true preference, hatred, or knowledge of love, is undeniable. This is what drove me, what gave me a path and focused my purpose. You see, Sheriff, when I had my children, my entire intent was to see if I could mold them into sociopaths even though they were inoculated with the Line."

Gray watched the doctor return to the tray and pick up a long, finely toothed saw. He ran a thumb over the ragged blade until blood seeped down its edge.

"You wanted to turn your own kids into psychopaths?"

"Precisely. And I did it. Well, at least I succeeded with Darrin and Adam. Ryan on the other hand resisted, which I must say, still troubles me. Regrettably, it also led to his death by the hand of your young deputy. But no experiment is perfect." Barder paused as if considering a minor inconvenience and then continued. "It was my hope that even though the sociopathic gene was nulled by FV5, I could use the tabula rasa and change them from the get go. The key, I found was beginning early with the children. I began all their *training,* so to speak, very young. I made them watch me cut myself, then I cut them, then I eventually moved them on to animals, and only recently did I graduate them fully."

"The Olsons," Gray said.

Barder laughed and shook his head. "No, Sheriff. The Olsons only came after both Darrin and Adam had tortured and killed in the root cellar I mentioned earlier. Both of their subjects were vagrants, men that no one would miss, but Ryan's was special since I saw he was resisting on some levels. I needed something unique to break through to him. Fate brought me Miles Baron."

Gray looked away from the doctor and studied the porthole in the door, watching for movement or shadows on the wall outside.

"You did a horseshit job pinning that on Hudson."

"Yes well, my boys were in charge of that. Also, I predicted that Hudson, being unstable and drug addled, would kill whomever went to investigate him, but once again you triumphed, Sheriff. Bravo."

"So I assume you saw the same opportunity with the women from Widow Town. You chose the ones who had no close relatives and wouldn't be investigated thoroughly if they went missing," Gray said.

"Sheriff, I applaud your deductions. You really were getting somewhere." Barder moved to the instrument table again and donned a pair of latex gloves. "But I didn't see an opportunity in Widow Town. I *created* it."

The smile that crawled across Barder's face was something reptilian. Comprehension punched Gray like a horse kick to the chest.

"You-you caused the explosion in the mine."

Barder nodded. "I did a lot of research on the families that lived in the development. Most were far from home without ties to the community. They were vagrants of the working class, traveling wherever the jobs were. They were perfect prey."

"Rachel's husband, he got blamed for the accident, but it was you. And you're wearing his cologne right now, aren't you?"

For the first time, Barder seemed surprised. He cocked his head at Gray, appraising him again.

"Astute, Sheriff, astute is the word for you. Yes, I was able to persuade Ken that evening to set up the charges specifically to create a cave-in. He complied, but what would you expect a man to do when the other scenario was me shooting him and then returning to his house to kill his wife and unborn child." Barder smiled again. "And I did fancy his cologne."

"You're a fucking monster."

Barder shrugged. "I am, that is all. That's all any of us are, Sheriff."

"You should do yourself a favor and put a bullet through your brain now so it saves me the trouble of killing you myself."

The doctor laughed, a hearty sound that rang throughout the room.

"I really like you, Sheriff, I do. You're something of a renaissance man; part detective, philosopher, historian, but you need to get in touch with your own id, I have a feeling you're a lot darker on the inside than you think. Most people are."

Gray clenched his fists and then released them. His temples pounded like drums, but the strength was slowly returning to his arms and legs.

"Are they dead? Joslyn, Rachel, Siri, their children?"

"Weren't you listening, Sheriff? My whole purpose was to bring back what the world had lost, the ones like me. So what better place to start than a development full of women without husbands, children without fathers. I may take another woman from Widow Town, but for now Joslyn, Rachel, and Siri will all be our Queens, so to speak. My sons will impregnate them whenever they're eligible to carry another child, I'll deliver the babies, and then begin their training when they're of age. Joslyn's son as well as Rachel's will be the first of the next generation of my experiment, and I expect it to go well. I'm preparing them just as I did my own children. They will experience all the wonders I have to offer them. And when the time comes, their first victims will be their own mothers."

The door banged open and Darrin followed by Adam came into the room wheeling a tall, rectangular frame of steel with casters bolted onto the bottom of its supports. It was almost eight feet tall and twice as long as the medical bed against the wall. From its center, Joslyn and Rachel dangled upside down by their ankles, their heads inches from the floor. They wore scrubs that matched Barder's, and their hands were bound similarly to Gray's. Lengths of rubber hose gagged their mouths. They swung and swayed like turkeys on a slaughterhouse conveyor line. Joslyn made a soft whimpering sound in the back of her throat, but Rachel was stoic, taking in the sterilized room along with Gray seated in the chair.

The two men brought the apparatus holding the women over the large drain and stopped it there, locking its wheels. Without a word they exited the room and returned moments later. Darrin pushed a cart that carried two little boys, their eyes wide and staring. One of them Gray recognized as Ken, Rachel's son, but the other was a bit larger and unfamiliar to him. Both kids were silent and watched their mothers dangling before them. Adam entered the room, and Gray's heart stuttered. The huge man had Lynn by the shoulders, guiding her like a child. When she saw Gray a look of relief and then horror flooded her features.

"Mac!"

"It's okay, honey, it's okay."

Adam half walked, half carried her to the medical bed, and amidst her protests, strapped her to it with wide, Nylon bands.

"Thank you, boys. Have either of you checked on the fire?" Barder said, his eyes floating over his new audience.

"The wind shifted and slowed it down, it's about a mile from here. The planes and helicopters are still flying but there's no visibility over a hundred feet with the smoke," Darrin answered, looking at Gray with what bordered on hunger.

"Good. I want you both to go to the house and gather up the rest of the food. I had it partially packed in the trunk of the car when the good sheriff interrupted me. Bring some of it down here and some to the root cellar. If a rescue crew decides to take a peek in our shelter it will look like that's exactly where we survived the fire."

Darrin nodded and motioned Adam toward the door but stopped beside Gray's chair on the way.

"I don't know how you managed to get out of that house but it didn't do you much good did it, Sheriff?"

"We'll have our dance once I get out of this chair, junior."

Darrin shifted his gaze from one of Gray's eyes to the other and then snorted, walking away from him and out of the room.

"They're still learning restraint and how to be careful," Barder said, walking to the instrument tray. "Eventually they'll understand tact." He selected a shining tool with two handles and a round hole lined with dual blades in its center. It looked like a miniature tree pruner. "We're going to do our own experiment today, my friends. It will be an experiment in empathy."

Gray watched him pick up the long saw again and pace to the stand holding Joslyn and Rachel.

"Empathy interests me to no end, mostly I suppose since I seem to lack it completely myself. I tried, I really did, to experience it while I was working with my subjects. I tried to feel something for them or what I was doing to them. I tried to feel sorry then and after they were dead, but—" Barder shrugged. "Nothing."

Barder examined the woman's bindings holding them upside down.

"Are you familiar with 'sawing', Sheriff?"

"I'm guessing not in the sense that you're referring to, no."

"Sawing is an ancient method of torture and execution that came out of Rome and Persia over fifteen hundred years ago. What it entails is the condemned is hung upside down like our two ladies here and then sawed in half lengthwise from the groin to the throat. Now the key, Sheriff, is how the person is positioned. Being upside down keeps the blood in the brain and makes it more difficult to pass out from the pain. In our case, so will the adrenaline shots I've given both of them."

Joslyn began to cry in earnest, tears dripping up over her eyebrows and onto her forehead before falling to the drain beneath her. Rachel's nostrils flared, but her eyes never left her son's face.

"Don't you touch them," Gray said just above a whisper.

"Now here's where the empathy experiment begins, my friends, or I suppose we can call it a game," Barder continued. "You and your lovely ex-wife are going to be the contestants. You'll be calling the shots, Sheriff, you'll be controlling fate. To start off, I'm going to remove one of Lynn's fingers with this," he said, squeezing the shears in his hand. The hole containing the blades spread apart and then snapped together with a shushing sound.

"Take my finger, do it to me," Gray said, offering out his hands.

"Ah, that's where the empathy portion comes in, Sheriff. I know you're the hero type and would endure a massive amount of pain, I mean look at what you've been through already. But there's no fun in that, no interesting results. I want to see what you'll choose. Now after I remove Lynn's finger, you have a choice to either let me take another one from her hand, or if you can't stand to see your beloved in agony, I'll saw one of the other women in half and Lynn will live."

"She'll live to be imprisoned here, raped by your two psychos, and eventually murdered by her own child," Gray said through gritted teeth.

"Well, Sheriff, I never said the options were perfect, but at least she'll be alive. And besides, you don't even know these other women, they're nothing to you when compared with how you feel about Lynn, I'm sure. I'm making quite a trade here, my friend. I'm giving up having the pleasure of watching one of my small protégés here eventually execute their own mother. Can you imagine it? The feat of changing someone from a typical path of dreary sameness to something wholly unique? It speaks volumes about what I'm trying to understand about empathy if I'm willing to give that up. In fact, I'll make you a deal right now. Say the word, and I won't even touch Lynn. I'll just saw Joslyn or Rachel, whichever you choose. No one outside of this room will ever know, Sheriff."

"I'll know."

Barder straightened. "Ah yes, the inimitable conscience, the enemy of the id. Last chance, Sheriff. You can save Lynn right this moment, and as an added bonus, I won't put you through hours of torture, I'll have Darrin shoot you and be done with it. One decision, and you can spare yourself and Lynn untold amounts of pain."

Gray sat silent, eventually bringing his gaze to Lynn's. Her jaw trembled as she watched him, but finally her mouth formed a solid line and she nodded once, imperceptibly. Gray brought his eyes to his own feet and sat still.

"All right, it appears you've made your decision. At any point you can tell me to stop, Sheriff, and I will bandage Lynn's wounds and shift my attention to one of the other women. If you say nothing, I'll keep cutting until she's dead."

Barder turned on his heel and strode to where Lynn lay. She tried to struggle again, to hide her hands beneath her, but the doctor brought her left arm out, grasping it by her slender wrist. She balled her hand into a fist but slowly Barder worked it open, splaying her fingers with his own.

"What do you think, Sheriff? The ring finger has some symbolic significance I would say."

Barder slipped the shears over Lynn's third finger and squeezed the handles.

There was a sharp clack and blood flew in a crimson ribbon down the length of the medical bed. Gray made a strangled grunt as he lunged forward again, the chains at his ankles and wrists snapping tight. Lynn held onto her scream for a heartbeat and then let it peal out, the room ringing with misery.

"You bastard," Gray growled, settling back into the chair. There was a singeing sound like an egg hitting a hot pan and Lynn cried out again, her back arching against the restraints. Barder turned and strode to Gray's chair, holding something in his hand.

"Don't worry, Sheriff, I cauterized the stump so she won't bleed out, but I thought you might want to hold this." He tossed Lynn's severed ring finger into Gray's lap. Her nail polish was the same color as the blood leaking from its opposite end.

Gray looked up at the doctor, the smugness of the other man's face a solid mask.

"Doc?"

"Yes?"

"Fuck you."

Gray clapped his boots together and the knife blade shot through the bottom of his sole.

He pistoned his legs out, kicking Barder's knee. The knife sliced beneath and then through the other man's kneecap, cutting the flesh, cartilage, and tendons like they weren't there. Barder's eyebrows went up as he looked down and saw the four inches of steel protruding from his leg.

Gray twisted his feet.

The knife turned and tore out of the doctor's leg, gouting a cupful of blood onto the pristine floor. Barder tried to take one step and then toppled, a howl crawling up out of his throat as he hit the floor.

Both of the little boys began to cry in their cart, their small arms waving as tears rolled down their cheeks. Lynn's eyelids fluttered and she turned her head, looking in Gray's direction. Gray put both feet on the ground and pushed. The handle of the knife slowly rose from the top of his boot and he sat forward, straining to reach it. The pain in his stomach built to a crescendo, and hot blood leaked down his side and into his lap. He reached farther and snagged the handle, pulling it free of his boot, the whole time keeping his eyes on Barder.

The doctor gasped as he cradled his knee, fleshy white lumps of sinew poking between his fingers. He blinked, first looking at the ceiling and then bringing his vision down to where Gray sat with the knife in one hand. Barder's mouth was a spittle-slick O that trembled like a fish pleading for water. He let go of his knee and began to slide himself toward the instrument tray.

Gray guided the knife beneath the strap at his waist and slit it free, then bent forward again, retracting the blade into the handle. He placed the butt of the weapon on the floor and threaded the chain binding his ankles together over the blade slot before triggering the knife again.

The chain link nearly exploded.

The wide blade shot through the chain's steel like cardboard, expanding the link out into a diamond shape before breaking it in a brief flicker of sparks. Gray paused to glance at Barder who had bypassed the instrument tray along with Rachel and Joslyn's hanger, and was scooting toward the dual doors of what could only be an elevator. Blood spewed from his ruined kneecap and spread out behind him like a rusty comet tail.

Rachel gurgled something unintelligible from behind her gag, and Gray realized she was urging him on. Retracting the knife blade again, he positioned it

204

under the chain that bound his wrists together and wrapped it as tight as possible before pressing the button. The alloyed weapon had the same effect as it had on the lower chain. A cracking and the smell of burned metal and then Gray's hands were free.

There was a rushing sound above the constant crying of the toddlers, and the air in the room changed. The doors to the elevator opened and Barder half crawled, half slid himself inside. Gray rose from the chair, a bout of dizziness nearly bringing him down before he moved forward, the broken chains clinking about his feet. Barder saw him coming and dragged his feet inside the small compartment.

"Level one," the doctor wheezed, and an electronic voice repeated his command before the doors began to slide shut.

Gray lurched around the apparatus the two women hung from, and sped toward the door as fast as his body would allow. He drew back his arm, readying to throw the knife at the man through the closing gap, but held up as the doors snicked closed. The last he saw was Barder's pale face concentrated in a grimace, his eyes clearer and full of hate.

"Mac," Lynn said, her head raised off the bed.

He hurried across the room to her, pausing only to look out the porthole in the door. There was short deserted corridor beyond but no visible lock on the door when he searched for one. He stopped at Lynn's bedside and began to loosen the straps holding her flat.

"Are you okay?" he asked.

"I think so." She sat up and examined her left hand. Her ring finger ended behind the second knuckle in a blackened stump. The end was flattened and shiny from the cauterization.

"It hurts like hell though."

"Can you walk?"

"Yes."

"Let's get you out of here," Gray said, helping her off the bed. Lynn made her way to the boys in the cart while Gray went to the instrument tray and found a small, indiscriminate key that fit the shackles on his wrists and ankles. In less than a minute he freed Joslyn and Rachel from their bindings. Rachel pulled the gag from her mouth and fell against him when she stood, her arms holding him tight.

"You came, oh God, thank you for coming."

"It's fine, you're okay. Let's get moving," Gray said, gently extracting himself from her. She turned and rushed to her son who held his arms out. Reaching. Tear tracks stained his small face and Rachel clutched him to her, burying her face against his neck. Joslyn held almost the same pose except she was kneeling on the ground, hugging her son tight.

Gray walked to the door again and checked the hallway. It was still empty and no sounds met his ears over the soft crying of the reunited mothers and sons. Lynn's hand gripped the inside of his arm and she pulled him close, her body shaking against him. He put an arm around her shoulders, and then turned back to the rest of the group.

"Okay, we have to move and move fast. The boys might be coming back down here right now. I'll go first and take the brunt if one of them stops us. If they have a gun, run back here and pile everything you can against the door. Then hide in the elevator if they get past me."

"I'm going to fight if they're out there," Rachel said. "There's no way they're locking us up again."

Gray appraised her for a moment before Joslyn spoke.

"Me too. You have no idea—" Her words broke off in a horse sob as she hugged her son tighter.

"Okay. We fight no matter what," Gray said, shifting his gaze to each of the women. A deep resolve burned in each of their eyes.

Rachel nodded and hitched her son up higher upon her hip while Joslyn nuzzled her child, whispering something that Gray couldn't hear. Lynn walked to the instrument tray and returned holding a wickedly curved scalpel.

"Let's go," she said.

They pushed through the door into the quiet hallway, only the sounds of their footsteps speaking back to them. Gray propped the door open with one of the empty shackles upon seeing the electronic locking mechanism on the outside of the doorframe. When he was sure it wouldn't slide shut behind them, he and Lynn led the group away from the operating room, their shoulders brushing from time to time. The hallway turned after several yards and then stretched away with heavy doors interspersed on either side. They moved down it, Gray pausing by each cell to listen. Nothing. A small alcove held a rolling cart and on its surface was the Raging Bull along with the two Tin-Snippers. Gray snatched the gun up and spun the cylinder out, his heart falling when he saw it was empty. The bottom level of the cart was bare, and when he rolled it away from the wall there was nothing but cobwebs and a ball of dust. He tucked the gun into a loop in his coveralls and slipped the Tin-Snippers into an opposite pocket. The knife he kept ready in his hand. As they neared the end of the corridor he noticed another camera mounted in the upper right corner. He gave it a look and then touched the door handle that sealed the hallway.

The handle moved down and up, swinging free without opening the door.

"They're electronically locked," Rachel said. "I got out before and none of them would open."

"Shit," Gray said, half turning. "We need to go back and look for a—"

His words were cut off as the door burst open, striking him hard on the shoulder. He fell, the knife clattering to the floor out of reach. His body exploded with a map of pain that marked each prior injury. The women screamed in a cacophony of sound that fluttered his eardrums. When he looked up, he saw Adam step through the door, but the younger man's face was obscured by something.

Adam wore a polished set of steel jaws that protruded from his face where his mouth should have been. Gleaming fangs interlocked amongst one another and fitted plates covered the man's jowls. Two black straps ran from where the mask met his face and stretched back around his neck and over the top of his skull. As Gray watched, the jaws opened, revealing Adam's real mouth and teeth behind the steel.

Adam opened his mouth wider and the mask did the same, the wickedly pointed teeth stretching like the yawn of a lion. Gray saw Adam shut his mouth just as the steel jaws followed suit, slamming together, creating a horrible crunching sound that rang like clashing sabers. In that moment Gray knew what had made the bite marks on the bodies of the Jacobs family.

Adam stepped forward, kicking the knife down the hallway. He leaned over, bringing his face to Gray's in a semblance of a kiss, the shining maw widening again. Gray kicked the younger man in the chest, shoving him backward. There was a flash of movement and Lynn lunged forward, swinging the scalpel down in a stabbing motion. The instrument plunged into Adam's shoulder as he tried to block the attack and he issued a muffled yowl from behind the device. He shoved Lynn and she flew back, tripping over her feet as she went down and landed in a heap. With a hiss, Adam withdrew the three inches of steel embedded in his shoulder, a flower of blood blossoming on the material surrounding the wound.

"Oh bitch, you're gonna pay for that one." The jaws snicked together and apart as Adam spoke. "I'm gonna bite you to pieces, and then I'm gonna eat some of you."

Adam aimed a kick at Gray as he scuttled backward, trying to regain his feet. The blow caught him in the thigh and he cried out, numbness shooting down the length of his leg. Rachel stepped forward, holding Gray's knife out before her like a pointed offering. Adam began to giggle.

"What are you gonna do with that, bitch? You don't put things into me, I put things into you, remember?" Adam laughed again and Rachel lunged forward with a yell. He caught her arms as she tried to drive the knife into his stomach, and held her there while she squirmed.

"I'd bite your face off, but I like it too much," Adam said. He tightened his grip and began to force Rachel's arms down, his mask rubbing against her cheek until she issued a hoarse sob and dropped the knife. With a backward kick, Adam sent the weapon sliding behind him on the floor and shoved Rachel away. Gray began to stand, his leg threatening to drop him, and Adam sent a looping fist into the side of his head.

The hallway dipped as if it were inside of a plane caught in turbulence. Gray stumbled back, running to keep upright. His hand went out in a final effort of balance and he found the edge of the rolling cart. He fell and took it with him, its heavy top thudding to the floor beside him. One of the Tin-Snippers escaped his pocket and rolled out, bumping against Rachel's shoe.

"He's gonna be so proud of me," Adam said, stopping to look at them. "Why don't you all be good and just go back to the hospital room. Hey, how did you get out anyway?"

Gray reached for the ball bearing, but his fingers wouldn't grip it. His lungs tried to pull air in, but they were small and ragged. He saw Rachel bend down and pick up the Tin-Snipper.

"Throw it and get down," he wheezed, locking eyes with her.

She looked at the polished egg of steel in her palm and then down the corridor to where Adam stood, his hands on his hips as if awaiting an answer. Gray watched her wind back her arm and whip it forward.

"Get down!" he yelled at Lynn and Joslyn who each pulled the little boys to the floor, covering them with their bodies.

The Tin-Snipper sailed down the hallway and Gray pulled the cart closer, hoping he would hear the sound of the sphere hitting Adam's mask. Instead, it bounced harmlessly off the giant's ample belly and shot straight up into the air. Adam laughed.

"Was that supposed to hur—"

The Tin-Snipper hit the floor at Adam's feet and detonated.

The concussion struck them first, driving the cart against Gray's outstretched hands and legs. There was no definable sound, only a thick buzzing in the air as if bees had returned from their extinction and swarmed the hall. Then the vacuum was punctured by a fading roar, followed by inhuman screams. They reverberated off the walls like things alive, cutting through the waning aftershock of the explosion.

Gray turned to the women and boys, searching for missing limbs or lacerated torsos. They were all sitting up slowly, the children crying in hushed tones, Rachel and Joslyn clinging to them. Lynn reached toward him, a haze of disorientation covering her eyes.

"What happened?"

He more read her lips than heard the words. The bees hadn't left his eardrums, but the floor had stilled. He gathered his feet beneath him and stood, a swarm of vertigo coming and receding within a heartbeat. He held out his hand to Lynn and helped her up. The screams were still coursing past them, a river of sound, and when he turned he saw why.

Adam's legs were gone from the hips down.

He lay in a muddled ocean of gore with shattered spars of bones poking their bleached heads through the red swells. Strings of muscle were splattered against the walls, and one especially long strand hung from the ceiling like a party decoration. Adam screamed over the top of his mask's lower jaw, the upper portion had been torn off in the blast and lay farther down the hall. The inner mechanism still worked and the piece of steel that hung from his face snapped upward with each bellow.

Gray rounded the overturned cart and saw that shrapnel had obliterated the lowermost tray. Dented constellations covered the underside of the second level. He moved forward, careful not to slip in the organic spray that used to be Adam's legs. The man squirmed in his own fluids, his palms slapping the wet floor, sending up droplets of blood. Gray came even with him and Adam turned his spattered face toward him, his breath coming in short hitches between shrieks.

"Help me! Help meeeee!"

Gray surveyed the pulped ends of the man's thighs, arterial blood jetting from them in rapid pulses. Miraculously, from the waist up Adam appeared unharmed. Gray knelt beside him, and began to open the pockets on the prone man's shirt. The plastic card was in the second one he checked. He drew it out, turning it over in the dim light.

"Daddy! Help me!"

Gray stood and walked past him, fragments of bone crunching beneath his feet. He passed the card over the electronic eye beside the handle and felt a click. He opened the door and looked around the corner at a set of steps leading up to a vacant landing.

"Let's go," he said over his shoulder, and held the door open.

They filed past the dying man on the floor. Rachel came last, and paused, turning Ken's face away toward the wall. The pumping blood was arcing out of Adam's ruined legs slower and slower. He reached toward her with one hand, trying to grasp her shoe and failing. Rachel leaned toward him and spit into his face before stepping on his hand and continuing down the hall. She moved past Gray without a look and began to climb the stairs.

Gray watched Adam reach toward his missing lower half, shock finally overwhelming him, his fingers feeling the tattered stumps and sharp femurs. With a final look, Gray let the door swing shut, and moved past the women toward the landing.

Joslyn had picked up his knife and offered it to him as he passed, but he motioned to Lynn instead.

"Give it to her," he whispered.

Lynn took the weapon and nodded once when Gray put a hand on her shoulder.

"I'm all right."

"Are you sure?"

"Never better." She gave him a wavering smile.

He climbed to the top of the stairs and waited, listening over the ringing in his ears. He eased one eye around the corner.

Another hallway, this one shorter, ran two dozen steps and ended in a set of stairs leading up and out of sight behind a wall. Two doors, identical to the ones below them, were set in the right side of the hall. The space seemed deserted.

Gray drew the remaining Tin-Snipper out, holding it at his side. He scanned the passage, searching for a camera, and spotted one hanging above the first tread of the stairs. After two more cautious steps he paused by the last door and turned to the landing.

"I think we're okay," he said.

A sharp bang came from the door beside him.

He flinched, spinning and bringing his arm up, ready to release the bearing at the slightest movement. The pounding came again from inside the door, and then a voice, high and unmistakably feminine saying words he couldn't understand.

"Siri," he said, stepping forward.

With a swipe of the card, the door released and he opened it, ready to slam it back shut if it was some kind of trick. Siri leaned against the doorjamb inside, her dark hair hanging in sweated strips around her flushed face. One hand was bleeding from the bottom of her palm, and the other held her swollen belly.

"Sheriff?"

"Siri, thank God."

He moved to her side as a cloudburst of pain crumpled her face, and caught her as her left leg trembled then gave out. The floor was wet beneath his boots, and when he looked down he saw the front of Siri's pants were soaked a darker blue than the rest of her outfit.

"My water broke two hours ago," she managed, bringing her face up to his. Her eyebrows knitted together and her mouth opened in a soundless cry as she nearly doubled over. "The contractions are less than a minute apart."

Chapter 42

Gray helped her to the Spartan bed and eased her down as the rest of the women filed into the room.

Lynn kneeled beside them as Rachel and Joslyn continued to comfort their boys. Over the quiet crying of Joslyn's son, Siri's jerking inhalations filled the air.

"She's having the baby," Gray said, propping a pillow behind Siri's head.

"We have to get her out of here," Lynn said.

"No time. The fire's almost here and we don't know where Darrin is. She's going to have to have it here."

"Mac, we don't know if the smoke from the fire will seep down into these rooms. What if the air gets cut off or it gets too hot."

"It's the chance we have to take. Barder was planning on staying here so if he was confident that it would be safe, that's all we have."

Siri moaned and began to shiver. Lynn stood and spread out a thin blanket over the shaking woman.

"He killed him, Sheriff. Darrin killed Joe," Siri whispered before she gasped for breath again.

Gray found her hand, hot beyond fever.

"I know, kiddo. I know. I'm sorry." He watched Siri close her eyes, nodding once as sweat poured in delicate streams from her temples. He let her hand go and wrapped the blanket up in her palm for something to grip.

"If the baby comes, you'll have to deliver it," Gray murmured to Lynn, standing and taking a step toward the door.

"What? Mac, I don't know how to deliver a baby, I'm not a doctor! Wait, where the hell do you think you're going?"

"I have to find Darrin before he finds us. We're completely vulnerable here. We have no weapons other than this grenade and that knife."

"We can lock the door," Lynn began.

"And if he figures out we're in here, which he will, all he needs to do is get a gun, open the door, and pick us off one by one."

"Mac—"

"Listen." He lowered his voice. "We will die in here if I don't deal with him first. If I find a gun, or ammo for the one I've got, I'll come right back."

Lynn watched him, her eyes filming over and then clearing. Her lips clenched white and she shook her head.

"Damn you, Mac."

"I'm sorry."

"I know. Go."

"Have someone stand by the door with the knife. I'll knock twice before I come back in. If there's no knock, stab whoever comes through that door in the throat."

Lynn nodded, gripping the knife tighter in her good hand. He looked her face over once more, committing it to memory though he didn't need to.

"Hey Adam, get your ass up here!"

The yell stiffened them all where they stood. Even Siri quieted and let a silent breath of pain slither out between her clenched teeth, her eyes bulging. Gray turned to the door, expecting Darrin to step into view any second, a surprised expression erupting over his handsome features at the sight of the prisoners all gathered where they shouldn't be.

Without a word, Gray turned and strode to the open door, peering out while holding the Tin-Snipper ready in his left hand. The hall was still devoid of life, but Darrin's voice rang down the nearby stairway again, clear and sharp with its command.

"Adam, quit fucking around down there. You better not be bothering the pregnant one, he said not to touch her until after she gives birth."

Gray hefted the small grenade, weighing it and his choices before covering his mouth with one hand and turning his head away from the stairwell.

"Coming," he barked, trying to make his voice amorphous. There was a pause and then a scuffle of feet at the top of the stairs. Then nothing.

He moved down the hallway and stopped beside the stairs, readying himself. Every muscle ached. Every bone burned beneath his skin. A pale light spilled down the stairway, giving the shadows a liquid quality. They lay in ashen tangles amidst the dark, and he tried to blend with them as he took the steps upward.

The stairway he'd fallen down had seemed to go on forever when he'd tipped into it. Now it was only ten steps, the treads covered in gritty dirt that snapped beneath his boots. He winced but continued at a steady pace, keeping his vision locked on the hatch above him, waiting for Darrin's form to darken it and fire a round into his chest as he realized that it wasn't his brother coming to meet him. He moved upward, the air growing warmer with each step. The hoarse roaring, like static from another room in a house, became louder as he climbed. The fire was nearer, and from what he could see of the silo, the air had thickened with its noxious breath. He came even with the submarine hatch and crouched, looking over the rim of the floor.

Darrin stood with his back to him a short ways off, gazing out of the open man-door to the yard that was filled with sulfurous-looking smoke. The air glowed yellow, and it carried the quality of a failing fall evening instead of a late August afternoon. The younger man leaned against the doorway as if admiring a stirring sunset instead of the raging destruction that was coming toward them. In one hand he held a pistol, pointed at the floor. Grit crunched beneath Gray's boot and he hesitated, waiting for Darrin to spin around. Instead, he spoke.

"It's beautiful, Adam. It's all burning away. There'll be nothing but charred remains left behind it. It's cleansing; clean in a way that only belongs to nature. Speaking of burning, where did you put the big bastard's body?"

Gray climbed silently from the stairway and wound his arm up, throwing the Tin-Snipper as Darrin pivoted. It flew across the distance between them, and Darrin caught sight of it just as it was nearing the space beside him. He dove in the opposite direction, hurling himself to the ground as it struck the steel wall, and was lost to Gray as the snipper exploded in a flare of thunder. Gray ducked, shielding himself behind the propped hatch door. The silo repeated the explosion until it was a fading whisper of itself, and deadly, tinkling shrapnel peppered the walls, leaving holes where it punched through.

Gray rose, searching the floor for another weapon but saw nothing that would suffice. His hands. They would have to do if there was any breath left in the murderer. He strode through the smoke, moving fast, watching for shadows that might leap toward him, but none did. He edged the pile of grain, feet cracking the wheat that housed life for the next season. Cordite smeared the air, and where he thought Darrin should lay dying, there was only a matted pool of blood, boats of seed floating between its shores.

He had only a moment to realize his mistake, following the trail of crimson where it led beneath the pile of chaff.

The wheat burst apart as Darrin launched himself from it. A myriad of grain flew, mimicking the Tin-Snipper's display, and in the center was a devil grin of malice plastered across the killer's face. Blood coursed from his arms, but the hands that latched onto Gray's neck were solid stone, cement come to life. He fell back under the younger man's weight, pressing down, the thumbs at his neck finding arteries and digging into them.

His head cracked against the floor hard enough to send flickering gray spots to the sides of his vision like a spilled bag of marbles rolling away to darkness. He blinked and brought his knees up, creating valuable space between him and Darrin's smothering bodyweight. The other man's face was inches from his own, blood-flecked teeth white against the yellow air. Gray threaded his hand and arm between Darrin's wrists, then the other, before scissoring them downward. Darrin's hands slid free of his throat, and he breathed in, tasting the tainted air and welcoming it like water in the desert. With an up thrust of his neck, he bashed his forehead against Darrin's. Once, again, a third time, until an unfocused look clouded the young man's eyes.

With a grunt, Gray rolled him over, switching their positions, and brought an elbow down to Darrin's nose. It broke with a sound like a pine knot popping in a fire. Blood spewed from both nostrils and the bone within slanted the once regal feature far to the left. Gray rained blows down upon him, some landing, some blocked by the younger man's upraised forearms. There were cuts and missing chunks of skin on his arms where the Snipper had tasted him with its many tongues. Gray postured up and sliced an elbow down between Darrin's outstretched hands, connecting with his forehead. A splotchy bruise rose and split open on his scalp, and just as Gray thought the other man was dropping into unconsciousness, Darrin grasped a handful of wheat and dust and threw it into his eyes.

A thousand biting insects were in his vision. He swiped at his face, trying not to rub the sharp grains deeper, trying not to scrape his iris and corneas raw. Darrin sat up and struck him below the jaw with an open hand. Gray's throat closed like a shutter being thrown. He choked and fell sideways as Darrin shifted his weight.

The younger man scrambled toward him and drove a knee into his side where the gunshot dribbled fresh blood. Gray screamed, a sound like a strangled bird coming from his mouth, and clawed at him, raking a runner of red down the side of his neck, but Darrin struck him again, his knee a wrecking ball of bone. Gray blinked, his eyesight like looking through a windowpane left to the weather for years without cleaning. Darrin's shape stood and moved a short distance away, bending over as if to look for something. Gray rolled to his stomach and pressed himself onto his hands and knees.

"You got me a bit there, Sheriff," Darrin said before hawking and spitting a ball of blood onto the floor. "Definitely a better fighter than your shithead deputy was. He died flopping on the floor and pissing his pants. Take that thought with you into the nether."

Gray's vision watered and then cleared enough for him to see Darrin pick up the pistol from an inch of seed. Launching himself up like a sprinter coming off the blocks, he ran the three steps between them as Darrin tried to bring the weapon to bear. He caught the younger man's wrist and swung it high over his head, a pulse of three shots erupting from its barrel into empty space, before bringing it down over his knee.

Darrin's arm broke, both bones folding over so that it bent in three places instead of two.

The pistol escaped his grip and bounced, disappearing into the wheat pile once again. Darrin let out a moaning grunt and pulled a cylinder from behind his back with his functioning arm, a long needle-like tip springing from one end. Gray shoved him backward, running with him toward the wall and the waiting grain elevator that leaned there.

Gray slammed him into one of the large bins that scooped up the seed, and Darrin strained forward, stabbing the pointed weapon at his face. The tip of the needle traced a line of fire across Gray's cheek, and he turned, wrapping his hand around Darrin's wrist. He wrenched the younger man's hand at a painful angle and stared into his defiant eyes. Slowly the weapon rolled out of his grasp and Gray ripped it away.

With a flick of his hand, he spun the cylinder around and plunged its tip it into Darrin's chest.

There was a muffled, wet snap and Darrin's eyelids widened, his eyes rolling up into his head. Gray looked down at the handle and saw that his thumb rested on a smooth button set within the weapon's grip. Darrin's legs jittered once, and then his knees folded beneath. Gray let him drop to the floor where he tipped face-first into the wheat. He landed on the weapon's handle, and several shimmering points poked from his back, glazed with blood. Darrin's body shuddered once and then was still.

"You really are something, Sheriff."

Gray spun away from the corpse and watched Vincent Barder enter through the open man door. Smoke whirled around him in wreaths of yellow, and a manic grin cut the bottom of his face. He held an oblong, black tube in both hands, a stubby handle attached to one end. A light blinked in a green dot on its far side. The man's injured leg was wrapped in a white, elastic bandage stained red at its center, and he limped slightly before stopping a dozen yards away.

"I'm surprised Darrin wasn't able to best you, he's wily and tougher than my other two boys. Was, I suppose I should say. I'm assuming you killed Adam as well since you've made it this far."

Gray said nothing and shifted his eyes to where Darrin's pistol had vanished beneath the seed.

"I wouldn't make any sudden moves, Sheriff. This is a tranquilizer that shoots accurately within a hundred yards. I've taken the liberty of loading it with darts holding lethal doses of tetrodotoxin. If one strikes you, you'll be dead in under a minute."

"How did you get up here?"

"Oh Sheriff, do you think I would build such an elaborate underground system without making sure I had more than one way out or in? By the way, that was a nice trick with the knife down in the operating room, I didn't check your boots, something I won't overlook again. Nonetheless it wasn't something I couldn't fix with some bandages, pain killers, and a little snifter of adrenaline."

The doctor's eyes shone, not a trace of color was visible around the black holes that had once been his pupils.

"Let's take a walk, shall we?"

"Where?"

"Downstairs. I'm sure you've located Siri, and the other women are held up with her in the room if I'm correct. I'm guessing you also have some sort of signal to tell them it's you before you enter, so let's go round them up and get back down to the business you so rudely interrupted us from."

A flicker of movement over Barder's shoulder drew Gray's attention, but he looked back at the doctor's face quickly.

"One question for you, Vincent."

"Yes?"

"You retain all the knowledge of your medical training even when you're your true self, right?"

"Yes, why?"

"Just wondering."

A large shape darkened the doorway behind Barder.

He sensed it and tried to spin, bringing up the tranquilizer, but a massive hand caught its barrel and stopped its motion.

Danzig glowered down at the doctor for a split second before sending a fist into the side of his head. Barder fell as if heart-shot and lay spread-eagle on the cement, a line of blood drooling from his open mouth. Danzig spun the tranquilizer around and aimed it at the doctor's limp form.

"Dan, no!" Gray yelled, rushing forward.

Danzig raised his eyes from sighting down the barrel and squinted at him.

"Why the hell not?"

"Siri's about to give birth and this sack of shit is the only one qualified to help her."

Danzig stared at the back of Barder's head and Gray almost expected him to fire the tranq anyway, but after a moment the giant lowered it to his side.

"Holy shit, Dan, I thought you were dead."

Danzig's eyes watered for a split second, and then he began to cough. Big ratcheting coughs that rumbled up from deep within him. He bent over from the exertion and finally hacked out a globule of mucus the same color as the air.

"Fucking smoke. My lungs are on fire. I was holding back that cough for the last twenty minutes. You haven't seen my mask, have you?"

"No. They took the rounds out of my pistol too. The only reason they didn't lock up the Snippers was because I don't think they knew what they were. You still didn't answer me. How the hell did you take a shotgun blast to the back and not have your guts hanging out the other side?"

Danzig managed a small grin and opened his coverall. Beneath was a black, mesh-like shirt that glinted in the dim light. Gray moved closer and put his fingers on the clothing. It wasn't cloth at all. The shirt consisted of miniscule links of dark steel, like a fishing net, yet infinitely smaller and more finely woven.

"I'll be damned," Gray said.

"It's the prototype I took off the wall in my shop the other day. Mixture of tungsten carbide and titanium. Flexes like clothing but becomes solid in a microsecond when hit with a high-velocity projectile. Turns into a shield. Nothing short of an armor-piercing round can get through."

Danzig tapped his chest once and the shirt jingled. The giant smiled.

Gray threw an arm over the other man's shoulders and hugged him before drawing away.

"Unbelievable," Gray said.

"Still hurt like hell and knocked me out. But don't go getting all misty on me."

Danzig began to cough again, the ragged hackings so raw it made Gray wince.

"Let's get this bastard downstairs and wake him up so he can help Siri, and we'll see if we can't find your mask."

Danzig managed to nod and grabbed ahold of Barder's arm, hauling him off the floor as if he weighed no more than a sack of flour. Gray pressed a hand to his throbbing side, his palm became warm and sticky at once. He moved to the man door and peered out into the gloom.

The sky was on fire. A red haze, boiling into orange, coated the horizon from end to end. The trees quaked and wavered before its light, worshippers before their alien god finally arriving from some other world. The wind blew in revolt against the flames, but they were coming. There would be no stopping the fire.

He turned to find Danzig standing near the hatch holding Barder over one shoulder like a child.

"Let's go," Gray said.

Chapter 43

After knocking twice, Gray slid the card over the electronic eye and opened the door.

Lynn was ready, off to one side holding his knife in white fingers, her face a rictus of strain. When she saw him and then Danzig close behind, she visibly sagged and came forward, closing her eyes as she leaned into him.

"Told you I'd be back," he said.

"No you didn't."

"Sorry to get your hopes up."

She laughed and released him, turning to Danzig as he set the doctor down. She pecked him on the cheek, standing on her tiptoes to do so.

"Darrin?" Lynn asked, turning back to Gray.

"Taken care of."

"So what are we doing with him?"

"He's going to deliver Siri's baby."

Rachel looked up from where she sat, holding Siri's hand. Joslyn stared at him while cradling both the small boys.

Lynn took a step back. "What? No. Absolutely not."

"Lynn, there's no other choice. What if there's a problem with the baby? We could lose it and Siri."

She shook her head. "You want to have the monster that brought her here, held her against her will, deliver her baby? Screw that, Mac."

"He's all we have. The fire's too close to leave now and the baby's closer than that."

Barder groaned from where he lay on the floor. His arm waved weakly and he licked his blood-sodden lips with an equally red tongue.

"We ask Siri," Lynn finally said, looking at the awakening doctor. "We do whatever she says." Her gaze left no room for argument and, when he looked at Rachel and Joslyn, their faces mirrored Lynn's.

"Okay."

He moved to Siri's bedside and knelt, putting a hand on her wrist. Her eyes had been squeezed shut, but she opened them when he touched her.

"Siri, you have to make a decision. Barder is here and he's under our control. Now we can lock him in another cell, or we can have him help deliver the baby, it's your call."

Siri looked around the room, her gaze finding each of them as they watched her. Her face crumpled as another contraction washed over her and she held Gray's hand, nearly crushing his fingers into a single digit. She panted, blowing lungfuls of air out that made her sweat-soaked hair sway like a dark curtain in a draft.

217

"I want my baby to live. He helps, but if he does anything, you kill him."
She held his gaze for a moment and then gritted her teeth, bearing down before
releasing a short cry.

Gray stood and moved to where Barder stirred. He flipped the doctor over
with one toe of his boot. Vertigo consumed him for a span of seconds. It was as if
the room were being tossed end over end. His feet were light and then heavy on
the floor, simultaneously losing and gaining gravity, over and over. A hand fell on
his shoulder, steady and sure, and Danzig was there close beside him.

"You need to sit down, Mac, you've lost a lot of blood."

"I'm okay."

"Bullshit."

The room was gray, tinged with black at its corners, like his house after
the fire. Ashes and char.

He was falling.

Danzig caught him and eased him to a sitting position in the corner of the
room, and someone was taking the key card from his pocket. Lynn's face was
there and then gone, words floating back to him as if through a thick fog in early
morning when the sun hadn't had a chance to burn it away. There was a long
buzzing drone and then the sound of wind blowing through a partially open door.
The static crackling of burning things. An inferno raging, devouring the world.
The flames were eating him, he was burning, his side was on fire.

Gray opened his eyes and saw Lynn's face and the ceiling beyond. His
back was pressed against cold cement and the bullet wound felt as if a hot coal
had been shoved inside. He hissed and tried to sit up.

"Relax, I'm putting a coagulant gel on it. It was leaking blood and you
passed out."

A high keening came from the far side of the room and he searched
Lynn's face for an answer.

"She's having it right now. Barder's delivering it."

"How long have I been out?"

"Ten minutes, maybe. I just gave you a shot of erythropoietin. Barder told
me it would boost red blood cell production. I made him take a shot of it first to
make sure it wasn't harmful."

"Get me up."

"Mac, no—"

"Up."

He got an arm beneath himself and levered into a sitting position with
Lynn's help. His head spun for a sickening span, and then slowed and stopped.
His vision doubled and then melded together which caused his stomach to leap for
the back of his throat, but he swallowed, taking deep breaths as Siri cried out
again.

Barder was at the end of the bed, his hands between Siri's legs. Her lower
half was covered with a stained sheet, and a large stainless steel pan sat on the
floor full of soapy water that steamed into the air. Danzig stood two feet behind
the doctor, the tranquilizer gun pointed at the center of his back. Siri's upper body
was propped on four pillows, her cheeks two blazing points of red that made Gray

think of the fire above. Rachel and Joslyn held each of Siri's hands in their own, their voices low, speaking encouraging words to the laboring woman. In the furthest corner the two young boys sat side by side, miraculously giggling as they took turns trying to tickle one another.

"Okay Siri, I want you to breath for just a second, and don't push," Barder said, his face a mask of concentration. "The head is almost out."

Siri breathed in puffs, inhaling only after every fourth exhale. Her face twisted and her head fell back as another cry escaped her and became a full scream at its end.

"Good, good. Okay, now—" Barder paused and scooted closer to the bed.

"No funny shit or you're dead," Danzig growled, prodding the doctor in the back with the tranq's barrel.

"The cord is around its neck, I have to free it," Barder replied.

Gray managed to get his feet beneath him and accepted a bottle of water Lynn held out. He drank, pouring the liquid down his throat so fast he didn't know if he'd actually taken time to swallow.

Danzig looked over Barder's shoulder and then flicked his eyes to Gray's. He nodded once and then stepped back to give the doctor room. Siri breathed faster, moaning in closer and closer intervals.

"There," Barder said, sitting back on his heels. "Push now, Siri, hard as you can."

Siri's hands were claws, gripping the other women, her knuckles like pearls in the light. She took a deep breath and then held it, tipping forward until she sat almost upright. A cry came out from between her teeth that brought the hairs up on Gray's neck. Barder worked beneath the sheet, pausing every so often to wipe a bead of sweat from his forehead. The gloves he wore shone wetly, the fingertips tainted with blood.

"Come on, Siri, again. Push, harder this time, we're almost there."

Gray moved closer to Danzig, his legs gaining more and more feeling as he walked. Lynn stood by his side, her shoulder pressed against his arm. Beneath the sheet the baby's head was fully visible as well as one shoulder. A ropy length of umbilical hung down in a fleshy U. As Siri strained, the other shoulder appeared, and the baby slid out of her in a single slick movement.

Barder's hands caught it with delicate finesse Gray was sure only surgeons possessed. Quickly he began to work mucus free of the infant's mouth and nose by gently stroking its neck and throat in opposite directions. One of the baby's arms, beet red and shining, stretched out, flailing as if it were asking for help.

There was a moment of complete silence in the room as everyone waited, balanced upon the sound they strained to hear.

A blob of viscous fluid fell free of the newborn's mouth and it let out a clucking cough that coalesced into a shaking cry. Its arms flailed, quivering in movement common only to new life.

"It's a boy," Barder said, looking down at the tiny body he held. "A boy."

A beat went by and Gray tensed, noticing Danzig raise the tranquilizer to the side of the doctor's neck.

"Give him to Siri," Danzig said.

Barder remained motionless for a second and then looked up, his gaze taking them all in as if he'd forgotten they were there.

"I will, but first I need to cut the umbilical. Someone hand me the plastic clamp."

Lynn stepped forward to a small tray resting beside the still steaming disinfectant bowl. She plucked a short, plastic-wrapped item from it and opened it, taking care to not touch the clamp directly. Barder placed the instrument around the glistening cord an inch from the infant's stomach, and clicked it shut as the tiny boy continued to wail.

"Don't you cry, little one," Barder sang almost beneath his breath as he stretched the cord out straight beyond the clamp. "There's no reason to pout, a miracle inside your mommy, and now the doctor brought you out."

"Don't you sing to him, you sick fuck." Gray said, stepping forward. "Don't you dare."

Barder glanced at him and then looked back at the child in his arms. A short smile flitted across his lips and was gone. He turned and grasped a clean sheet from the table beside the bed, wrapping the squalling boy in its folds.

"Give him to me," Siri said in a breathless voice. Her arms shook, but she raised them anyway, reaching for the bundle.

"He'll need to be cleaned, and someone else can do that, but the cord needs to be cut."

"We can cut it, give him to Rachel," Gray said.

"What are you going to use? There's nothing sterile in this room."

"We'll wash my knife, now give the baby to Rachel or I'll kill you where you stand." Gray reached his hand out and Danzig placed the tranq in it without a word, the sight never leaving Barder's head.

"Okay, okay. We all need to calm down here, I mean we just experienced a miracle."

"Now," Gray said.

Lynn knelt by the pan of sudsy water and began to wash the knife's blade as Rachel came forward, her eyes and hands steady but her movements unsure, as if she were approaching the open door of a lion's cage. Barder smiled at her and offered the baby out, the newborn's aching cries growing louder. Rachel reached for him.

Barder yanked the baby back to his chest and kicked the bowl of hot water.

Lynn screamed as the scalding liquid splashed up her arm and onto her face. Water spattered Gray and Danzig, stinging droplets burning more than Gray guessed they would. Rachel and Joslyn cried out, and the little boys in the corner began to yell for their mothers. Amidst the chaos Gray heard one sound that made his stomach plunge.

The knife clattered to the floor at Barder's feet.

Gray tried to secure a shot, but the doctor moved with the same liquid grace he'd displayed earlier, scooping the knife from the floor as he'd caught the baby from Siri's womb. With a short flick of his wrist, he cut the infant's cord and slid the blade to the child's throat. Oblivious to the danger, the boy continued to wail.

"No!" Siri yelled from the bed, and tried to rise, the umbilical still trailing from between her legs.

"Drop it, Barder!" Gray said, keeping the tranq's bead on the man's face while eyeing his exposed legs.

"Ah, I wouldn't, Sheriff. You try to shoot me and I stab him, and you don't want two children's deaths on your conscience." Barder grinned, and shifted his gaze to everyone in the room. "That goes for all of you. No one make a move or the little one's dead."

Siri and the children sobbed. Lynn picked herself off the ground and wiped her face free of water, the skin where it had splashed an angry red. Barder edged toward the door, his eyes flicking to each of them in turn. A fevered grin pulled his features into something hideous, and Gray could see the doctor was enjoying himself.

"Now it's time to disappear, folks. It's been real fun, but my welcome's worn out in this town so to speak."

"There's a forest fire outside, where the hell do you think you're going to go?" Gray said, still following the other man's movements with the tranq.

"I'll figure something out, I always do."

"You won't make the county line before I cut you down," Gray said.

"I can see you mean that, Sheriff, but I have resources stocked away just for an occasion such as this and I'll be fine." Barder hefted the baby and readjusted his hold on the knife. "Actually, we'll be fine."

"Bring him back," Siri moaned. "Bring my baby back, please."

The doctor moved so that his back was to the wall. He slid sideways, forcing Gray and Danzig to rotate away from the open door.

"Lynn, give me the door card," Gray whispered.

He didn't release his gaze from Barder, couldn't look away, but felt Lynn put the thin card into his outstretched palm. The newborn continued to flail within the sheet, kicking its legs and twisting its flushed face in and out of view. Barder reached the doorway and backed out, watching them all with buzzard eyes.

"Goodbye my friends," he said, and kicked the door shut.

Gray leapt forward, stretching out the hand that held the key card. The door slammed home and he waited to hear the lock engage, but no click came. When he looked down he saw the card bent into the door's frame covering the locking mechanism.

"Did it not—" Danzig began.

"Shhh," Gray said. When all was still for another ten agonizing seconds, he pushed on the door.

It stuck solid for a sickening beat and then swung into the deserted hallway.

"He didn't wait for it to lock," Danzig said, staring hard at Gray.

"Nope."

"I'm coming with you."

"You won't last a minute outside in the smoke."

Danzig started to argue again but Lynn silenced him with a touch to his bicep.

"He's right, Dan. I'll go instead."

"No," Gray said, starting out the door.

"MacArthur Gray, you are not going alone. You'll die without help this time, and it's not just your life you're risking, it's Siri's son's too. Now cut the macho bullshit. You need me."

He glanced at her, taking in the aggressive stance, the set of her jaw.

"Okay."

He squeezed Danzig's arm once and shook his head when the big man tried to speak.

"Keep them safe," Gray said, and turned away.

They crept down the hall without another word. Gray swept the stairs with the tranq as they neared them and chanced a look all the way up. The hatch was open, the silo thick with smoke. It sounded as if a train were running on a track directly outside the building.

Gray motioned to Lynn and they moved up the stairway single file. The silo was a hazy murk. They could have been on the bottom of a disturbed lake, floating sediment all around them. He turned in a slow circle, scanning the space, but saw nothing. There was no place to hide with the loud infant, not in this echoing place. He coughed, the air dry and tangy with a taste that went past his tongue and followed straight to his lungs. The familiar burning that he'd felt in Hudson's barn returned.

"You okay?" Lynn asked.

He quelled the coughing by swallowing a half dozen times.

"Fine."

They moved to the door and he noticed the heat again. It was exponential with each step. The steel walls radiated it and his hair curled with its touch. The yard glowed, smoke lit in ambient flames without definition. The fire whipped and flowed like something alive, its gnashing jaws the only sound audible, but indefinable behind the roiling fumes.

Over the cackling of the fire, a baby's cry floated to them.

"Toward the field." Lynn pointed and Gray followed her finger.

A darker shadow hovered in the choking swirls, its shape resembling a man but monstrous in the misgiving light. Barder's form grew, elongated into a stilted figure out of an ancient carnival, and then shrank as the waves of smoke rolled past them.

Gray grasped Lynn's warm hand and they set off from the silo. The heat was worse in the open air, too large for lungs to breath. They tried to get below the smoke that rolled past them, closer to the ground, but it wasn't much use and Gray felt a coughing fit rising within him. He bit down on the insides of his mouth, drawing blood, and swallowed.

They reached the border of the barnyard and cornfield and stopped. The baby squalled again somewhere to their left and they moved, the pliant earth of the field becoming crusted by the approaching heat. The fire roared behind them and then over them. Gray ducked, yanking Lynn down with him while the roar become a thudding beat.

The helicopter exploded from the smoke overhead, a stone's throw above the ground. Its twin rotors cut the air and fanned the noxious clouds down and away. It continued on toward the tree line, dropping the last of its chemical retardants on the withered leaves before fading from sight.

They picked themselves up from the ground and went on, walking careful and quiet. Gray held the tranq at waist level, searching the smog. The infant cried out, a long heartbroken wail that drew them forward onto a path leading toward the dense trees lining the field.

A flapping came from ahead like some great bird trying to take off. Gray put a hand on Lynn's arm, halting her. The baby screamed its protest which led into a stream of minute coughs. A shape began to form as the wind shifted, blowing away the curtain of smoke.

Barder was there, not a dozen yards before them, uncovering something beneath a featureless tarp. Siri's son lay on the ground, the long grass bent beneath him like an archaic cradle. As they watched, Barder yanked on the tarp again and the shape was revealed.

A new four-wheel-drive pickup sat amidst the swaying grass and overhanging trees. Its paint glistened as if it had just been recently washed. Barder opened the door and set something inside on the passenger seat before turning toward the infant.

At the same instant, he noticed their presence. Gray brought the tranq up and fired.

The moment he pulled the trigger he knew he'd missed. The dart containing the poison was barely visible, its flight streaking across the distance in half a second. It flew by Barder's chest close enough to make the doctor cry out and take a step in reverse.

"Get away from him," Gray said, pulling the trigger again.

Barder bared his even teeth and ducked behind the truck's fender as the second dart skipped off the hood, marring the pristine paint. Gray ran forward, putting himself in between the other man and the infant thrashing in its swaddles. When he rounded the truck, Barder was gone. He swung the weapon back the way he'd come, covering the opposite side in case the doctor tried to flank them.

"Lynn, get him."

But she was already picking up the newborn and cuddling him close to her chest. She let out a bray of coughing, hoarse and racking, as she stood, her eyes watering but from the smoke or relief of holding the baby, he didn't know. Movement caught his eye from the right and he saw Barder coming around the rear of the truck, the knife held point down in his fist. Gray raised the tranq and fired again, the dart singing over the doctor's head as he ducked.

"Nice try, Sheriff. I'd tell you never to use another man's weapon, but that's hypocritical since I'm holding your knife."

Gray rounded the front of the truck as Barder stood, smiling through the drifting smoke. He centered the gun on the doctor's chest and pulled the trigger.

The tranq clicked empty.

"The other reason you don't use another man's weapon is you never know how many rounds he had in it. In this case I only had time to load three."

With a grin that became a snarl, Barder rushed forward, bringing the knife up over his shoulder. Gray backpedaled and flipped the tranq around so that he held it by the barrel. He swung it like a baseball bat, bashing the doctor in the side of the face. Barder partially blocked the blow with his forearm and slashed the blade in a wicked arc past Gray's chest. The tranquilizer snapped near its grip, leaving him holding only the barrel which became surprisingly light without its handle. He danced backward, feinting to the left and right, inches out of reach of Barder as he pinwheeled the knife over and over, the blade cutting ribbons of smoke as it sang through the air. Daring a look to his side, he found Lynn watching helplessly as she cradled Siri's son.

"Go! Run to the silo!" he yelled as Barder attacked again, stabbing this time at his stomach.

He caught the other man's wrist and pulled him forward off balance. With his opposite arm he threw an elbow that smashed under the doctor's right eye. The skin split open there and drizzled blood onto his cheek. With an upward slash, Barder broke free of Gray's grip, cutting a strand of cloth from his coveralls and skimming his arm with the knife's tip. Gray stepped back and the reaching touch of the corn met him. With an overhand swing, he brought the tranq's barrel down, aiming for the other man's skull. Barder sidestepped, deflecting the blow with the knife. The steel slipped in Gray's sweaty fingers and he lost his hold on the makeshift baton. It fell to the ground behind Barder, disappearing from sight.

Gray kicked forward, feeling the lancing pull of the bullet wound as he did. His foot met the doctor's stomach and Barder stumbled back, his breath knocked from his chest. Gray flicked his eyes to the left and was awestruck in spite of the doctor slowly straightening himself.

The fire was there.

It was a wall fifty feet high, its naked flames finally visible without the cloistering wrap of smoke. It walked and swayed to an orchestra of crackling earth, peeling trees, and boiling life. It surged toward them, and as he watched, the flames overcame Barder's home. In an instant the roof was consumed and the siding ignited. It swept forward like a tidal wave washing forward after an oceanic meteor impact. And before the open maw of hell, Lynn ran with the baby. She made it within forty feet of the silo and then halted as if she'd hit a fence. She turned, shielding the baby and bent forward, coughing without sound as the fire howled over everything. With a final push, she tried again and then turned back toward the field, the heat herding her the way she had come.

Barder screamed and leapt forward, stabbing at Gray's heart. He twisted, but it wasn't enough. The blade slid into and through the muscle of his chest. There was quick burning and then numbness where the steel had entered his body. His mind reeled, registering he'd been stabbed, while at the same time seeing Lynn pelt past them into the rows of the field, the child a flash of white cloth in her arms. Gray clamped a hand onto Barder's wrist as the doctor tried to withdraw the blade, and then slammed the other into the man's throat as they fell together into the corn.

Barder landed on top of him, driving the blade deeper. Gray grunted and slapped the side of the doctor's head with a cupped palm, forcing air into his eardrum hard enough to perforate it. Barder cried out and shook his head like a dog that'd just emerged from a lake. The doctor balled up his free hand and struck Gray between the eyes, releasing a grenade of pain into his broken nose. The world drained of its color, first at the edges of his vision and then from the center, leeching his sight into a pallid haze.

The knife slide out of his chest and the beautiful numbness receded with it, leaving a tide of agony where it had been. Above him, Barder pushed himself into a sitting position, his knees dug into the hot soil to either side of Gray.

"End of the line, Sheriff. Great ride but it has to stop sometime. Should be able to make it to the truck and run down your lady before the fire gets here. We'll have to see."

Barder raised the knife above his head, holding it with both hands like some past tribal chief, offering a sacrifice. He plunged it down, driving it toward Gray's exposed throat.

Gray's hands came up and caught the doctor's wrists, stopping the blade's descent. He gritted his teeth and wormed his fingers in between Barder's clenched fists, finding the small bump he was looking for.

The button depressed beneath the pad of his finger and the blade vanished into its handle.

An astonished look crossed Barder's face and Gray wrenched the knife free of his hands, batting it away into the dirt. The doctor jabbed a fist into Gray's side, finding the bullet wound perfectly. Gray curled into himself, wrapped around the pain that reverberated in his gut. He took a shuddering breath tainted with dust and smoke. The heat from the fire fell over him like a blanket as Barder struggled to his feet and coughed before wiping a hand across his mouth.

"You're a stubborn one, Sheriff. Guess I'll just let you burn."

Barder turned, taking one step before Gray swung his foot up and around as hard as he could, catching the other man in the side of his injured knee.

The joint popped like a firework.

Barder had a split second that he used to scream before his leg folded inward and back, the bandage around it unraveling and sliding up his thigh. He fell to the ground, clutching at cornstalks as he went, their too-green trunks folding beneath his weight. He thrashed there, a beetle overturned on its shell, one hand tracing down the length of his leg to where it bent at an ugly angle.

Gray got to his hands and knees, then to his feet, shaking with the effort. He swayed there and turned toward the flames that licked up the side of the silo and highlighted its soaring height. He watched the fire churn within itself, its colors blending then parting, spewing black smoke from the tips of its orange fingers.

Barder screamed again, trying to turn himself over so that he could crawl, and reached for Gray's boot. Gray pulled his foot away and stood looking down at the man covered in the dark soil. Finally he walked away, swaying a little, drunk with the solid heat of the air. The doctor called after him, saying something with words that didn't make sense anymore. His side was sticky again and he tried brushing the dirt from it as he walked, but it stung too much so he stopped.

His skin tightened the closer he got to the truck, the trees beyond backlit by flame. A portrait of desolation so bright and horrible, he couldn't help but stare. His fingers grazed the warm steel of the truck and he looked down, seeing his hand on the handle. He pulled it open, blinking against the smoke and fatigue building inside his head. The interior of the vehicle was immaculate. A large bag sat on the passenger seat, its mouth partially open. Gray felt along the ignition for a key or fob but there was nothing.

"Truck, on," he said in a voice of gravel. Nothing happened.

A cinder landed on his shoulder and seared through the coverall to his skin. He brushed it away without looking. His arm was a chunk of lead, but he managed to grasp the bag's strap and pull it closer. The interior was crammed with money. Thick stacks of bills clipped together with plastic holders. He shuffled the bag around, searching for a key but there was none to be found.

Gray leaned back out of the truck and shut the door, the nape of his neck warming past the point of comfort. He looked out across the expanse of corn, the wind coursing white and yellow smoke through its rows in swirling channels.

"Run fast," he said, and his legs gave out.

His hand brushed the truck's mirror on the way down but couldn't hold on, and he collapsed in a heap. He coughed, his throat burning like the trees around him. He could almost feel his lungs blistering. He rolled to his side, reaching out into the grass and trying to sit up. His fingers grazed something hard there. A log or stone. The last throne of the world upon which to watch everything burn. He gripped it and pulled himself forward, sure he could rise one last time, but then his fingers met nothing and a darkness consumed him beyond black as the fire went out.

~

The baby struggled against Lynn's chest as she ran, its movements spastic, but weaker than earlier. She choked and coughed, the white smoke that pursued them down the rows of corn catching up and blocking their path ahead. She didn't look back but could feel the heat rising, a step or two behind the smoldering air.

"It's okay, it's okay, it's okay," she repeated, a mantra in time with her falling footsteps.

The ground tried to hold her feet down, the soft dirt becoming hands grasping and pulling. She stumbled and fell, managing to get one arm out to break their fall while keeping the little boy tucked close to her body. She coughed again, a dry pain building in her lungs as nothing came out of her mouth. She spit and stood, the row before her obscured white as a blank page.

A crackling sound filled her ears. Filled the world. She turned, throwing a look over her shoulder.

The cornfield had caught fire.

It sprang into flame as if the stalks were coated in gasoline. The fire leapt forward, jumping from one row to the next, its massive height crouching down to feast on the fertilized corn.

Lynn faced forward and raced on, her legs burning as if the flames had already reached them. The wind swept toward them, peeling the smoke back enough for her to see the field stretched out another half mile or more. They would never outrun the blaze. The breeze shifted again to her back and the field was lost in the white haze. She sobbed, tears drying instantly on her face. She slowed and then stopped, crouching down as low as she could get before collapsing completely. The baby cried, struggled against her. She exposed his face.

He was beautiful.

Even smudged with afterbirth and soot from the fire, his large eyes shone with awareness. They closed as he wailed and then opened, looking her fully in the face.

"Hush honey, it's all right. I won't let the fire get you," Lynn said, slowly balling up the loose fabric that swaddled the child. She wept, her heart slamming so hard against her breastbone the sound blocked out the crackling flames that rushed toward them. She took a last look at the infant's face and saw it was Carah she held now. Her daughter, so sweet and small, her little body hot against hers.

The cotton she had balled up to smother the baby with, fell from her hand and she shook with silent sobs. Her heart thrummed louder, making the ground shake and the corn tremble and bend. She knew then that it was the end, they would burn together.

The helicopter emerged from the smog and circled directly over them, pounding the smoke away and flattening the corn. The wind from the rotors whipped her hair about like striking snakes that snapped at her face. Lynn raised her head from her daughter and saw the chopper come closer, its door sliding open to reveal a man wearing a bright orange jumpsuit along with an oxygen mask hiding his face. He leapt from the aircraft when it was still ten feet from the ground and ran to them, his steps sure and strong.

"Come on! Get up! We have to go!" he yelled, helping her stand. His fingers found the inside of her arm and he pulled her along the row where the chopper touched down, its landing struts sinking deep into the soft ground. They ducked as they neared the door, and then they were inside, and the man in the mask was buckling her into a wide bench seat. The ground dropped away just as the fire reached the chopper, the heat so intense she squeezed her eyes shut, knowing the fuel tanks would ignite and they would be blow apart in a single, hot flash.

But then they were airborne. The sinking sensation in her chest was gravity doing its best to keep them on the earth, and losing. The field angled away and trees took over the view before the craft leveled out.

"Ma'am, let me take the baby from you, okay?"

Lynn held the bundle tighter, staring at the man's mask, his eyes two reflective black discs. There was no way she was giving up Carah, not now, not after waiting for so long to hold her again. The man peeled the oxygen unit off revealing tightly cropped blond hair and a razorblade nose.

"It's all right, I just want to make sure it's unharmed." He held out his hands.

Lynn looked down at her baby, at Carah, but it wasn't her little girl. It was a newborn, his eyes wide now, staring back at her in wonder, pink hands beside his cheeks. She smiled at him and his mouth crinkled at one corner, the suggestion of a grin.

She transferred the baby to the man, who laid him on a padded stretcher ten times too large for his small form. Lynn watched for a time, closing her eyes whenever they skimmed over a rough patch of air, and finally looked away, focusing her gaze out the window to where the earth burned below.

Chapter 44

It took twelve hours for the area to be deemed safe before Lynn could lead the authorities back to the Barder farm.

The wind continued to blow out of the east, shoving the fire onward at a relentless pace. It consumed everything in its path and left behind a scorched landscape, appearing as if God had created the world in charcoal instead of color.

Sheriff Enson drove the cruiser Lynn rode in, and wouldn't speak or look at her as they wound the roads into the farmstead, stopping only to push the occasional fallen tree out of the way. When they arrived with three other units behind them, she got out and jogged ahead, not waiting for the portly sheriff to catch up. Enson waddled behind, his steps unhurried as he glanced around at the smoldering pile that once was the Barders' home.

When he entered the Silo where Lynn had disappeared, he spoke.

"I'd like to remind you again, Lynn, Vincent Barder is a highly respected member of the community in both our neighboring counties and your statements are—"

He lost the rest of his words as he saw Lynn emerge from the hatch in the floor with two women in tow who in turn carried small boys, neither older than two years of age. His mouth slowly worked, trying to form the rest of his sentence but stopped when Danzig climbed out of the hole carrying Siri in his arms.

"Bitchel, shut your worthless mouth and get a fucking ambulance out here," Danzig rumbled.

Several deputies strode into the silo, took one look at the bedraggled group, and went sprinting back to their cruisers. In less than ten minutes, an ambulance, lights flashing in strobed timing with its siren, came barreling up the drive and stopped beside the blackened structure.

"Are you sure?" Siri asked Lynn for the third time as she was loaded onto a stretcher and hauled toward the waiting doors of the vehicle.

"He's fine, darling. He's waiting for you at the hospital. You'll be in the same room with him."

"Thank you." Siri's eyes sparkled with tears. Squeezing Lynn's hand she asked, "Sheriff Gray?"

Lynn blinked, her lips pressing together. She shook her head.

Siri's fingers unclasped from her own as the EMTs gently lifted the stretcher into the back of the ambulance and let it lock into place. As the vehicle drove away, moving slower this time, a forensics van pulled to a stop in the yard, a group of people piling out already wearing white jumpsuits. They moved to the rear of the van and began to unload several cases of equipment.

Lynn turned away and walked toward the charred field that had been an emerald expanse the day before. The early morning sun was hidden beneath a ruffled mixture of clouds and the air was finally cool. Danzig fell into step beside her as she walked.

"Shouldn't go down there, Lynn."

"I know."

"Then let's go back. I don't want to see if…" His voice trailed off.

"I need to."

They reached the edge of the field and she swept it with her eyes.

There was no evidence that the plain had ever held crops. Its surface was a black rubble caked with ash. Clumps of matter smoked, trailing slender lines into the sky where they blended with the clouds. A humped form drew her attention and she strode to it, her heart picking up speed with each step.

The man's body lay partially on its stomach and side. It was shrunken to the size of an adolescent, the skin and muscles blackened and hard over bone that shone through it drab patches. The skull was tipped back, mouth open to reveal pebbled teeth studding its exposed jaw. One of its knees was bent inward, the lower part of the leg jutting at a ninety-degree angle away from the body. Its arms were out in front of it, one hand dug into the ground, the other reaching for something.

"It's not him," Lynn said, stepping away from the body. She made to move past Danzig to where the burnt husk of the pickup sat beneath a fallen tree. Danzig caught her by the shoulders and pulled her to his chest. She tried to push him away, to struggle free, but he was too strong. When he began to stroke her hair, the tears came flooding out that she'd held onto all night.

"It's okay, it's okay," he said, and she was reminded of speaking the same words to Siri's boy in the burning corn. A teardrop landed on her hair and soaked in as the big man heaved a sigh, deep and slow.

They stood that way for long time, the sky above mirroring the land below, the wind smelling of slag.

When they had both quieted, she detached herself from his arms and they walked toward the silo which bustled with activity. Deputies and forensics personnel moved past one another in hurried strides. Another ambulance had arrived, its lights running in silence. Mitchel Enson sat on the hood of a cruiser, staring at a spot of ground several feet in front of his boots. He didn't look up as they passed.

When they came even with the silo door, a young deputy holding a digital clipboard spotted them and held out a hand.

"You two aren't thinking of leaving, are you?"

"She needs her rest and so do I," Danzig said.

"Hold on, I need to ask you a few questions first."

"Can't it wait?" Lynn said.

"I'm afraid not, ma'am. First off, how many men did you say were holding your group?"

She sighed, her shoulders drooping with resignation. "Three. Dr. Vincent Barder and two of his three sons, Adam and Darrin. Ryan Barder is dead too, but I have no idea where his body is."

"Okay. See that's where we're running into a problem because we've got a fourth person down there, the EMTs are bringing him up now. He was found in a sealed room adjacent to an elevator system. There was an open hatch a lot like the one in the silo in the adjoining room."

Lynn frowned and looked at Danzig who shook his head.

"He's alive?"

"Yes ma'am, barely. Looks like he fell in through the hatch. His face is a little burned, and it looks like he was beaten badly. He's also got a gunshot wound on his side—"

She didn't hear the rest since she was already sprinting to the silo door, heart clamoring in an unsteady rhythm—*alive, alive, he said 'alive'.*

She skidded to a stop at the top of the stairway as two EMTs emerged carrying a stretcher between them.

Gray lay upon it, his eyes closed.

His face was red, as if he'd spent too long in the sun on a hot day, and a white bandage, blazingly clean against his filthy coveralls, was blotched with blood on his stomach. But even from a distance, she saw the rise and fall of his chest.

Then she was at his side, holding his bloodied hand, stroking his arm that was devoid of hair from heat. She kept pace with the EMTs, her breath shuddering in and out, yet she couldn't take her eyes off his face.

"Holy shit," Danzig said, taking a place on the opposite side of the stretcher. "I can't believe it."

The pale light fell on Gray's face as they stepped into the day, and his eyelids scrunched shut further. Lynn laid her palm against his face.

"We're here, Mac, you're safe. You're going to be okay, honey."

His eyelids fluttered at the sound of her voice and they came open, his pupils dilating and then finding her. He blinked and tried to smile, only one side of his mouth rising, just like the child's had in the helicopter.

"Took you so long?"

She laughed. "Apologies."

He licked his cracked lips as Danzig squeezed his arm.

"Hey brother," Danzig said.

"Hey yourself. Fucking luck, huh?"

"Fucking luck."

Gray shut his eyes, and for a moment Lynn thought he'd passed out again, but then he squeezed her hand.

"If my legs still work after this, I'd like to take you dancing."

"You were a terrible dancer before, I'm guessing you couldn't get much worse."

He smiled again as moisture fell on his cheek.

"Don't cry, honey," he said as they neared the back of the ambulance, its rear doors open and waiting.

Lynn smiled and smoothed back his hair.

"I'm not. It's raining."

The EMTs slid the stretcher into the vehicle as Lynn and Danzig climbed in, holding their positions at his side. The doors slammed shut, and then they were moving down the long drive as the rain fell in great drops that became solid sheets and hissed against the embers that winked out with their cool touch.

The End

Author's Note

First and foremost, thank you for reading. To know that you've spent your time on something I've created is the highest compliment, and I hope you enjoyed the ride.

So I had this idea, and it began the wonderful way many writer's ideas begin with in the form of a question: What if?

What if there were no sociopaths or serial killers stalking the streets of the world, hiding in plain sight? What if we'd conquered that particular mar on society by finding a gene that, when active, could give way to those tendencies? Would anyone have a problem with inoculating their children at a young age? Of course not, we do that now to ensure they don't catch terrible diseases that could end their lives. But could we ever be rid of pure evil in that form forever? Would we be able to control it, or would life find a way?

These are the questions I asked myself while pondering Widow Town. The Tabula Rasa, or "blank slate" theory immediately came to mind while I was researching, and this was one of the bases I built the premise on. The balance between nature and nurture has been debated for centuries, and it's a terrifying thought to realize that each one of us perhaps has the potential to become something terrible given the right circumstances. I also asked if there were a gene that could contribute to a person developing without empathy, without a conscience, could it be turned off? And if it could, would there be any other way for evil to form, through environment and treatment of the individual? This led me in the direction of placing this particular tale in the future. I do enjoy science fiction, but it isn't my forte, so I stayed near the shallow end of the pool when developing technology or referring to some new breakthrough. I also wondered, how much does the world really change over time? Our technology changes of course, along with methods in science, religion, politics, but at the center of it all, do *we* really change?

Of course there is no "murder gene", but the what-if in this case swept me away with possibilities about how a society would react to a threat that they thought was gone. How they wouldn't be able to fathom that a monster in human skin could live next door, and they'd never know it; how they would treat a man who believed in something preposterous.

Once again, I hope you enjoyed the book, and I appreciate any and all feedback, whether it be a review online or a simple email to tell me your thoughts. Thank you for accompanying me on these journeys, and I'll continue to make my best efforts in creating new places for us to travel.

Joe Hart
February 2014

Other Books by Joe Hart

Lineage (novel)
Singularity (novel)
EverFall (novel)
The River Is Dark (novel)
The Waiting (novel)
Midnight Paths: A Collection of Dark Horror (collection)
The Line Unseen (short story)
The Edge of Life (short story)
Outpost (short story)

Printed in Great Britain
by Amazon